"Are you okay?"

He knelt next to her, bending those long legs and folding his arms over his knees. He pushed back the black cowboy hat and peered at her. He looked concerned.

She took a breath and waited.

"Of course I am." Breezy made sure to smile. "Why wouldn't I be?"

Jake grinned. "Well, you were almost toast out there with that bull."

"I *am* glad you came along when you did."

"Me, too," he replied. His voice was soft, like wind through the trees, and it undid her a tiny bit. "Here, you're probably cold." He slipped off his jacket and eased it around her shoulders. "This should help."

Words failed her. Yes, the jacket helped.

Or did it?

It smelled of Jake Martin, like pine, mountains in the fall and cold winter air. She wanted to bury her nose in the collar and inhale his scent. At the same time she wanted to tell him she didn't need his jacket or the unexpected emotions it stirred in her.

Brenda Minton lives in the Ozarks with her husband, children, cats, dogs and strays. She is a pastor's wife, Sunday-school teacher, coffee addict and sleep deprived. Not in that order. Her dream to be an author for Harlequin started somewhere in the pages of a romance novel about a young American woman stranded in a Spanish castle. Her dreams came true, and twenty-plus books later, she is an author hoping to inspire young girls to dream.

Glynna Kaye treasures memories of growing up in small Midwestern towns—and vacations spent with the Texan side of the family. She traces her love of storytelling to the times a houseful of great-aunts and great-uncles gathered with her grandma to share candid, heartwarming, poignant and often humorous tales of their youth and young adulthood. Glynna now lives in Arizona, where she enjoys gardening, photography and the great outdoors.

A Rancher
for Christmas

Brenda Minton

&

High Country
Holiday

Glynna Kaye

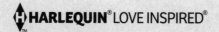
HARLEQUIN® LOVE INSPIRED®

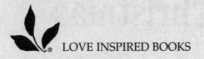

LOVE INSPIRED BOOKS

Recycling programs for this product may not exist in your area.

ISBN-13: 978-1-335-97118-0

A Rancher for Christmas & High Country Holiday

Copyright © 2019 by Harlequin Books S.A.

A Rancher for Christmas
First published in 2014. This edition published in 2019.
Copyright © 2014 by Brenda Minton

High Country Holiday
First published in 2014. This edition published in 2019.
Copyright © 2014 by Glynna Kaye Sirpless

www.Harlequin.com

Printed in U.S.A.

CONTENTS

A RANCHER FOR CHRISTMAS

Brenda Minton

Dedicated to my sweet ladies at the residential care facility. Your prayers, hugs and love have meant so much to me. Lola, this one is for you.

And to friends who are always just a phone call away: Pam, Lori, Tracie, Steph and Shirlee.

Melissa Endlich, as always, thank you!

Not that I speak in respect of want: for I have learned, in whatsoever state I am, therewith to be content.
—*Philippians* 4:11

Chapter One

Breezy Hernandez stood in front of the massive wood door on the front porch of her brother's Texas Hill Country home. When she'd met Lawton Brooks two months ago, he had filled in the missing pieces of her life.

Now he was gone. In one tragic accident Lawton, his wife and his mother had been taken. The lawyer in Austin had given her this address. He'd told her in Martin's Crossing she would find Jake Martin, executor of the estate.

She knocked on the door and then looked out at the windblown fields dotted with small trees, waiting for someone to answer. No one did. There was no muffled call for her to come in, or footsteps hurrying to answer the door. She leaned her forehead against the rough wood, her hand dropping to her side. Her heart ached.

After a few minutes she wiped away the dampness on her cheeks and reached for the handle. It wasn't locked. She pushed the door open, hesitating briefly before stepping inside. Why should she hesitate? Nothing would change the reality that Lawton and his wife had been killed in a plane crash two weeks ago. She'd missed the opportunity to see him again. She'd missed the funeral and the chance to say goodbye.

But she could be there for his girls.

As she stepped inside she flipped a switch, flooding the stone-tiled foyer in soft amber light. The entryway led to a massive living room with stone flooring, textured walls in earthy tan and a stone fireplace flanked by brown leather furniture.

Enveloped by silence and the cool, unheated air, she stood in the center of the room. There were signs of life, as if the people who had lived here had just stepped out. There were magazines on the coffee table, a pair of slippers next to a chair. Toys spilled from a basket pushed against the wall. Her throat tightened, aching deep down the way grief does.

"It isn't fair," she said out loud, the words sounding hollow in the empty space.

She should have come to Texas sooner but she'd needed time to come to terms with what Lawton had told her. His father, Senator Howard Brooks, had an affair with her mother, Anna, a drug addict from Oklahoma City. Breezy was the result of that brief relationship. She'd known for years that she wasn't the true granddaughter of Maria Hernandez, the woman who had taken her in years ago. Maria had given her that information shortly before she passed away.

Now she knew who she was. But what good did that do her?

She left the living room and walked to the kitchen. The room was large and open, with white cabinets and black granite countertops. She moved from that room, with sippy cups in a drainer next to the sink, to the dining room.

A table with four chairs and two high chairs dominated the room. On the opposite wall were family portraits. She stopped at the picture of an older man in a suit, a flag of Texas behind him. Her father, Senator Howard Brooks.

In the next picture his wife of over forty years stood next to him. They looked happy. Evelyn Brooks hadn't known about her husband's brief affair or his daughter. He'd confessed the secret on his deathbed one year ago.

Breezy drew in a breath and fought the sting of tears. She'd never been one to cry over spilled milk. Not even if that meant she might have had a real family.

This was different, though. This was a family lost. Her family. She had a habit of losing family. It had started more than twenty years ago, after her mother's death, when she and her siblings were all separated. Mia was adopted by the Coopers and Juan went to his father's family. Breezy had been taken in the night by Maria because she had worried they would eventually learn the truth, that Maria's son wasn't really Breezy's father.

Out of fear, Maria had kept them moving from town to town, living in cars, shelters and sometimes pay-by-the-month hotels.

Breezy brushed off the memory. It was old news.

A wedding photo hung on the wall. She studied the image of her brother and his pretty bride, both wearing identical looks of joy. At the last picture her heart stilled. Lawton, his wife, their two baby girls.

Just then, a sound edged in, a door closing. Footsteps, heavy and booted, echoed in the empty house. She held her breath, waiting.

"Who are you?" The deep male voice sent a shiver of apprehension up her spine.

Breezy turned, not quite trembling in her shoes, but nearly. The man filled the doorway. His tall, lean frame in jeans and a dark blue shirt held her attention, and then her eyes connected with pale blue eyes in a suntanned face. His dark hair was short but messy, like he'd just taken off a hat. She let her gaze drop, almost expecting a holster, Old West style, slung low on his hips.

Of course there wasn't one.

"I'm Breezy. Breezy Hernandez." Chin up, she swallowed a lump of what might have been fear.

His eyes narrowed and he frowned. "The missing sister."

She wanted to argue she hadn't been missing. She hadn't known she was lost. She'd needed time to process that she had this brother. She'd needed time alone to figure out what it meant to find out who her father was. The ache in her heart erupted again. She'd been on the run for most of her life; it had become second nature to take off when things got a little dicey. Maria Hernandez had taught her that.

"So we know who I am. Who are you?" She managed to not shake as she asked the question, meeting his somewhat intimidating gaze.

"Jake Martin."

"Of Martin's Crossing." The town in the middle of nowhere that she'd driven through to get here.

"Yes, Martin's Crossing."

"The girls?" She glanced back over her shoulder and saw that he was moving toward her.

"They're safe." He stepped close, smelling of the outdoors, fresh country air and soap. "I got a call from Brock, the attorney in Austin. He said he told you to come here and talk to me."

"Yes, he told me about Lawton and asked me to find you." She shook her head. "I missed the funeral, I'm sorry."

She didn't give him explanations.

She guessed the Goliath standing in front of her wouldn't want to hear explanations. He wouldn't want to know how much it hurt to know that all these years she'd had another brother. And now he was gone.

"Right." He looked away, but not before she saw the sorrow flash across his face, settling in his eyes. She started to reach out but knew she shouldn't. Her hand remained at her side.

Maybe they were feeling the same sense of loss but he didn't seem to be a man who wanted comfort from a stranger. From her.

"So, you came for your inheritance?" He dropped the words, sharp and insulting.

"Is that why you think I'm here?"

"It would make sense."

She shook her head. "No, it doesn't. It's insulting."

He shrugged one powerful shoulder. "Your brother was my best friend. His daughters are my nieces. I have every right to keep them safe."

"I'm not here for any reason other than to see them." She turned and walked back to the kitchen.

"Running?" He followed her, light on his feet for a man so large.

"Not at all. I need a minute to cool off so I don't hit you with something."

At that, the smooth planes of his face shifted and he smiled. She was slammed with a myriad of other emotions that seemed more dangerous than her rage. At the sink she filled a glass with water and took a sip. He scooted a chair out from the island in the middle of the big room and bent his large form to fit the seat. She ignored the lethal way he sat, like a wild cat about to attack. She ignored that he had beautiful features, strong but beautiful. She could draw him, or chisel his likeness in stone.

Or grab a chunk of granite and…

His eyebrows lifted, as if he guessed where her thoughts had gone.

"I'm not here to take what I can and leave." She remained standing on the opposite side of the island, not wanting to be anywhere near him. She needed that force of wood and stone between them.

"Really." His voice was smooth but deep, and full of skepticism.

"Yes, really. I had a father and a brother that I never got to meet. I wanted to come here because this is where Lawton lived. I thought I might somehow…" She shook her head. "Never mind. He's gone. I want to meet his daughters. Please, just let me meet them."

Jake stood, rethinking what he'd come to tell her. Rethinking her. She stood on the other side of the counter, as if the granite could protect her. As he eased out of the chair, she moved a little to the right, her back against the counter. Brown eyes the unfortunate color of caramel watched him.

Unfortunate because her eyes were strangely compelling. And more, there were emotions that flickered in their depths—sadness, anger, loss. He hadn't expected to feel anything for her other than distrust.

"I'm going to get a glass of water, nothing else," he said.

He opened the cabinet and found a glass, filling it with cold water from the fridge. He took a drink and studied the sister of his best friend, looking for similarities. She had long straight dark blond hair that framed a face that he'd call beautiful but strong. She was tall and slim but not thin. The peasant skirt and blouse gave her a bohemian look. She would stand out in Martin's Crossing. If she stayed. He doubted she would. She had city written all over her.

Yes, she looked enough like Lawton for him to believe she was his sister. Lawton had obviously believed it. Even before the DNA test.

"Well?" she asked.

"You remind me of your brother."

"I hope that's a compliment."

"It's an observation." He watched her, still unsure. He'd been unsure from the beginning when Lawton first told him about her. "I need to head back to my place. You can meet me over there."

Jake poured out the remaining water and put the glass in the dishwasher. She had moved away from him again. He didn't comment, just walked past her and headed for the front door, grabbing his hat off the hook on his way out. She followed.

He had more on his mind than a sister who suddenly showed up when it looked as if the gravy train might have derailed in her front yard. Back at his place he had a mare about to foal. He'd lost a good cow that morning and now had a calf to tend to. He had fifty head of cattle heading to the sale tomorrow and a brother who couldn't get his act together.

They both stopped on the porch. The temperature, typical of late November, had dropped fifteen degrees while they'd been inside. Clouds were rolling, gray and full of rain.

"How far?" She looked past him to the open land and seemed unsure. Then she focused her attention on the horse he'd tied to the post.

"Not far." He untied his horse, tightening the girth strap and watching her over the top of the saddle. "Since I'm riding, you'll need to go back down the drive, turn left and in a mile take a left at the entrance to the Circle M."

"How long before you get there?"

"It'll take me a little longer but I'm cutting through the field, so not much." They stood there staring at each other and he noticed the softness in her brown eyes. The last thing he wanted was to give in to the softness. Lawton had immediately trusted her. That wasn't Jake's way. He had to be the one to draw lines and make sure no one got hurt. But he wasn't an ogre. "I'm sorry."

She gave a quick nod her eyes registering surprise. "Thank you."

"He was a good man." More words of kindness. His brother Duke would have been proud. He'd told Jake to be nice to their new sister. He'd almost laughed at that. She was *not* their new sister.

Jake didn't need one more person to watch out for. His plate was full of siblings that couldn't seem to stay out of trouble.

With a goodbye nod, he put a foot in the stirrup and swung himself into the saddle. She shot him a wary look and headed for her car.

He watched her go, holding the gray gelding steady as the horse tossed his head, eager to be on his way. The car was down the drive when he turned the horse and headed for home. The rain had blown over but the air was damp and cool. It felt good, to let Bud loose. The horse was itching to run. So was Jake. But he knew he couldn't outrun the problem that was driving to his place in a compact car with Oklahoma tags.

Fifteen minutes later, with his horse unsaddled and back in the pasture, he headed for the house. Breezy was standing on the front porch of the stone-and-log home he'd been living in alone for more years than he cared to count. He'd be thirty-four soon. He guessed that made him a crusty bachelor.

"Pretty place," Breezy said when he reached the front porch of the house.

"Thank you."

He nodded toward the door. Time to get it over with. He figured she'd be here another ten minutes, and then she'd be gone and he wouldn't have to worry about her. He'd hand her a check and they'd go their separate ways.

Today he'd said a few prayers on the matter and maybe it was wrong, but he'd prayed she'd take the out. Of course he knew God didn't exactly answer prayers based on Jake Martin's wants. But he'd sure be grateful if the good Lord made this easy on him.

"Let's go inside." He led her across the porch with the bentwood furniture. Ceiling fans hung from the porch ceiling and in the summer they made evenings almost bearable. Not that he spent a lot of time sitting out there.

"Do you live here alone?" she asked, turning a bright shade of pink. "I mean, do you have family here? In Martin's Crossing?"

"This is my home and I do have family in Martin's Crossing." He didn't plan on giving her the family history.

What would he tell her? That he and his twin sister had helped raise their younger siblings after their mom had left town, left their dad and them? This ranch had been in their family for over one hundred years and keeping it going had put his dad in an early grave. Now he'd lost his sister, and he was determined to find a way to keep the family together, keep them strong, without her.

But no, he wasn't alone. He had his brothers, Duke and Brody. They had their little sister, Sam. Short for Samantha.

Duke lived in the old family homestead just down the road.

Their little brother, Brody, only came around when he needed a place to heal up after a bad ride on the back of a bull. The rest of the time he stayed with friends in a rented trailer in Stephenville.

Sam had been in boarding school and was now in college. Out of state. That was his idea, after she couldn't seem to keep her mind off a certain ranch hand. Their dad, Gabe Martin, hadn't seemed to connect with the thought that his family was falling apart. It had all been on Jake.

The house was dark and cool. He led Breezy through the living room and down the hall to his office.

He flipped the switch, bathing the room in light, and motioned for her to take a seat. He positioned himself behind the massive oak fixture and pulled out a drawer to retrieve papers.

Breezy took the seat on the other side of the desk. With a hand that trembled, she pushed long blond hair back from her face. Lawton had mentioned she sang and played guitar. Something about being a street performer in California. Jake had taken it upon himself to learn more.

"Why didn't you come back here with Lawton?" Jake asked, pinning her with a look that always made Samantha squirm. He didn't have kids of his own, probably never would, but he knew all the tricks.

She looked away, her attention on the fireplace.

"Miss Hernandez?"

"Call me Breezy," she whispered as she refocused, visibly pulling herself together. "I needed time to come to terms with what he'd told me. I didn't know how to suddenly be the sister he thought I would be. Or could be. And I have a sister in Oklahoma."

"I understand." It had come out of nowhere, this new

family of hers. "Lawton's dad kept his skeletons hidden pretty deeply. But as he got older—" he shrugged "—guilt caught up with him."

"I see." She bit down on her bottom lip. "I could have been a part of their lives."

His heart shifted a little. And sympathy was the last thing he wanted to feel.

"Yes, I guess."

"And Lawton's wife. She looked very sweet."

That's when his own pain slammed him hard. He cleared his throat, cleared the lump of emotion that settled there. He hadn't yet gotten used to the loss. "Elizabeth was my twin sister."

She bit down on her bottom lip and closed her eyes, just briefly. "I'm so sorry."

"So am I."

"So why am I here?"

"Because Lawton came home from Oklahoma and changed his will." He brushed a hand over his face, then he reached for the manila envelope on his desk. "He left you his house, money from his dad's estate, as well as a small percentage of his software and technologies company. He left the twins a larger percentage as well as a trust fund. The business manager, Tyler Randall, also inherited a small percentage of the company."

"I see." But she clearly didn't understand. He was about to make it clear. And he prayed she'd take the out.

"Breezy, Lawton and Elizabeth left us joint custody of their daughters."

He and this woman were now parents to two little girls.

Chapter Two

"No." Breezy shook her head. This couldn't be happening. No one would give her custody, even shared custody, of two little girls. "He couldn't have done that."

"I'm afraid he did."

She met his blue gaze, knowing he disliked her. Or at the least, disliked the situation he'd been forced into with her. He knew these little girls. They were the children of his twin sister. Of course he was angry. She was angry, too.

What had made Lawton, a man she barely knew, think this was a good idea? She'd never stayed in one place longer than six months until she moved to Dawson, Oklahoma. She'd never had real family until her sister, Mia, found her. She definitely didn't know how to raise a child.

"I'm not sure what to say," she admitted.

"That makes two of us. I never planned on losing my sister and my best friend. And I certainly couldn't have seen this coming."

Jake Martin studied her. His blue eyes were sharp; his generous mouth was a straight, unforgiving line.

He shook his head and hit a button on an intercom. A woman answered. "Okay," he said.

She sat quietly, forcing herself to maintain eye contact with him. The door behind her opened. She didn't turn, even when he looked past her, smiling at whoever had entered the room. There were footsteps and quiet voices.

Curiosity overrode her desire to hold his gaze, to not feel weak. She glanced back over her shoulder and the room spun in a crazy way that left her fighting tears, trying to focus. Twin girls toddled across the room wearing identical smiles on identical faces.

"These are your nieces." His voice came from far away.

"Oh." What else could she say? The toddler girls were smiling as they bypassed her to get to Jake Martin.

"The lovely lady behind them is Marty, their nanny," he explained, nodding toward the older woman who had remained in the doorway. He leaned down, holding out his arms. The girls ran to him and climbed onto his lap. He hugged them both tight.

"They're beautiful." They were dark-haired with blue eyes and big smiles. After all they'd been through, they could still smile. Though she didn't want to, she attributed that to the man sitting across from her.

"They are." He kissed the top of each dark head. "And we are their guardians."

"You should have told me."

He shrugged and looked at the girls, who had picked up pens and were drawing on the papers on his desk. He moved the envelope out of their reach.

"I think I just did."

"I meant from the beginning."

"Really? I should have disclosed this to someone I've never met?" He shook his head. "I'll do whatever I need to do to keep them safe."

"I get that." She kept her voice soft, not wanting the girls to hear anger. She had too many memories of loud and unforgiving voices as she hid beneath the bed with Mia and their brother, Juan.

Was she really angry with him? As she studied the little girls on his lap, she thought not. He wanted to protect them.

He grinned at the girls and they reached up to pat his lean cheeks. "Rosie and Violet, this is your aunt Breezy."

She had nieces. She wanted to hug those little girls close. She wanted to hold them forever. They were looking at her, wide-eyed, curious but not ready to come to her.

"Hi, girls." What else could she say? Her vision blurred. She raised her hand to wipe away the tears that drifted down her cheeks.

Jake Martin looked at the little girls he held, his gaze serious and then he refocused on Breezy. He studied her, as if looking for a sign that she might run. He pushed a box of tissues across the desk, never removing his eyes from her. She wouldn't run. She didn't know what he knew about her, about her past, but she wouldn't run. She couldn't. Not now.

"Marty, why don't you take the girls back to their playroom?" He set the girls down, easing them onto their feet. They walked around the desk and Breezy wanted to touch them. Rose smiled up at her and toddled close, little legs and bare feet peeking out from her colorful sundress, white with big brightly colored flowers. Violet held back, letting Rose take the lead.

They were identical, but not. Rose had a slightly rounder face. Her dark hair had a bit of wave. Violet's dark hair was perfectly straight.

"Hi, Rose." She leaned and the little girl walked up, unafraid, her little face splitting in a dimpled grin.

"Hi, Rose," the toddler repeated and giggled. Breezy smiled.

"You're both very pretty."

"Very pretty," Rose repeated and Violet giggled.

"And smart."

"Smart a…" Rose started what sounded like something inappropriate.

"No!" Marty jumped forward. "Uncle Duke is a bad influence."

"I know he is." Jake shook his head. "He's going to start putting money in a college fund if he doesn't watch his language around them."

Marty took the hand of each girl and they left the room with soft words, giggles and the patter of their bare feet.

"They're precious." Breezy turned to face what felt like her judge and jury. He had leaned back in the big leather chair and his booted feet were on the desk.

"Yes, they are. And I will do anything to protect them."

"I'm sure you would." She studied him for a minute. "But you don't have to protect them from me."

"That's the problem. I don't know you, Breezy. I know you were Lawton's sister and he had the crazy idea that this would be best for his girls. But he also didn't plan on dying so soon."

"You don't want me in their lives?"

He exhaled sharply and shook his head. Of course he didn't. "I'm not sure what I want."

The answer surprised her. "Did you hope I wouldn't show up?"

He shrugged. "It would have made my life easier."

"Right, but I'm here and those little girls are just as much my family as they are yours. Tell me what I need to do."

Jake Martin tapped his pen on the desk and studied her.

"Lawton left us joint custody as long as you remain here, in his house. But there are stipulations. If you leave, you lose custody and ownership of the house. If I see a reason that you're not capable of this, I take full custody. If either of those should happen and I should take full custody, the house goes to the girls. The money is yours no matter what happens. He had hoped…"

"That I would be in their lives."

"Yes. He said you'd lived a life of independence and adventure. He wanted his daughters to learn that from you." He brushed his hands through his hair and she saw the lines of exhaustion around his eyes. "Lawton had a very different life. *Structure* was the senator's favorite word."

"I see." She let her gaze travel to the windows that offered a view of the rolling fields dotted with cattle. Craggy, tree-covered hills rose in the distance, gray and misty, as clouds spread across the sky.

Her brother had seen her life as adventurous. She guessed it had been, if a person wasn't fond of knowing where one would sleep or where their next meal would come from.

Jake moved in his chair. His shoulders were broad, his arms corded with strong muscles. Breezy had always been taller than average. She wasn't a petite little thing who backed down easily. She had street smarts, and a black belt.

All of that aside, Jake Martin intimidated her. He was lethal, she thought. The type of man who had always had power, never felt afraid or out of control of his life.

"I guess you'll have to trust me," she said after several minutes of trying to get a handle on her emotions.

"You have the option to take your money and leave." He slid a check and a few papers across the desk.

She took both and he sat there like a rock, a solid mountain of a man with a strong chin and a mouth that shifted the smooth planes of his face when he smiled, making him less intimidating.

She considered the offer, to take the money and leave. That was the option he wanted her to take. And maybe he had the right of it. How long could she stay here without feeling caged? What about her life in Dawson with Mia and her adopted family, the Coopers? Did those two little girls really need someone like her?

Martin's Crossing was another small town. For a girl raised in cities, she wasn't used to small-town closeness, church on Sundays, people who knew her story. A picture of those two little girls on his desk caught her attention, making her rethink who she used to be and forcing her come to terms with the person she needed to be now.

"I'm not going anywhere." She sat back and gave him a satisfied smile that trembled at the edges. Hopefully he didn't notice it, or how her hands shook as she took the check and looked at the amount. She repeated her mantra. "I'm staying here with my nieces. If this is what Lawton wanted, then I owe it to him."

"For how long?" His jaw clenched. "What would it take to buy you out, to make you leave?"

"I'm not for sale. I have two nieces who have lost both of their parents."

He sighed and stood up, obviously not happy with her response.

"Okay, fine. So here's the deal, Breezy." He walked to the window and then looked back at her. "I don't want the girls to be upset by this situation. They've been through enough."

"I agree."

"That means you'll understand that I make the rules."

"Why is that?"

"Several reasons. Lawton left the decision-making to me. They're comfortable with me, and with Marty. I'll bring them over to the house so they can get to know you."

"Joint custody?" she reminded him with a voice that unfortunately shook.

"Right, and that will happen. But first we'll go slowly. You'll visit with them. I'll supervise. If all goes well, we'll come up with an arrangement that works for us both."

"When do I get to spend time with them?"

"Tomorrow." He picked up the hat he'd dropped on his desk. "I have work to get done and you'd probably like to settle in."

"I guess that's my cue to leave." She stood, picking up her purse and waiting for him to say something.

He rounded his desk and walked with her to the door. "I'm sure you'll find what you need at Lawton's place." He pulled a key out of his pocket and handed it to her. "Anything else you need, you'll find in Martin's Crossing."

"Is there a grocery store?"

"Yes. Grocery store, gas station, restaurant and feed store. There are a couple of little shops, antiques and the like."

He opened the front door and motioned her out ahead of him. She shivered as she stepped outside, surprised by how cold it had gotten. With this weather, she could believe Christmas was coming. She'd been looking forward to spending the holidays with Mia.

"Do you have any other questions?" Jake asked.

"None." She nodded at him, her final goodbye. And then the case of nerves she'd been fighting hit and she couldn't get her feet to move forward.

Her brother and sister-in-law were gone. She had two nieces who needed her. She needed them just as much. The man standing next to her seemed to be calling all of the shots. Everything inside her ached.

"Are you okay?" His voice rumbled close to her ear. She shivered at his nearness.

"Yeah, I'm good." She swiped at her eyes and looked away from his steady gaze, taking a deep breath. A hand, strong and warm, touched her arm, sharing his strength.

"It'll all work out. Maybe it doesn't seem that way right now, but it will. And I'm sorry, that you and Lawton didn't have a chance to spend more time together."

She nodded and closed her eyes. The hand remained on her arm. But then it slipped away. She opened her eyes and took in a deep breath. She could do this.

"Thank you." She looked up at him, surprised by the way his presence gave her more strength than she would have imagined.

Maybe someday they would be friends, even allies.

He pulled a business card out of his shirt pocket and a pen, quickly writing something on the back before handing it to her. "That's the information for the alarm system. And you can call if you have any problems. I'll see you tomorrow at noon."

She took the card, glanced at it then slipped it into her purse. "I'll make lunch."

He gave her a look but then he nodded. "You can do that."

Breezy walked down the stone steps to her car, her mind reeling. As she backed out of the drive Jake Martin still stood on the porch. He raised a hand as she pulled away and she returned the gesture.

It was the beginning of a truce. Truce, but not trust. Jake Martin wasn't the type of man who would give trust easily. She understood because she was the same way.

Jake walked back inside. He found Marty waiting for him.

"Are the girls down for a nap?" he asked on his way to the kitchen, knowing Marty would follow.

"Yes. They were asking again." She shook her head, and he knew that meant the girls wanted their mommy and daddy. "They're a little lost, of course."

Jake tossed his hat on the counter as he went for a glass of iced tea. "Aren't we all?"

"Yes, but I worry about you, Jake, about you taking on one more burden."

He shook his head at that. "The twins are family, not a burden."

"You've raised a family. You've been taking care of people your whole life."

Of course, he'd raised a family. His brothers and sisters had been counting on him for as long as he could remember. He'd made sure they were fed. He'd been the one to hire Marty years ago when his dad was sick and not really paying attention. He'd made sure the ranch kept making a profit.

Now he'd make sure Rosie and Violet were loved and protected.

Marty handed him a cup of coffee and then patted his arm the way she'd been doing for a long time, since she and her husband first came to town. Long before she was the cook and housekeeper, she'd figured out what life was like at the Circle M for a bunch of ragtag kids trying to make do with a mom that had left and a dad who had checked out.

"Brody called," she said as she moved back to the counter and a bag of carrots that suddenly held her interest.

"And?" His younger brother had a knack for finding trouble.

"He and Lincoln had a fight. He's coming home."

Brody and his roommate and traveling partner were always one argument away from killing each other so Jake wasn't surprised. He shrugged and took a drink from his cup. Marty started peeling carrots again.

"Well, I guess he'll figure it out. The bull-riding season is almost over. He's probably tired of being on the road."

"He does get homesick, even if he doesn't admit it."

He set the glass in the sink and leaned a hip against the edge of the counter, crossing his arms over his chest as he waited for Marty to tell him what he needed to do. She was good at giving him advice. And, even if he wouldn't admit it, she was usually right.

"Don't lecture him," she finally said. "I heard something in his voice."

"I'll go easy on him. He's a grown man. It's time he made his own decisions, anyway."

Marty put a hand on his arm. "Is it really possible for you to do that?"

He grinned at her fairly unsympathetic tone. "No, probably not. What's for dinner?"

"I'm making beef stew."

"Okay." He waited, watching. He could see the furrow in her brow and knew she had more on her mind than the stew.

"It's okay for you to let this young woman help. I know you have reservations…"

"Because we don't know her at all," he reminded.

Marty shot him a look that he couldn't fail to understand. He was being too "Jake" for her liking. He did like to take control. He liked to know his family was taken care of and safe. Old habits were hard to let go of.

"You've raised your siblings. Now you're looking at raising two little girls. And I'm sorry, but they need more than you, Jake. I think Lawton was right. These girls need Breezy. I might not know her well, but I think I'm a good judge of character and she seems like someone you can trust."

"It's possible she won't stay."

Marty stopped dicing up an onion. "Because of her childhood? All I see is a young woman that was a victim of her situation."

He grinned and kissed the top of Marty's head. "I love you, Marty."

She sniffled and wiped at tears trickling down her cheeks. "Silly onions."

"Onions never make you cry."

"Oh, hush. Go to town."

As Marty cried, he placed a hand on her shoulder. She covered that hand with her own.

"I'm okay."

"Of course you are."

She was always okay. He'd known Marty most of his life. She and her husband had moved to Martin's Crossing to pastor the Community Church at the edge of town. That had been close to twenty-five years ago. After Earl passed away, Marty had stayed on. She'd been the cook and housekeeper for the Martins. Then she'd gone to work for Lawton and Elizabeth after the girls were born.

"I need potatoes," Marty said on a sigh.

"I'll get a bag in town."

"I should have planned better."

He shrugged it off. "I'm sure there are other things

we need. I've got a calf to check on, then I'll come back in for a list."

As he reached for his hat, she stopped him. "Give her a chance. I don't think she's had a lot of them."

"That's the Marty I know and love. You always see the good in people."

"This is the Marty who knows that God doesn't need us to judge for Him. That doesn't mean she gets a free pass. Our baby girls come first."

He laughed at that. "And there's the Marty who protects her little ones."

Her smile returned, settling in her gray eyes. "You'd better believe it."

Jake believed it.

And he'd do his best to give Breezy a chance. But flat-out trust? That was something he'd have to work on. He'd learned—in life and in business—to reserve the right to form opinions at a later date.

Time would tell, he told himself as he headed out to the barn. She'd stay or she'd go. While she was in Martin's Crossing he'd do his best to treat her like family, because that's what Lawton would have wanted.

Chapter Three

⌒∾

Breezy was standing on the porch when Jake pulled up to Lawton's house the next day. She could see two little girls in the backseat of the truck. Her heart thumped hard against her ribs. This was it. Her new life.

She'd spent the rest of yesterday and this morning wondering how she would do this. How would she stay in Martin's Crossing? How would she know how to take care of two little girls? After cleaning a layer of dust off the furniture the previous evening, she'd sat down and tried to list the pros and cons of staying in Martin's Crossing.

And she'd gotten stuck on Jake Martin, on the wariness in his eyes, on the way he'd questioned her, on the way his hand had touched her arm. Jake Martin had trust issues. Breezy had her own issues. She didn't know how to settle, how to put down roots.

Sticking around now took on a lot of importance, for herself and for two little girls. She watched Jake unbuckle the girls from their car seats. Staying meant everything. She headed his way to help.

If he would let her.

It shouldn't bother her. She'd grown up used to people giving her suspicious looks. She'd spent her life adjusting to new people, new situations. She knew how to reinvent herself. She could be the person two little girls needed her to be. Once she figured out who that person was.

She stepped close to the car, watching as he unbuckled one of the twins. Then he placed that little person in her arms. Dark hair straight, face thinner than the other little girl. "Hello, Violet."

The little girl just stared, her eyes big and unsure. Yes, Breezy was getting used to that look. It mirrored the expression on Uncle Jake's face. The man in question pushed the truck door closed. He held Rose in one arm against his side and the little girl patted his cheek with her tiny hand. Breezy watched the change that took place when he was in the presence of these little girls.

The twins made him human. They softened the distrust in his blue eyes.

"Are you ready for us?" he asked with a grin that surprised her.

Breezy nodded. "I'm ready."

She walked in front of him, Violet in her arms. The little girl smelled like baby soap and fabric softener. Her arms had gone around Breezy's neck. They reached the front door and Jake reached around her to push it open, a small touch of chivalry she hadn't expected.

As they stepped inside, Violet struggled to be free. Breezy let the little girl down and Violet toddled as quickly as her little legs could carry her. In the center of the living room, she looked around, unsure. And then she cried.

"Momma!" Violet wailed, walking through the room. "Momma!"

Jake went after her, scooping her up with his free arm. "It's okay, baby girl."

By then both twins were crying and clinging to Jake.

"I'm sorry." Breezy stood helpless and unsure of how to help. Should she reach for the twins? Maybe she didn't have the mom gene. How could she, really? She'd never truly had a mother of her own.

Jake noticed and his expression softened although the concern remained in his eyes.

"It isn't your fault. It's just too soon to bring them here."

Breezy looked around, trying to come up with something. "They have toys here. Let's pull out the toys and let them settle down. I'm not sure that avoiding this house is what they need. They lived here. It's familiar to them."

"I think I know where they lived."

"I think you should give me a chance." She reached over and this time Rosie held her arms out and fell into Breezy's embrace. The toddler's arms around her neck took her by surprise.

"I'm working on it," he said in a raspy voice.

Of course he was. She sat down on the edge of the sofa and Rose slid off her lap and headed for the guitar Breezy had left leaning against the wall. The little girl moved quickly. Breezy moved faster, getting the instrument before the child could grab it. But she held it, letting Rose pluck the strings. With a few strands of hair on top of her head in a pink bow, Rose smiled and jabbered.

"Do you want a song?" Breezy asked, settling on the sofa again. Rose rested against her knees.

Jake had moved to the nearby chair, still holding Violet. As Breezy started to play, the child slid down from his lap and joined Rose. Breezy swallowed past the lump of emotion that lodged in her throat. She managed not to cry. Instead she sang a Christmas song because it sounded like one a child would be soothed by.

As she sang, Rose clapped a few times and sounded as if she might be singing along. But it was hard to tell in the language of a two-year-old. She finished and set the guitar back on the floor. Violet had wandered back to Jake and was leaning against him, her thumb in her mouth, twirling dark curls around her finger.

He cleared his throat, and the little girl looked up at him. He scooped her into his arms. "We should feed them."

"Yes, of course."

If the music had soothed the girls, it seemed to have had the opposite effect on Jake. He headed off to the kitchen like a lion with a thorn in his paw. She remembered the folk tale, and knew, with certainty, that she wasn't the mouse who would offer to remove the thorn. She wouldn't want to get that close to the lion.

"I made soup and grilled cheese." She walked to the stove, ignoring the man who had taken the girls to the dining room. "I have the sandwiches ready to grill and the soup is warm."

She wasn't about to admit that she'd pondered for a

very long time over what to feed the girls. She had no idea if they could eat a sandwich or if they were still eating baby food.

"They'll eat that." He settled Violet in her high chair and then reached for Rosie.

Breezy watched from the doorway but then turned to the kitchen and the job of finishing lunch. She turned the griddle on and pulled the already buttered bread out of the fridge, along with the cheese slices she would put in the middle. When she had them on the electric griddle, she found Jake Martin in the doorway watching her.

"You play well," he said in an easy tone.

"Thank you," she said, turning back to the griddle. "What would you like to drink?"

"I can get our drinks. The girls are buckled in and I can see them from here," he offered as he took glasses from the cabinet.

She nodded, as if she wasn't making a mental list of parenting dos and don'ts. One: always make sure they are buckled and within line of sight. Yes, those things seemed like common sense, but what if she forgot something? What if there was a rule that most people knew but she didn't? She'd learned a lot of those rules when she'd moved in with Mia, but Mia's stepson, Caleb, was almost seven now. He didn't require safety seats or high chairs anymore.

"Are you talking to yourself?" He opened the fridge and pulled out the pitcher of tea she'd made that morning. Tea should never be instant. Mia had taught her that rule. There were other rules, too. Going to church on Sunday was another one.

Had she been talking to herself? She bit down on her bottom lip and shook her head, hoping that was the right answer. "No, of course not. I was telling you there are sippy cups here and milk in the fridge."

"Of course. Because the word *milk* sounds like *rules*."

"It could," she hedged. She flipped the sandwiches off the griddle onto a plate.

He laughed. "You're kidding, right?"

She started to feel a little bubble of laughter coming to the surface. She didn't want to laugh, not with him. Laughing with Jake would make them feel like friends and he clearly was *not* a friend.

"There aren't rules, Breezy."

"Aren't there?"

She ladled the soup into bowls, adding just a tiny amount for the twins. How much soup would they eat?

"A little more than that," Jake responded to her unasked question. "And I guess there *are* some rules."

Great, she loved rules. She might as well ask now and get it over with before she broke them all and found herself dismissed from the lives of her nieces. He'd made it clear he had the power to do that.

"Okay, tell me the rules."

Jake cut up the sandwiches and placed them in front of the girls. She'd forgotten to do that. Next time, sandwiches in four triangles. That was simple enough. She set the soup on the table. Jake moved it back.

"What?"

"Soup out of reach or it'll be on the floor before we can turn around."

"Rule one, no soup."

He laughed, the sound a little rusty but nice. He should laugh more often.

"I didn't say no soup," he clarified. "I said out of reach."

She handed him a glass of tea and he took the seat next to Violet. Breezy took that as her cue and moved to the seat next to Rose. The little girl had already reached for a triangle of sandwich and was nibbling crust.

"Next rule?" Breezy asked as she reached for her sandwich.

Jake held out his hand. "We pray before we eat."

Of course. She let out a sigh and took the hand he offered. She ignored the fact that with one hand in his and one hand holding Rose's, she felt connected.

And a little bit trapped. No, she couldn't ignore that.

Jake took a bite of sandwich and nearly choked. "What in the world is that?"

Next to him Violet gagged. Rose continued to nibble as if it was the best thing she'd ever eaten.

"It's grilled cheese."

"That is *not* cheese," he pointed out.

"No, it's not," she admitted. "It's cheese substitute."

Jake put the sandwich down on his plate and took a long drink of tea, hoping it was real tea. It was. After he washed the taste of fake cheese out of his mouth he pinned the woman across from him with a look. "Rule three, no fake cheese. That's not even real food."

She laughed a little and smiled at Rose, who was happily chowing down. Rose grinned up at Breezy. Drool and cheese slid down her chin.

"Rose likes it," she informed him.

"Rose doesn't know better." He pushed back from

the table and headed for the kitchen. "I think we'll have more soup and crackers, if you haven't found a substitute for those."

When he returned to the dining room, she looked less than sure of herself. "I thought it would be healthier for them."

"They're two, they need to eat dairy." He ladled more soup in the bowls and tossed a sleeve of crackers in front of Breezy. She had taken a bite of sandwich and made a face.

"It is pretty gross."

"So you're not really a vegetarian?"

She shook her head. "No, I just thought it sounded like the right thing for children."

He laughed and then she laughed. Maybe this is how they would get through this mess, with laughter. Maybe they would work out a friendship and he would learn to trust her. But he wasn't ready for that. Not right now. He sat back down and pushed the sandwich away. "I think maybe next time we'll stick to real cheese."

"Right," she said. "And maybe we should go over the rest of the rules."

He leaned back in his chair, his gaze settling on Violet's dark hair as she sipped soup from her spoon. "It isn't as if I've made a list of rules, Breezy. I'm not trying to make this difficult. I just have to be the person who keeps them safe."

"You think you're on your own with this?"

He didn't answer the question because he didn't want to explain that having Sylvia Martin for a mother meant he'd been taking care of children since he'd been old enough to reach the stove.

He didn't know how to let go. And in his experience, women had a tendency not to stick around. At least not the ones in his life.

"I'm not on my own," he finally answered. "But I'm the head of this family and I will always make sure these little girls are taken care of."

"Maybe give me the benefit of the doubt and understand that I want the same for them. I want them happy and healthy. I want to be part of their lives." She leaned a little in his direction. "C'mon. Give me the rules. You know it'll make you feel better."

"I don't know what the rules are." Even as he said it he found himself smiling, and surprised by that. She did that, he realized. She undid his resolve with a cheerful smile and a teasing glint in her golden-brown eyes.

"You have rules," she said. "Should I get some paper or do you think I can remember them all?"

"Okay. Church. We always attend church."

She smiled at that. "Because it's a law in Martin's Crossing or because you are a man of faith?"

"What does that mean?"

She shrugged. "You made it sound like a law," she said. "If broken, they'll what? Stone me in the town square?"

"No, they won't stone you in the town square and yes, I'm a man of faith."

"Okay, Rule Number Three, church. I can do church."

There was a hesitance to her voice that he wanted to question but he didn't.

"We eat as a family on Sunday afternoons."

"Am I considered family now?"

"You're family." He hadn't planned this, for her to be

in their lives, a part of their family, but she was. Man, she complicated his life in so many ways.

On the other hand, the rules made him smile, because he'd never intended to list them. He hadn't even thought of them as rules until she pointed it out.

"Okay, church and Sunday dinner. That's nice. What if I bring the tofu pizza?"

"Rule Number Five…"

She laughed. "No tofu?"

"Never." He pushed back from the table and she did the same. "I need to check on the cattle."

"Is checking on cattle a rule?" She grinned at him.

"No, it isn't a rule. It's something that has to be done."

"Can I help you do things here? I mean, I'm going to be around, I might as well earn my keep."

He unbuckled Violet and lifted her from the high chair. He hadn't expected Breezy to offer her help. What was he supposed to tell her, that he'd been looking for an excuse to get away from her for a few minutes? He hadn't expected her to tease, and he definitely hadn't expected to enjoy her company.

"You want to help out with the cattle?"

She looked a little unsure. "Well, maybe. I mean, is there a way I can help?"

"Have you ever lived on a ranch, Breezy?"

"My sister was raised on a ranch in Oklahoma."

"But you, have *you* ever lived on a ranch?"

"I've seen cows." She said it with a wink.

He held Violet close but he smiled at the woman opposite him. "You've seen cows but thought cheese came from a plant?"

"Okay, let's not mention that anymore, and I promise to never buy nondairy again."

"Thank you. I can't even believe they had such a thing at the store in town. And we still have a few rules to cover."

"Such as?" She had Rose in her arms and the little girl's eyes were droopy. Breezy kissed her cheek and stroked her hair, causing those droopy eyes to close and her head to nod. She'd be asleep in a few minutes. So would Violet.

He headed for the living room and she followed. "If you are here long enough to date, we don't bring dates home, or around the girls."

"That's absurd. Are you planning to stay single until they're eighteen?"

He didn't like the question, and as he settled into a rocking chair with Violet he tried to ignore it. Bottom line was he wouldn't let a mother walk out on Violet and Rose. The twins had already lost enough.

Violet nodded off in his arms. Rose was already on the sofa, a blanket pulled up over her. He started to get out of the rocking chair with Violet but Breezy moved to take her from him, her blond hair falling forward. The silky strands brushed his arms as she lifted his niece. Their hands touched and he looked up to meet her gaze head-on.

The strangest feelings erupted as she moved away from him with Violet in her arms. It made him want to reach out to her, to know her better, to trust her.

He shook off those thoughts because they didn't make sense.

He watched as she carried Violet away from him,

cradling her gently and then settling her on the opposite end of the sofa from her sister. He remained in the rocking chair, as she covered the little girl with a pink afghan. She kissed Violet's cheek and brushed her hair back from her face.

If she was going to leave, he hoped she left before the twins got used to her touch, to her softness.

"I'm going to the barn," he said, heading for the front door. She didn't have a chance to question him. He didn't need more tangled-up emotions to deal with. He needed fresh air and a few minutes to clear his thoughts.

And a few rules for himself when it came to Breezy Hernandez.

Chapter Four

Thursday morning, just a few days into this new life of hers, Breezy stepped outside with a cup of coffee. It was cool, crisp, but not cold. She breathed in the slightly frosty air as she settled in a rocking chair on the front porch. The land stretching forever in front of her was different than Oklahoma, yet similar. The terrain surrounding the house was flat with small trees; the leaves had turned and were falling. An old barn stood in the field, gray wood against a backdrop of a foggy morning. A short distance away the ground rose in rugged hills, also dotted with trees. She knew there was a lake not far from Martin's Crossing, and the creek that ran through this property emptied into that lake.

The sun rose, turning the frosty air to morning fog and touching everything in pinkish-gold. It made her think of faith, of believing in something other than herself. She'd tried, since she was little, to capture that faith.

Not just the faith, but what came with it. The sense

of having purpose, of belonging, of Sunday dinners and laughing families.

She wanted that life. She wanted a home that would always be hers, with belongings that were hers. Maybe she wouldn't have to leave. Maybe she could fill this house with pictures and things she collected.

Her gaze drifted in the direction of the metal barn, a newer structure, part lean-to for cattle and part machine shed for farm equipment. Something was off. She tried to figure out what was different. And then she saw the cattle moving outside an open gate.

They definitely shouldn't be out. She would have to do something about the problem.

She set her cup down and slipped her feet into her slippers As she ran across the yard and then down the dirt track to the barn, she was struck with the realization that she didn't have a clue what she needed to do once she reached the cattle. Of course she knew she should put them back in the field. But exactly how did a person go about putting up a small herd of cattle?

As she ran she shouted and waved her arms. The cattle continued to drift, separating into several small groups. They were gigantic black beasts. One eyed her with a glare. She glared back.

"Back inside that gate, you wooly mammoths." She waved her arms and ran at the animals.

For the most part they stood their ground. A few moved out of her way but definitely not toward the gate. Several dropped their heads to graze on winter-brown grass. One took several cautious steps in her direction.

She paused to watch, hopeful he wasn't going to charge her but not really positive. Time for a new tactic.

"Back in the field. If you please, Sir Loin."

She shooed him with her hands. He shook his massive head. She started to run at him, slipping a little on the frosty grass.

"Listen, hamburger, I was giving you the benefit of the doubt when I thought you were a gentleman, now go." She charged at him, waving her arms.

He snorted and took a few quick steps away from her before turning back to face her again. It clicked in her city-girl brain that she wasn't going to win a battle against a one-ton animal. Plus, she had nowhere to run. The small herd of cattle were between her and the barn. The house was a few hundred feet behind her. There were definitely no trees to climb.

Her legs suddenly grew a little shaky and she started to worry how much it would hurt to be trampled by a bull. He had turned his attention back to her. The other cows were grazing and moving away. Maybe she should have started with them because they definitely looked less aggressive.

Walk away, slow and easy. It was the same advice she'd given herself on city streets at night when someone walked a little too closely behind her or came out of an alley looking for trouble. Never let them see your fear.

She started to walk, glancing over her shoulder to make sure he wasn't going to charge. He seemed content to watch. But as she moved toward the barn, she heard him moving. She looked back over her shoulder and he was trotting toward her, his head lowered.

"No!" She started to run.

Sharp barks and the sound of a horse's hooves broke

through her fear-fogged brain. She saw the flash as a dog rushed past her, heard his warning barks, and then a horse moved next to her. She looked up, her entire body turning to jello as her heart tried to beat itself out of her chest.

Jake Martin smiled down at her and then he swung, with casual ease, from the saddle. He landed lightly on the ground, all six-plus-feet of him.

"Having some troubles, Miss Hernandez?"

"Oh, no, I just felt like playing with the cattle, Mr. Martin. They seemed lonely. I thought the bull would like to play fetch."

"Yes." He grinned. "Bulls do love to play fetch. I hate to ruin your fun, but what say we put your playmates back in the field and figure out how they got loose."

"Good idea." She peeked around his horse, a red-gold animal that was huge, because a man like Jake Martin needed a huge beast to ride.

The dog, a heeler, was having a great time circling the cattle and bringing them toward the gate.

"Why don't you wait inside the barn?" Jake pointed and she nodded in agreement, her insides settling now that he was there.

He swung back into the saddle and the horse spun in a tight half circle, going after a few cows that were making for the house and the yard. Breezy watched from the door of the barn, somewhat entranced by the beauty of it. Jake's horse seemed to obey with the slightest touch of his hands on the reins or his knees on its sides. The dog kept an eye on the cattle and an ear perked toward Jake, waiting for various commands.

Within minutes the cattle were back in the field

and the gate was closed. Jake slid to the ground again and wrapped the reins around a post. The dog plopped down on the ground and proceeded to lick his paws.

Jake walked toward her, no longer smiling but giving the place a careful look. When he got to her, he peeked inside the barn.

"Have you been in there?"

She shook her head. "No. I was sitting on the porch with a cup of coffee when I saw that they were out and this door was open."

"The door was open?" His brows came together and his eyes narrowed. "You haven't been out here at all?"

"No, of course not."

"I'm sorry, I'm not accusing you, just trying to figure things out. Stay out here."

"No!"

He smiled, his features relaxing. "Chicken?"

"No, of course not. But why would I stay out here if you're going in there?"

He pushed the door open a little wider and motioned her inside. "By all means, be my guest."

She stepped inside the hazy, dark interior of the barn. Jake was right behind her, his arm brushing hers as he stepped around her. Without a word he headed down the center aisle for the open door at the other end.

"You haven't seen anyone? Any cars? Any sounds last night?"

"Nothing."

He slowed as he reached the open door. For the first time she felt a sliver of fear. It shivered up her spine as she stepped close to the wall. Jake eased close to the room and looked inside. And then he stepped through that door, leaving her somewhat alone.

"Is everything okay?" she whispered.

He stepped out of the room, shaking his head. "The office is ransacked. I'm not sure what anyone was hoping to find in there. But I'm going to call the police and file a report, just to be on the safe side."

So much for her calm, peaceful existence in Martin's Crossing. Breezy sank with relief onto an overturned bucket and watched as Jake paced a short distance away from her. He spoke quietly on his cell phone, making it impossible to hear him. But she couldn't help wondering if he suspected her. Why wouldn't he? She'd showed up in town, the mysterious sister of Lawton Brooks. She was a woman who had lived on the streets. Her resume included panhandling, singing for change and an arrest record—although no charges were ever filed. Why wouldn't he suspect her? Most people did.

Even her sister Mia's husband, Slade, had been a little on the suspicious side when he first found her. He'd looked into her past and dug up what dirt he could find. He'd done it for Mia. Even bringing her to Oklahoma had been for Mia, not for Breezy.

It had worked out, though. And had given her a taste of what it was like to belong. It had only been a few days, but she wanted to belong in Martin's Crossing. Belong to a town with a small grocery store and neighbors who asked how she was doing.

Jake ended his call and walked back toward her. With his long, powerful strides he was there in a matter of steps. He kneeled next to her, bending those long legs and folding his arms over his knees. He pushed back the black cowboy hat and peered at her. He looked concerned.

She took a breath and waited.

"Are you okay?"

"Of course I am." She made sure to smile as she said it. "Why wouldn't I be?"

His face split in a grin. "Well, you were almost toast out there with Johnny."

"The bull's name is Johnny? How ridiculous."

Eye brows arched. "Really? What would you name him?"

She shook her head. "I thought perhaps Sir Loin. But then he didn't seem very chivalrous for a knight, so maybe Johnny is better."

"He usually isn't aggressive, but he does like to play. And when a bull his size decides to play, that makes you the bouncy ball."

"I'm glad you came along when you did."

"Me, too," he replied. His voice was soft, like wind through the pines, and it undid her a tiny bit. "You're probably cold."

She was cold. She'd been wearing yoga pants and a T-shirt when she'd gone on this wild adventure. And her slippers were soaked from the damp morning grass. As she considered her pathetic condition, he slipped off his jacket and eased it around her shoulders.

"This should help."

Words failed her. The jacket smelled of Jake Martin, like pine, mountains in the fall and cold winter air. She wanted to bury her nose in the collar and inhale his scent. She wanted to tell him she didn't need his jacket. Without his jacket she was safe. Not tangled up with him, longing to be a part of something she'd never be a part of. In her experience, wanting always ended with disappointment. What she wanted was always taken from her or left behind when she moved on.

Jake watched as a train of emotions flickered across her face. He'd seen gratitude when he'd first put that coat around her, then he'd seen fear and maybe regret. He wished she wasn't so easy to read. She'd be less complicated if she could be as composed as she thought she was.

Breezy was poetry, classic novels and maybe the Bible, all rolled into one very open book. It was a book he thought he might like to read. In any other life but his own.

For Violet and Rose's sakes, he couldn't mess this up. He'd seen, even in their short introduction to Breezy, that the girls would need this woman in their lives. But he couldn't need her. His entire life was a juggling act. The ranch, his career, the twins, his family. One more thing might set the whole mess falling fast around him.

But he would handle the moments when she made him smile, made him laugh. He was selfish that way.

"Do you want to go back to the house?" he asked, needing to get past whatever vibrated in the air between them.

She shook her head; he'd known she would. "I'm cold, but I'm not going to faint or fall apart, Martin."

He smiled again. "I didn't begin to think you would, Hernandez."

At that she actually smiled, and he saw her vulnerability slip away. She was strong again. Snuggled in his jacket that she would leave scented with her lavender-and-citrus fragrance.

"If you need to do something, go right ahead," she offered. "I know you didn't come over here with the intention of rescuing me and then solving a mystery."

"No, I came over to feed. To do that, I'll have to get the tractor and hook a round bale. I'll be gone in about fifteen minutes."

"I haven't forgotten how to protect myself. I've been doing it a long time."

He had no doubt she could protect herself. And he also knew that was her way of telling him she didn't need him to look after her. He walked away, taking a spare jacket that had been left inside the tack room and heading out the side door to the tractor. He climbed up into the big green-and-yellow machine and closed the door, blocking out the sounds and thoughts that were bombarding him this morning.

But one thought wouldn't be evaded. When was the last time anyone had looked out for Breezy? Had she ever been made to feel safe, to feel protected?

It wasn't his job, that role of protector. She did have a sister in Oklahoma. And she had made it clear that she relied on herself, her own abilities.

Jake had the twins, Samantha, Brody and sometimes Duke to watch over, to keep out of trouble and to protect. Lawton had put Breezy in his life but he hadn't made Jake her guardian.

With that settled in his mind, he drove out through the field with a round bale on the back of the tractor and cattle following behind him. He'd hired a kid to do this job but it hadn't worked out. James had been twenty-one and wanting to save up to go to welding school. After a week of taking care of things at Lawton's place, James had stopped showing up.

That left it to Jake. Maybe when Brody came home he'd help out. And Duke would do what he could.

As he headed back to the barn to park the tractor the county deputy was pulling up in his car. Mac the blue heeler greeted him, his stub tail wagging. Jake knew the deputy. They'd gone to school together a long time ago.

When he stepped back into the barn after parking the tractor, Deputy Aaron Mallard was in the office. Breezy stood in the doorway answering questions and apologizing because she really hadn't seen anything other than loose cattle and an open door.

The deputy nodded in greeting when he saw Jake. "Jake, been a while."

"Aaron, yeah, it has. I didn't touch anything, but I can tell you it wasn't like this yesterday."

"Didn't figure you left it a mess. And I know Lawton was a stickler for neatness. Someone was looking for something in the filing cabinet. It's pried open. Funny, because I'm not seeing anything but feed bills and farm equipment receipts."

"That's really all that we kept in here."

"Anything in the house that someone would want?"

"I guess there could still be paperwork or research in Lawton's office. He took most of his work to Austin but sometimes he worked at home," Jake responded. He tried to remember anything Lawton had said or even hinted at. Had they had prowlers before? It wasn't un-heard-of these days.

The country used to be safe. They hadn't locked their doors for more years than he could remember. Yeah, life had changed. People didn't mind stealing from neighbors. Worse than that, now they even stole from the church if they got a chance.

What had happened to respect? Leaning against the door frame, he shook his head at the turn of his thoughts. "I'll take a look around, and see if I can find anything that might have been interesting to a burglar."

"Could be it isn't a burglar, Jake." The deputy closed the filing cabinet drawer and walked out of the office. "Could be they're searching for something and it isn't a random break-in. Lawton developed some pretty serious financial software. Could he have left something around here that he was working on? Something new?"

"Yeah, maybe," Jake agreed, trying hard not to think about how this put the twins, and Breezy, in danger. If someone was searching for Lawton's latest project, what would they do to get their hands on it?

"I'll make sure we send a patrol by here a couple of times a day, and you all keep the alarm system acti-vated." The deputy gave Breezy a look this time. "And keep the doors locked."

Jake walked Aaron out. They discussed the odds of it being someone they knew. They talked about the weather and Christmas. As they talked, Breezy walked out of the barn, closing the door behind her. She told Jake she'd meet him at the house.

She was still wearing his jacket. He watched her walk down the driveway, his dog next to her. He knew.

her scent would linger on his jacket. Every time he pulled it on, he'd smell that light spring fragrance.

Jake had been around awhile. He knew temptation when he saw it, when it walked away with his dog and his coat. And maybe took a little of his common sense with it.

It had been years since he'd met temptation head-on like this, but he still recognized it for what it was. And he still knew where that road led. He knew he wasn't going there.

Chapter Five

After Jake left, Breezy decided to unpack her few belongings. She'd been putting off the task of settling in,
thinking something would happen, preparing for the reality that this, too, could be taken from her. She'd kept
her clothes in her suitcase and her toiletries in the bag
she'd put on the bathroom counter. Unpacking meant
staying. Unpacking meant a commitment to remain
here and help raise two little girls.

It meant staying in Jake Martin's life. For a long,
long time. Always being the person he tolerated. A
person he'd rather not have in his world.

She had news for him. He was no picnic, either.
But they were stuck with each other and she'd make
the best of it.

The decision to stay meant picking a room. There
were two bedrooms and a craft room upstairs. She had
picked a spare room on the ground floor, close to the
room that had belonged to the twins. A room those
twins would return to in time. They would spend nights
with her. Maybe even weeks.

Breezy's new room was pretty with tan, textured walls and another wall of stone, with a fireplace in the center and French doors that led to a patio. She stood in the middle of that room and tried to imagine herself living there. She tried to picture herself helping Jake Martin raise two little girls, picture them growing up. She would be there as they went to school, as they started to think about boys and dating, and then someday they would leave. And where would she be then? Still in Martin's Crossing, still single and wishing she could find a place to belong?

What if she grew to love this town?

How would it feel to grow old in Martin's Crossing? For some reason, images of Jake Martin popped into her mind. Unattainable, undeniably gorgeous, a man with rules, a man of faith. She would be coparenting those little girls with a man who was everything she'd never been.

She headed down the hall to the kitchen, where she quickly made a list of things she needed from the store. What she really needed was to get out of the house. Breezy headed for Martin's Crossing, AKA: The One-Horse Town. As she drove she called Mia. She needed to tell her sister everything that had happened. She also needed to know she still had an ally, someone who trusted her.

"Hey, sis." Mia sounded bright, happy. Of course she was happy; she'd found the man of her dreams in Slade McKennon and the two of them were having a baby. "How are you?"

"I'm good. It looks as if I'll be staying here awhile."

"Really? But…"

"Lawton left me something in his will." Her voice choked as she said it, and she blinked away the threat of tears.

"Breezy, are you okay? Do you need me to come down?"

Breezy cleared her throat. "I'm good. Mia, he left me joint custody of his little girls."

"Girls. As in children?"

"Twins. They're toddlers." She paused, because saying it would make it real. "I'm going to have to stay here."

"Oh, Breezy, no. You were just getting settled. You still have your things at my house."

A few things in boxes she'd never unpacked. Even at Mia's she'd had a hard time believing she had a place to stay. And there wasn't much in those boxes. A few stray seashells, a photograph of herself singing at a coffee shop in Pasadena and a Christmas ornament. Because families had Christmas ornaments they kept and hung up each year. She'd bought one for her tree at Mia's.

"I'll be able to come up eventually. But for now, I'm going to have to stay close to Martin's Crossing."

"Are you sure you're okay?" Mia, a former federal agent, couldn't let go of that instinct to look beneath the surface. Breezy smiled, thankful, so thankful, for her sister. They'd spent almost twenty years apart but they'd been busy reconnecting, making up for that lost time.

"I'm really okay. I've been in worse places." Homeless shelters, on the street, alone.

"I'll be praying for you."

Mia's words came so easily. Her life with the Coopers had been grounded in faith. She had a foundation, one that included a loving and stable family. Breezy's path had been different. She hesitated to answer and Mia knew.

"Breezy, it gets easier."

Believing, having faith, trusting. Yes, she was sure it would get easier. "I know. I'm going to work through this, Mia."

"I know you will. So tell me about the girls."

She smiled. "They're beautiful. They're two and almost identical. They have dark hair and blue eyes."

A long pause. "And who are you sharing this guardianship with?"

"Lawton's brother-in-law, Jake Martin."

"Oh."

Breezy smiled a little. "Don't say it like that. He's horrible, an absolutely straitlaced grouch."

"And there's nothing worse than straitlaced grouches, right?" Mia teased. "Who, other than you, calls a man 'straitlaced'? Does he wear cardigans with elbow patches, maybe he has thick glasses and…"

Breezy laughed at the image. "Stop! He's just… Well, he has rules."

Their discussion of Jake unfortunately brought an image of the man to mind, and it sure wasn't straitlaced. He was a man who made a girl dream of chivalry, of being rescued, of being protected. She'd never counted on being rescued, and she'd learned at an early age that she could only count on herself.

For years Mia had been on the list of people she didn't count on. As a little girl, Breezy had spent several years waiting for her sister to find her, to rescue her. Because as children it was Mia who looked out for her. Mia had made sure she didn't go hungry. But Mia hadn't shown up and Breezy, the child, hadn't understood that her sister had been a child, too.

"Shudder! A man with rules," Mia said, bringing her back to the conversation.

"You're not helping."

"No," Mia agreed, "I'm not. I'm sure he's perfectly horrible. I think I'll look up Jake Martin of Martin's Crossing on Google and see what I come up with."

"Please don't." Because she knew that would only convince Mia to begin plotting Breezy's demise. Or marriage. "Just say your prayers for me and I'll keep you posted."

"I love you, Breeze," Mia said. The words, even spoken from so far away, made all the difference.

"Love you, too."

Breezy ended the call as she drove past the city-limit sign of Martin's Crossing, population 678. She wasn't quite to town. There were a few farmhouses with barns scattered about, and a flea market with a gravel parking lot a little farther in. The building that housed the flea market was decorated for Christmas with lights wrapped around the posts, and plastic deer with red bows on their necks placed along the exterior. A tree, big and tacky, had been decorated with garland and big ornaments.

Ahead of her she could see the gas station on the left. On the right was the Martin's Crossing Community Church and fellowship hall. Next to it was a large open area and a park. A block down from the church she knew would be a left-hand turn that was the main street of Martin's Crossing. A street that was wide, and had a couple of businesses on either side. She'd noticed a restaurant called Duke's No Bar and Grill, just down from it was the feed store and across from that was the grocery and a tiny gift and clothing store. She had seen a couple of other businesses that she would check out in time.

Welcome to Martin's Crossing.

She pulled into a parking space in front of the grocery store and got out. In front of her a man had just opened a ladder and was climbing up it, holding a string of lights. The building in front of him was tiny and narrow, with a single door and a window. The sign on the window claimed it to be the home of the wood-carved nativity. Above that sign was one that heralded the name of the building as Lefty's Arts and Antiques.

"Hey there, young lady." He smiled down at her.

"Hello."

"You must be Lawton's sister."

Breezy was surprised. "How did you know?"

He grinned. "Word travels fast in a town like Martin's Crossing."

"Yes, I'm sure it does."

"Could you hand me up the string of lights and hold them as I hook them up to this overhang?" He grinned down at her again. He had white hair, gray eyes and a smile that took away her reservations, that part of her that always held back.

"Of course." She held up the lights and he pulled a hammer out of the tool belt hanging from his waist.

"Thank you. My name's Lefty. Lefty Mueller. I've been in this town all of my life."

"I see," she said, not knowing what else to say. His gray brows drew together as he squinted, watching her with equally gray eyes.

"And your name is…?" he asked as he raised his arms to hook lights along the overhang.

"Oh, I'm sorry. I'm Breezy Hernandez."

"Lovely, very lovely. Well, I'm glad you've come to Martin's Crossing, Breezy Hernandez." He grinned. "We can always use a fresh breeze."

She smiled at the turn of phrase. "You're very charming."

"I do my best." He slipped lights over another hook. "And I love to think that I help bring Christmas cheer to this little town. I've got these lights now. You go on inside and look around."

She glanced toward the grocery store, wondering what time it closed, then gave up and walked through the door of Lefty's little shop. As she stepped inside a Christmas carol played, ending abruptly when the door latched. The interior of the store made it easy to believe that Christmas was less than four weeks away.

The tiny shop was a maze of tables filled with all types of nativities. A nativity mobile hung from the ceiling in the center of the room and another nativity lit with candles spun in a slow circle on the counter. Breezy stopped in front of one that had the tiniest baby Jesus, his minuscule hands reaching for his mother as Joseph looked over Mary's shoulder with obvious pride. A music box attached to the side had a switch and she flipped it. "Away in a Manger" played in soft, music-box tones and the angel on top of the manger spun with wings spread.

The door opened. She turned, smiling at the creator of this art that she never would have imagined in a town like Martin's Crossing.

"Do you like it?" Lefty stepped close, settling a pair of wire-framed glasses on his rather large nose.

"They're all beautiful," she answered.

"This one is yours." He indicated the one she'd been looking at.

"No, I can't. I mean…"

He smiled back at her. "Breezy, you should have a nativity. Do you have one?"

She'd never had one in her life. She'd seen them in front of churches, sometimes homemade, sometimes made from brightly colored plastic. She had loved the one that Mia's family put up in their home each year. But she'd never had one of her own. She didn't want to think about all of the things she hadn't had because they'd moved so often. She'd had a few dolls, but each time they moved on the dolls were left behind. The books were left. Friends were left. She'd learned early that getting attached hurt.

It had become easier to not have, to not get attached. Lefty Mueller stood behind the counter, staring at her over the frames of his glasses. She managed a smile and he nodded, as if that meant acceptance.

"It's yours, so don't argue. It's my welcome gift to you. You see, my great grandfather was German. He settled here, where he continued to do his wood carvings, and he taught his son, who taught his son. What good is such a gift if it can't be shared with people we meet?"

"But you can't just give it to me. I can buy it."

"Then it wouldn't be a gift, my friend. It wouldn't

be a story you can share someday, about an old man who shared a piece of Christmas with you."

As he'd been talking, he had been wrapping the nativity in paper and then settling the pieces in a box.

"Thank you." She spoke softly, afraid she would cry at his kindness.

"You're very welcome. Someday you will tell stories about this nativity. Let them be stories of faith, of an old man who carved what he knew best, a savior."

She nodded as he handed her the box. He came out from behind the counter and she gave him a quick hug. He chuckled as he hugged her back.

"I will treasure it forever, Lefty."

"And I hope you find the meaning of it all, Breezy."

"Yes, of course."

He opened the door for her and she walked out, putting the nativity in the front seat of her car. Across the street, a car door slammed. She looked that way and saw Jake Martin. Of course it was. He would be everywhere in this small town. He waved, then proceeded to pull a pine tree from the bed of his truck. He wore gloves and a long-sleeved shirt. His hat was pulled low.

She turned away from him and bumped into a man coming down the sidewalk. He steadied her but then moved back. Breezy studied the elderly man with an oversize coat, dusty, bent-up hat and several days' growth of whiskers on his craggy face.

"I'm so sorry," she said quickly.

"No need to apologize, miss. I wasn't really watching where I was going, either." He grinned a little, holding tight to a potted poinsettia. "But I wasn't watching Jake Martin, either."

"Oh, I…"

"No need," he said. "I would guess you're the aunt of those two little girls."

"I am." Did *everyone* in town know her business? She didn't even know this man's name. "And you are?"

"Joe, I'm Joe."

"You live here in Martin's Crossing?"

His smile shifted and she saw sadness in his eyes. "Oh, I guess I do. I'm passing through, eventually. But it seemed a good place to spend Christmas."

"Yes, it does seem like it would be." She studied his face, his eyes, and she thought she understood Joe.

"Let me offer you this lovely welcoming gift." Joe held out the plant with its bright red flowers.

"But I… I couldn't take your poinsettia."

"Nonsense." He smiled and pushed the potted plant at her, settling it in her hands. "I've nowhere really to keep it and there's nothing better than a poinsettia to put a person in the holiday mood."

"But it's yours."

"Now it belongs to you."

And with a tip of his dirty, bent-up hat, he left. Breezy watched him walk down the street. Then she put the poinsettia in her car, setting it next to the nativity. After locking the car door she looked in the direction Joe had gone, but he'd already vanished from sight. She headed for the grocery store.

The Martin's Crossing grocer had hardwood floors, three aisles and a meat counter in the back next to produce that was labeled Locally Grown and Worth It.

A woman came out from the back of the store through swinging doors, wiping her hands on an apron that hung from her waist. She was middle-aged with short brown hair and an open smile.

"Well, hello."

Breezy smiled as she filled a basket with fruit. "Hello."

The woman followed her down the cereal aisle. "I'm Wanda Howard. My husband, Gene, and I own this place. And you must be Lawton's sister."

"Yes, I am." She smiled and held out a hand. "I'm Breezy Hernandez. I believe I met your husband the other day."

"Yes, you did. And we're looking forward to having you with us at church on Sunday."

"Yes, of course."

Because that's what a person did when she lived in a small town where everyone knew her name—she went to church. That person would also have a plant and even a nativity to set out for Christmas each year.

As she walked back to her car with her bags of groceries, she saw Jake on the long, covered porch of Duke's. He wore faded jeans, work boots and a shirt with the sleeves rolled to his elbows. She thought that a person who lived in Martin's Crossing would also manage to be friends with Jake Martin.

Friendship was easy.

And then she thought of his many rules and she added one for herself. *Rule Number Five: don't lie to yourself.*

Jake unloaded the tub of decorations for his brother Duke and headed across the street to the grocery store to have a talk with Miss Breezy Hernandez.

"Where are you going?" Duke called out from the door of his restaurant.

Jake glanced back at his brother. "I need a word with Breezy."

"You could…"

Jake kept walking. He didn't need Duke's advice. Duke had always found it a little easier to smile, to joke. Duke hadn't been the oldest. He hadn't been the one begging their mother not to pack her bags. Duke hadn't been the one holding Samantha, just a toddler, as their mother drove away. Or trying to keep Brody from chasing her car.

That memory was the one that always undid him.

He raised a hand as he headed across the street, silencing his brother who continued to call out to him. Breezy had come out of the store carrying two bags of groceries. He watched her heft those bags and he couldn't help but smile. He hoped she wasn't buying more fake cheese. Or something as un-Texas as veggie burgers.

The wind whipped her pale blue skirt, wrapping the cotton material around Western boots. She wore a denim jacket and her hair was pulled back in a ponytail. She saw him and smiled.

It made his step falter a little. It took some of the steam out of him and made him forget what he'd been so determined to tell her. He didn't know how she did that because it didn't happen often, that someone sidetracked him.

"Mr. Martin."

"Jake," he corrected.

"Of course, Jake."

He took one of the bags of groceries and followed her to the little economy car she drove. "There's a truck in the garage at Lawton's. You can drive it."

"I'm okay with my car."

He waited as she opened the door and then he set the bag inside, next to a package from Lefty's and the poinsettia he'd seen her accept from Joe.

After she'd closed the car door and stood facing him, he cleared his throat and remembered that he'd approached her for a reason and it had nothing to do with carrying groceries, the lavender scent of her hair or the way she studied him with eyes the color of caramel.

"I saw you with Joe."

"Oh, yes. He gave me a poinsettia."

"You need to be more careful," he started, but stopped when her eyes narrowed to a glare. "I mean, you are going to be a parent. You'll have the girls to think about."

"You're telling me who I can and can't talk to?"

"I'm asking you to be careful with someone you don't know," he explained.

Her smile lit up her eyes. "I don't really know you."

"You're being purposely difficult."

She laughed. "Yes, I am. Are you being purposely bossy?"

No, he was being derailed, sidetracked and maybe even a little convicted for what he'd said about Joe. "I'm not bossy, I'm careful."

"I'm a black belt. I'm very capable of taking care of myself. And that man, Joe, only wanted to do something nice for a stranger. Everyone has been kind today.

Lefty gave me a nativity. Mrs. Howard gave me a basket of fruit."

"Joe isn't from Martin's Crossing. We don't know anything about him."

"Do I need to remind you that you don't know anything about me?"

He could have disagreed. But disagreeing would have meant admitting to the private investigator he'd hired when he'd first learned of the will. He should tell her about it. Marty had told him that if they were going to raise the twins together, they needed to be honest and trust each other.

"I don't know everything about you, Breezy. But what I'm learning is that you're too trusting."

"I'm not that trusting. And I'm not afraid of Joe. I've been Joe. I know what it's like to be on the streets. If you're worried about Joe, you should be worried about me."

"I'm not worried about you." He glanced toward Duke's. This wasn't getting them anywhere. "Let's get a cup of coffee."

She stood there, wind whipping that blue skirt around her legs. She held her hair back with her hand and smiled at him as he made the offer. They had to start somewhere.

Because, like it or not, they were in each other's lives. Lawton and Elizabeth had tied them together, two unlikely people raising two little girls. When Lawton had mentioned it, Jake had tried to talk him out of it. There were better people than him. And Breezy, she was just an unknown.

Lawton had asked him who would be better. They

had no one else they would trust the way they trusted Jake. Breezy, they'd told him, would help him get through.

It shouldn't have been like this. It should never have happened at all.

"I don't drink coffee." She paused, studying his face. "But tea would be good."

Jake walked with her across the street, aware that anyone who happened to be in town would be watching the two of them. He'd really stepped in a mess this time. And all because of Joe.

Joe was a man who had done odd jobs around town, been to church a few times, and really hadn't done more than appear to be suspicious. Because no one knew where he'd come from, where he was staying or when he'd be moving on.

They walked up the steps of Duke's. The building was wood-sided, rustic with a long covered porch. In good weather Duke put tables and chairs on that porch for people who wanted to eat outside. This wasn't exactly good weather. The tables were gone and Duke was decorating for Christmas.

The holidays and life would go on. Without Elizabeth and Lawton. They would all continue to live each day. They would raise the twins. They would be happy. They would laugh again, tell jokes and move on with their lives.

All of that made Jake real friendly with the punching bag his dad had strung up in the barn years ago. It gave him something to take his anger out on. Even way back when his mom had walked out on them. She'd left without looking back, occasionally sending a letter to let them know how happy she was in whatever state she lived in.

He'd used that punching bag when he'd caught his ex-fiancée, Alison, cheating on him two months before their wedding. He'd used it when he'd caught Samantha with a hired hand, not doing anything too serious, but serious enough Jake had wanted to hurt the younger man.

He'd used the punching bag a lot the past couple of weeks as grief had torn him up inside. But the woman standing next to him didn't need to know that. He reached past her to open the door and she said a soft "Thank you."

It was midafternoon and there were few customers in Duke's this time of day. Even though the sign said to wait to be seated, he motioned her to a booth on the far wall. He waved at John Gordon, owner of the garage next to the gas station.

"Jake, did you get that backhoe going the other day?" John asked.

"Sure did, John. But I'll probably still bring it in."

John nodded his head and gave both him and Breezy a careful look before returning to the piece of pie on his plate.

As they sat down, the doors to the kitchen opened. Duke walked out, a giant with a goatee, shaved head and big grin.

"Hey, brother, did you decide to come back and help?"

"Brother?" Breezy repeated.

"That's me. Little brother of Jake." Duke grinned and pulled a chair from a nearby table to sit at the end of their booth. "And you must be Breezy Hernandez?"

"That's me." She smiled at Duke, and Jake didn't know what to make of that. How in the world did Duke, who looked like he brawled behind buildings, put everyone at ease?

"My big brother isn't being too hard to get along with, is he?" Duke said it with a grin directed at Jake, for which Jake wasn't too thankful.

"No, of course not."

"That's good to know."

Jake turned over the coffee cup that was on the table, settling it in the saucer. Maybe Duke would take the hint.

Instead Duke, younger by two years, stretched and settled in. Relaxed. Jake hadn't known many moments in his life like that, when he could let go and pretend everything would get done, everyone would be taken care of.

"You're going to help me put those lights up, right?" Duke gave Jake a kick in the shin. He managed to not flinch.

"Yes, I'm going to help. I dragged them to town for you, didn't I?"

"Yes, you did." Duke continued to study Breezy. "We're kind of big on Christmas here in Martin's Crossing," he explained. "It won't be easy this year but we'll all be together."

Including Breezy, if she stayed. Family now included her. Jake knew it hadn't been Lawton's intention to make him feel responsible for her, but that's the way it worked.

"Christmas is a good time for healing." Duke's voice was low, sending a strong hint. "I think what we all need is a deep breath and something to help us focus a little."

Right, Jake thought, because it was that easy. To forget a sister, a best friend and that the twins had lost their parents.

Duke nailed him with a look. "It isn't going to be easy," Duke responded to Jake's unspoken thoughts. "But we'll get through the way we always do. We're family."

"Yes, family." Jake moved his empty coffee cup. "Do you have a waitress who could pour a cup of coffee and get Breezy a glass of tea?"

"When did you get so impatient?" Duke grinned as he eased out of the chair, unbending his six feet eight inches of solid muscle to tower over them. Jake was only a few inches shorter than his mammoth brother, but even he was a little intimidated. He looked up, smiling at his little brother, as he liked to think of Duke.

"Oh, are you the waitress?" Jake asked. "You need a little cap, or an apron, I think."

Duke's eyes narrowed and he growled a little. "You're asking for it, brother."

As Duke walked away, Jake made eye contact with the woman sitting across from him. She drummed her fingers a little on the table and he wondered what in the world he'd done now.

"So, Christmas with the family. Rule Number Six. Or is it Seven?"

"Are you really going to keep track?"

"It seems like the easiest way to stay out of trouble. Church. Check. No scary vagrants. Check. Real cheese. Check."

He added, "Christmas with the family. Check."

"Gotcha."

"You don't like Christmas?"

"I do. I'm just…"

He waited for her to explain. Duke returned with the coffeepot and a glass of tea. "Pie?"

"Might as well. What do you have?" Jake asked as he reached for the creamer. "Homemade chocolate?"

"Made it myself." He stood there for a moment looking from Jake to Breezy, then back again. He grinned a little too big. "I'll get you a piece and then I guess I'll make myself scarce."

"Sounds like a good idea," Jake agreed.

Duke disappeared through the door to the kitchen. Jake's gaze connected with Breezy's, and he wondered a little more about her past. He wanted more than the sterile facts uncovered by the private investigator. For a brief moment he saw shades of vulnerability in her eyes and then, quickly, the look was gone. She didn't like to be vulnerable. She was all about being independent. She was about being in control. Yeah, he got her.

But understanding her was the last thing he wanted or needed. What he'd like most would be for her to decide Martin's Crossing was the last place she wanted to be, tied down to him and two little girls. He had a feeling that she wasn't a quitter. He needed to adjust because she was in his life. For better or worse.

Chapter Six

By Friday Breezy was starting to get a routine going. She'd spent the morning with the twins while Jake worked. After they'd left she'd baked some halfway-decent bread. She was teaching herself to cook. People who lived in one place baked. And cooked. Probably from recipes handed down from generation to generation.

She wanted those recipes. She'd searched through the kitchen hoping to find a book with things like "Grandma's Vegetable Soup," or "Aunt Iva's Homemade Rolls." So far she'd only found a few cookbooks.

If she was going to continue her cooking adventures, she needed more ingredients. Late in the afternoon she cleaned up the kitchen and grabbed her purse. She would head to town, do some shopping and maybe treat herself to dinner at Duke's. She liked Jake's younger brother. He was uncomplicated and easy to talk to.

He didn't make her feel like she should leave. Or make her want to run far and fast.

She parked in front of Oregon's All Things shop. It had been closed for a few days but today it was open.

Breezy grabbed her purse and headed toward the front door. As she did, she saw Joe a short distance away. He waved a gloved hand and she waved back, forgetting all about Jake's silly rules.

The bell over the door clanged as she entered Oregon's. The shop was small and cozy. It smelled like freshly baked apple pie, compliments of a candle burning on the counter. There was a row of skirts and tops on one wall. On the adjoining wall were shelves of handmade Christmas ornaments. She noticed one that was hand-painted with a picture of the manger scene. In tiny writing was the author's signature: Oregon.

The door at the back of the shop opened and a woman stepped out. She was small with dark hair and dark eyes. Her smile, when she saw Breezy, was sweet and welcoming.

"Hello, I'm sorry it took me so long to get out here. I had to wash paint off my hands." The woman held out a hand, still slightly damp. Breezy took it in hers. "I'm Oregon Jeffries. And you must be Breezy."

"I'm beginning to wonder if there's a neon sign over my head," Breezy lamented as she moved from ornaments to clothing, all with the tags stating they were original designs by Oregon.

Oregon laughed. "There is. It flashes your name and the word *newcomer*. Don't worry, the novelty will wear off and then you'll just be one of the folks that lives in Martin's Crossing."

"I'm looking forward to that," she said. She looked around, amazed. "You do all of this?"

Oregon's cheeks turned pink. "I do. I've been sew-

ing my whole life, and painting. It seemed like the best
way to keep myself out of trouble."

"I've never sewn." She would add that to her list of
things a person staying in one place should do. "I took
a sculpting class once, years ago."

"Maybe you'll take it up again?"

Breezy shook her head. "No, I think it was a passing phase. But you, on the other hand, have a gift."

"Sewing and art were my escape from reality," Oregon explained. "My mom moved us around a lot. She
had a hobby. Marriage."

"I really understand the moving part."

Oregon smiled. "Yeah, I think you probably do."

Breezy turned back to the Christmas ornaments.
She picked one with an angel and a Bible verse and
the one with the manger scene. She would add these
to her meager collection today. Ornaments she would
keep, that she wouldn't have to leave behind.

"I'll take these two."

"Perfect. I'll wrap them for you." Oregon walked
behind the counter with the two ornaments. "Are you
going to join us tonight at the church? We're decorating the park and the church for the annual Christmas
bazaar and the community festival."

"I'm not sure. I didn't know if…" What should she
say? That she didn't know if she was included? She
wasn't a member. Didn't she need to be a member or
a real citizen of Martin's Crossing?

"If?" Oregon asked as she wrapped the decorations.
"If you're invited? Of course you are. This is a community event and I've heard it's a lot of fun. They decorate,
practice for the community caroling and then have a

potluck. There are probably five churches in the area and they'll be working on floats for the parade. The fire station has one, too."

Before Breezy could respond, a girl of about twelve ran in from the back room. She had dark hair and blue eyes. She looked from Breezy to Oregon.

"Did you finish cleaning for Mrs. Walters?" Oregon asked her.

"I did. And she said to remind you to bring that vegetable thing that you make. And now I'm going over to Duke's. He said if I'll sweep the porch, he'll pay me."

Oregon's smile faded. "When did you make that deal?"

"Last week. Come on, Mom. You said if I want a horse, I have to raise the money and pay for it myself."

"Right, of course, but…" Oregon turned to the register, pushing a few buttons and then handing Breezy a receipt. "But I didn't know you were going to be all over town."

"I'm not all over town. And I am twelve."

"Right, you're twelve. Okay, go sweep, Lilly, but don't be a nuisance."

"Love you, Mom." And out the door the child went.

"She's beautiful," Breezy commented as she pulled out her money.

"And a handful. We've only lived here for six months but she's managed to involve herself in every aspect of the community. She wants to barrel race now. I've tried to tell her it isn't cheap."

"She seems willing to work for it."

"Yes, she does," Oregon answered a little wearily. "So I'll see you in an hour?"

"An hour?"

"At the Community Church."

"Oh, right." Breezy picked up her ornaments. "I'll be there."

An hour later, Breezy walked up to the Community Church. From the sidelines she watched as lights were strung from pole to pole on the outside of the building. The nativity, a homemade affair with a shingle roof, barn-wood sides and carved wooden figures, was the center of everything. Behind it was an outline of an ancient city in glittering white lights.

Inside the stable Joseph and Mary kneeled behind a manger. The display was large enough that real animals would be brought in the night of the Christmas festival. They would have a parade that night and the churches in the area would join together for caroling.

A week before that community event, there was a craft bazaar that brought people from other communities to shop in Martin's Crossing.

Breezy watched all the activity, unsure of where she fit. People were stringing lights in obvious holiday shapes. These people belonged. To Martin's Crossing, to the church and to each other. She considered quietly slipping away. Because she didn't belong.

That was ridiculous and she knew it. She'd always been able to make herself a part of things, to blend in. She'd done it in Dawson, as Mia's sister and as an honorary Cooper. She could do it here. And deep down it meant more to be a part of this town, these people.

A movement to her side stopped the melancholy

thoughts. She turned, spotting old Joe. He nodded a greeting as he stepped closer.

"This is the way it should be celebrated," he said with a sad smile.

"I'm sorry?"

He glanced at her, and then looked away. "Christmas. It should be about community. People reaching out to each other."

"Yes, it is nice. I've always thought it should be like this, too." For her, though, it had always been another day.

No, that wasn't true. It had been different. Even for her. It had often been a day when they might have lined up at a soup kitchen or gone to a shelter where gifts were handed out to children.

"It wasn't like this for you?" Joe asked, buttoning the top button of his canvas jacket.

"No, not really. Last year I spent Christmas with my sister. And that was a lot like this."

"Come inside and get cocoa." Joe pointed toward the church fellowship building. "And food. Fill up a plate, get warm and then I bet they'll find a job for you. Pastor Allen is a decent man and you'll enjoy this congregation."

She thanked him for the invitation and allowed him to lead her inside the metal-sided building next to the church. The sign over the door said Community Church Family Center. As they entered, most people smiled. A few were obviously curious about the newcomer and Joe.

She turned her attention back to her escort. "Have you eaten, Joe?"

"I have. And you don't need to worry about me, Miss Hernandez. I'm taking good care of myself."

Of course he was. But was he warm? Did he have a roof over his head at night? She wanted to ask but wasn't sure how. He let her off the hook with an easy, unconcerned look.

"Get yourself that cup of cocoa and some dinner," Joe encouraged, and then he was gone. He was her only friend, it seemed, as she stood there with no one to talk to, no one who knew her.

She was rescued by a familiar giggle. Rose headed her way, toddling on chubby two-year-old legs. She had a doll in one arm and a smudge of chocolate on her cheek.

"Brees." Rosie growled the toddler version of Breezy's name.

"Yes, Brees." She picked the little girl up, holding her close and quickly changed her mind about closeness. "And you do not smell good, little girl."

"Poop." Rosie cackled as she said it, like it was the best news ever.

So what in the world was she supposed to do with a messy little girl? She looked around, wondering where the diaper bag might be. She spotted Jake heading her way, Violet in his arms. He grinned and her heart tumbled a little. The stink no longer mattered, not really. Not when Jake Martin smiled. Truly smiled.

"I see you found my runaway," he said as he settled Violet on his shoulders. "I told her she needs her diaper changed."

"Yes, I kind of noticed. If you have the diaper bag somewhere, I can do it."

"Gladly." He pointed to a table in the corner. "And I'll owe you one."

She was okay with that. The idea of him owing her was suddenly very appealing. "Where should I change her?"

"The nursery is through that door." He pointed. "But I'll show you."

They were almost to the nursery when they were stopped by a woman with light gray hair and pretty brown eyes. She wore jeans and a sweatshirt but she had class that couldn't be denied.

"Jake, this must but Breezy." The woman held a handful of lights but switched them to the other hand and held out her right hand to Breezy.

"Yes." Jake leaned in to kiss the woman's cheek. "Breezy, this is my aunt Patty."

Breezy had to switch Rosie to her other arm to free her hand. Rosie wasn't cooperative. She wanted down.

The woman patted her arm. "No, don't worry. I think you have your hands full."

"She is a handful," Breezy agreed. "And she needs a diaper changed."

"I'll let you go, then. And make sure you get something to eat." Patty started to walk away but stopped and turned to Jake. "Did you hear about the anonymous donation to the church? To buy Christmas gifts for children in the community. It was a big check."

"I hadn't heard." He shrugged. "But it'll come in handy."

"Yes, it will," Patty answered. "And I see Hailey so it's time for me to go. We're wrapping lights around the frames of the wise men."

"She seems very nice," Breezy said, making conversation as Jake led her into the nursery.

"She's the best. She raised three girls, and did her best to help out at our place."

"Help out?"

He didn't answer. His gaze settled on the door behind her and he frowned. All evidence of the lighthearted Jake Martin disappeared in a matter of seconds.

"Problem?" she asked as she spun around to see what had caught his attention.

"No, not a problem. Just a little brother returned to the fold. I'll have to catch up with you in a few."

He handed Violet over, leaving Breezy the job of wrangling both twins. She held one on each hip and watched him head for the young man who had entered the building, a cowboy hat pushed down on his dark head, his jeans hanging low around slim hips. He had a black eye and a huge scowl on his face. Jake descended on him acting more like an angry parent than an older brother.

That explained more about the man than any questions he might have answered for her. Each time she learned something about this man, it felt as if a tiny chisel had taken aim at her heart, tearing off another small chunk of the armor she'd always thought indestructible.

Jake didn't know what he planned on saying to Brody. What did you say to a kid that should have been an adult by now? Duke had recently told Jake that the blame for Brody not acting responsible was Jake's fault, because he bailed him out too often. Jake had been too easy on him when it came to the ranch.

It looked like high time someone stopped being easy on Brody. From the looks of things, someone had already taken a piece off his hide. His black eye and the gimpy way he walked said a lot.

"Well?" Jake stopped in front of his younger brother, aware of their audience and not willing to let another Martin family squabble be the thing people remembered about this night. "Head outside."

"I'm not going anywhere with you. I want to see the twins."

"You can see the twins later."

Brody shot a look past him, his smile, complete with dimple, appearing out of nowhere. "Hey, is that the new sister?"

"She isn't our sister."

Brody gave him a knowing look. "I guess that's something to be thankful for."

"I'm not too thankful for anything right now, Brody. What happened to your eye?"

"Aren't you going to ask me about the other guy?" Brody walked away with a casual swagger. Jake followed.

"Who was the other guy?"

"Lincoln," Brody admitted with a shrug. "I'm hungry."

"You're always hungry. Why did you fight with Lincoln?"

"Because he's…" Brody shook his head. "Let it rest. We had a difference of opinion. You might not think much of me. I know I let you down a lot. But I am a Martin and you have taught me that people ought to be treated right. Women ought to be treated right. Lincoln and I had a disagreement and we parted ways permanently."

"That bad?" Jake let go of his frustration with his younger brother.

Brody shrugged, as if it wasn't worth discussing. Jake knew it had to be tough. Lincoln and Brody had been inseparable friends for years. Even when they didn't agree.

"I'm going to get some food," Brody said. "If you don't mind?"

"Go ahead. And mind your manners with Breezy."

Brody stopped and landed a careful look on Jake, even with one eye nearly swollen shut. "Gotcha, big brother. I'll keep my hands off your…"

"Watch your manners," Jake warned in a growl he hadn't intended.

Man, this is not what he needed, for both his brothers to think that Lawton pushing him and Breezy Hernandez together as the girls' guardians made the two of them a couple. They had been unwillingly forced into a situation neither of them had expected. End of story.

"Of course." Brody tipped his hat and walked away.

Jake shook his head at the retreating back of his younger brother. Nothing really bothered Brody. Or at least it always seemed that way. But whatever had happened with Lincoln had definitely gotten under his skin.

"We're all cleaned up, Uncle Jake," Breezy said as she walked up.

He smiled at Breezy and the twins. He held out his arms and Violet fell into his embrace, her head resting on his shoulder and her thumb instantly going to her mouth. It was getting late, the girls were tired and he still needed to help put up some lights.

"Do you want to take them home with you tonight?"

he asked. It made sense. He could get more work done if the girls were in Breezy's care. And neither of them would get work done if they had to wrangle twins all night.

Breezy's eyes widened and she glanced down at the little girl in her arms. "Of course. I think."

"Nervous?"

"No, no, of course not. I can do this."

If he'd guessed her next sentence, the one she hadn't said, it probably would have been something to the effect that she was going to have to do it sooner or later. He agreed. If she was going to be a part of their lives, she would have to get used to having the girls for longer than a few hours at a time.

"You can do it. And if you need anything, I'm just a phone call away." He kissed Violet's cheek. "I'll help you get them in car seats."

"Thank you."

It probably looked easy from the outside, turning those girls over to her. It was anything but.

People probably thought he should be relieved. After all, he'd already helped raise his siblings. He had a ranch and a business to run. Someone taking part of that load should make him happy.

As he walked out the door with Breezy and the twins, he thought of all the reasons why this should be the best thing for him and for the twins, maybe even for her. As he helped carry car seats to her car and helped strap the twins in, he probably should have been thinking that, for this one night, he didn't have to worry.

Instead his worry doubled. Tonight he would worry about all three of them.

Chapter Seven

On Sunday Breezy pulled into the parking lot of Martin's Crossing Community Church. The main building was a traditional white-sided structure with a tall steeple and stained-glass windows. Next to it was the fellowship and community center, a metal building with a tall wooden cross standing next to it.

After meeting so many of the community members on Friday when she'd helped decorate, it was easier to come here than she had imagined.

Not that she didn't have her doubts. She'd almost talked herself into staying home, but she couldn't. She had promised Jake she would do this. They would go to church as a family. She wanted to make this work for the twins, the two little people counting on her to be in their lives.

This weekend had been a good start. The twins had stayed with her Friday night and all day Saturday. Yesterday, Jake had stopped by in the late afternoon to pick up the twins but he'd stayed for dinner. After they had finished eating the twins played in the living room. Only one thing had dampened the mood. Once as they all sat in the living room, Violet had looked around and said, "Mama?"

Breezy knew that someday it would hurt less. At that moment, knowing there was no mama and knowing Breezy couldn't fill Elizabeth's shoes, it had hurt.

So for the twins, and maybe for herself, she was going to church. It wasn't that she had something against church, or even against God. She believed. She even prayed. But church, it was all about the past when it came to church.

Someone rapped on her window, and she jumped then frowned at the man smiling at her. He opened the door, cowboy cool in a plaid button-up shirt, jeans and boots. He had shaved off the stubble that had covered his cheeks the previous day. As she stepped out of the car she realized he smelled good, like country air and expensive cologne. A combination she could cuddle up to, if it were any other man. Chivalrous and Old West he might be, but safe? He was anything but safe.

"Nervous?" he asked as she just stood there next to her car.

"A little." She glanced around. "Where are the girls?"

"I've already checked them into the nursery."

"Oh." She studied the building. It felt like looking at her future, all wrapped up in a neat package with a Christmas bow on top. This town, the church, the twins and even Jake.

She wanted to accept it, to believe it. This was her life now. But how many times had she thought she might be able to stay, to put down roots, only to have it ripped out from under her?

Even her life in Oklahoma with her sister.

"You okay?" he asked.

"I'm good."

One brow arched and he studied her face, and then surprised her by reaching for her hand. "Good but a little shaky?"

"You grew up here, didn't you? You've always lived in this town, with these people who know you and this church that has been there for you?"

"Yes, of course."

Of course. Because it was Martin's Crossing. Duke had told her that their great great grandfather had settled this area, building up a farm and starting the general store. And that grandfather's brother had been the law in these parts. Family history.

Breezy's family history was of a drug addict who overdosed and a man whose life story she didn't really know.

"Breezy?"

His voice was soft, husky, and he was standing too close. She pulled herself together and gave him an easy look, the kind she knew how to give. The smile that said she was okay. Everything was good.

"I'm ready," she said. "I have gone to church. I went while I lived in Dawson. It's just… I've had a different experience than you have."

And she was so tired of starting over.

"What was your experience?" he asked as if he really wanted to know. But how did she tell him?

Maria had used churches. She had used Breezy. But how did she explain that to a man who had lived this perfect, American dream kind of life?

He would never understand the embarrassment of being dragged from church to church. He wouldn't get how it felt to sit in a classroom where every other kid had families, homes and nice clothes.

She stopped walking, wondering what to tell him. There was so much about her life that people didn't understand, so she didn't share. Not even with Mia. But she and Jake were raising children together. That changed everything. "My experience was that church was the place where I never really belonged. We were always passing through."

He started to comment but she put a hand up to stop the words that would be some variation of "sorry, shouldn't have been, this will be different." They were facing each other on the sidewalk and somehow her hand settled on his arm.

"This will be different," he assured her. His gaze held hers and he looked like he meant it. And she believed him.

Of course it would be different. She wasn't that dirty little girl anymore. She no longer stood on street corners with her guitar, hoping someone would throw a few dollars in the case. Maria wasn't here, telling her to play along at church, to listen to the stories about God and fishes and loaves, just long enough to get money for a room or food.

The difference between Breezy and Maria was that Maria hadn't believed. She'd only used the people who had been kind enough to put their faith into action. Breezy had wanted to know more. She had wanted to understand the stories, the faith, the hope that the teachers spoke of.

She had always wanted a home, a place to plant roses, maybe a garden. A place to stay. And now she had it, even though it didn't feel like her life. It felt like she was borrowing Lawton's. The idea of staying scared the daylights out of her. And the longer she stayed, the more she grew to love the twins, the more she feared it might all be taken away.

"What should I say?" he asked as they walked toward the building.

"Nothing, really. Just understand that you grew up here, where this was a safe place. I grew up being used by a lady who took me to church to get money."

He nodded, and she was glad that he didn't say anything else. He touched her back and then dropped his hand to his side. The brief gesture cause a shiver to race up her spine.

"I have a roast in the Crock-Pot for lunch," he said as they walked up the steps of the church.

"Is that an invitation?"

"Yes, it's an invitation. It used to be a big family event. There are fewer of us these days but we still have lunch together every Sunday. Today Marty has plans with friends, so it will just be you, me, Duke, Brody and the twins."

"Can I bring something?"

"No, Marty's taken care of everything. And Duke is bringing pie."

Duke's pie. She'd had a slice the other day when she'd had coffee with Jake and it was the best pie she'd ever had. Even better than Vera's at the Mad Cow in Dawson.

They stepped through the doors of the church. A

man wearing bib overalls over a dress shirt handed her a bulletin. His gray hair was combed back, and his beard was neatly trimmed. He winked.

"How do you do? I'm Robert Carter."

Breezy took the hand he offered. "I'm Breezy Hernandez."

"Good to know you, miss. And I see you dragged in this scoundrel. How you doing today, Jake? Looks like you're hanging with a better class of people than normal."

"I hope you haven't told Duke he's outclassed," Jake said with a grin.

"I'd say he already knows it." Robert pounded Jake on the shoulder. "You'd best get a seat. And, young lady, watch out for those Martin boys. They're trouble."

Breezy smiled at that as they made their way to the front of the church. Duke was indeed waiting for them. He'd left two seats to his left empty. As they approached he stood, a welcoming look on his face. Breezy breathed a little easier. Duke made people feel at ease. He held a hand out to her and pulled her to the seat next to his.

"Smile, sunshine, or they'll think we're holding you hostage. You know, back in the old days…"

"Don't tell stories, Duke." Jake sat down.

Breezy smiled and took the seat between the two brothers. For a moment there was peace. She glanced around, not wanting to be conspicuous as she surveyed the building. The walls were wood paneled but painted white. A cross hung at the front, behind the pulpit. The band was tuning up. A drummer, guitar player and pianist. Someone stepped forward with a violin.

After a song service that had the church on their feet, the pastor stepped forward. He didn't wear a suit, just jeans and a button-down shirt. His hair was buzzed short and he looked to be not much older than Breezy. But as he spoke, she stopped thinking about his appearance and focused on a message that asked his congregation to really think about what Christmas means to them. Not as Christians, but personally.

How does it change their lives? How does it affect their choices and the way they reach out to others? What makes them different than everyone else in the world?

Breezy leaned in a little, listening to his words. What did Christmas mean to her? As a child it had been a hard time of year, spent in shelters and run-down motels. They'd rarely had a tree. They hadn't spent the day with family, enjoying a big meal. It had been a holiday when churches would reach out to people like Breezy and Maria. She would get a few gifts, maybe new socks and a sweater, sometimes gloves or a jacket. She'd always felt embarrassed taking those gifts, but she'd always wanted them. She'd wanted pretty packages, something new. She'd opened each silly little gift as if it were…

She held her breath and closed her eyes as an image of three wise men kneeling before a baby flashed through her mind.

Duke patted her arm in a brotherly way and told her to take a deep breath. She tried but it came out as a sob. Christmas had changed her life because for one day each year she'd mattered to someone. The kindness of strangers had mattered.

How could she make that difference in other people's lives?

When the service ended, she didn't move, not right away. She needed time to reflect on how, in one message, Christmas had changed for her. Pieces, broken and scattered, had come back together. Jake stood, his blue eyes reflecting understanding.

"Are you okay?"

She nodded. "Yes, I'm good. Thank you."

He nodded and walked away, leaving her alone with her thoughts.

Jake headed for the nursery to get the twins. He should have stayed and said more to Breezy, but he hadn't known what. She'd been sitting there in a prairie skirt, denim jacket and a pastel scarf around her neck, looking like someone who needed a hug. He was the last man for that job.

Duke was there. He was a hugger. They all had their roles in the world. Duke was better at sympathy and compassion. Jake was the brother who made sure everyone was taken care of.

When he walked up to the nursery the girls ran at him, tackling his legs with chubby arms that held tight. The nursery worker, Janet Lester, told him the girls had been good but that Rosie seemed to have the sniffles. He picked both girls up and Rosie did look a little the worse for wear. Her nose was red and her eyes a little misty. Jake's aunt Patty appeared from the back of the nursery, a sympathetic look on her face.

"She's not feeling her normal happy self."

"No, doesn't appear to be," he agreed.

He kissed her forehead the way he'd seen Elizabeth do. Thinking about his sister brought a sharp ache to his heart. His own twin, the person he'd always counted on to share the burden of raising their ragtag family, was gone. Now her little girls needed him to protect them, to raise them and love them.

Without really thinking, he stepped away from the nursery, forgetting for a moment to thank Janet and his aunt Patty. He turned at the last moment and called out to them. They waved and went back to the children whose parents hadn't yet picked them up.

Outside the air was cool but not cold. He headed toward his truck and Duke waylaid him.

"You invited Breezy for lunch, didn't you?"

"I did. Where is she?" He shifted the girls. Duke reached for Violet, taking half the load.

"Talking to Margie Fisher. Margie is in charge of the caroling this year and I mentioned to her that Breezy sings. I thought it might help her to adjust if she felt included. I think they're also discussing the decorating committee. When Margie finds a willing volunteer, she hangs on tight."

"You're not getting her involved. You're throwing her to the wolves."

Duke grinned at that. "Yeah, well, everyone needs to feel included."

"Right." He glanced around and saw Breezy on the sidewalk. Margie stood in front of her, talking nonstop. Margie, with her dark gray dress, neat gray bun and glossy black cane looked like a formidable woman at first glance. But as starched as she appeared on the outside, she was spun sugar on the inside. No one had a bigger heart than Margie Fisher.

Duke tickled Violet and she giggled. Then he blew raspberries on her cheek. She giggled more. Rosie was a dead weight in Jake's arms, sound asleep.

"Rose not feeling good?" Duke asked.

"Doesn't appear to be."

"Take her on home. I can make sure Breezy escapes."

Jake nodded but his gaze caught and held on the woman in question. The wind picked up and she caught her hair and held it back with her hand, but tendrils drifted free and blew across her cheeks. Her hair smelled like sunshine, he knew. It bothered him more than a little that he'd noticed.

But thinking about Breezy was less disturbing than thinking about the sermon that had stabbed at his conscience. Because what was Christmas to him? A time to bring family together? Traditions of a big meal, a tree decorated with ornaments that had been kept for years, maybe generations? What else? Community parties, events that kept them busy for the holiday season?

He let his gaze shift to a man walking out the double doors of the church. Joe with no last name. He'd been in church and now he was walking next to a mom with two small children. Jake didn't know their names.

"I have to go. Can you hand Violet over to Breezy? I think she has a car seat in her car."

"Sure thing. I have car seats, too. We're all prepared. Is Brody at the house?"

"Yeah, at least he was when I left. See you there."

"Yep." Duke shifted Violet to his other arm and the two waved goodbye as Jake headed out with Rosie.

The young mom and Joe were still walking, the kids staying close to their mom as she tried to shelter them from the rain. Joe took off his jacket to hold it over the little ones. Jake hurried to his truck, unlocked the door and buckled Rose in the car seat.

A few minutes later, he pulled up next to Joe, the mom and those two kids. The rain was falling a little harder now. He rolled down the window and they all looked at him. Joe smiled and tipped that bent-up hat he wore. The mom, who might have been in her early twenties, looked worn down.

"Do you need a ride?" he offered, leaning a little to look down at the two kids, who had backed away but were grinning like the idea of riding in his truck was the coolest thing ever.

The mom started to shake her head but Joe opened the back door of the truck and the kids piled in, wet hair and damp clothes. "Of course she does. It's really coming down and she lives a half mile out. I told her someone would give her a ride."

"Of course," Jake agreed. "Joe, you get in, too."

"I don't have far to go," Joe answered. The mom had climbed in the front. Jake pushed the armrest back to open the middle seat. She scooted and Joe stood, unsure.

"Nevertheless…" Jake paused. "We have roast on at the house. There's plenty for all of us."

"I'd never turn down roast." Joe pulled himself into the truck. "Thank you, Jake."

Jake glanced back over his shoulder where the boys

had buckled in, looking drenched and cold. He introduced himself to the young woman, who was trying hard to tell him he didn't need to feed them. He cranked up the heat.

"No reason to let a good roast go to waste," he argued back. "Unless you have other plans."

She shook her head and her arms went around her two boys. "No, sir, we don't have other plans."

What did his faith mean to him? He glanced at the man sitting next to him and the three people in the backseat and he wondered if he'd have thought to give them a ride last week. How had he gotten so wrapped up in his own life that he'd stopped thinking to look around him?

And what had made a difference this week? A sermon? Or the woman sitting next to him during that sermon? A woman he didn't know that well, but knew without a doubt would have driven this unlikely four to their destination and fed them along the way.

Chapter Eight

Breezy followed Duke, who'd offered to carry Violet, through the house. She'd been in Jake's house before but only as far as the office. Today she walked down a wide stone-tiled hallway to the kitchen. The home was stone and log on the outside, and the interior walls were the same. The massive kitchen looked like a restaurant. The counter formed an L-shaped bar around the cooking area. Bar stools were arranged around the counter. There was a wood-plank-style dining room table in the open section with French doors that led to a deck overlooking the hills in the distance.

The room was already crowded with people. She smiled at Brody, whom she hadn't been officially introduced to. He had Rose in his arms and was tickling her until she bent over, giggling. Joe was stirring something on the stove. A young mom and two little boys were sitting at the counter bar looking half-scared and out of place. Breezy gave her best encouraging smile and the mom shrugged thin shoulders.

"Hey, looks like a houseful!" Duke grinned big and

the little boys shrank against their mom. Of course they did. It wasn't every day a kid learned about Goliath at church and then went to lunch with someone that looked like he might *be* Goliath.

Breezy stepped next to the giant. "Ease up, you're a little bit scary."

He glanced down at her. "I'm handsome, not scary." He grinned again at those little boys.

"No," she countered, "you're scary. If I didn't know you, I'd want a slingshot and some rocks."

He laughed at that. "Breezy, I've been described a lot of ways, but you're the first to call me a Philistine."

"Well, if the shoe fits." She glanced at his feet. "But do they make shoes that fit?"

He laughed again, then the two little boys laughed and their mom broke into a hesitant smile. Breezy stepped away from the friendly giant. "I'm Breezy, and you are?"

"Cora," the mom spoke softly. "And these are my boys, Ben and Jason."

"It's really nice to meet you guys."

"Do you live here?" the smaller of the two asked.

"No, I don't. I'm just…" What was she, exactly? She sensed the boy wasn't the only one waiting for her answer. She glanced at Jake. He stood at the counter but he'd turned to watch her, those blue eyes narrowed, waiting to see what she'd say.

Was she just visiting? Passing through? She met his eyes and he arched a brow, pushing her to answer.

"I live down the road." She finally settled on the easier explanation.

She let her gaze settle on Jake, and saw from the corner of her eye that Duke was giving him a look. She had an ally in Duke, she knew that. He'd told her that the twins needed her. She sometimes thought they might.

"If someone would set the table, this is almost ready." Jake shifted the direction of her thoughts with the proclamation.

"I can do that," Breezy offered. She turned slowly, looking at the abundance of cabinets. "If you'll tell me where to find plates."

He pointed and she opened the cabinet. Cora slid off the stool, telling her boys to stay put. "Can I get the glasses ready or anything?"

Jake pointed to another cabinet. "Glasses up there, ice in the fridge door and tea is already made."

It felt like a family gathering, Breezy thought. Brody was entertaining the twins. Duke was cutting pie and Joe was moving serving dishes to the table. She thought she could learn to feel like a part of this life, this family. Even though they weren't quite a family. Cora and her boys, Joe and even Breezy were strays brought in out of the rain.

As they settled down to eat, Jake's phone rang. He apologized and answered it. As he spoke, he glanced at Breezy. He nodded, said it would be okay and then ended the call.

"Who was that?" Brody asked as he piled roast on bread.

"Marty." Jake passed salad to Cora.

"And?" Brody pushed.

Breezy wondered how he could have been raised in this home and not realize it was a bad idea to push Jake. She considered kicking his shin since she sat closest.

Jake sighed, shook his head and passed the plate of bread. "She is stuck in San Antonio for a few days. Her sister is in the hospital."

"Oh, that's rough. You, the ranch, twins." Brody whistled as he poured gravy over the food on his plate.

Breezy watched the mound of food grow and looked from the plate to the man sitting next to her. Not that Brody was a man. He had to be close to her age but he seemed younger. He wasn't tall like Jake and Duke, and he was lean and wiry. But he obviously could pack away the food.

He caught her staring at his plate and grinned. "You don't think I can eat it?"

"I have a feeling you will," she countered.

He laughed and dug in. Jake cleared his throat. "I don't think we've prayed."

Everyone stopped. Jake reached for the hands of the people on either side of him and around the table hands joined. They all bowed their heads. As Jake prayed a blessing on the food, Breezy prayed she'd survive.

After the meal was finished and the dishes were done, Duke offered to give Cora, Joe and the boys a ride back to town. Brody disappeared with the excuse that he had work to do in the barn. Breezy watched as little by little everyone left. The twins were sleeping. It was just her and Jake. And he looked restless.

"Is there a problem?"

"A small one," he admitted.

"Okay, well, why don't you tell me? Or is this another rule, 'don't question Jake'? Or is there a rule that you have to do everything on your own without help?"

She was goading him, she knew. But she didn't

know any other way to get the man to open up, to let her in. Not that she really needed or wanted all of his deep, dark secrets. As a matter of fact, after thinking about it, she was considering pushing Rewind and leaving him to his misery.

As she considered making her exit, he sighed and brushed a hand through his hair, leaving the dark brown strands in disarray. When he looked at her, his blue eyes were troubled. Okay, she did care. He needed someone to take part of the load or he'd work himself into an early grave.

The person to do that was her.

"Tell me," she spoke softly. "Listen, I know you love your family, but you can't do it all alone. What good will you be to the twins if you don't take care of yourself?"

"You're probably right."

"I know I'm right." She said and for some crazy reason took a step closer. Why? Why did she suddenly feel the need to comfort this man? Jake Martin wasn't a man who invited hugs and easy touches. But she touched him anyway.

She put her palm on the smooth planes of his face, aware that she should step back, aware that the room had gone still except the wild pounding of her heart. He didn't move away; in fact his hand slid to her waist and pulled her close. For a long moment they stood toe to toe, forehead to forehead, her hand on his cheek, his hand on her hip.

Breezy knew that they were both waiting for common sense to return. But it didn't. Slowly, ever so slowly, his head bent toward hers and their lips touched.

He kissed her slowly, taking his time it seemed, and she closed her eyes.

She moved her hands to the back of his neck. He raised his head for a brief moment then leaned in again, brushing his lips against hers and then moving to her cheek.

The front door slammed. Jake stepped back, releasing her from his hold. She stared up at him, waiting for him to say something, to undo the moment. He didn't. He gave her a long look, rubbing his hand against the back of his neck, and then he put distance between them.

Breezy thought she might cry.

Jake had stepped away from Breezy but it hadn't been an easy thing to do. It should have been. He should have stepped back, said a polite "thank you for the kiss" and let it end. Instead he stood there looking at her, wondering if there would be a repeat, and kind of wishing for one.

That proved he hadn't been getting enough sleep. He rubbed his hand across the back of his neck, ignoring his brother. Brody shot the two of them a curious look and mumbled something about his horse and antibiotics. Jake guessed he should listen but didn't.

"Jake, the problem?" Breezy called him back to planet Earth with that question. She was right, they'd been discussing a problem.

"Right. Marty won't be home for a few days. And I'd been counting on her to help with the twins."

Breezy's eyes narrowed and her pretty mouth, the one he'd just kissed, formed a straight line of disapproval. "You understand that you're not raising the twins alone anymore? There is a will, I think, and it appointed us both guardians."

Brody hurried past them, head down, hands up. "I'm a neutral party but she's right."

"Get out of here," Jake growled.

Brody obliged.

Breezy didn't give him a chance to interrupt. "You're arrogant, Jake Martin. You have this idea that you are the only person capable of doing anything. You run this ranch. You run your family. You are now trying to run me, and that isn't going to work because I'm not yours to run."

"I kind of got that."

"No, I don't think you have gotten it. You're worried about how you'll take care of this ranch, take care of the twins, and probably worried about taking care of me. Well, I can take care of myself. And I think I can even help you take care of those two little girls." She hesitated, locking those caramel-brown eyes on him. "*Our* little girls, Jake. As much as it hurts, they are ours."

It did hurt. Hurt enough that it felt as if she'd physically pushed him. He took a deep breath that shuddered on the exhale. She started toward him but he held his hands up to stop her.

"I'm sorry." She said it softly and it felt like rain coming down on him. "I'm sorry that you lost your sister and I'm sorry you lost Lawton. We're in this together, though. And you have to let me help you. Maybe that's what Lawton wanted. Maybe he knew you'd need someone from outside the family who couldn't be bullied and who maybe, just maybe, would bully you back."

Had Lawton thought that? It made sense, but Jake couldn't delve into the psychology of Lawton's plan. Not now.

"I have to take cattle to an auction tomorrow and I need to make sure the guys move a herd from one field to another. I also have to make contact with a firm in Fort Worth. Lawton and I were putting a system in their office and it has a few kinks. I was counting on Marty."

"Yeah, I get that. Now you'll count on me."

"Right, I'll count on you."

She smiled at that. "See, that wasn't so hard. Now, why don't we get their bags packed and you can bring them over this afternoon?"

He agreed to her plan. What other choice did he have?

Later, as he pulled up to Lawton's house, he realized it was the only option. And it was the right choice to make. She shared custody with him and it was time for him to let go. As he looked at the house, he realized it was time to stop calling it Lawton's house. It was Breezy's house now. It was her car in the drive. It was Breezy who would open the door when he walked up the steps with the girls.

She was right, it was time to face that Lawton and Elizabeth weren't coming home. This wasn't temporary. The girls were his. They were Breezy's.

Accepting reality meant accepting her in his life. It also meant he'd have to trust that she wasn't going to sneak away in the night. That thought unsettled him a little. He could see that the twins needed her. They were getting used to her songs, to her hugs, to the way she talked to them.

As he'd known she would, she greeted him on the front porch, taking Rose from him. She kissed the little girl's cheek and then leaned to kiss Violet's cheek.

"All ready for this?" he asked as they walked through the front door.

"I think so. I have real food and I put clean sheets on their beds. I'm a little worried how they'll adjust to sleeping in their beds again."

"They usually do better if they sleep in one crib together," he offered.

"Oh, I should have thought of that."

"It isn't something that makes or breaks you, Breezy. But it might make your night a little better."

They walked into the living room. Violet and Rosie were fresh from their nap and ready to play. Violet wiggled from his arms and Rosie was already pulling a doll from the basket of toys next to the couch. He looked around the room, noticing that it still looked exactly as it had when she'd moved in.

"You know, you can change things. Put out your own stuff." Weren't women big on personal touches?

She glanced around the room and then looked back at him and shrugged. "I know. It's a strange concept for me. I've never really had a place of my own and I guess I still think of this as Lawton's house that I'm staying in. Like he and Elizabeth will be back. They'll want their lives, their girls…"

She covered her face with her hands and shook her head.

Jake pulled her close. Her hands were still on her face and her arms were between them. She sobbed as he held her. He guessed they both had some adjusting to do. He stroked long blond hair until she stopped crying.

"Shh, it'll get easier. We both have to figure this out."

She nodded into his shoulder, her head resting there, fitting perfectly. Common sense, which had been in short supply lately, told him to pull back. But she felt good in his arms and he didn't want to let go, not yet.

The twins were playing, sitting close together the way they sometimes did, heads practically touching, their dolls between them. He wondered if they communicated that way. Did they discuss the situation, wonder together where their mommy and daddy had gone to? Those thoughts ached inside him and suddenly he needed this woman in his arms as much as she needed him.

Eventually he let her go and she wiped her eyes and sniffled. "I'm sorry."

"No need to apologize." He sank onto the sofa and watched as she took a seat in the rocking chair. "Breezy, we have to accept this. I have to work on letting you be my partner in raising the girls. You have to make this your home."

She seemed pale in the dim light of the lamp and her eyes shimmered. She eventually nodded. "I know."

"A home where you stay," he pushed.

Because that was still his fear, that the twins would get attached and she'd leave.

"Why do you think I'll leave?"

"I know you aren't used to staying in one place."

She shook her head, leaning a little in his direction. "Yes, that's been true for most of my life. But for most of my life I didn't have a reason to stay. But your trust issues, those are your issues to work through."

"Trust issues?" So in a matter of days she thought she knew him?

"I've been here almost a week and…it's a small town." She caught her bottom lip between her teeth and studied him for a minute.

"Yes, it's a small town." Suddenly he was uncomfortable with the direction this conversation had taken.

"I know about your mom, and I know that when she left, you took care of things. You were just a boy and…"

He held up a hand. "Don't start picturing me as a little boy in need of a mother. I was twelve and I survived."

"Of course you did," she said. "You and I have that in common. And now we have those two little girls counting on us to help them survive."

He stood, because it was time for him to go. He wanted to be upset, because leave it to a woman to think a man had to get in touch with his emotions in order to deal with life. He wasn't upset, though. Because Breezy pushed him in a way that few people did. The twins needed her strength. Maybe he did, too.

"Jake, I'm sorry." Her hand reached for his. He looked down at those fingers with pale pink polish holding on to his, not letting go.

"Don't be," he finally answered. "We'll get through this. But I'm just about talked out so I'm going to head to the house and get some work done."

"I'll see you tomorrow." She stood on tiptoe and kissed his cheek before he went out the door.

Jake got in his truck and headed back to the ranch,

to work left undone. His phone rang as he drove. A county deputy was on the other end, letting him know they'd checked out a few leads on the break-in but so far weren't any closer to figuring out who might have been at Lawton's the other day. They had one print, a half print actually, and it wasn't in the system.

Great. One more thing to worry about.

Chapter Nine

Breezy and the twins were gone. Jake walked through Lawton's place two days later, looking, listening. He could admit to a good case of the nerves settling over him the minute he'd walked through the door, calling out to Breezy and the twins and getting no reply. Her car was in the drive. He'd checked the garage and the truck was parked where it had been for weeks.

He walked out the back door and headed in the direction of the barn. Halfway there he heard laughter, Breezy's and the twins'. The sound drifted on the wind and seemed to come from the field behind the house. He opened the gate and paused, waiting for more laughter, maybe conversation that might lead him in the right direction. After several seconds he heard Breezy yell, "Timber!"

That did it. He ran in the direction of her voice, coming to a sudden stop as he spotted her, the twins and an Arizona cypress toppling to the ground. She stood a good distance back from the tree. The twins were in a wagon that had been kept in the garage. She was holding the handle of the wagon with one hand and a saw in the other. When she spotted him she waved the saw and then pointed to the fallen tree.

"What are you doing?" He smiled at Rosie and Violet. "You girls having fun?"

Rosie nodded. Violet pointed to the tree, her mouth open and her eyes wide. "Tree," they both said.

"Yes, a Christmas tree." Breezy looked far too pleased and that only annoyed him more.

"What in the world are you thinking?"

"That if I'm going to make this house my home, I need a tree." She looked surprised and a little bit annoyed.

"I could have gotten you a tree. As a matter of fact, there's probably one in the attic."

"I wanted a real tree. I've never had one."

She brushed at a few strands of hair blowing in the wind even though she wore a cap pulled down tight. Her eyes were bright toffee and her pink lips parted in an excited grin.

How did she do that? How did she look like a child and a fantastically gorgeous woman all at the same time? He allowed himself a minute to look at her, at all of that blond hair flowing out from beneath a white knit cap. She'd worn an old canvas coat, probably Lawton's, with a white sweater, jeans and brown riding boots.

"Anyway," she was saying, "I thought it wouldn't be hard to cut one down. I hope it's okay to do that."

"Yes, it's okay." It wasn't okay to turn him inside out this way. It wasn't okay to look like a woman he wanted to kiss. Again.

None of this was okay and Lawton should have

known better. He was angry. Angry with himself, with her for being so tempting, and angry with Lawton for leaving them alone in this mess.

"Jake?"

He brushed a hand over his face and then raised that same hand to stop her. He just needed a minute. She started to say something. He held up one finger. Surely she could understand. He needed a minute. One quiet minute to get past the loss of a sister and his best friend.

He needed more quiet moments to figure out what exactly she was doing to his calm, very ordered existence.

When he opened his eyes, she was still watching him and the twins were staring, as well. They wore identical looks of doubt. Of course they did. All three of them were doubting his sanity and his ability to take care of them. And that's what got him. Lawton hadn't added a partner, he'd added one more person Jake felt the need to care for.

The empty house had shaken him. He tried to write off this roller coaster of emotions as fear. He hadn't expected to find her gone. He had panicked. But they were fine.

"Let's get that tree back to the house." He pulled gloves out of his jacket pocket and put them on. Without anything further said, he grabbed the end of the tree and trudged along next to Breezy, who pulled the wagon.

"I'm sorry," she whispered halfway to the house. The twins had climbed out of the wagon and were walking alongside the tree, telling him in their toddler voices that they could help.

"No need to be sorry." He said it with an ease that

surprised him. "You wanted a tree. I should have gotten you a tree."

She glanced at him then. She looked mad. Maybe close to furious. They didn't know each other, didn't know the right words to say or what the other person was thinking.

When people had children together, it was a given that they would know each other. He and Breezy were walking through a field of land mines.

"I don't need for you to get me a tree, Jake. I don't need you to take care of me. That isn't why I'm here. Lawton didn't leave me to you. He didn't ask you to take care of me, too. I'm here to help you. I've taken care of myself for a long, long time."

"Right, of course."

"Jake, I'm not the kind of woman that needs a man to run to my rescue. I won't ask you to hang curtains, kill wasps or slay dragons."

He wondered why she was so against allowing a man to do those things for her. He didn't ask. Asking would have dragged him further into her life. She was kind enough to give him an out and he should take it.

He dropped the tree in the yard. He would have to find a stand for it. And she'd have to clear a space in the living room. He would have explained but she trudged up the steps ahead of him. The twins following close behind.

As they entered the house he noticed what he hadn't before. It smelled wonderful. The kinds of smells that made his stomach rumble with hunger.

She must have heard because she laughed. "You're welcomed to stay for dinner."

"That isn't tofu, is it?"

She shook her head as he followed her to the kitchen. "No, it's bread and homemade stew."

"You cook?"

She nodded and lifted the lid from the slow cooker. "I'm learning. I've never had a kitchen of my own, not really. In Dawson I worked a lot, waitressing, and I ate at the restaurant. Before that I lived in California in an efficiency that was less than efficient. It was one room with a bed, microwave and dorm-size fridge."

"Why did you stay there?"

She stirred the stew and then took a careful taste. He waited for an answer and wondered if it was too much to ask. Maybe they didn't need to know each other's stories. But then, she knew his.

"I stayed because I didn't know what else to do. I don't have a real education so I couldn't get a decent job. My income kept me where I was."

"You didn't call your sister?"

She shook her head. "I was five when Maria took me. I didn't remember Mia's last name. I didn't know where she'd been taken to."

"What happened to Maria?"

The lid clanged a little on the cooker. She righted it and set the spoon on a plate. "She died when I was nineteen." She cleared her throat. "This will be ready in an hour. Let's put the tree up."

"Breezy…"

She shook her head. "No. Let's stop with the past. We all have one and we all have to make choices about how we live today, how we live tomorrow. I've had great experiences and bad experiences. I define who I am today."

"Experiences do change who we are."

"Right, but they don't have to destroy us. Those experiences don't have to take our joy or make us afraid to take chances."

"I guess you're right."

She grinned and he noticed the slight dimple in her left cheek. "I know I'm right."

After Jake put the tree in a stand, he disappeared into the garage to find ornaments. Breezy brought a box from the kitchen and set it on the table. The twins peered inside, smiling and reaching for the decorations they'd made with dough. She'd found the recipe in an old cookbook, one that said it had belonged to Lawton's grandmother. At last she'd found family recipes. It made her feel connected. She'd had a grandmother. She had a past, ancestors, connections. She now had what so many people took for granted: her history.

"What's this?" Jake returned carrying a tub that he sat on the floor next to the tree. He sat down on the sofa and watched as she strung ribbon through holes in the baked and decorated dough decorations.

"We made these." She handed a star to Rosie and a tree to Violet.

Jake picked one up, tapped it, held it to his mouth. Breezy watched, not sure he would actually take a bite. Surely he wouldn't. He started to.

"Don't eat it!"

He pulled it back and shot a look at the twins. Both

girls wore big grins and now had their decorations up to their mouths, ornery looks in their blue eyes.

"No eating, girls," he said in mock seriousness.

They giggled at him, all three of them. Breezy wanted the moment to go on. She wanted to decorate a tree, maybe drink hot cocoa and eat the cookies she'd also made that morning. Maybe this would become a tradition, their tradition.

"So we have a tub full of decorations and yet you felt inclined to make your own?" he asked as he pulled lights and a few other decorations from the tub.

She shrugged slim shoulders and he noticed a faint pink in her cheeks. "It seemed like the thing to do."

"Making decorations?" He really didn't get it. Maybe he didn't need to.

"I found the recipe in a family cookbook and there were paints and glitter in a craft room upstairs. I hope that's okay." She had felt strange, wandering through the house last night after the girls had gone to sleep.

"Of course it is. I'll repeat, you live here."

Yes, it was her house, but it wasn't. The craft room had an abundance of supplies and a half-finished tod-dler-size dress on the sewing machine. The bedroom that had belonged to Lawton and Elizabeth still had towels hanging next to the shower.

She'd found family photo albums with pictures of her father, his parents, his siblings. There were pictures of Lawton with his parents. She'd sat for a long time with that photo album, picturing herself in their lives and being unable to, because she hadn't existed to them.

But she had her own life. She had memories of who she had been and where she had lived. It was tough but she had to blend who she had always been with the person she now knew herself to be. The daughter of a senator.

"Let's decorate the tree." She stood, ready to let go of the thoughts that brought her nothing but regret. She reached for the ornament she'd bought at Oregon's shop.

"That's new." Jake took a closer look.

She nodded and hung the ornament up high on a sturdy branch. "Do you want to string lights before we get too far into the process of hanging decorations?"

"Sounds like a plan." He opened the tub and pulled out a box of lights. "You'll have to help."

She shifted away from the tree and noticed the girls were still sitting with their decorations. They looked perfectly innocent.

"You girls sit and as soon as the lights are up, we'll hang your ornaments."

They smiled at her, perfectly sweet smiles. She looked to Jake. He glanced at the girls, then at her. "Suspicious."

"Very." She shrugged it off. "If you go behind the tree you can string them on that side and pass the lights for me to wrap around this side."

From her side of the tree she watched as he started the lights at the top of the tree and then wrapped them around, handing them off to her. She took the lights and wrapped them around the front, passing back to him. And down the tree they worked. At times their hands would touch briefly and she would wonder how this would be in a year or five years. What if he found someone and married?

What would it be like if he had his own family? Would he still include her and the twins? Would they all get together on holidays? Would the twins spend half of their time with him and his family? Round and round the thoughts went, like the lights being wrapped around the tree, and she had to stop.

"Where'd you go, Hernandez?" He pushed the string of lights at her.

"I'm here."

"You're quiet." He handed her the strand of lights for the last time.

She finished and the two of them stepped back to survey their work after Jake plugged the lights in. The clear lights twinkled and the tree was beautiful, even with just the one ornament in place. The twins were in awe. At least for a moment.

"Come on, girls, let's hang your ornaments." Breezy held out the box to Jake and he took several. "You get the top half."

Violet and Rosie hung their ornaments side by side and came back for more. Violet took an angel. Rosie took a shepherd. Each time they hung their ornaments side by side, jabbering in a language only they understood.

Jake pulled another box of ornaments from the tub. He handed Breezy one that told the birthday of the twins and their names on one side. On the other it had a picture of them as newborns. She hung it closer to the top so it wouldn't fall and get broken. Jake hung a snowflake with a family picture—Lawton, Elizabeth and the twins.

Each ornament felt like a piece of history, a piece of

her family. As Jake finished, holding the twins to hang decorations on the higher branches, Breezy stepped back to survey the job they'd done. Jake caught her eye and she gave him a thumbs-up before picking up the box with the nativity Lefty Mueller had given her. She touched the hand-carved pieces, took them out and arranged them on the fireplace mantel with Christmas lights behind them. Jake came to stand near her right shoulder.

"One of Lefty's?"

She nodded as she watched the lights twinkle and the nativity caught the soft glow. "Yes."

"It's beautiful."

"Yes, it is. I've always wanted one." It was one of her contributions to their new traditions, but he wouldn't understand. He wouldn't understand what it meant to have keepsake ornaments, a nativity and something handmade with the twins to keep year after year.

This was the place where she would stay. She would be here next year to carry on these traditions with Rosie and Violet.

She would create memories for all of them. And stability that made them feel safe each night, not afraid to sleep, not afraid of where they would be the next day or next week. She would give them everything she'd never had, including family.

"I think we should finish the tree and then eat, because I'm starving," Jake suggested. They stood shoulder to shoulder. He touched his fingers to hers.

Something came over her. She wanted to lean against him, put her head on his shoulder. Instead she pulled away, coming to her senses. Better late than never.

"Yes, we should definitely eat."

"I think the twins are having an appetizer." He nodded toward the girls. "They're eating your popcorn."

She laughed at the sight that greeted her as she turned. The twins were sitting on the floor with popcorn she'd spent the previous evening stringing to make a garland for the tree. As they kept a careful eye on the adults, they nibbled kernels of popped corn off the string.

"I hope you weren't planning to use that again next year," Jake teased.

"No, I hadn't planned on it. And I think our helpers are definitely ready to eat."

Traditions started this way, she thought. As she sat at the table she also realized that Christmas was far more than these traditions. But the traditions reminded people of the real meaning of the holiday.

Throughout the Bible people had held to traditions and celebrations in order to remember what God had done for them. Passover, Hanukkah, Palm Sunday, Easter each holiday held a tradition that was a reminder of God at work.

For Christmas, the tree, the lights, the nativity, all were reminders, but the real meaning went so much deeper. And this year the reminder touched a little deeper because Breezy could look at the people sitting with her at that table and she could see what God had done for her.

He'd given her what she'd always wanted. She had a family. She had a home. She even had a plant. The poinsettia Joe had given sat in the center of the table, a reminder that she was staying. People who stayed had plants.

After they finished dinner, Jake helped by clearing the table and doing dishes. Breezy gave the girls their bath. He found them when they were out of the tub and wearing matching pink gowns and matching polka-dot robes. He peeked in the room they shared and waved.

Breezy ran a comb through Violet's hair. "They're ready for a story and then bed."

"I could make coffee while you get them down."

"I'd prefer hot tea," she answered.

The conversation was so normal it took her by surprise. They weren't a couple. They didn't end their evenings with coffee and discussion of the day's events. As kind as Jake might be, she knew he still didn't trust her. She knew he had his own life and she was added baggage.

"I can make hot tea," he offered.

"You don't have to. I mean, if you have things you need to do." But she was lonely and company, any company, would be so nice. The closer they got to Christmas, the more she missed Mia and the people she'd met in Oklahoma.

"I don't have anywhere I have to be." He leaned against the door frame. "Do you have a hot date?"

She snorted at that. He really didn't know her. "I don't date."

"Interesting." One dark brow arched and she turned her attention back to the girls. "Is that a warning?"

He should go now. She thought about telling him to

leave. But the twins were pulling away from her, wanting their uncle Jake.

"No, not a warning at all. It's a simple statement."

He grinned and she was startled by how much that smile of his changed everything.

"I think Lawton might have thought…"

She pulled Rosie back to her lap. "Lawton couldn't have planned that."

He shrugged, picked up Violet and hugged her before setting her back on the ground. Both of them were silent. They looked at each other and looked at the twins.

"Herbal tea," she reminded. He exited the room and she was left with the girls, with tears she tried to hide and with doubts. So many doubts.

Each day got a little easier as she got to know the twins and understand this new life. But each day also grew a little more complicated as she got to know Jake and felt her heart moving a little in his direction.

Jake was the kind of man most women dreamed about. She'd had her share of dreams over the years. Long, long ago she'd thought maybe someday a man would rescue her. But dreams were not reality. Men like Jake didn't date women like Breezy. They didn't take the girl home to meet the family, or even want the family to know about her.

As she joined him in the kitchen, she reminded herself it was nothing more than a cup of tea and a minute to catch up. They would do a lot of this in the coming years. Now was the time to adjust and accept his presence in her life.

Chapter Ten

On Thursday evening Breezy made it to town for the choir practice Margie Fisher had asked her to be a part of. She had wrangled the twins into warm clothes, fed them pasta and green beans. She'd even managed to do the dishes and throw in a load of laundry.

And she was exhausted. She had always thought children would be a lot of work. She knew babies took time and love. She didn't know that *two* could turn a person's world upside down and inside out. As she'd tried to put one girl in pants, the other had taken off running, giggling and losing hair clips as she made her escape. She'd chased Violet with Rosie under her arms and managed to snag her only to have Rosie escape and run through the house like a wild thing on the loose.

At Oregon's All Things shop she parked, got out of the car and for a minute she stood there, unwilling to unbuckle the twins from their car seats. She closed her eyes and took a deep breath, needing a moment to give her strength to get through this night. She had no idea how Marty managed, but she now realized the woman deserved a medal.

She wasn't a quitter, but the girls had definitely worn her out. A part of her had almost expected them to tie her up and ransack the house! A quick peek in the window of the car led her to wonder how such innocent little girls could wreak such havoc on a house!

She leaned back against the car. A few deep breaths and she'd be ready for round two.

"Hey, you okay?"

She opened her eyes and saw Oregon. "I'm good. Just needed a breather."

"Those twins are something else, aren't they?"

She nodded and closed her eyes again. The air was cool and the sun had set, leaving a dusky, lavender light on the western horizon. She worried that if Oregon said anything too sympathetic, she might actually cry. It had been that kind of day. The kind that made her wonder if she was really cut out for raising two little girls.

The western horizon reminded her of times in the past when Maria would say, *I think it's time for a new adventure.*

Sometimes Breezy had looked forward to those adventures. And other times she'd wanted to just stay, to let her feet stay rooted in that spot, let it become familiar.

"Breezy?"

"I'm good. I'll get them out and meet you at the church?"

Oregon closed the shop door. Breezy noticed then that her daughter, Lilly, was with her. Lilly grinned and held up a puppy.

"Want one?" Lilly asked. "They're nearly weaned and Mom said I can't keep any of them. Well, except the mama dog, Belle."

"What kind are they?" She opened the car door and started to unbuckle Rosie. Oregon moved to the other side of the car and did the same with Violet.

"They're mutts," Oregon offered. "The mother is a border collie. Dad is anyone's guess."

Breezy glanced back at the fawn-and-white puppy that Lilly was holding. The girl had moved closer and her blue eyes fairly twinkled. Breezy studied the girl more closely, taking in her dark hair, her blue eyes. Interesting. She smiled and refocused on the puppy.

"How long did you say you've lived here?" she asked Oregon.

"Breezy, the puppies are almost weaned. I'm sure the twins would love one." Oregon returned to the subject of puppies. "Really, a person with twins should have a puppy. That border collie half might be good at keeping these little girls rounded up." Oregon bit down on her bottom lip and gave Breezy a look. The subject of puppies was safe. The subject of Lilly was off-limits.

"A puppy, huh?" She looked back at the dog again, noticing its slightly long hair, gentle brown eyes and the way it leaned into Lilly. "I've never had a pet."

Lilly practically gasped. "No way."

"Yes way," Breezy confirmed. "I've never had a dog or a cat. I've never stayed anywhere long enough to have an animal."

"You're not going anywhere this time, Breezy." Oregon had Violet out of the seat and was kissing her cheek. "I love these little girls."

"Me, too," Breezy said. They were a part of her. They weren't little strangers shoved into her life. They were her flesh and blood, her DNA. They were her family.

Oregon joined her and the five of them, plus the puppy, headed down the sidewalk in the direction of the church. Lilly put the puppy down and held its pink leash as they crossed the road. The little dog wagged her fluffy tail and sniffed the ground as they walked.

"You don't have to take a puppy," Oregon offered.

"I think I'd like to have one. Is it a boy or a girl?"

"That one is a girl. We call her Daisy, but you can call her whatever you like."

"Daisy." Breezy looked at the dog and the girl holding the leash. "I'll take her when she's weaned."

As they walked, Joe joined them on the sidewalk. He was wearing his usual tan jacket, tan pants and work boots, his bent-up hat pulled down on his thin gray hair. But today he looked tired. His skin looked as gray as his hair.

"Are you okay, Joe?" Breezy asked as he stepped next to her.

He peered at Oregon, who didn't really seem to notice. "I'm good, thank you. And you, Breezy? How is motherhood?"

"Exhausting."

"I'm sure it is. Although I've never been a mother." He smiled at that. "And I wasn't able to be a father to the one child I had."

"I'm sorry, Joe." Breezy shifted Rosie, who was squirming in her arms to get down.

"No one's fault but my own. I let too many years

go by. Years I'm sorry for. I hope to someday make it up to her."

Breezy studied the older man in the dim light of the street lamp. "I think we all live with some regrets."

"Yes, I suppose we do. But this is Christmas. It's a time of hope. It's a time of celebrating our faith. Because without this one event, what would we have hope in? We have a lot to be thankful for. And you, Miss Oregon." Joe shifted to look at the other woman, his eyes gentle. "How are things at your shop?"

Oregon's smile came with hesitancy. "It's better. The Christmas traffic has helped."

"Keep your chin up, my dear. Don't give up hope."

"Yes," she responded, but Breezy didn't think that Oregon looked all that hopeful.

The light display in the park next to the church lit up the entire block, lending a glow of twinkling lights to the darkening sky. The nativity graced the center of the display and music played from a speaker inside the manger.

"Where will you spend Christmas, Joe?" Breezy asked as they walked up to the church. Lilly had run off to talk to friends, dragging the dog that was soon to be Breezy's with her.

"I'm sure I'll find somewhere to spend the holidays. Of course I'll be here for the town celebration the night before Christmas Eve. And then maybe I'll go somewhere warm."

"You should be with friends or family." She put Rosie down and held the child's hand. "I'm sure you could spend the day with us."

He touched her arm. "I appreciate that, Breezy. It's

good to know I have friends. And you, Oregon, what will you do for the holidays?"

Oregon held Violet's hand now and she looked up, surprised and unsure. "Lilly and I will be together."

Breezy reached for her hand. "Spend the day with us."

"You don't have to do that." Oregon held tight to Violet, who was pulling to get away.

"But I have a home." Breezy reached for Violet and held both twins so they couldn't escape. "I've never had a home to invite friends to."

"But what about the Martins?" Oregon reminded.

"What about the Martins?" Jake walked up behind her. She spun to face him, the twins giggling at the movement.

"Oh, I... We were discussing Christmas."

"And?" Jake reached for Rosie and Breezy allowed him to take the child.

"Oregon and Joe don't have family in the area."

Jake looked from Joe to Oregon. "I see. Of course they're welcome to join us at the ranch for Christmas."

"I wouldn't want to impose," Oregon assured him with Joe echoing the sentiment.

"No imposition. We'll all be together. There's always room for a few more."

A few more. Including her.

She felt unsettled at the thought. The twins were her family. She didn't know how to fit into Jake's family. He had an aunt and uncle, cousins, brothers and a sister.

But for the sake of the girls, she was willing to try.

Jake watched as Oregon and Joe both bid Breezy farewell. He hadn't meant to make them feel uncomfortable. He hadn't meant to sound like the ruler of clan Martin. Old habits died hard.

"I'm sorry." He moved Rosie to one hip and took Violet from Breezy. He didn't miss the dark shadows under her eyes, a good indication chasing after two little girls had left her exhausted. With Marty home she'd have a break tonight.

"No need to apologize. I should have thought before making additional plans. I just…" She shrugged and looked at the floor. "I've been Joe and Oregon, the person with nowhere to go, no one to spend the holidays with. I've had too many years of spending Christmas with strangers."

"And in a sense, you'll be doing it again this year." His understanding even surprised him.

"In a sense, yes."

"What would you have done for Christmas in Oklahoma?"

She had a faraway look in her eyes. Homesickness? Regret? He wanted to ask, but he also didn't want to take that step, to know too much about what she felt.

"I would have spent it with my sister and her extended family. But this is my family now. The twins are my family."

"We're your family," he offered.

"Right, of course."

He'd had his family around him always. Almost to the point of needing a break from them. She'd had the exact opposite. Curiosity got the better of him.

"Breezy, why did Maria keep running? Why didn't she rent an apartment for the two of you?"

"I didn't realize it when I was younger, but she was

afraid the police would find us and take me from her. She wasn't all bad. She was a lonely lady and she'd cared for my mom, cared for us kids. She also didn't know what would happen to me since I was the child without any known family, so she took me and ran. She wasn't emotionally healthy." She looked away from him, not letting him in. "There was so much I didn't understand."

"I'm sorry."

She brought her gaze up. "She loved me. She did her best."

What could he say to that?

"You're defending the woman who took you from your family and kept you from having a home?"

"I know you don't understand."

"Probably not."

Because he was looking at a beautiful, talented woman who hadn't lived the life she should have lived. Senator Brooks might have found her, might have taken care of her. But it was all water under the bridge.

"They're starting to practice." She headed toward the front of the fellowship hall. "And there's Brody."

Jake's younger brother headed their way, wearing a giant-size grin. Violet ran over to him and he picked her up.

"Did the two of you hear that someone bought Cora a van, had it delivered to her little house yesterday along with a trunkload of groceries?" Brody asked when he reached them. The news about the young mom who had eaten Sunday lunch with them came as a surprise.

"I hadn't heard." Jake watched as Breezy drifted

away from the two of them. He watched her go and wondered about a woman who had spent her life with nothing but had recently inherited enough for several lifetimes. Was she playing Santa to the poor in Martin's Crossing?

"Yeah, that and the check the church got, and Anna Cranston got a surprise yesterday. That roof of hers has been leaking. Someone must have noticed because a crew showed up to fix it." Brody held both twins now. They were patting his cheeks and pulling at his hat.

Jake glanced from his younger brother to the woman now taking her place at the front of the church. She looked comfortable there in her long skirt, boots and a sweater. She fit in. She glanced his way. He tipped his hat to her and started to walk away. He was at the church for a business meeting, and to help plan the order of events for the Christmas celebration. He wasn't there to watch Breezy.

When he started to turn away, Brody stood in his way.

"You think it's our new sister?" Brody asked, grinning as he rocked back on his boot heels and peered up at Jake.

"She *isn't* our sister," Jake warned.

Brody laughed at that. "No, she isn't, is she? Glad you noticed."

"What are you getting at, Brody?"

"Nothing, don't be so touchy. I wondered if you thought she might be the one playing Santa."

"No, I don't think so." He managed another quick look at the woman in question. "I don't know, maybe."

Brody stood next to Jake, still holding the twins.

Violet had his hat on her head. "I'm going to take them to the nursery. But, Jake…"

The tone, serious, a little sad, caught Jake's attention. And he knew. It happened every Christmas. Every year the questions started for Brody. He was the one who had never given up hope that Sylvia Martin would come back. Jake guessed he didn't blame his little brother. Jake had been twelve, but Brody had only been in preschool when she left.

The kid had needed a mom.

"Go ahead, Brody. Ask."

Brody shifted the twins, hugging Violet tightly enough that she protested by wiggling and he set her down. She moved to Jake, holding his legs. He picked her up, wondering if it had been confusing for them, being back in their home with Breezy.

"Don't you ever wonder where she is?" Brody finally asked.

"Yeah, sometimes I do, Brody. She used to write. A few times from Florida, once from New York. The letters stopped a long time ago."

"Do you think she's alive?"

Jake didn't have an answer to that, but he didn't want his kid brother to have false hope. "I'd say she probably is."

"I've thought about hiring someone to find her."

Jake tamped down his temper. Violet had her head on his shoulder but she looked up at him, big blue eyes questioning and a little worried. He managed to keep his tone soft for her sake. "Brody, why? She didn't want to be a mother twenty-two years ago. I doubt she feels any differently today or she would have come back."

Brody looked like a kid who'd lost his favorite toy. Jake hated that. He didn't want to feel like the guy who kicked the dog. It made him angry all over again. He'd been picking up the pieces for years, and each year at Christmas he picked them up all over again. For Brody. Maybe for Samantha, too.

This year there would be four missing spaces in their lives and at their table. Parents, a sister, a brother-in-law.

He looked over to Breezy and watched as she spoke to Dotty Williams, a sweet old thing with too many cats. Everyone avoided Dotty's pies at church potluck dinners. Those cats were notorious for climbing on counters and inside mixing bowls.

Breezy laughed at something the woman said and then hugged her. Breezy filled up the empty spaces. He was waiting, unwilling to completely trust that she would stay.

He realized that was the difference between himself and Brody. His kid brother kept waiting for a mother who wasn't coming home.

Jake refused to believe that anyone would stay.

Chapter Eleven

Breezy pulled into the drive long past ten that night. Choir practice had been wonderful. The people of Martin's Crossing had welcomed her into their group, made her feel like a part of things. After parking she sat in her car for a minute. It felt good, to have this town and these people. It felt good to have the twins, as exhausting as they were.

Violet and Rosie had gone home with Brody and Jake. Marty was home and the girls seemed ready to go back to what had become their normal routine at Jake's house.

That meant Breezy was alone again in this house, with the memories she was trying to piece together, and the missing spaces that would never be filled. She reached into the backseat for her purse and, exhausted but happy, climbed out of the car. As she walked up to the front door something stirred in the grass.

She stopped, listening to the softest sound. Maybe it was just a rabbit or a stray cat. She reached into her purse for her keys and raised her hand to unlock the door. She heard it again. The hairs on the back of her neck stood on end. A chill swept through her, setting her nerves on edge.

Wanting her hands free, she put her purse on the chair next to the door and kept her arm bent, ready to take aim at a face if someone sneaked up behind her. As she put the key in the lock she tried to tell herself it had been her imagination. She was used to living in cities and the silence of the country must be getting to her.

Who lived in places this quiet? This dark? She laughed a little at her own apprehension. Of course that's all it was. The wind had rustled the shrubs and she'd panicked. She pushed the door open and reached for the alarm system, then thought better of it. She had a minute to punch in the code. A minute to make sure she was alone, that there wasn't really someone out there.

As she reached back to get her purse, the body came at her from the dark end of the porch. He shoved before she could prepare herself. She fell back against the door and tried to steady herself.

"I'm not going down without a fight!" she yelled. As she went at the man, pushing her palm into his nose and then kicking him in the gut, he fought back, knocking her sideways. Her head hit the wall and her legs crumpled.

The alarm went off, screeching into the night air, breaking that country stillness with a vengeance. Her attacker ran for the back office. Breezy grabbed her purse and found the pepper spray. But as she ran through the house, she heard the back door slam. He was gone.

The house phone rang. She picked it up, answering the call from the alarm company. They asked her if she was okay. She told them she needed the police. No, she didn't need an ambulance. And then she sank back to the floor.

Headlights flashed before blue lights. She pushed herself to her feet and walked to the door with her head pounding, feeling less than steady on her feet. Jake jumped out of his truck. Behind him another truck pulled up. Duke got out, racing his brother to the house.

Martins to the rescue, she thought. She giggled, but that hurt, too. She pushed her fingers against her temple and winced.

"What happened?" Jake shouted as he headed up the sidewalk.

She shook her head only slightly. "Could you not yell?"

"Is he still here?" Jake continued.

Duke had joined them. "Maybe give her a minute?"

Jake took a deep breath and Breezy shot Duke a grateful look. "Thank you. No, he ran out the back door. He was waiting for me to open the door and deactivate the alarm, I think. Good thing I heard something and decided to not deactivate the alarm."

Duke grinned at that. "Good thinking, sis."

Jake came closer than was necessary. Or at least that's what Breezy thought. She closed her eyes and his fingers brushed her temple, pushing her hair back and then settling on the knot that had come up on the side of her head.

"That should probably be checked out."

"I'm fine, just a little loopy from getting pushed into a wall."

"Right, of course you're fine. But we'll still get that checked."

"At the Martin's Crossing E.R.?" she teased.

"No, we'll have to take a drive to Austin."

"I'm not interested," she argued. But her vision wavered a little. "But I would like to sit down."

Jake picked her up. It happened in one swoop. His arm was around her shoulder one minute and the next his other arm swept beneath her knees. "I can walk. I…"

"You want to keep arguing until you pass out?" He grinned in the dim light of the porch. "Relax."

They walked inside. Or Jake and Duke walked. Breezy allowed herself to be carried, to be the damsel in distress, just once. She told herself she wouldn't do it again. She'd been taking care of herself a long time. And it wasn't the first time she'd been on the receiving end of a man's fist. But it felt good to be in his arms. It felt safe there. Why wouldn't she rest her head on his shoulder, breathe in his scent? Any woman in her position would.

She might have suffered a concussion but she hadn't been knocked senseless. She sighed as she relaxed in his arms.

Outside the window, blue lights flashed and a siren wailed. Duke took a careful look around the house as Jake settled her on the sofa. He reached for the afghan on the back of the rocking chair and covered her with it.

"I really don't need a blanket."

"Of course you do." He tucked it up to her chin.

"I'm really okay."

"Yeah, I know you are. But humor me."

Duke reappeared with a bag of frozen corn. He handed it to Jake, who settled it on the side of her head. She flinched as the cold touched her skin.

"You should see the other guy." She teased, even though her head did ache.

He laughed a little. "I bet. Did you manage to get a good shot when you hit him? And did you see his face?"

"I think I probably broke his nose." She grinned up at the cowboy leaning over her, his blue eyes searching her as if looking for other signs of injury. "And no, I didn't see his face."

She told herself not to be too overcome by his hero act. He took care of everyone. He would have done this for a stranger.

Commotion at the front door ended the conversation and her rush of emotions. Duke spoke to the officers and led them inside. One took off through the house, the other approached her.

"Do you need an ambulance?" he asked as he stood over her. Why did the cops always look imposing, even when they were on her side? She shivered a little and shook her head.

"I'm good."

He asked questions then, about the suspect, about his build, any identifying traits, if she'd seen a vehicle. The only thing she knew was that he had been about her height and he probably had a broken nose. The officer smiled at that and wrote information on the tablet he'd carried in with him.

The other officer returned. "There's some blood in the kitchen."

"From the broken nose." Jake laughed as he said it.

They discussed evidence. The door to the office had been opened but because the alarm had gone off the guy had left, running out the back door.

"He could have had a gun." Jake pulled a chair close to the sofa.

Breezy opened her eyes and looked up at him. "But he didn't. Or if he did, he wasn't interested in shooting me. He's looking for something."

"Right, and he was willing to slam you against a wall."

"Jake, I'm fine."

As she said the words she knew that she wasn't fine. Not really. Maybe she would be physically, but emotionally she knew she had a real problem. For the first time in her life, she wanted to be taken care of. She wanted to be protected by this man, held in his arms.

And that scared her. More than the intruder ever had.

The deputies finished their investigating and told Jake that unfortunately they couldn't find much to go on. He walked them out, then returned to the living room, where a medic from the local first-responder unit was examining Breezy. He'd insisted it was either the local guys or he would take her to Austin.

Duke had left. Jake thought it would be a good idea for one of them to be at the Circle M, just in case their prowler thought he might find what he was looking for in Jake's office.

"How is she?" Jake asked the medic as he sat down on the edge of a chair. Breezy touched the knot on her head, wincing. He guessed that was his answer.

The medic, a guy who had been in Afghanistan twice in the past few years, gave her one last look. "I think she's okay. She said she never lost consciousness. I do think it would be a good idea for her to stay awake for several hours. If the headache changes, speech slurs, you know the symptoms to watch for."

Jake did know the symptoms. Brody had been riding bulls for ten years. They were concussion experts.

"We can handle it. She'll be at my house where Marty and I can keep an eye on her."

"I can stay here!"

"Of course you would argue." He leaned back, watching as the medic packed up his stuff. Boone was a good guy. He'd grown up on a ranch outside of town, and his folks had gone through some tough times.

"Ma'am, no arguing with this," Boone said. "You really have to be with people tonight. And you have no idea who this guy is and if he'll come back."

She looked around the house, now lit with overhead lighting. Jake watched as her gaze landed on the nativity she'd put on the mantel and then the tree. He'd told her to make this house her own, add her stuff. And she had.

He thought he understood her reluctance. "It's a day, two at the most, Breezy."

She nodded and moved to the edge of the sofa. "I need to pack a bag."

"I can help," he offered.

A smile broke across her face. "No, you can't. But thank you."

A few minutes later, they were heading down the road to the Circle M. He shot a cautious look at the woman in the truck next to him. The light was dim and he couldn't make out her expression, but he heard her weary sigh, saw her lean a little toward the window as she clutched her overnight bag in her lap.

"You okay?"

"I'm good. I just thought it would be different here. It isn't supposed to be like this."

"Care to share?"

She shook her head. "No, not really."

He pulled up to his house, easing the truck into the garage. Duke's truck was parked out front in the circle drive. He had caught sight of his brother sitting on the front porch in the cold. Jake guessed he wasn't the only one with the burden of needing to protect.

They walked in through the garage door that led through a utility room, a breakfast room and then the kitchen. The giant-size kitchen that the woman who had agreed to marry him insisted she would need. Only she hadn't really wanted a kitchen in a ranch house in Texas Hill Country. She was now married to a doctor in Austin. Jake hadn't quite met her standards.

The same way his dad hadn't met Sylvia's standards. She'd wanted to be a socialite, not a rancher's wife.

He shrugged it off. "Want a cup of coffee? I can plug in the Keurig."

She sat down on a bar stool, dropping her bag on the floor next to her. "Sure, if I have to stay awake, I might as well have coffee."

The machine was already plugged in and the water reservoir filled. Marty must have anticipated they'd need it. From the living room he heard the door click and then the alarm system computer voice said, "Alarm activated."

Duke walked into the room a few minutes later. "Coffee?"

"Yes. I guess you want a cup." Jake pulled three cups out of the cabinet.

"Might as well if we're going to be up all night."

Breezy spun on the chair to face him. "You don't have to stay up. I'm really okay."

Duke took off his hat and tossed it on the counter. "Listen, sis, none of us is going anywhere. That's how we Martins roll. We stick together."

"I'm not a…"

He patted her hand, silencing her. "Yeah, you're one of us. So relax. Let Jake take care of you or he'll break out in hives."

"Jake has enough on his plate without the burden of me. I don't think that's my reason for being in Martin's Crossing."

"Oh, I think it is." Duke headed around the counter to make his own cup of coffee. Jake shot him a lethal glare.

"What's going on?"

Jake pushed a cup under the spout of the Keurig. "Nothing. How do you like your coffee?"

"Since I don't drink coffee, I'll take it however you think is best."

"Cream and sugar," Duke offered. Jake shot him another look. "What did I do now? You know, I think I'll head to the living room and put my feet up."

"Good idea." Jake spooned sugar into the cup and added cream. He set it in front of Breezy. She rested her elbows on the counter and laced her fingers together to rest her chin on her hands. He thought she looked done in, and guessed by morning they'd all look a little worse for wear.

"Thank you." She pulled the coffee to her and raised it to take a sip. Her eyes closed and she sighed. "Why haven't I ever been a coffee drinker?"

"Maybe you haven't had the right coffee?"

"Could be."

Jake made his coffee and sat down next to her. "Breezy, what happened?"

"A guy broke into my house."

He sighed and placed a hand over hers. "In California. On the streets."

"Oh, that."

Pain flashed across her features. Sadness and anger followed.

"Yeah, that. You said you thought it would be different here. I want to make sure it's different."

He wanted to give her a home that no one took from her, a place filled with family and friends. He couldn't stop thinking about the sister they'd taken her away from. Or Lawton had taken her from. He knew she'd wanted to stay in Oklahoma and build that relationship.

"You're very sweet, Jake." She moved her hand, turning it so that their hands were palm to palm, and then she laced her fingers through his and brought his hand to her lips, kissing his knuckles.

"And you won't tell me?"

She shrugged slim shoulders beneath the sweatshirt she'd changed into before leaving. "There isn't a lot to tell. We moved from town to town. My social life was rather nonexistent. It wasn't as if I dated, went to a prom or hung out with friends. And there were times along the way that men thought, because of our situation, that I, that I…"

He wouldn't make her say it. "You deserve better."

She released his hand. "Most people do. I'm really okay, Jake. Tonight took me by surprise, that's all."

"I think it took us all by surprise. In a day or two, as soon as I know we're safe here, I'm going to take a trip to Austin and talk to some of the employees at Lawton's company."

"Should I go? I mean, what if it's one of them and I need to identify someone?"

"I think we'll know him by his broken nose."

She laughed the slightest bit and then they finished their coffee in silence.

Sometime close to dawn he allowed her to go to sleep. She curled up on the sofa and in minutes she was out. Jake watched her as she succumbed to sleep and then he stood to leave. He had chores that wouldn't wait. Marty was standing in the doorway. She didn't say anything. Better for him to pretend she hadn't been watching with those eagle eyes of hers.

"I'm going to get some work done, and make sure the guys know what needs to be done today." He marched toward the back of the house.

"Is that all you're going to say?"

"Nothing else to say." He grabbed his jacket off the

hook by the back door. "And I already know you want to say something. Please don't."

He was thirty-four years old. He didn't need to have his housekeeper tell him what he was feeling.

If she didn't say anything, he could keep telling himself that Breezy was one more person he needed to take care of and nothing more. Then he wouldn't have to admit to himself that he *wanted* to take care of her.

Chapter Twelve

Breezy somehow slept for hours on the sofa in Jake's living room. She slept through the twins poking at her face, Duke arguing with Brody and Jake going to town to order grain. She knew all of this because Marty told her.

The two of them were in the kitchen going through recipes when Jake walked through the back door. She looked up from the notebook she was using to copy recipes and made cautious eye contact with the man walking through the kitchen. His mouth eased into a smile.

Marty cleared her throat and pushed an index card across the counter. "What about this one for gumbo?"

Breezy looked at the recipe. "Sounds great. Have you made it?"

Marty nodded and looked a little teary. "I used to make it twice a month on Fridays. Earl and I would have friends over for dinner to play games and I'd make the gumbo. One of our friends would bake bread. Those were wonderful times."

"Then I definitely want this recipe."

"And here's one for pizza crust that's so easy." Marty pushed that card to her, as well.

"Thank you. This means so much to me, Marty."

"I'm glad to do it. We never had children so it means a lot to me that someone will be using these and passing them down."

Breezy glanced over her shoulder to check on the twins. They were being very quiet. They had plastic bowls, lids and spoons that Marty had given them to play with. Sometimes the bowls were musical instruments, sometimes they pretended to cook.

Violet turned a bowl over and pounded on it and Rosie tried to take the spoon. A squabble ensued. Breezy started to hop down off the stool but Marty put a hand on her arm, stopping her.

"Give them a minute. They aren't pulling hair or biting, so they might work it out," the older woman advised.

It wasn't easy to sit back and watch. But eventually Rosie gave up on the spoon. Big tears welled in her blue eyes and she stood and toddled to Breezy. As Breezy reached to pick her up, Rosie sobbed a little. "Mama."

Breezy held the child close, patting her back. "Aunt Breezy, honey."

Marty shook her head. "Mama is who you are, Breezy."

"No, they have, they..." She buried her face in Rosie's dark hair, inhaling the lavender and chamomile scent of her baby shampoo.

Marty rubbed Breezy's back much the way she rubbed Rosie's. "They have you. They have Jake and of course they have all of us."

"I don't know how to do this, Marty. I'm not prepared."

"You're doing it, though. Maybe you weren't prepared. We hardly ever are prepared for life's challenges. But we manage. I think if we knew the challenges were coming, instead of taking them on, we'd run."

Violet had pushed aside her bowl and spoon and joined them. Marty pulled her to her lap. That's how Jake found the four of them. Breezy wiped her eyes with her hand as he walked back into the room, his expression puzzled.

"From recipes to tears. What are you two doing?"

Breezy chuckled a little, the sound mixing with a sob. "We just had a moment."

Marty pointed at Breezy. "Mama."

Jake's smile faded. Breezy wanted to say something, to stop him from walking away. She didn't want to take his sister's place, to replace her.

"Jake," Marty called to him as he walked away.

"Just give me a minute," he called back.

"I should say something." Breezy started to get up. Again, Marty stopped her.

"One thing you learn is that when a Martin says he needs a minute, you give him a minute. He and Elizabeth were close, Breezy. They practically raised this family. They cooked. They kept things clean. They kept their dad functioning and sometimes kept him off the drink. Losing Elizabeth was like losing a part of himself."

He took care of everyone else. So who took care of Jake?

She heard the front door close.

Marty took Rosie from her. "You go. I've got these two. He'll be in the barn. But don't be surprised if he runs you off."

"I'm not easily frightened."

Marty grinned at that. "And that's why he needs you."

Jake needed her. She shook her head at the thought. Jake didn't seem to need anyone. But something small inside her had ignited and she wanted to be the person he needed, the person who was there for him.

She hurried out the back door, grabbing her coat as she went. She hadn't been to the barns on the Circle M. There were several. There was an old barn in the field behind the house. It was wood-sided, gray and weathered with a new metal roof and obvious repairs. To the west of the house was a metal structure. It housed equipment and hay. And then there was a metal building with wide doors that pushed open and a standard door to the side of that. Horses grazed in the field to the right of the barn. In the distance a tractor hauled a big round bale of hay to cattle. She picked this as the right barn.

She didn't know what she would say to Jake but she knew that it was time he let someone be there for him.

The barn was lit with overhead lights down the center of the tall ceiling. On one side were half a dozen stalls. On the side were various doors. She called out for Jake but he didn't answer. She knocked on the first door and got no reply. She opened the door to find a feed room and tack room. The next room held trophies and saddles.

And then she heard a pounding sound and the sound

of feet scuffing the earth. She started to knock on the door but knew he wouldn't answer. She turned the knob and opened the door slowly, peeking in as she did.

Jake stood in the center of the room. No, he wasn't standing. He was boxing. The room was a gym. There were weights, a treadmill, a television, chairs and the boxing bag on a stand in the center of the room. He jabbed at it, letting it come back to him and then jabbing again. As she watched, he went at it, pounding hard with both fists.

He was breathing heavily and in the noise she heard his sobs. She should go, let him grieve in piece. But how could she walk away? How could she let this be one more thing that Jake Martin seemed to do on his own?

As she stood in the doorway contemplating her next move, he spotted her and shook his head.

"Go away," he said in a quiet voice that rumbled like thunder through a stormy night.

She shook her head. He was stubborn. She could show him she was just as stubborn, if not more so. He needed her, whether he wanted to admit it or not. Maybe that's what had brought the two of them together.

Maybe God had known she needed a place of her own and He'd known that Jake Martin needed someone strong enough to stand toe to toe with him, strong enough to be there for him.

He reached for a towel, wiping it across his face before wrapping it around his neck. She closed the distance between them. As she reached for him, he pulled her hard against him, holding her tight.

* * *

Jake hadn't expected her. He hadn't expected her to search him out. He hadn't expected to need her. He'd come to the barn thinking he'd do what he always did. He'd box. Maybe he'd go for a ride. He'd think, figure it out, move on. But the pain had followed him, pounding against him as he'd pounded that punching bag.

It was relentless, wave after wave of grief.

Breezy's arms were around him as he held her tight against him, soaking up the comfort in her embrace, in the words she whispered. He didn't really hear them, but they were there, pouring over him like summer rain.

He pulled her head to his shoulder and kissed her brow. Man, he needed this woman. For how long, though? How long would she be here, soaking up his pain, his grief? How long would she be here to make him smile when only weeks ago he'd wondered if any of them would ever be happy again?

"You can lean on people, Jake." The words were muffled against his shoulder, her warm breath permeating his shirt. He stroked his hand down the softness of her hair, thinking through the words that she spoke as if they made perfect sense.

What did he say to that? How did he lean on people? If he leaned on someone, how did he stay strong? He hadn't leaned on anyone since…never? Maybe he'd leaned on Elizabeth. Sometimes, every now and then, he leaned on Duke. But Duke joined the army at twenty-one and for eight years he'd been gone.

A long time ago, the day their mother left, Jake tried to lean on his dad. But Gabe Martin had pushed him away, told him to figure out how to turn on the oven if they were hungry. If they were out of groceries, he told him to drive to town but don't get caught.

Elizabeth had been a mess, the same age as him but needing a mom. Duke had been angry and had rode off on his horse. Brody had been about four and still trying to run from the house to chase Sylvia down. Samantha had been little more than a baby.

The grief had finally left their dad but he hadn't been there to lean on. Ever.

When he didn't answer Breezy, she looked up at him, for all the world looking like she had meant her words of comfort.

"You can at least lean on me," she said with conviction. "We're parents together. That's what parents do."

He brushed a kiss across her cheek and sighed. "Yeah. Parents."

And parents were called Mom and Dad. It was natural for the twins to begin to see her as mom, him as dad. He thought that in time they would need that connection. Look at Brody, a kid who'd never had a mom. He was still looking for her.

"Thank you." He finally croaked out the words.

"Do you have water in that fridge over there?" She nodded toward the fridge at the far side of the room.

"Yeah." He pulled her with him to open it and grabbed two bottles.

"Is this where you go when you're upset?"

He looked around the room. It had started with a punching bag and he'd built it into this. "Yes, this is where I go."

"Try going to a friend once in a while."

She smiled up at him and he felt like a puzzle with the pieces coming together. He brushed a hand across her cheek, tangling his fingers in the silky strands of blond hair. With caramel eyes, melting, darkening, she looked up at him. He leaned, tilting his head to find the right angle as he closed his lips over hers.

She kissed him back, her free hand going to the nape of his neck, sliding into his hair. He tried not to need people.

He couldn't lie about needing her. He needed to pour his hurt into her and have her hold him until it started to heal. He brushed his hand up her back and she stood on tiptoe, her lips soft beneath his.

He eventually pulled back. He had a lot of questions about himself, about her, about the future. They'd have to figure out the answers. Because Lawton had planned this. He'd told Jake when he mentioned making the two of them guardians that he thought they'd both be single, even twenty years from now. Single and lonely, waiting for the right person to come into their lives, so they'd make the perfect guardians for the twins.

Lawton hadn't meant to leave them now. Jake leaned back into the woman standing close to him. Her arms circled his neck and she placed a kiss against his chin.

"Let's go for a ride," he suggested, amused when her eyes widened.

"Ride? In your truck, you mean?"

"Horses. Come on. It's warm and there's no rain."

She was his rain. He needed to soak her up like the land after a long drought. For today, maybe just for the moment, he needed her close. Later he'd figure out what to do with these feelings.

She pulled back on his hand as he tried to tug her toward the door. "I've never ridden a horse."

"You live in Texas. It's time to learn."

How long had it been since he'd flirted with a woman? Or even let down his guard long enough to enjoy being around a woman? How long since he'd taken a few minutes to relax, to not worry about who was taking care of things? He needed this. And she must have realized because she allowed him to lead her through the barn.

"I'm not sure if this is a good idea," she said as she stood in the doorway that led to the corral.

He winked. "You'll do great. I'll be right back."

With two lead ropes he trudged through the corral to the gate. He whistled and the horses looked up, ears twitching as they watched him. He shook a bucket of grain and that got their attention. The small herd, just five of them, headed his way. He opened the gate and culled the two they would ride. A big chestnut he'd been riding lately and a small bay gelding for Breezy.

After the horses were saddled he led her to the corral and helped her up. She put her left foot in the stirrup and swung her right leg over, landing with a thud in the saddle. She looked down at him, unsure, unsteady but with a definite spark of adventure in her eyes.

"You'll do great with Montego."

"Montego?" She brushed her hand down the horse's neck, still looking more than a little nervous.

"Bay." He grinned. "Montego Bay."

He gave her a short riding lesson and then he swung himself into his saddle and rode up next to her. He'd closed the gate to the field and opened the gate leading out of the corral. There were plenty of back trails, and with some daylight left they'd have a good ride.

"Where are we going?" She rode next to him and he had to give her credit, she didn't look like it was her first time in the saddle. She had a natural ease, holding the reins lightly, her heels down and her legs relaxed.

But he could see the slight tremble in her hands, the occasional clenching of her jaw.

"Not far." He nodded toward the hills in the distance, a half mile back. "There's a pretty stream at the base of those hills. Sometimes there's a deer or two, so don't get too relaxed and drop your reins. If you horse starts, go with the motion and keep a firm hand."

Her eyes widened. "Will he startle? I thought he was gentle."

"He's as gentle as they come, but any horse can startle. Get used to the feel of him. Even with a saddle you'll feel him tense. Right now you can feel that he's relaxed."

She rode for a few paces and nodded. "Okay, I've got this."

"That's good. Never think you've got this. Be confident, but always expect the unexpected."

Expect the unexpected. She was the unexpected and she'd sure caught him off guard. He'd expected her to take the money and run, not be tied down to two little girls she didn't know.

He hadn't expected her to be all-in the way she'd proven to be. She'd even made herself at home in Martin's Crossing.

But these weren't the thoughts he wanted to go over again. He needed to clear his head. He eased a look in her direction and shook his head. Yeah, he needed to get it together. Because he was thinking of kissing her again. That couldn't happen.

If he complicated their relationship this way, how would they manage to go on, raising the girls together? He hadn't thought of that before, because for two weeks he'd been trying to figure out how to manage being parents together.

He'd been trying to figure out how to trust her in their lives and trust that she wouldn't leave.

Now he had to face that they were in a situation that required them to be more than parents. They were in each other's lives. Day in, day out, counting on each other, turning to each other. It was a given that someday one, or both, of them would want to settle down, get married. To someone else.

But this relationship, allowing it to become a flirtation, or even casual dating, that would only end in disaster. Because if it ended, they would still have to face each other every day and still be the best parents they could be to the twins.

Kissing her again was the last thing he should be thinking about.

After the ride Breezy sat on the step to the tack room and watched as Jake unsaddled and brushed the horses. He'd insisted she should watch this time, and next time he'd let her help. So she watched, because who wouldn't want to watch a cowboy in faded jeans that fit just right brush a horse? She watched as he lifted hooves and cleaned them with a pick. She watched as he untied first one horse and then the other and led them to the gate.

"You're quiet," he said when he returned. He reached for the jacket he'd left on a hook and tossed it to her. "It's getting cold."

"Thank you. I was just thinking that I feel okay and I'll probably go back to Lawton's."

"There's no reason you can't stay here," he said, holding out a hand and helping her to her feet.

"I know, but my stuff is at Lawton's. And I can't run in fear."

They walked out of the barn. He flipped off the lights as they left. He'd been right, the air was colder. The sky was steel-gray, no evidence of the setting sun. She shivered in the warmth of a jacket that smelled like Jake.

"You have to start calling it your place, Breezy," he said quietly as they walked. The dog had joined them and it raced ahead, chasing something, then came back.

"Easier said than done."

"Yeah, I know. I think we're both having a hard time taking possession. Of the twins, the house…" He paused.

She filled in the empty space. "Lawton and Elizabeth's life."

He only nodded, his gaze faraway. An arm went around her waist, pulling her close to his side. "You don't think it's Joe, do you?"

She shook her head. "Too tall."

"Good."

They walked in silence and Breezy knew she was in trouble. She knew the comfort from his arm around her waist was trouble. It anchored her in a way that a plant, a nativity, an ornament only hinted at. It made her feel as if she had found a home, and it was in Jake Martin's arms.

That was when she knew that she really had to make her escape back to Lawton's.

Chapter Thirteen

Breezy went home the next day, and life slipped back into an easy routine. During the day the girls were often with her, and in the evening they went back to the Circle M. Jake sometimes stayed around while they were with her. He would work outside and then they would eat dinner together in the evenings before he took the girls home.

Breezy poured through the recipes Marty had given her. She made casseroles, soups, breads and anything else she thought Jake and two little girls would eat. And they did.

Christmas was a little over a week away and she had shopped in town, finding gifts that she wrapped and put under the tree. She had shopped at the antique store and found small things to put around the house to make it feel like her home. A braided rug for the kitchen, a picture in her bedroom, a pretty clock for the living room.

She and Jake had developed an easy friendship. And wasn't that what they needed in order to raise two little girls? It should have been one of their first rules, to be friends. But their friendship could easily get blurred around the edges because, even as their friendship grew, Breezy remembered how it felt to be held by him. And every now and then when they stood too close or accidentally touched, she knew that he felt it, too. It was an indrawn breath, a moment of stillness, a certain connection when their eyes met.

But another rule seemed to be that they not mention that attraction for fear that it would undo their friendship.

On a cold Friday night they met in town for the annual Christmas block party. The stores were open late. Duke was serving hot drinks and pie. A few vendors had set up around the park, in tribute to their German ancestors selling handmade toys and crafts, brats and other treats. The Christmas lights were lit up and each building was decorated.

Breezy found Jake at a vendor buying bratwursts for him and fries for the girls. He had them in a stroller built for two. From several feet away she watched as he pulled off his gloves to pay for the food. He tested a fry before handing them to the girls.

He must have sensed that she was there because he nodded at her. She greeted the twins first. It was easier. It gave her heart time to calm down, to realize she wanted what she couldn't have. Hadn't she learned that it could only lead to a world of hurt?

She squatted in front of the stroller, kissing first Rosie and then Violet. "You girls look perfect tonight, like cotton candy."

They were dressed in puffy pink coats, pink stocking caps and pink gloves. Their jeans were tucked into pink-and-brown boots.

"Candy!" Rosie shoved a fry in her mouth.

"Too big a bite, little girl." Breezy opened her hand and Rosie gave her a look and kept chewing. "Okay, but small bites."

Rosie took another fry and bit a small piece off the end. "Small bites."

"Bites." Violet giggled.

"Do you want a brat?" Jake asked.

She stood and turned to the vendor. He was looking past them at people starting to form a line. "Yes, that would be good."

While they waited, she pushed the girls' stroller to the side, making room for the crowds that were starting to form. It surprised her, to see so many people in this little town. There were people admiring the lights, people walking in and out of shops.

Jake handed her the brat and then his gaze slid past her. She looked in the same direction, not sure what he saw. There were people. Few of them were familiar to her. She saw Joe walking in the crowd, talking to a member of the church. Farther in the distance she saw Brody walking with a young woman.

"I'm sorry. Can I leave the twins with you for a minute?"

Breezy shrugged as she finished a bite of brat. "Sure. Is something wrong?"

"Tyler Randall is here. He's the man in charge of Lawton's company. I'm surprised to see him here."

"Go ahead. We'll wander around. I'm sure we'll find stuff we want."

He grinned at that, then he leaned a little closer. For a second she thought he might kiss her. Instead he brushed his finger across her cheek. "Mustard."

"Oh." She managed a smile and then she watched as he walked away, her heart beating a million miles an hour.

After finishing her brat, she pushed the stroller down the sidewalk, admiring local arts and crafts. She stopped at a lighted tent filled with handmade wooden toys. A rocking horse caught her eye. Two rocking horses. They couldn't have just one or there would be fights.

As she admired the horses, Oregon entered the tent. The other woman joined her. "They're precious."

"Yes, I think they would make perfect Christmas gifts for the twins." She flipped the price tag and was surprised by a price much lower than she would have expected.

"How are things going?" Oregon asked as she looked at painted wall plaques.

"Good. I'm still learning but I think we're managing," Breezy answered as she waved to the vendor and pointed to the two rocking horses.

"You'll always be learning. Lilly is almost twelve and I'm always one step ahead of her or two steps behind."

"So you're telling me it doesn't get easier?"

Oregon shrugged "There are easier moments."

"How's your shop doing?" Breezy listened to the man tell her the price of the horses and she pulled out her wallet. "Aren't you open tonight?"

"I am. I wanted to take a few minutes to browse so Joe is watching the shop."

Breezy paid for the horses and asked the vendor to hold them for her until she could arrange free hands to carry them to her car. She and Oregon walked out of the shop together.

They were strolling toward a hot apple cider stand. Oregon stopped walking, her hand on Breezy's arm to bring her to a halt.

"What's up?" Breezy pulled the stroller back so she was closer to her friend. Oregon glanced around, her bottom lip between her teeth. "Oregon?"

"Someone bought my building."

"They did what? Are they going to make you move out?"

"No, they bought it and signed the deed over to me," Oregon explained.

"Who?" Breezy looked around to make sure they weren't attracting attention. Fortunately they'd found a somewhat quiet spot. In the distance a small group stood on a corner caroling. A car honked and someone laughed. But she and Oregon were alone.

"I'm not sure. A lawyer showed up the other day and told me the building had been bought and that I was the new owner. I'm not sure what to think."

"I think you've been given a wonderful opportunity. Now you don't have to worry as much about the winter slowdown after Christmas." Breezy knew that had been on Oregon's mind. She had some internet business from her website, but from what Oregon had told her, it wouldn't have been enough to cover expenses.

"Yes, a great opportunity. But who does something

like that? Who gives a young mom a new van, a church a five-figure check and me a building?"

"Someone with a big heart and a lot of money?"

Oregon was looking at her, dark eyes suspicious. "Some people think it might be you."

Breezy laughed. "It isn't me. Not that I don't consider myself bighearted, but I'm barely registering my new circumstances enough to allow myself to write a check for groceries."

They started walking again, the hot cider luring them in.

"I'm really thankful," Oregon said, her voice soft. "But I'm also suspicious."

"Don't be. Whoever is doing this is obviously trying to help people at Christmastime. I think that's what Christmas is all about. I know that there were a lot of years when I wouldn't have had Christmas, period, if someone hadn't donated money."

"It must have been tough," Oregon said.

Tough. Yes, she guessed it had. It had been tough. And frightening at times.

"It was tough," she agreed. "But it wasn't always bad. Maria usually found a way to get us a room, usually efficiency apartments. She made sure I studied. She would find school books at used book stores. She made sure I got my GED."

They bought hot apple cider and headed for the light display. There were lights in the shape of the nativity, the wise men and a star that stood on a tower above the entire display. There were camels that seemed to move, shepherds in a field and angels singing.

If everything continued to go well she would live

here for a long time. She would visit this park every Christmas, and shop in these same stores where people knew her name.

She stood listening to the carolers on the sidewalk in front of the church and she realized that most importantly she seemed to have found herself here in Martin's Crossing. She had found a home. A place to belong.

The star, dozens of feet up in the air, twinkled in the night as snow flurries drifted down. They were big flakes, the kind that didn't last long, but looked so beautiful as they fell.

The most important thing, she realized, was faith. Because in this town of traditions she had finally realized that God loved even her. She'd always wanted to believe, to have faith, but she'd wondered if God even knew she existed. Sometimes in life she had felt that invisible.

He not only knew she existed, but He cared.

The choir sang "Joy to the World." Oregon sang along. Breezy joined her. The snow continued to fall and a crowd gathered with everyone singing together. Breezy looked around. Vendors had stepped out of their shops. The crowds had stopped walking.

The snow fell a little harder. Breezy pulled the top out on the stroller so that the twins were protected and found blankets to tuck around them.

This is how home felt. And she smiled.

Jake could hear the carolers but he couldn't get away to join Breezy and the twins. He studied Tyler Randall's face and wondered if he trusted the man.

"Anyway, Jake, things are going well. I'm hoping for a government contract on that new software."

"Sounds good, Tyler. You've always known how to bring these deals together. If you need my help, let me know."

"I think I've got it."

He still didn't get what Tyler was doing in Martin's Crossing. The story Tyler told him was that he'd heard Lawton talk about this festival and he'd wanted to see it for himself. There were a lot of Christmas festivals he could have attended. Most were bigger. And definitely closer to Austin.

"Where's the heir apparent?" Tyler asked just as Jake was thinking to make his excuses and walk away.

"Heir apparent?"

"The senator's daughter." Tyler grinned, even winked. Jake couldn't quite push down his dislike of the man.

"Tyler, I'm not sure what's going on with you, but she's Lawton's sister and she deserves respect."

"Oh, so Lawton got his way?"

"What does that mean?"

"Lawton thought two lonely people deserved each other. I guess he hadn't planned on bringing you together this soon in this way."

"He was my best friend, Tyler. And Elizabeth was my sister. We lost a big part of our family in that plane crash. I'm not sure I see the joke in all of this."

"I think you're being overly sensitive," Tyler pushed, still smiling.

Some people just didn't know when to quit.

"Tyler, you might want to remember that I own a portion of this company. That makes me your boss"

Tyler's hands went up in surrender. "Right, gotcha."

"And now, if you don't mind, I have two little girls that I'm supposed to be spending time with."

He walked away because that seemed the safest thing to do. He wasn't sure what would happen if Tyler said anything else that rubbed him the wrong way.

It took him a few minutes but he spotted Breezy and the twins. Snow had begun to fall and they were standing a short distance away from the carolers. They were silhouettes with the lights of the nativity behind them.

He paused to watch as Breezy leaned down, giving sips of her drink to the girls. She tucked their blankets a little closer. When she stood she looked over at him. He waved. She raised a gloved hand and said something to Violet and Rosie. The twins laughed and waved, but not really in his direction.

The music ended. He walked up to Breezy, greeting the twins first. "I'm sorry I got tied up."

"Is everything okay?" Breezy asked as they started walking.

He wasn't sure. But he didn't want to ruin the moment with snow falling and lights twinkling around them.

"Do you want anything else?" he asked.

Breezy shook her head. "No, I just thought we'd walk along the path and look at lights. I take it you don't get a lot of snow here?"

"Very little. This is perfect, though. It isn't freezing cold and this won't amount to much."

"It is perfect."

They walked through the light display with the twins pointing and jabbering. By the time they reached the sidewalk and turned back toward Main Street, the girls were asleep and the crowds had thinned out.

Jake saw Joe walking down a sidewalk away from the shops. He wondered where the old guy went. He guessed everyone was wondering. As he considered what he should do, he saw Duke come out of the restaurant and call Joe over. Duke wouldn't let him sleep on the streets.

"I don't want you to stay at the house alone tonight," Jake finally admitted as they got to her car. That had been on his mind since his meeting with Tyler. He just hadn't known how to bring it up.

"Why?"

He took the keys from her hand and opened her door. "Because I'm not sure why Tyler Randall is in town and I don't trust him."

"Tyler?"

"The employee that I spoke to earlier."

"Oh, right." Breezy tossed her purse in her car. "I have to pull over to one of the vendors and get the rocking horses I bought the twins."

He smiled at that. "They'll love to have those under the tree on Christmas morning."

He watched her go somewhere, drifting on distant memories, he imagined.

"I think they will." She shoved her hands in her pockets. "I really will be okay at the house, Jake."

"I know you will. I know you can take care of yourself. I would appreciate, though, if you would do this for me." He leaned in close. "Because I don't want anything to happen to you."

Her lips parted just slightly and he knew she planned on arguing. Of course she would argue. And he couldn't let her. Not this time. He had a hinky feeling about Tyler. A man with a good dose of greed and jealousy might be willing to do anything to get what he wanted. And Jake was pretty sure Tyler was the man they were searching for.

Before she could say anything he brushed a hand across her cheek and settled it on her neck to pull her to him. He lowered his lips to hers, knowing he shouldn't but unable to resist. Her lips tasted like cherry lip balm and apple cider. He closed his eyes, lingering in a kiss that could have gone on forever.

What was it about this woman?

He brushed his lips across her cheek, heard her sigh as she leaned close, moving to rest her head on his shoulder. He wanted to know that she would stay, not just for the twins, but for him.

He wanted to trust her.

The rangy kid who had watched his mother leave town had a hard time with trust. And that kid was still buried deep inside him, warning him not to get too close.

Chapter Fourteen

Three days later, both twins had a cold. Their noses were runny and their eyes were watery. Breezy, still at the Circle M until Jake decided her house was safe, sat in the recliner with them, rocking gently. Jake had gone to Austin the previous day. He had shopping to do and business to take care of, he'd said. She thought it more likely that he was digging around, trying to learn if Lawton had been working on something new that he hadn't known about.

As much as Breezy wanted to go back to her own place, she enjoyed the extra time with the twins. She loved holding them, cuddling them against her. She loved when they woke up in the morning and before breakfast they wanted to sit quietly and watch their favorite cartoon. And it broke her heart when every now and then one of them called her Mommy. Marty had told her it would happen. It had to happen.

No one was being disloyal to Lawton and Elizabeth. The twins were babies who needed that connection with a mommy and daddy. It was only natural,

Marty had said. Breezy kissed first Violet and then Rosie on the top of the head. Rosie reached up and patted her cheek.

"I need to ask Marty what to give you to make you feel better," she said, kissing the hand that continued to pat her cheek. Marty had gone to visit her sister for a few hours after lunch.

Rosie whispered, "Pancakes."

"Yes, Marty makes pancakes." Breezy pushed the recliner with her feet. "But it isn't breakfast, sweetheart. Maybe fruit would be good."

"Fruit is good," Rosie said, leaning her head against Breezy's shoulder again.

Violet was sound asleep now. Rosie, from the looks of things, would be joining her. And what in the world should Breezy give them to make them feel better? Fever reducer, maybe? She leaned her cheek against Rosie. She did feel a little warm. She hoped they wouldn't be sick for the Christmas celebration at the end of the week.

She heard the rumble of a truck coming up the driveway. The flash of dark blue meant Jake was home. She leaned back, relieved. Because he was there to help with the twins. She told herself that had to be the reason she ached to see him.

It couldn't be more. Because more meant putting everything on the line, opening herself up to pain, to rejection. It had been a long time since she'd wanted to take the chance.

Right now, with the twins counting on her, with a new life and new opportunities, maybe it wasn't the right time. It might be better to be content with friendship.

As she rocked and the twins slept, she told herself that she had to draw the line between herself and Jake. Friendship. Anything else and they risked hurting the twins. And that was the last thing she wanted to do, to have a broken relationship with Jake that would hurt Rosie and Violet.

Jake walked into the living room a few minutes later. When his gaze immediately slid from her face to the twins, it grew concerned.

"Are they sick?"

She nodded. "Just a cold, I think."

He leaned down, touching his lips to Violet's head. "She feels warm."

"I know. If you're going to be here for a little while I'll run in to town and get medicine. Marty isn't here but I know Oregon or Wanda, at the grocery store, can point me in the right direction."

"Let me help you get them into bed." Jake reached for Violet. Even in her sleep the little girl reached for him, wrapping her arms around his neck.

As Breezy stood, she allowed herself a quick look at Jake. He'd dressed for business in dark gray dress slacks, a light gray button-down shirt and black boots. He smelled expensive, the kind of cologne a girl notices. Something a touch oriental but all masculine.

She must have made a sound because he gave her a cautious look. She widened her eyes at him and went all innocent.

"Something wrong?" he asked.

She shook her head, situating Rosie against her shoulder. "Hmm, not that I can think of."

Other than the fact that he made friendship a very difficult task.

She followed him to the room that belonged to the twins when they stayed at the Circle M. Jake placed Violet in the crib and stepped back for Breezy to settle Rosie next to her. The twins curled against each other. Breezy covered them with a light blanket.

"I have something for you," Jake said as they walked back to the living room. It had grown overcast and the room was shadowy but sparkled with lights from the Christmas tree.

"For me?"

He held up a finger. "Stay here."

She waited while he disappeared into the kitchen. A moment later he was back. He handed her a box.

"Is it for Christmas?" She shook it just slightly.

"No, you can have it now."

She slowly pulled the red foil paper off the package. Inside was a cardboard box. Jake pulled a pocketknife out of his pocket and slit the tape. She looked up at him and then at the box, lifting the flaps to look inside.

Her eyes filled with tears as she pulled out a glass ornament. On one side it had the year. On the other side was a picture of Breezy with the twins. A picture Jake had taken a little over a week ago as she and the twins made cookies.

"It's beautiful." She held it up, studying the picture, the happy looks on their faces.

"Are you crying?" He grabbed a box of tissues off the coffee table.

She took one and wiped her eye. "I'm not crying, I'm just… I'm touched. And I want to hug you."

"Hugging leads to kissing." He grinned as he warned her. But she saw that, like her, Jake meant to keep this limited to friendship. And of course they should.

"I know, but this…" She put it back in the box and set the box and the tissues on the table. She took a step toward Jake, not really thinking about repercussions. "Why?"

He traced a line down her cheek to her chin with a finger, and tilted her face so that her eyes met his. She melted at the touch.

"Because I know that it's important to you to feel as if you belong here. I've watched as you've collected your ornaments, decorations, plants and even recipes. I'm not sure why those things mean so much, but I know they do."

"They mean staying," she explained. "I've lived my life leaving things behind. Friends, dolls, pictures and books."

If she had these small things, it was proof that she would stay and not have to leave anything or anyone behind again.

"You won't have to do that ever again, Breezy. This is your place now, your community and your family."

She nodded, wishing she could believe it as easily as he said the words. Maybe collecting those things was her way of convincing herself. His finger had dropped and now he held her hand. He pulled her a little closer and she looked up at him as he leaned to brush a sweet kiss across her lips.

"You won't have to leave it all behind," he assured her.

She loved the thought behind his words. She loved the idea that she would always be here. But she knew that Lawton's will stipulated that Jake, if he ever saw reason, could undo her guardianship. He could take the twins from her.

He could break her heart.

Jake watched as Breezy left to go to town. She'd withdrawn after he'd kissed her. She'd told him again how much she loved the ornament. She'd picked it up and carried it out with her. Probably because she wanted it on her tree. It symbolized something for her. All of the things she'd collected, even the puppy Oregon had promised, symbolized putting down roots.

He went to his office, flipping on the light as he entered the room. He knew what worried her, or at least he thought he did. The thing they both knew was in Lawton's will: the stipulation that Jake could remove her from guardianship.

Jake also knew what Breezy wanted to keep hidden and what probably haunted her every day. He picked up the private investigator's report. He'd hired the man before Breezy had showed up. He'd wanted a way to protect the girls. Now he felt that old weight bearing down on his shoulders. The need to also protect Breezy.

Lawton had done that, had put her in his care. It might look like joint custody, but it was also Lawton's way of keeping his sister safe, and of giving her what she should rightfully have had.

Jake tossed the paperwork in the trash. A few petty crimes, a mistake that anyone could have made, it was all history. She deserved to have her past left in the past. Didn't everyone?

If she'd trusted him enough to tell him, he would

have explained to her that no one should have their past weighing down on them. He knew, because he'd allowed his to be a weight around his neck for too long.

But she didn't trust him. He got that. Trust didn't come easily to someone like Breezy. She'd never really had anyone she could trust. Her mother had never protected her. Her father hadn't acknowledged her. Maria Hernandez had never given her the basic necessities. And now she had to trust that he wouldn't take her nieces from her.

Somehow he had to assure her that wasn't going to happen.

Breezy went back to her place before going to town. The medicine for the twins was her main reason for going to Martin's Crossing, but she had another. It was cold and Joe would be out in this weather. As she drove into town, she came in from a side road onto Main Street.

When she saw him, it took her by surprise. He was at the end of the block, standing by a light post that was wrapped in twinkling red lights. He was obviously watching Oregon's shop.

Breezy pulled up and rolled down the passenger window of her car. "Joe?"

He looked away from Oregon's shop, unsmiling and lost.

"Joe, are you okay?"

He wiped at his eyes and cleared his throat. "Of… of course I am."

"Can I do something for you? It's going to be cold tonight and I thought maybe we could find somewhere for you to stay." She handed him the thermos of coffee she'd prepared at her place. He took it in his gloved hands.

"You're a kind person, Breezy. Back a few weeks ago when Pastor Allen asked what our faith means to us, I think you were searching."

"Yes, I was searching," she admitted.

"But I think you're figured out what your faith means. Its more than all of this." He swept his arm in a wide arc. "All of this is pretty. It makes people happy. But without faith, it's just empty lights and tradition."

She watched as he poured himself a cup of coffee and she didn't know what to say. She agreed, faith was more than tradition. But traditions helped people remember their faith.

"Joe, you can stay at my place."

He shook his head. "I don't think Jake Martin would appreciate you opening your home to me, Breezy. But that's very kind of you."

"Joe, you can't stay outside tonight."

"I won't be outside." He took a sip of the coffee. "Very good coffee. Thank you."

"You're welcome, and I know you won't be outside. I know you're sleeping in the nativity."

He chuckled, his eyes twinkling in the dim light of late afternoon. "It's warm. The light is a heat lamp. I think Pastor Allen did that on purpose. And there's a soft bed of hay behind Mary and Joseph."

"That's all very cozy and nice, but it isn't a home."

"Breezy, don't worry about me. I'm making up for my past."

"The past doesn't have to hold us prisoner. If we believe what we say we believe, then aren't we set free? Isn't that the purpose of that baby in the manger?"

"Whom the Son sets free is free indeed," Joe quoted. "Yes, Breezy, you're right. I've been set free from my past, from the many things that nearly destroyed my life. But I have something I have to do, and until it's done, I'll be staying in the nativity. If it was good enough for that baby, it's good enough for me."

How could she argue with that? "If you change your mind…"

"If I change my mind, I'll let you know." He winked, held up the coffee in salute and walked away.

Breezy watched as he made his way back to the nativity. She wondered how no one else had noticed that Joe slept there every night. But then, no one else had really been watching. They were all trying to figure Joe out, wondering if he was safe, where he'd come from and when he'd leave.

They had no idea that Joe was making their lives better.

Breezy considered him a friend.

After picking up the medicine for the girls, she headed back to the Circle M, worrying that Jake would wonder what had taken so long. She thought of Joe and his determination to make up for the past. She was just as determined to let go of hers. Maybe letting go meant telling Jake?

When she pulled up to the house, she saw Jake waiting on the front porch. She got out of the car and held up the bag of medicine. Jake walked down off the porch to meet her. A caged lion came to mind. He looked as if he'd been pacing.

"I'm sorry. I saw Joe and I wanted to make sure he's okay. It's going to be cold tonight."

"I know it is." Jake took the medicine from her. "But you should have called. I was worried."

"Are the twins still sleeping?"

"Yes, and Marty's making dinner. Breezy, I'm serious about this. You need to understand that until we prove who has been breaking into the house or catch them, you're not safe."

She slipped her arm through his. "I know. And I'm sorry. But you also have to trust that I'm being careful. I'm not going to put myself or the twins in danger."

"But you went to your house."

"Just to get coffee for Joe," she admitted.

"Next time, don't. Or at least let me go with you," he said.

"Right, okay. I do have to go over there tomorrow. There's a horrible smell in the fridge. Something has to go."

Right, okay. Just make sure you activate the alarm while you're in the house."

"Yes, sir. I'll activate the alarm," she agreed, teasing him. He mock-scowled at her.

It was nice to have someone worrying about her. But it was still a new feeling to Breezy, and she was afraid to get used to it.

As they stood in the living room, the lights from the tree twinkled. Christmas was just around the corner. Somehow they would make this work. They would make a family out of the remnants and they would survive.

Chapter Fifteen

Breezy left the girls with Marty when she drove over to her place the next afternoon. Jake had been out in the barn, talking to Brody about some cattle the younger Martin wanted to buy. They'd been at it for hours and she hadn't bothered to let Jake know she was leaving. Marty knew. And Breezy would keep her promise and set the alarm.

As she walked in the front door, she answered her phone. It was Joe.

"Hi, Joe, what's up?"

"Am I speaking to Breezy Hernandez?" It wasn't Joe's voice.

"Yes, this is Breezy." She turned to push a code into the alarm and then waited to close the door and make sure it was activated.

"Miss Hernandez, I'm calling from Austin Community General. We have a patient, Joe Anderson. He asked us to call you and let you know that he's here. He's had a heart attack and he's in serious but stable condition."

"Joe?"

"Yes, ma'am. Mr. Anderson wanted someone to know."

"I'll be there as soon as I can."

She hung up and stood there for a minute. She wasn't sure what to do. Did he have family? Was he alone? She would go to him, of course. Everyone deserved to have someone. A person to call, to turn to.

She walked through the house, uneasy. She really disliked that someone had taken her peace, her joy in living in this house. It was her home. She had a plant. She had a nativity. And she was getting a dog. That's what people did when they had a home.

The fridge was her main goal for the day. That and more clothes. She opened the fridge door and held her breath, grabbing contents and tossing them in the trash. Something really stunk.

A noise caught her attention. She told herself it was nothing. And then she tried to convince herself it would be Jake coming to check on her. But Jake would have announced himself. He wouldn't be in the office and that sound definitely came from the office.

Slowly she closed the refrigerator door. She opened a cabinet drawer and pulled out a rolling pin. Anything could be a weapon. She eased along the wall, taking careful steps. As she walked she reached into her pocket for her phone and came up empty. She'd left it on the table in the living room.

Wonderful.

Go after the prowler or get her phone? The phone. And the alarm. She eased across the living room and as she reached for her phone he came running. She hit Redial, knowing it would ring to the ranch.

"Might as well hang that up," he said. He was tall with blond hair. She didn't know him but he looked like someone you would say hello to on the street.

"Who are you?"

He smirked. "What does it matter?"

"Well, if you think you're going to hurt me, I'd like to know the name of the man I'm going to knock out," she informed him with what she hoped was a confident look.

"Aren't you going to wait for Jake to rescue you?"

"No, I typically don't wait for a man to rescue me. You're in my home and I'll handle you," she said. "And your name?"

"Tyler Randall, the man who should have had twenty percent of a business, not ten. But you managed to get my share. You showed up, and claimed to be the senator's daughter."

"I never made the claim. Lawton found me and…"

He waved his hand in the air. "I don't really care. I'm just letting you know—" he raised a file "—that I'm getting what is rightfully mine."

"And you think I won't stop you?"

"I think unless you want Jake Martin to know that you were arrested on suspicion of murder, you won't say a word."

She froze, looking at the phone in her hand, hearing Marty yelling, asking if she was safe. Her breath came in ragged gulps. How could she be okay? Someone knew. And if he knew, Jake would know.

And she would lose the twins.

"Oh, I've upset you." Tyler Randall took a step toward her. "I have an idea. You sign your share of the business over to me and I won't tell Jake that the aunt of his nieces has a criminal past. Of course there's a chance his P.I. will eventually uncover this information, but for now you'll be safe in your stolen life."

Her stolen life. She shook her head. It wasn't stolen. It was hers and it was real and it meant everything to her. The twins meant everything to her.

Jake. She let go of the pain that threatened to steal her breath. He had hired a private investigator. He hadn't trusted her. She couldn't let that be a distraction, not now.

"I'm not signing anything over to you. I'm calling the police." She raised the phone. Marty was still talking, still trying to convince her help was on the way. She pushed End and called 911.

Tyler rushed her, but she stepped to the side. Maria hadn't been a perfect parent but in little ways she had shown she cared. She had made sure Breezy could protect herself.

"You won't get away from me." Tyler laughed, not as confident as he'd been a minute ago.

He reached for her and she grabbed his arm, kneed him and then elbowed him in the nose. He went down on his knees, screaming in pain.

"Self-defense, Mr. Randall. I'm not anyone's victim."

She had been once, a long time ago. But she would never be a victim again. She pushed him down on the floor and held him with her knee in his back as a car roared up the driveway. When Jake walked through the door, she stepped away.

He nodded and then he jerked Tyler to his feet. There were sirens in the distance. It was over.

She walked out of the living room, leaving Jake to clean up the mess. On her way out of the room she looked at the nativity on the mantel. In the kitchen she walked past the poinsettia she'd watered and cared for. It stood two feet tall and was covered with red blooms.

Jake could now effectively take the twins. Why would he be loyal to her? She was the sister who came out of nowhere to claim a portion of Lawton's life, his inheritance, his children.

He had hired a private investigator. That knowledge hurt. Where trust might have been, she now had the knowledge that even as they'd been forming their own family with the twins, he'd been looking for a way to take that family away from her.

As the thoughts rolled through her mind, she knew they weren't logical.

Logic didn't seem to matter when nothing made sense. Her heart feeling shattered didn't make sense. Her anger didn't make sense.

What made sense was leaving. She had to go to Joe. He needed a friend and she could be a friend. As she headed for her car, Jake caught up with her.

"Where are you going? The police need to talk to you," he said.

"I need to go."

"Breezy, you can't leave. You can't just walk away." He reached for her hand. "Come inside and talk to the deputies."

"Right, okay."

"Why do you think you have to leave?"

She blinked a few times. "Because I'm always going

to be the homeless girl in your eyes. You are never going to trust me, not completely."

"We need to discuss this."

She shook her head. "No, I need to talk to the deputies. Just let me get this over with. The one thing I can't do is talk to you right now."

"So you want me to back off?" he asked. "When have you ever backed off and left me alone? You forced me to admit that everyone needs someone. You need someone right now."

"You hired a private investigator," she accused. Pain tightened in her throat and tears burned her eyes.

He didn't deny it. "I had to protect the girls."

"Right, of course. Now I have to talk to the police and then I have to go. I have a friend and he needs me."

He put his hands up and backed away. "Fine, go talk to the police."

She nodded and walked past him, pretending she didn't need him.

Jake wasn't going to argue with her. He wouldn't chase her and plead with her to stay in their lives. No way would he tell her how much they needed her.

He remembered trying to tell his mother they needed her. He'd pleaded with her to take Samantha and Brody, to not leave the little ones. She had shaken her head and told him she was sorry. She couldn't stay and be a mom.

The police questioned Breezy. She told them everything Tyler had confessed to. She told them how she'd defended herself. And then she thanked them and said she had to go.

She walked over to the Christmas tree and took her ornament off, the one he'd given her. When she approached him she did so with her chin up, her brown eyes soft. She looked like a woman preparing herself for a battle. "I'm leaving. It's easier than waiting for you to tell me to go. But I'm taking this. I'm not leaving everything behind. And I'd like to be able to see my nieces from time to time."

He should stop her, he thought. But he couldn't. That twelve-year-old boy who had begged his mother to stay wouldn't let him. If people didn't want to stay, they couldn't be forced.

"Take whatever you want."

She opened her mouth as if she meant to say something, but she shook her head and walked away. He watched her as she got into her car and drove away.

Jake turned back to the house. Tyler was being put in the back of the police car. The deputy gave Jake a few more details. They would follow up, letting Jake know what charges would be filed. Jake listened but his mind had drifted off, to the pain that flashed in Breezy's eyes.

He should have told her about the private investigator. He should have told her it didn't matter. Not anymore. But he'd waited too long and someone else had told her. No matter what he said, he looked guilty. He looked like a man who didn't trust her.

When he pulled up to the house, Marty came out. She watched him walk up the steps, across the porch. She stepped aside to let him in the house. "Well?"

"She's gone." He kicked off his boots.

"What do you mean gone?"

He brushed a hand across his face. "What does gone usually mean?"

"In this household it means a stubborn man doesn't know what's good for him and didn't fight to keep what he wanted."

Jake plopped down in the recliner and looked up at her. "Really? And what does this man want?"

"That woman?"

"I'm not going to chase after her and try to force her to stay."

"No, you wouldn't want to do that. Why try to talk out a misunderstanding when you can let it hang between you? After all, words are so useless." Marty shot him an accusing look and then she dusted the table with the towel she'd carried in with her.

"I learned a long time ago that you can't beg someone to stay in your life."

"You learned that, did you?" Marty sat down on the edge of the sofa. "Did you ever learn that sometimes a person needs to hear the truth so they can make an informed decision?"

"I've learned that, but I also know that Breezy is not a woman who stays in one place long. Maybe she was looking for this out?"

"I don't think so. She loves it here and she loves those girls." Marty let a hefty pause hang between them. "And I think she probably loves you. Although I'm not sure why."

"Must be my charm."

"Go after her."

"I don't know where she went," he admitted. "Maybe

she went back to Oklahoma. If so, then maybe that's where she wants to be. Her sister's there."

Marty studied him for a moment. "What's in that report?"

"That's her business to tell."

"Do you care about her?"

Jake shrugged at the question. "I've known her three weeks. I don't know what I feel."

"Oh, I think you do."

Maybe he did care for her, but he'd been wrong before. What if he was wrong again?

Chapter Sixteen

Breezy walked down the hospital corridor to a room at the end. The nurse had informed her that Mr. Anderson was in a private room. And then the woman had said that Joe was quite a charmer. Yes, Joe was. But a private room? She thought back so many years ago and shivered at the memories.

For a long moment she stood outside the door of Joe's room telling herself that this moment was nothing like Maria. Joe wasn't going to die. The nurse had told her that he'd definitely improved and that he was now stable. Though it had been touch and go when the ambulance had brought him in.

Ambulance? What had Joe been doing in Austin?

There were a lot of questions and only the man himself could answer them. She rapped lightly on the door, waited for him to invite her in, then peeked inside the room to make sure it was indeed the Joe she knew. He waved her inside.

"Joe, how are you?"

"I'm going to be just fine, Breezy. It's this old ticker

of mine. It hasn't been the healthiest the past few years. I never expected it to knock me down, though."

He indicated a chair next to the bed. She looked around the room with the small sleeper sofa, recliner and even a dorm-size refrigerator. It was better than the apartment she'd lived in back in California.

"This is nice, Joe. Much better than the nativity," she observed.

"If the nativity was good enough for the King of Kings, I think it is good enough for one old man who has done a lot of wrong things in his life."

"Joe, is there someone I can call?"

"No, there's no one."

"No family, no children?" she pushed.

He brushed a neatly manicured yet shaky hand over his face and shook his head. "No, I think not."

Now she was confused. "You think you don't have children or you think I shouldn't call?"

The nurse came in, took vitals and checked the IV. She then moved around the room to take care of other small tasks and then asked Joe if he would like some coffee. Joe pointed at Breezy.

"No, but my guest might."

Breezy shook her head. The nurse smiled at them and left.

"Joe, are you sure you're okay?"

"I will be. It's just time for me to make things right."

And then Joe told her a story about a young man who had come from a good family, a wealthy family, but he'd had a drinking problem that no one but his wife knew about. He'd been a mean drunk, he admitted. And his wife, rightly so, had left him. She'd taken their child with her, and a good deal of his money. She'd also forced him to sign paperwork stating he would never try to see their child.

"I'm so sorry, Joe." What else could she say? "But why were you living on the streets in Martin's Crossing? Judging from this room, you don't have to be homeless."

"No, I don't have to be. I chose that life for the past year. I guess you could say I'm a senior citizen runaway."

She smiled at that. At least Joe had options.

Joe reached for her hand, patting it in a fatherly gesture. "I'm sorry for worrying you."

"It's okay." She removed her hand from his. "Joe, you're the one who has been helping people out, aren't you?"

"You won't tell, will you?"

She shook her head. "No, I won't tell."

"Thank you. I'm going to rest now. And you don't have to stay. I know you have those little girls and Jake Martin. I wouldn't want them to worry."

She didn't bother telling him she didn't think Jake would worry about her. He was probably looking at the guardianship papers right now, wondering how to take the twins away from her. But she wouldn't let him.

She wouldn't let him break her heart. And she wouldn't let him take Rosie and Violet from her. She wouldn't allow him to take the life she was building for herself.

"Are you still with me, Breezy?" Joe's voice, gravelly with sleep, broke into her thoughts.

"I'm here. I'll step out for a moment."

"You don't have to stay," he argued.

"I'm not leaving you alone."

She had left Maria. Even now it hurt to remember how it had felt to leave her. Breezy had been nineteen when it happened. She'd found a day job and on her way back she'd seen the ambulance, the police, the crowd on the street corner where she had left Maria that morning. Maria had insisted. She'd planned on selling papers, hoping to make a little extra money so they could get a room. But rooms didn't come cheap.

They said someone had taken the money and pushed her. Breezy went to the hospital that evening and she'd stood a short distance away from Maria's room, gathering the courage to go inside, to say goodbye to the woman that had raised her. Instead the police had found her and taken her into custody. They'd questioned her about Maria, about why she had run when she saw the police. They'd questioned her about where she came from.

Why had she run? She'd been afraid of the police, but how could she explain that? Maria had taught her to never trust them or give them information.

Standing in the hall of this hospital it was easy to remember that young woman and how alone she'd felt when the police had told her it was too late. Maria had passed away from a heart attack she suffered during the mugging. Later they allowed her to leave the police station because they'd determined that she and Maria were family. They'd even driven her to a shelter for the night.

She sat in the bed at the shelter, alone, afraid and unsure of how she would live the rest of her life with no family, no home and no real education. She had even tried to remember Mia's last name, because Mia had taken care of her when they'd been children, hiding from their mother and her string of boyfriends.

Pushing the past away, she called Jake. Not to give him explanations but to tell him she would be back. She loved the girls and she wasn't leaving.

When he answered the phone, she hesitated.

"Breezy, where are you?"

"I'm still in Texas. I'll be home in a day or two."

"You're okay?" He actually sounded concerned. She wanted his concern. His friendship.

Silly heart. It had soaked up his friendship like a dry sponge soaks up water. It had wanted more than a plant, Christmas decorations and a puppy to prove it belonged in Martin's Crossing.

"Breezy?"

"I'm here. I'm just…"

"I'm just going to ask one thing of you. Don't walk out on these little girls. They need you."

"I'm not walking out. I don't walk away, Jake." She closed her eyes and did her best to not cry. "Don't take them away from me. I know that you must know about Maria, but I can explain it better than a private investigator."

"We'll talk about that when you get back."

"Okay. Thank you," she whispered at the end of the conversation.

The call ended. At least he hadn't said he would take the girls from her. That was something. She stood for a long time leaning against the wall, her eyes closed, her heart feeling squeezed. Eventually she took a deep, shaky breath, opened her eyes and told herself she would get through this. She always survived. She always managed to get back on her feet. This time would be no different.

Jake avoided looking at Brody and Duke as they brought in the cattle they needed to work before bad weather hit. Breezy had been gone for two days. They didn't know exactly where or what she was doing. And Duke was none too happy. If Jake cared to explain, he could have told his brother he wasn't too happy, either.

The twins weren't happy. They'd already lost enough. They didn't need to lose Breezy. He should have kept his focus, not allowed himself to get distracted. By her. After all of these years of keeping his priorities straight, he'd dropped the ball when the twins needed him focused.

"Hey, get that heifer," Brody yelled. "Jake, are you anywhere near this farm?"

Jake shot his little brother a meaningful look as he kneed his gelding and the animal shot around the cow that had been trying to make a break for it. He circled her, bringing her back to the herd.

"I got her." He gave Brody a pointed look. "And I don't need your…"

"Could we not fight?" Duke interrupted.

"Not fighting," Jake said. "But you know, this job should have been done months ago when these calves were easy to handle. Not now when we're going to have to run them in a chute plus deal with mommas that don't want their babies taken from them."

"So it's my fault you're in a bad mood?" Brody

flashed him a look that was a little too confident and went after a rangy steer that was trying to head back to pasture.

"Yeah," Jake growled, "it's your fault."

Duke laughed, pushing his hat back a smidge as he rode up next to Jake. "You know you're just mad because you've never been good with the ladies and this time, when one was handed over to you like a Christmas present, you let the past get in the way."

"I..."

"Her past and yours," Duke continued.

"This has nothing to do with the past." Jake eased up on the reins when his horse started tossing his head. "Could we just get these cattle in the corral?"

So they did. The herd moved through the open gate. Brody jumped down and closed them in, limping a little.

"You okay, little brother?" Duke asked.

Brody nodded as he flung himself back into the saddle, gathering up the reins and turning his horse toward the barn. "I'm good. But thanks for asking. I'll get the stuff."

"Don't forget the rubbing alcohol," Jake called out after his retreating back.

"I never do," Brody half snarled.

"You have to stop treating him like a kid. He's twenty-six, not fifteen." Duke pulled his right leg loose from the stirrup and hooked his knee over the saddle horn.

"Then he needs to act twenty-six."

Duke shook his head. "Stop being the parent, Jake. That's half your problem with Breezy. You like her, but you won't let yourself because you're punishing every woman for Sylvia's crimes."

"I'm not punishing anyone," Jake insisted.

"Yeah, you are. You're even punishing yourself. You think you have to take care of the whole family and half the town. After all, Mom left, Dad left. Who does that leave in charge, the noblest of creatures, Jake Martin? Stop."

Jake leaned forward in the saddle and pointed at Duke. "You think I don't want to stop. But how do I stop when I have two little girls who now need me to raise them."

"Get yourself a wife. Loosen up a little and enjoy life. When was the last time you went on a date?"

"I don't date."

Duke pointed at him. "That's right, because Sylvia left, so how can any woman be trusted? If I was you, and I was this twisted up inside over a woman, I'd try to get her back."

"She's coming back," Jake admitted. Man, he was exhausted. He wished Duke would let it go. But as much as Jake thought he had to take care of their family, Duke thought he had to keep them all hugging and smelling the flowers.

"Why aren't you happy about that?"

"Duke, this isn't a relationship. Breezy and I are raising the girls together. End of story. Maybe for a little while I forgot that. I might have crossed lines I shouldn't have crossed."

"Jake Martin crosses lines?" Duke whistled. His horse sidestepped and Duke, even though he didn't appear to have control, brought the horse back around with no problem.

"Breezy and I are going to have to sit down and discuss our relationship."

"Why don't you just date the woman, Jake?"

Jake leaned to open the gate and rode through. "We have work to do."

"Yeah, there's always work to do. Why don't you answer my question?"

Jake eased his horse through the gate and Duke followed. They knew what to do without actually discussing it. They would separate calves from mommas long enough to take the calf through the chute, give him his immunizations and tag his ear.

Brody had walked back to the corral. He had a bucket with the tags, alcohol, giant-size needle and everything else they would need. Yeah, he was growing up. Whatever had happened between him and Lincoln had hurt him, but Brody wasn't a kid anymore.

"Jake, you didn't answer me."

"I don't want to answer you. I want to get this work done. I have Christmas shopping to do and some other errands to run."

And he didn't want to explain that anything more than friendship could ruin things not only between himself and Breezy but also for the twins. The twins had to be his priority.

For now and forever.

Chapter Seventeen

❧

It took Breezy ten minutes to find a parking place. Martin's Crossing just days before Christmas was a busy place. She hadn't realized it would be like this, that the entire town would show up for this early Christmas celebration. Down the block she could see the parade lining up. The floats were lit with Christmas lights. A school band was warming up.

She stood next to her car waiting for Joe to get out. He'd been released from the hospital that morning. They'd gone to his home so that he could pack a few things. It had surprised her, Joe having a home.

He joined her and they walked across the street and down the block to the park. In the distance a horse whinnied. Of course there would be horses in the parade. Breezy scanned the crowd looking for Jake and the twins. She ached to see them. But she was afraid.

"You'll be okay, Breezy. And so will those little girls."

She put a hand on his arm. "Thank you."

The church choir was warming up. They would be

singing outside because the weather was good. Breezy, with Joe at her side, walked toward them. She didn't know if she would still be included. Her acceptance here had a lot to do with her acceptance by the Martins. She knew that. And she wanted their continued acceptance.

She wanted this Christmas to be special. It would have been if she hadn't crossed lines with Jake. If she had remembered that relationships never worked in her favor.

No, she shook her head as she chastised herself. This Christmas would be special. She had a home, she had Rosie and Violet. And she had friends in Martin's Crossing. She would have a big dinner and invite Oregon, Joe and anyone else who might be alone for the holidays.

A flat trailer was being used for a stage. Breezy headed that way. Margie spotted her. The older woman called out and waved Breezy forward. The others noticed and many of them called out, friendly smiles on their faces.

"Breezy, I was so worried you wouldn't be here for your solo. But here you are. And Joe, too. I'm so glad to see you both." Margie gave Breezy a quick hug and then handed her a songbook. "We'll sing right after the parade and then before cookies and warm drinks in the community building."

"Okay." Breezy held the songbook and glanced around. "Have you seen the twins?"

"They're with Marty. I saw her pushing the stroller. Those little girls have grown, I think," Margie said.

"You go catch up with them and we'll see you after the parade."

She drifted away. Joe had left her. She knew that he planned on helping serve cookies and drinks. Like her, he had found a place in Martin's Crossing. She hoped, no, she prayed that things went well for him in the future.

As she walked toward the street she spotted Marty and the twins. She called out and Marty turned. Breezy stopped, waiting to be beckoned forward, waiting for Marty's reaction. The older woman smiled and waved. Something eased inside Breezy.

She hurried forward, catching up with them as Marty positioned the stroller so the twins could watch the parade. The girls spotted her and started to cry her name. But garbled in the word *Brees,* she also heard *Mama* and she knew that she wouldn't leave. Jake would have to make the decision to take away her rights to the twins. And she knew he wouldn't.

They would work out a way to be friends. They would spend Christmases together for years to come. So this year was important. She had gotten off track with wishful thinking. But she was back on track now. She would be able to smile at Jake and pretend nothing had happened.

She would pretend he didn't shake her world to the core.

"Rosie, Violet." She kneeled next to the girls and gathered them in hugs, kissing their cold cheeks. Rosie patted her face and Violet pulled herself out of the stroller to cling to her neck.

"They missed you." Marty said it with a kind look that didn't include censure. "I missed you, sweetie."

Those words meant everything. With both girls clinging to her, Breezy stood and allowed Marty to take her, with the twins, into a motherly hug. She breathed in, fighting the sting of tears.

"It's good to be home," Breezy said as she backed away, wiping at her eyes.

"You're okay?" Marty asked as she moved them all toward the street and the approaching parade.

"I'm good. Joe was in the hospital so I stayed in Austin long enough to bring him home."

"Breezy, you had quite a shock with Tyler Randall coming after you the way he did. I wish you hadn't left."

"I just needed a few days," Breezy explained. "And I'd gotten the call about Joe. I had to go to him."

"I know. We have all the time in the world to talk. But I want you to know you have people here who care about you."

She nodded, fighting tears. Marty sighed and patted her arm.

The parade was almost to them. At the front was a local band with only a dozen or so students. They played "Silent Night" as they marched past. Young girls carried the banner with the school name. The twins waved and bounced in Breezy's arms.

Breezy set the twins down. She held Violet's hand and Marty held Rosie's. Breezy pointed so that the girls could pick up the wrapped pieces of chocolate and lollipops that were tossed to the people lining the street.

For thirty minutes they stood there watching. The

floats from area organizations and churches came after the horses. Another band, this one playing "Joy to the World," walked by.

More candy was tossed and the girls would pick it up and hand it to Breezy to put in her pockets.

Near the end came the local saddle club. Jake, Duke and Brody road with them. Breezy held her breath as she made eye contact with Jake for the first time in several days. And it still hurt. His lack of trust hurt.

At the very end, the local fire department had decorated their old truck with lights and music blasting from speakers. Santa sat in the back. The truck stopped and more candy was tossed.

The crowds pushed closer, gathering more candy. Children rushed to greet Santa. Someone pushed close behind Breezy and she stiffened, waiting for an attack that didn't come.

"It isn't a big parade, but it's always been one of my favorites." The voice, low and husky, came from behind her.

Breezy hesitated before facing Jake, hoping she didn't look too desperate. "It has been fun."

"Welcome home."

"Yes, it's good to be back. Where's your horse?" she asked as she and Marty put the girls back in the stroller.

"Duke put him in the trailer so I could get over here to the girls. And to you."

"They loved the parade."

"I thought they would. They're old enough to enjoy these things a little more. Last year…"

She touched his arm. Last year his sister and Lawton had been here.

He cleared his throat. "Last year they were barely a year old."

"A lot changes in a year," she said.

"Yes, a lot changes."

"I need to go join the choir." Breezy looked down at the twins again. It was easier to focus on them than the man with the crystal-blue eyes standing in front of her.

"We'll be over there in a minute." Jake took the stroller from Marty. "I drive slower than Marty."

She managed a smile and walked away. For the twins she could do this. She *would* do this. But it was going to hurt. No two ways about it.

Jake ignored the look Marty gave him. The one that asked him what he was going to do. He didn't have an answer, and he didn't want to think about this. Not tonight.

It was hard enough that today he'd caught Brody on the computer searching for Sylvia Martin. He'd told his kid brother to let it go. He'd tried to find her once. He'd written her a letter when their father died. She'd responded and told him she was really very sorry and hoped they were all doing well. He tried to write and tell her they were great without her. That letter was returned, undelivered.

He had to acknowledge that Breezy wasn't Sylvia. Breezy had come back. As hurt as she was, he knew she would come back to the girls.

"Jake, you have to find a way to make this work. For the twins." Marty touched his hand as he pushed the stroller. He stopped pushing and looked at her, trying to find an answer for her and for himself.

"I will." Jake let the words out on a sigh. "I made a mistake, but I'm going to fix it."

"What mistake? Being attracted to Breezy?" Marty winked as she said that. "I can't see how you two falling in love is a mistake. Not for you, for her or the twins."

"I don't think I mentioned love," he said. "I meant I should have told her about the P.I."

"Yes, you should have."

The band played a few notes, warming up. Jake watched Breezy take her place on the makeshift stage. She stood up there in her long skirt, sweater and boots, blond hair down her back. She belonged. To this town. To him.

Man, he wanted to push his way through this crowd of people and take her in his arms. But he couldn't because he didn't know what he was feeling or what would happen come next week or next month.

Marty whispered for him to move forward and stop staring because he looked like a fool. He chuckled and shook his head. He pushed the stroller forward, joining the crowds.

"Lawton wanted us to become a couple," Jake shared with Marty.

She laughed. "He was your best friend and he wanted you as happy with his sister as he was with yours. Makes perfect sense to me."

"Not to me. Take two people with trust issues, toss them in a situation and see what you get." He walked around to the front of the stroller and handed Violet the drink she'd asked for.

He missed his sister at times like this. And he

missed Lawton. He pushed his hat back and took in a deep breath and let the pain out on the exhale.

The music started, giving him a much needed reprieve. Marty was as bad as his brothers these days, wanting to involve herself in his life. His relationships.

The choir started to sing. "Away in a Manger" came first. They included a choir of children for this song, letting the little ones sing the last verse without the band. The crowd's silence said everything. Especially since tonight the baby Jesus had been put in the nativity and the star above the little building was lit.

The last song of the night included Breezy's solo. He watched as she sang "Mary, Did You Know?" Their gazes locked for an instant, then she glanced away, her eyes widening on something or someone behind him.

Jake spun around, worried it was Tyler Randall, even though Tyler's bail was high and Breezy looked thrilled, not upset. A couple approached Jake, and a small boy of about seven walked with them. The woman was tall with long dark hair. The man next to her wore a cowboy hat and a protective glare. Family, Jake guessed.

The woman walked up to him, pinning him with a look.

"Jake Martin, I'm Mia McKennon. Breezy's sister."

He must have looked perplexed because the man next to her held out a hand and offered an apologetic look.

"Slade McKennon, and you'll have to overlook my wife. She's retired from the DEA but she hasn't retired from digging into other people's business." He gave his wife a look that Jake couldn't miss. He brought the boy up to his side. "This is our son, Caleb."

"It's good to meet you." Jake shook Slade's hand and then watched as Mia knelt next to the twins, her smile for them a lot different than the one she'd given him.

"Breezy didn't know we were coming down," Slade offered in a way that seemed to be another apology.

"Didn't she?" Jake said. Breezy was still on the stage. They were singing "Hark! The Herald Angels Sing." The crowd sang along.

After the song ended, Slade McKennon spoke again. "No, she didn't. Mia talked to her yesterday and said she got a bad feeling. Mia doesn't ignore her bad feelings. And I guess I've learned not to ignore them."

"I see," Jake said. He got the distinct impression they thought he was responsible for those bad feelings in Breezy's life.

As he watched Breezy hop down off the trailer, the only thing he could think about was loading her up in his truck and taking her for a drive somewhere, far away from all of these people and their opinions.

If they drove far enough, maybe they could outrun both of their pasts.

He'd like to hold her close as they sat on the tailgate of his truck watching stars. It had been a long, long time since he'd done anything like that. He couldn't remember the last time he'd even wanted to take a woman for a drive down by the creek. He wanted to hold her hand, maybe brush a kiss across her knuckles. He wanted like crazy to tell her that if they could be friends, maybe they could be more.

But all of those thoughts fled like darkness come

sunrise. Breezy's family had come to check on her, to make sure she was safe. What did they want after that? To take her back to Oklahoma?

Breezy hurried toward them. When she reached them, she pulled her sister into a hug, reaching for the boy, Caleb, as she did. The two sisters talked, laughed, hugged again.

Violet started to cry. Breezy broke away from her sister as she gave Violet her attention, leaning down to pick up the little girl who wanted to be held.

"They're beautiful," Mia said. Her hand, probably without her realizing, went to her belly. "I can't believe that by summer I'll have a little person like that."

"Maybe a little smaller." Breezy smiled as she said it, holding Violet to her shoulder.

Rosie, not to be left out, looked at Jake with big tears falling down her cheeks. He picked her up and she immediately reached for Breezy.

"I think they've missed you," he said.

"I could take them tonight. If you think…" Breezy shrugged.

"That would be good." Jake handed Rosie over. "I have some shopping to do tomorrow. By the way, if you haven't seen Lilly, she wanted me to let you know the puppy is weaned."

"Right, Daisy. I'll pick her up tomorrow."

"I can pick her up on my way home and bring it to your place," he offered.

"Okay, thank you, Jake."

"Mia and Slade are welcome to stay and join us for Christmas." He made the offer and Marty nodded her approval, then motioned that she was going to the fellowship hall for cookies.

Breezy looked at her sister, hopefulness in her expression. He knew she missed Mia. He knew this had been hard for her, being tossed into the lives of strangers.

"Of course we're staying," Slade answered, his arm sliding around his wife's waist. Caleb moved to the spot in front of his dad and Slade's hand rested on the boy's shoulder.

Jake gave the other man a cursory nod, then he looked at Breezy. "I'll see you tomorrow."

Breezy stepped forward. Her sister had taken Rosie and she had Violet in her left arm. With her free right hand she touched his cheek and then she stood on tiptoe and kissed where she'd touched.

"I'm sorry, Jake."

She really knew how to bring a guy to his knees. He didn't think she realized how she twisted him inside out. He didn't think she had a clue that he was fighting the urge to kiss her in a way that would show her that friendship just wasn't going to work.

He just stood there, watching as she stepped back, a sweet expression on her face.

"I'm sorry, too," he said. As soon as he could he would offer a real apology for the private investigator, for not trusting her.

As he stood there thinking about how to make amends, she walked away with the twins, a boy named Caleb, her sister and her brother-in-law. They looked like family.

And oddly, he felt like the outsider.

* * *

Breezy and Mia stayed up long after the twins, Caleb and Slade went to bed. They curled up on the couch with herbal tea and talked about home. Mia's home in Dawson, her family the Coopers, the Mad Cow Café where Breezy had worked and all of the other people Breezy had known while living in that small Oklahoma town.

"Are you homesick?" Mia asked.

Breezy had to think about that. She missed Dawson. But it would hurt Mia's feelings to tell her it hadn't been her home. It had been Mia's home, Mia's family and friends. Breezy had felt somewhat settled there.

"I do miss it," she admitted. "I miss you and your family."

Again, they were Mia's family.

"But?" Mia set her cup on the table next to the sofa and pulled an afghan up to her waist.

"This really does feel like home. I miss you all, but I'm supposed to be here. I'm supposed to raise Rosie and Violet. I keep thinking about how Lawton came into my life when he did. What if he hadn't found me? What if I'd never known him? I would have missed out on so much."

She wouldn't have known her brother. She would never have known who her father was. She wouldn't have had the twins. It would have been Jake raising those little girls alone.

And she missed him so much. Even though she'd just seen him, she missed *him*.

"So about your parenting partner," Mia started with

a knowing look, her mouth turning slightly and her eyes twinkling. "He's easy on the eyes."

"Yes, he is." There was no denying it.

"And the two of you are close?"

"Do we have to go there?" Breezy sipped her tea and dragged part of Mia's afghan to her own feet.

"Yes, we do. I'm worried about you. I'm worried that he is going to break your heart."

"He won't break my heart. We know what we need to do."

"And what's that, Breezy?" Mia jerked the blanket back to her side and grinned. They had missed out on so many moments like this because Maria had taken Breezy away. They had just found one another, just started to get reacquainted, and then Lawton had found Breezy.

But their reconnecting didn't have to end. They could visit, talk on the phone and share pictures. Breezy would definitely be with Mia when she had the baby.

Mia nudged Breezy with her foot. "Come back to earth."

"Jake and I have to be friends for the sake of the twins."

Mia barked a laugh and then covered her mouth with her hand. "That's hilarious. Friends, for the sake of the twins. There's electricity between the two of you. You look at each other and forests in other states catch fire."

"That isn't true."

"Oh, it's true," Mia said with a grin. "And if you think you can contain that in a mason jar like a lightning bug, you're fooling yourself. There's no lid tight enough to hold in that force. I know because I fought my feelings for Slade for a long, long time."

"I know."

Slade's wife, Mia's best friend, had died in a car accident. It had taken Mia a long time to be okay with what she felt for Slade.

"I want you to be happy, Breeze. You deserve to be happy. And to have this awesome home. And stuff to fill it with." Mia grinned and lifted her cup to her lips.

Breezy looked around the house, at the things she'd bought to make this house her home. She wouldn't leave it. She wouldn't take off in the night and leave behind the things she loved, the things she cared about.

She wouldn't leave Jake behind. Or the twins. Because when she thought of things she couldn't leave behind, it wasn't material things at all. It was the people she loved.

And she loved Jake Martin.

Chapter Eighteen

Christmas morning dawned and Jake was awake. He made coffee before Marty came to the kitchen to start cooking. She kissed his cheek and went to work on the meal that would feed their family. She could have gone to visit family in Austin or San Antonio, but she considered the Martin kids her kids. She had told him last night that she really wouldn't want to be anywhere else.

He was glad she felt that way. He knew without a doubt that they wouldn't be nearly as functional without her.

He plugged in the lights on the tree and the lights on the mantel while he waited for everyone else to wake up. And he waited for Breezy, the twins and Breezy's family. They would be there within the hour.

"I'm going to run out to the barn to take care of a few things." Jake walked through the kitchen on his way to the back door.

"I'll have breakfast ready when you get back. Over easy?"

"Yes, thanks," he called out as he headed out the door. When he got to the barn he stopped to check on

Breezy's Christmas gift. He was kind of proud of himself. He hoped Breezy would like it as much as he did. He planned on giving the gift to her here, in the barn. He wanted time to talk to her. Alone. He wanted time to explain that he'd been wrong and he wanted to make things right.

Her brother-in-law's truck was in the drive when he got back. He found them all in the kitchen, seated at the bar stools around the counter. Caleb, Slade's son, was wearing a cowboy hat today and what appeared to be new boots.

"Nice boots, Caleb." Jake leaned down to take a look.

The kid began to tell him all about the boots and how they were the best. Jake tousled his blond hair before stopping to see the twins, who were sitting on Breezy's lap. They were barely awake. Rosie rubbed a hand over her eyes and smiled up at him. And then she raised her arms in a silent request. He picked her up, holding her close.

"Have you been in the living room?" he asked.

Breezy shook her head. "No, we didn't want to give anything away."

"Good. I want to see their faces when they see…"

Breezy cut him off, a finger to her lips. "Shh, don't tell them."

"You know, it's all I could do not to come over last night and get them so they could have their gifts," he admitted.

Slade laughed at that. "Caleb got a new saddle and we gave it to him two days ago. I couldn't wait."

Mia gave her husband a sweet look. Jake thought

that look said it all when it came from a woman like Mia, who appeared able to take down small armies if necessary.

"We could take them now," Breezy offered.

"No," Marty said in a loud, firm tone. "Breakfast, then gifts. New parents always get ahead of themselves."

Jake looked at Breezy and saw it register in her expression. That moment when they realized this was it. They weren't going to wake up tomorrow and have this all be a dream.

She reached for his hand. He'd missed her.

Brody walked into the kitchen a few minutes later, rubbing sleep from his eyes and then smoothing hair down with his hand. He might be an adult but he still looked like a kid who woke up on Christmas morning half-asleep but ready to open gifts.

"Breakfast," he muttered.

Caleb took a long look at him. "You're a bull rider."

Brody narrowed his eyes and looked at Caleb. "Did we get another kid?"

Caleb laughed at that. "No, I'm Breezy's nephew. Those are my parents. They kiss a lot. Grown-ups do that when they love each other."

He said the last part as if repeating what he had been told often.

Jake wished the kid would stay around a little longer.

Brody looked at Caleb, one eye squinting. "So you're the new sister's nephew. I guess you can call me Uncle Brody. And yeah, I used to ride bulls."

"You don't ride bulls anymore?" Caleb continued to quiz even though Mia had put a hand on his arm.

Jake watched the exchange, interested in things Brody didn't really say to any of them. And yet he'd tell a kid he barely knew.

"No, I don't ride anymore." Brody grinned. "But I'm finding other things to do."

Duke showed up next. Caleb eyed him as he walked through the door. The kid's eyes widened. Duke poured a cup of coffee and hugged Marty, who handed him a plate of food. Everyone else was eating.

Everyone but Caleb. He spun in his chair to watch Duke take a seat at the table. "Are you a giant?"

Duke spooned a mouthful of eggs into his mouth. "Yeah."

"Cool."

Everyone laughed.

After breakfast they all walked to the living room. The twins held Jake and Breezy's fingers. They had been little last year and Christmas hadn't been like this, filled with awe and wonder.

Christmas music played on the radio and the smell of ham baking filled the air. Rosie and Violet stopped in the living room, their eyes widening at the sight of the tree and all of the gifts.

They had put the rocking horses under the tree with ribbons around their necks. Jake had bought some type of scooter for Caleb. It would work great in the driveway, the salesgirl at the toy store had told him. When Caleb saw the scooter he just looked at it.

Jake grinned at the boy and indicated with a nod that he should head for the tree with the twins. "I think you'll find something with your name on it, Caleb."

Caleb took the twins by the hand and led them over

to the tree. The girls climbed on those rocking horses and Caleb pulled the scooter out to give it a thorough look.

Jake put Brody in charge of handing out the other gifts. As he did, their other guests arrived. Joe, Oregon and Lilly. He watched as Lilly immediately went to Duke, showing him the ring she'd gotten from her mom and telling him how much money she had saved in her piggy bank for a horse.

Joe took a seat next to Marty and asked if she'd like some help in the kitchen. Jake saw Marty's cheeks turn red. Joe had secrets, but it was no secret that he was charming.

As things settled down, Jake walked up to Breezy. She looked up at him with a soft smile playing on her lips. "Merry Christmas, Jake."

"I have something for you," he said. "If you could escape for a few minutes."

She looked at the twins. They had unwrapped gifts and were busy on the floor with their new dolls. Next to her, Mia gave her a little push.

"Go. I'll watch them," Mia offered.

The day was cool so Jake handed Breezy a jacket from the hook at the back door. They walked outside together. He reached for her hand. As they walked, he wondered if this was the right gift, at the right time.

He'd soon find out.

Breezy hadn't expected more gifts from Jake. He'd given her a wooden box from Lefty's shop filled with family recipes. He'd also given her a bracelet with pretty charms and jewels. The gifts were sweet gestures of friendship.

Now he said there was more.

"Where are we going?"

He shrugged. He didn't answer.

"Jake?"

"Do you understand what a surprise is?"

She sighed and continued to walk with him, trudging across the crunchy, frosty ground. They reached the barn and she wondered if maybe he had given her boxing gloves. That would be nice. She'd like to hit something.

He led her through the barn, turning on lights as they went. A horse whinnied. Jake didn't say anything. Why didn't he say something?

"Are you going to give me a hint?" she asked.

"No need." He put his hands over her eyes and turned her. When he removed his hands she faced a stall. And in the stall a pretty golden horse with an almost white mane and tail stood watching them, its golden ears pricked forward.

"What?"

"It's a horse," he said, close to her ear. She could feel the warmth of his breath. She could almost sense his lips close to her cheek.

"Yes, a horse." She reached and the animal nuzzled her fingers.

"Merry Christmas, Breezy."

She turned to look up at him, awed, unsure. "You bought me a horse?"

"I'm hoping you're happy. I was really going for happy."

"Of course I am, it's just… I didn't expect a horse." A horse belonged to someone with roots, someone who stayed. She wanted a horse and all it implied.

He pulled her close. "That's the wonderful thing about a surprise. It's unexpected."

Yes, unexpected. Like Jake. "You didn't trust me."

He sighed. "I should have told you about that report. I started all of that before I met you. And then I didn't know what to say, how to tell you."

"You could have asked me to tell you what happened."

"I know," he admitted.

"So what do we do now?" She waited, knowing that she loved him more than she'd ever expected to love anyone. How did she keep boundaries when her heart had already made up its mind?

"I think we should agree that Lawton made a good decision and he knew what was best for the twins."

Her heart quaked a little because she didn't know what that meant. "Okay."

"Breezy, you're the best friend I've ever had. I don't want to lose you."

She pushed her hands through his hair and brought his head close to hers. Face-to-face she stood on tiptoe, touching her lips to his. "And yet, you make friendship more…"

He kissed her long and sweet, her arms around his neck.

"I make friendship more…?" he leaned in to her.

"More complicated. More interesting. More difficult. I'm not sure what we're supposed to do now."

"I think that what we do now," he said, "is move forward."

She waited, knowing there had to be more. Her heart needed more.

"I know you've left a lot behind, Breezy. I think you've left more than people and possessions. You've left pieces of yourself."

"Oh, Jake." Had anyone ever gotten it the way he did?

"I love you and I want to put all of our pieces back together and make us whole. Together."

She placed a hand on each of his cheeks and pulled him down, touching her lips to his. "Thank you."

"I messed up, Breezy. When you first came I was in a panic, trying to protect the girls. Protect my family. And I let you down. I didn't trust Lawton. And I didn't trust you. I should have."

"I think we couldn't have imagined this happening." She raised the hand she held and brushed her lips over his knuckles. "I love you, too. I'm not going anywhere. I want to be here. I want to be in your life and in your arms."

"That's where I plan on keeping you, Breezy."

"Forever?"

"Yes, forever."

He kissed her again. It was a slow, lingering kiss, the kind that made them forget the barn, the horse, the people waiting inside. Slowly they returned to themselves, and Jake took her by the hand and led her back to the house for Christmas with the family.

Their family.

Epilogue

Breezy loved Martin's Crossing. She loved it in the winter when Christmas lights decorated the entire town. She loved it in the spring with trees budding, flowers blooming and warm air reminding everyone that winter never lasted forever.

She realized that hard times were like winter. They sometimes seemed like they would go on forever, but they never did. Spring always came with sunshine and the promise of better days.

On a pretty day in late April, with flowers blooming and birds singing, she waited in a small classroom at the Martin's Crossing Community Church. Somewhere out there, Jake was waiting for her.

She smiled at her ladies-in-waiting, as she liked to call them. The Coopers were all present to help with wedding preparations. Mia was her matron of honor, even though she was due to give birth in a matter of weeks. Oregon was a bridesmaid. The twins were flower girls. Breezy thought the flower petals would end up everywhere but where they should be sprinkled.

"You look beautiful," Marty said as she arranged the veil. Marty was taking the place of mother of the bride. And she was happy to do so, as she had no children of her own.

The twins had recently started calling her Gamma.

"And the dress?" It had been Mia's wedding dress, and Breezy loved that they could share it, and share this occasion. A few years ago she hadn't dreamed of having a family. Now she had it in abundance. When God provided, He didn't skimp.

"Perfect," Marty concurred.

Heather Cooper handed her a bouquet of white and pale pink roses. "There's a guy out there, in the church. He has the sweetest smile."

Mia chuckled. "And we thought it would never happen."

Heather shot her a look. "Nothing has happened. I just wanted to know his name."

The door opened. Lilly ran through the room straight to her mother. She spotted Breezy and stopped to stare. "Wow, you're beautiful. I think my mom should marry Duke so I can be a bridesmaid…"

Oregon shot her daughter a look. And Breezy thought it wasn't the typical mom-embarrassed-by-daughter-talking-too-much look. It was a look of fear.

Mia must have noticed it, too, because she took over.

"I think we should probably find out if Jake is ready for his bride."

Lilly quickly volunteered and ran out the door. Breezy smiled down at the twins in their pale pink dresses. Caleb was the ring bearer. He was with the men.

Breezy winked at Oregon. Oregon didn't smile. Instead she looked as if she might cry.

But it was too late to ask questions. Lilly was back and informed them that it was time. Breezy walked out the door of the room and down the hall to the back of the church where Tim Cooper, Mia's dad, was waiting to walk her down the aisle. He smiled at her, patting her hand as she placed it on her arm.

The music started, and Breezy took a deep breath and prepared herself to meet the man she loved at the front of the church.

She loved him. She smiled at the memory of the night he'd asked for her hand in marriage, while slipping a ring on her finger. It had been Valentine's Day and they'd cooked dinner together at her place. She'd turned around and he'd stepped close behind her, waiting for that moment to pull her close.

"I love you," he had said as he'd kissed her. She'd seen the walls coming down, the trust growing. She'd known. God had known.

He'd seen two damaged people and He'd used faith, love and a little time to put them back together. He'd made a family out of those broken people and two little girls. He'd taught them to trust themselves—and to trust Him.

Today she would marry Jake and they would continue to build a new life, a new family.

Mia and Slade walked down the aisle ahead of her. Slade stepped behind Jake at the front of the church. Mia took her place to wait for Breezy.

Duke waited for Oregon to take his arm. She did, but didn't look at him.

And then Tim Cooper walked Breezy down the aisle. She beamed at Jake as she walked toward him, whispering that she loved him. He mouthed the words back to her.

Yes, they had gotten this right. She stepped next to him. Tim kissed her cheek and wished her all of God's blessings.

Pastor Allen recited the vows, words of honor, of love, of standing strong through good times and difficult times. During a quiet moment while they lit the candles, Breezy thought about all of the ways God had blessed her.

Pastor Allen then brought them together—Jake, Breezy, Violet and Rosie. "Breezy, this is your family. God has entrusted them to your care." He looked at Jake. "And, Jake, you have been given this wonderful blessing. A wife and two little girls. With everything else in life that you do, everything that keeps you busy, always remember this—this wife and these children are the most important thing God has given you to do."

Jake looked at Breezy, smiling as he held her hand. Rosie and Violet wandered off. The people in the church laughed softly as the girls went their own way, sprinkling flowers in their wake.

Pastor Allen cleared his throat and then he continued.

"Jake and Breezy Martin, by the power vested in me by God and the state of Texas, I now pronounce you husband and wife. Jake, you may kiss your bride."

Everything in her life had led her to this moment. She moved into her husband's embrace and he kissed her. She melted in his arms.

They left the church to a cheering crowd and music that celebrated love. When they reached the car that would take them to a resort a short distance from town where they would have a reception, someone shouted that she should throw the bouquet.

She paused, looking back at the crowd of people gathered to celebrate their wedding. A large group from Oklahoma had traveled to Martin's Crossing for the wedding. Not only the Coopers, but also Vera and several others. All of them mixed in with her family and friends from Martin's Crossing.

Tears gathered in her eyes as she saw this united bunch of people. They symbolized everything that had changed in Breezy's life. She had a place of her own. She had family.

A hand tugged on hers, reminding her of the most important change in her life. She had Jake Martin's love, and together they would raise their twin nieces.

She would build a life and a family here in Martin's Crossing. With a smile she tossed the bouquet, watching as women rushed to catch it.

Breezy smiled up at her husband and he leaned down to claim her lips in a kiss that would be hers, forever.

* * * * *

HIGH COUNTRY HOLIDAY

Glynna Kaye

To Aunt Nancy.

Thank you for being a part of my life.

But the angel said to them, "Do not be afraid.
I bring you good news of great joy that will be for
all the people. Today in the town of David a Savior
has been born to you; He is Christ the Lord."
—*Luke* 2:10–11

For He has rescued us from the dominion of darkness
and brought us into the kingdom of the Son He loves,
in whom we have redemption, the forgiveness of sins.
—*Colossians* 1:13–14

Forgive as the Lord forgave you.
—*Colossians* 3:13

Chapter One

"Three weddings next month? Are you kidding me?" Paris Perslow cast a look of dismay at the wall calendar in the back room of her father's real estate office on Main Street. The pastor of Canyon Springs Christian Church had to be out of his mind asking her to get involved with this. "December's only a few days away."

Outside the back window, a gust of wind swept snow through the towering ponderosa pines, filling the air with a reminder of the frosty holiday season. While it wasn't by any means the first snowfall of the year in this Arizona mountain community, she wasn't ready for winter.

Or Christmas.

Or Christmas weddings.

Another gust rattled the window, tendrils of cold creeping in around its wooden framework. She stepped away from the glassy panes, thankful for her cashmere sweater.

"My wife would kill me if she knew I was asking you to help." The voice of Pastor Jason Kenton carried over the phone in an apologetic tone. "You know, because…"

Yes, she did know. Because both he and his wife, Reyna, were aware she'd stepped away from responsibilities as a volunteer wedding coordinator when her own dream wedding three and a half years ago had taken a tragic turn.

"I'm sorry about Reyna's illness, Jason, but I don't see how I could pull three weddings together on such short notice." Not if they were anything like the over-the-top extravaganza she and her mother-in-law-to-be had once orchestrated.

"There isn't much left to do," he assured. "Jake Talford and Macy Colston have been planning their wedding since last spring. Sharon and Bill since the summer. And you know the Diaz clan—the whole family will be on top of Abby and Brett's special day. You'd be more of a go-to person representing the church, a reassuring voice for jittery brides and grooms."

Wasn't that *his* job? She paced the hardwood floor, the powerful music of Handel's *Messiah* that emanated from the CD player lending her strength to stand her ground.

"I don't have the time.…"

She'd scheduled church and community-related activities into her calendar months ago, including the Christmas charity gala for which she'd been voted the committee head. Dad, too, had expectations for seasonal entertaining. The holidays, even without a trio of weddings, could be exhausting when you and your widower father played a prominent role in the community.

A pang of apprehension shot through her. Dad

wasn't going to like what she intended to tell him after the first of the year…that she'd soon no longer be at his beck and call. That is, if she could garner the courage to make the break. Life away from Canyon Springs? Could she do it?

She had to.

"Would you be willing to think about it?" Jason coaxed. "Maybe pray about it?"

She could almost see his eyebrows rise in question as they often did during Sunday morning messages when challenging his congregation.

"I'm not sure I can commit to doing even that."

"Taking this on may help you work through things," he said gently, again broaching the issue they both knew stood between yes and no. "Weddings are meant to be happy times, Paris. A celebration of God joining two lives for His purposes."

"I understand, but…" While it was difficult seeing others caught up in their happily-ever-afters, the real issue behind her reluctance was one which Pastor Kenton knew nothing about.

"No matter how brides try not to let it get to them," he continued, "the tiniest of setbacks can throw them into a tailspin. But I have confidence you can help these gals keep the right perspective. Honestly, Paris, this shouldn't take much of your time."

A skeptical smile touched her lips. Maybe she'd better get his wife to confirm that. But Reyna hadn't yet been released from the hospital in Show Low, and Jason had mentioned earlier in the conversation that she had a long way to go to recover from a serious bout of pneumonia.

"Could I get back to you tomorrow?" Why was she even saying that? She couldn't allow herself to be sucked into a world of weddings and receptions and starry-eyed couples. Into a world where her "widowed" status drew misunderstanding and undeserved sympathy. But Reyna was more than the pastor's wife, she was a friend.

At her words, Jason perked up. "Tomorrow? You've got it. And no pressure. I promise. Take a look at your calendar and see if you can fit this in."

She knew what the calendar looked like and it wasn't pretty.

"Reyna and I would both be forever in—" He brought himself up short with a self-conscious laugh. "No, no pressure. Think about it. Pray about it. I know this isn't an easy decision to make."

There it was again.

Cody Hawk averted his gaze, pretending not to notice, but it disturbed him just the same. The expression was fleeting, evasive. Sometimes curious, suspicious or even—could he only be imagining it?—silently accusing.

But above all, it was a look of recognition, one that had become annoyingly familiar since returning to his hometown of Canyon Springs two days ago. Not even Christmas melodies piped onto Main Street the morning after Thanksgiving or snowflakes floating through the air made it any more palatable. You'd have thought that after a dozen years people would have forgotten about him and gotten on with their own lives.

Squaring his shoulders, he strode across the street

to the office of Perslow Real Estate and Property Management. A two-story natural stone building with a cheery pinecone wreath gracing the door, it exuded a rustic warmth suitable for drawing in newcomers to purchase or rent a piece of what was touted as a mountain country paradise.

Paradise.

The misnomer left a bitter taste in Cody's mouth. The community might be a dream come true for those who had the financial means to buy their way into it, but it showed a much different side to those with lesser resources.

Sleigh bells on the office door announced his entrance, jingling as if delighted to welcome him. Not likely. He closed the door to block a blustery gust, then stuffed his gloves in his pockets, unzipped his jacket and pulled off his baseball cap. A faint tang of pine emanated from a half-decorated Christmas tree in the corner. Several boxes of ornaments and a rope of tinsel lay neglected at its base as if a holiday elf had been suddenly called away.

Although the waiting room was devoid of visitors and no one manned the front desk, he could hear the distinctive strains of Handel's *Messiah* overriding a feminine voice coming from a partially open door. It was a one-sided conversation, as if someone was on the phone.

Had it really been a dozen years since he'd charged out of this place, boiling mad and head held high from having told his father's boss—Paris Perslow's father— what he could do with his job offer?

Dumb kid. He hadn't been old enough or smart

enough to know burning bridges could come back to haunt you. What was that parting line he'd tossed at Mr. Perslow that memorable afternoon? *Just you wait and see. Someday you'll be groveling at my feet. Sir.*

Cody groaned inwardly at the sarcasm with which he'd laced that final word of his tirade. Well, he might be only minutes away from being shown the door, but what choice did he have?

Reluctantly moving to the seating area, he'd barely lowered himself into a burgundy leather chair when the final notes of the classic Christmas choral piece faded away as the woman in the back room wrapped up the conversation. Her lilting tones now clearly reached Cody's ears.

A viselike sensation tightened around his chest.

It couldn't be, could it? But that voice…

He stood and moved swiftly to the door. This wasn't the time or place for a reunion. Not when anyone could walk in on them at any minute. Her dad. A coworker. *Her husband.*

"May I help you?" a melodious voice called from behind him as he reached for the doorknob.

He tensed, willing his heart to slide down out of his throat and back into his chest. *Please let this be a cousin. A long-lost sister.* With effort, he turned to look directly into the smoky-gray eyes of a woman far more exquisite than the girl he'd long remembered.

A soft charcoal sweater, jeans, English riding-style boots and dark brown hair pulled loosely into a low ponytail gave her the carefully casual appearance of an American aristocrat. High cheekbones touched by a whisper of rose and delicately arched eyebrows under-lined the air of seemingly flawless refinement.

But he knew the satiny gloss on a too-tempting mouth camouflaged a scar acquired in third grade. She'd been running from playground bullies, slipped on a graveled walkway and cut her lower lip. He re-membered the day well, his first at the new school as a fifth grader. He'd retaliated on her behalf by bloody-ing a few noses, got sent home…and forever lost his heart to Paris Perslow.

Or rather, Paris Herrington.

Mrs. Dalton Jenner Herrington III.

Heart pounding, Paris stared up at the boy she'd known since grade school. A man now. Tall. Muscu-lar. Rugged. A shock of raven hair slashed across his forehead and the high cheekbones gave credence to talk of Native American blood in his ancestry. Sharp, black-brown eyes pierced into hers.

"Remember me, Paris?" His words, tinged with the faintest of Texas accents, held a note of self-deprecat-ing humor as he no doubt recalled their last meeting.

How could she forget him? Not only had he been her self-appointed guardian from third grade onward, raising the ire of teachers, classmates and her father alike, but her last encounter with him had left her more than shaken.

"I'm sorry to hear of your father's stroke, Cody."

His jaw, graced with a five o'clock shadow even this early in the morning, hardened. "Bad situation."

"Is he… Has there been any improvement?"

A humorless smile touched Cody's lips. "He still

can't talk much. I'd say that's an overall improvement, wouldn't you?"

Paris flinched at the candid judgment. While the burly Leroy Hawk could be a charmer when he chose to be, his humor was sometimes biting and unforgiving. She'd often wondered why her father kept him on as an employee.

Clearly, though, there was still no love lost between father and son despite over a decade's separation. Which wasn't surprising. In elementary school, Cody had once furtively raised his ragged T-shirt to show her the ugly bruises—but only after he'd made her promise never to tell.

She hadn't told.

But she should have.

Ignoring Cody's harsh question, she restlessly moved to the Christmas tree and picked up a box of glass ornaments. "How is your mother holding up?"

Cody had adored Lucy Hawk, and Paris suspected that as a kid he'd deliberately drawn his father's anger in an effort to protect her from the short-tempered man's fists.

"Working too hard."

She always had, and now Leroy's health setback would make it even harder on her. Paris removed an ornament from the box and hooked a metal hanger into its loop. "I bought the wreath on the door from Dix's. It's one of hers. Canyon Springs is fortunate to have her working on the annual Christmas gala this year. She's a true craftsman—a gifted artist."

"I'll let Ma know you think so."

For several moments, neither of them spoke. What

more was there to say that *could* be said? A tremor of awareness skittered as Cody's dark eyes remained fixed on her, and she self-consciously hung the ornament on the tree. He'd always looked at her that way. It was in many ways the same look other men had long been known to give her—appreciative of her beauty. But with Cody there had been something else. A tenderness. An almost…reverence.

That had always been her undoing, and she'd long guarded against it. Abruptly she turned toward him. "I'm sorry, is there something I can help you with?"

He cleared his throat. "I'm here to see your father."

Regarding Leroy's job security? His insurance? His stroke wasn't workers'-compensation-related. Everyone in town knew he'd blown last Friday's paycheck on lottery tickets and booze, then when the multimillion-dollar winning number was drawn—and it wasn't his—he'd suffered a stroke.

Her own father had seemed more agitated about the whole thing than she would have expected. Had he anticipated this visit from Cody, asking special favors for his father, maybe applying legal pressure?

"I'm afraid Dad left for the Valley this morning. He'll be gone for a few days. Remember, this *is* a holiday weekend."

Cody's brows lowered.

"He left you here to watch over things?" His glance raked the office, then focused again on her. "All alone?"

Gazing up at the big man, a ripple of unease skimmed her spine. But that kind of thinking was preposterous. Cody might look menacing, but he'd never so much as attempted to lay a hand on her during the years she'd known him. Not even that last day when he'd stepped out of the darkness and frightened her half out of her wits with his crazy talk.

Nevertheless…

"Everett's here. And Kyle. Or at least they'll be back in few minutes." She moved behind the receptionist's desk, placing a barrier between them. She didn't know Cody now. She hadn't really known him back then, either. And although he'd never crossed any lines with her, he *was* a Hawk.

"I don't," he stated, "have business with Everett or Kyle."

"Perhaps there's something I can—"

"I need to see your father."

"I'd be happy to schedule an appointment for Monday." She did her best to keep her tone cheerful despite his terse responses. She'd warn her dad, of course, so he wouldn't be caught unprepared.

Cody exhaled a resigned breath. "First thing Monday morning then."

She opened the scheduling software program. "Nine-thirty?"

"There's nothing earlier?"

You'd have thought she'd suggested high noon. He'd been an early riser as a kid, with chores to see to before he came to school. Maybe old habits died hard?

"Dad often works late in the evening with clients, so yes, nine-thirty is customary."

"Fine."

He didn't sound as though it were fine, but she typed his name into the database. "May I let him know what the appointment concerns?"

"He'll know."

Did he have to sound so confrontational? That wouldn't go over well with Dad. It didn't go over well with her, either. Cody might never have had much patience with those in authority, but he'd always been more than polite with her.

As if coming to the same realization, he nodded toward the computer, his tone softening. "I mean, he'll know I'm here about my father's situation. I need to find out where things stand regarding his employment status and medical benefits."

She nodded and made the note. When she glanced up, he was watching her with that look that had been typical of Cody since the first day she'd met him. Self-consciously she ran her tongue along her lower lip. Across the scar.

"Well, you're all set," she said with a businesslike clip to her words. "Nine-thirty on Monday morning."

"Thank you." He placed his ball cap on his head, zipped his jacket and started to turn away. Then he paused to look down at her once again. "So you're filling in here while visiting Canyon Springs over the Thanksgiving holiday?"

"I live here. I'm a real estate agent."

His expression darkened slightly.

"Was there something else?" She held her breath, the pulse in her throat racing as his gaze lingered, indecision flickering through his eyes.

"No." He shook his head. "Have a good rest of your day, Paris."

And then he was gone, the sleigh bells chiming a farewell as the door closed behind him.

Exhaling, she leaned back in the chair and closed her eyes.

Cody Hawk had returned to town.

But he wouldn't be here for long. He'd made that clear. He had family business to take care of, then would disappear into the night as he'd done a dozen years ago. Thankfully, he hadn't attempted to express condolences for the death of her fiancé. Nor had he made reference to their last meeting.

When he'd confessed he loved her.

She'd been certain he intended to kiss her that night and, to her shame, she'd wanted him to. But when she'd come to her senses and rejected the outpouring of his heart—as her father would have expected of her—he'd had the audacity to claim that one day he'd return to town and she'd beg him to marry her.

She hurried to the windows to peek between the wooden-louvered slats at a departing Cody. Collar turned up against the wind-driven snow and hands rammed in his jacket pockets, he crossed the street with that same mesmerizing, masculine grace he'd grown into as a teen. He'd been all male from adolescence onward and even the nice girls noticed. But while a nice girl might dream a dangerous dream, in a little town like this she wouldn't dare throw away her—and her family's—reputation for a boy with kin like Cody's.

Paris herself had been more than aware of him those many years ago, aware of his slow, lazy smile and barely-under-the-surface interest evidenced in the way he looked at her. That look had both excited and frightened her youthful heart, for he was a Hawk. Forbidden territory for a Perslow.

She abruptly stepped back from the window, irritated at herself for gawking after the still-enticing man. She was twenty-eight years old now. He was what— thirty? He'd been living his life elsewhere, doing who knew what, far from the vigilant eyes of Canyon Springs. He'd probably been up to no good, just like his father and older half brothers. Dad always said even a shiny apple didn't fall far from the tree.

But that didn't mean it wasn't tempting.

She returned to the Christmas tree where she picked up another ornament. She wasn't a teenager now, given to indulging in silly daydreams. Cody would soon be gone and his return to Canyon Springs a mere blip on the radar of her life.

With an air of resolve, she slipped a hook into the ornament loop and placed it on the end of a branch. But before she could react, the too-fragile needles bent, sending the decorative glass ball tumbling to the hardwood floor where it shattered at her feet.

Chapter Two

Cody strode to the old Dodge pickup, jerked open the door and climbed inside. Then he slammed the door and sat staring blindly out the snow-streaked windshield.

It was clear Paris couldn't wait to send him on his way. He couldn't blame her. How old had she been back then—almost sixteen? He'd been nearly eighteen and old enough to know better than to do what he'd done that night. He could still hear her soft gasp when he'd stepped out of the shadows where she'd been relaxing on the porch swing. He'd been desperate to speak to her before he left town, daring to risk being caught by her father.

Looking back, he was lucky she hadn't called the cops.

And yet…for a fleeting moment, he thought he'd seen something in her eyes that sustained him with a glimmer of hope despite her firm but gentle turn-down. It kept him going as he endeavored to turn his life around and become a man worthy of a woman like Paris. That is, until the day four years ago when he'd come across her engagement announcement on the front page of the online local paper.

Yeah, he'd been a dumb kid in more ways than one. He wasn't that bright of an adult, either. He hadn't spoken to Paris in twelve and a half years, yet he'd neglected to say it was good to see her. He hadn't told her how beautiful she was. Nor could he bring himself to offer congratulations on her marriage into the Herrington clan.

Dalton Herrington.

Cody's fists clenched involuntarily at the thought of the hotshot physician marrying Paris. But with Dalton's professional status and upper-crust social standing in the community, he was exactly the kind of man she'd have been expected to marry. No surprises there. The future doctor had been in the same graduating class as Cody, likely finishing up medical school and heading into a residency program three and a half years ago. But even though he hadn't been one to give Cody grief like others in the popular crowd, Cody didn't want to think about them being a married couple who'd probably soon be starting a family of little high-class Herringtons.

For all he knew, they already had.

"Cody!" A sharp rapping at the driver-side window startled him back to the present.

He turned to find an auburn-haired, fiftysomething woman smiling at him and his spirits lifted as he stepped out to join her. Sharon Dixon, owner of Dix's Woodland Warehouse, had always been good to his mom. To him, too, come to think of it. Funny how you forgot things like that.

The once-robust woman had lost considerable weight, though, since he'd last seen her. Had she been ill? His mother hadn't mentioned it but, then again, after Paris's engagement he no longer checked online to see what the pretty Miss Perslow might be up to, and forbade Ma to share any Canyon Springs gossip with him.

"As I live and breathe," Sharon whispered, her former smoker's voice as rough as sandpaper. "I'd heard you were back in town, doll. I'm sure your mother is tickled to pieces."

He noticed she didn't include his dad in that observation.

"Look at you. All grown up." Her smile widened as she took him in from his booted toes to the baseball cap on his head. "I imagine you're beating off the girls with a bat these days."

He gave a dubious chuckle. "I can't say that's been much of a problem."

"It will be if you stick around here for long." She winked.

Right. While women elsewhere didn't seem to have any objections to what reflected back at him in his mirror, he doubted any in this town would line up to compete for a guy who'd grown up on the wrong side of the tracks.

"I'm glad our paths crossed today, Cody. I have something for you to give your mom." She dipped her fingers into a jacket pocket, then handed him a check. "It's payment for wreaths and table decorations she left on consignment last week. They sold out within days."

He glanced at the amount on Dix's Woodland Warehouse check stock, then raised a brow. He used to gather bags of ponderosa pinecones for Ma, but had no idea people paid that kind of money for homemade Christmas decorations. He pulled out his wallet and tucked the check inside. "I'll see she gets this."

When she wasn't with Dad.

"I've hesitated to contact her with all that's going on." Sharon gazed at him with sympathy. "But I have customers asking about future deliveries. There would be guaranteed sales if she can find time to put together more wreaths. The greenery or pinecone variety both sell well. Those quilted table runners are popular, too."

"Thanks. I'll let her know, Mrs. Dixon."

"It's Sharon." She wagged a finger at him. "I thought we went through this when you were a teenager."

They had, but he still felt funny calling her by her first name. His Texas-born mama had been a stickler for proper etiquette, Mister and Missus being drilled into him from infancy. Not that his manners had made any difference in this town.

"I'll give the message to her... Sharon."

She studied him for a long moment, windblown snowflakes lighting in her hair. "How is your father?"

Not many asked. Not many cared. But he knew Sharon's concern, like Paris's, was genuine, not merely fishing for gossip to share with neighbors who clucked their tongues at those no-good Hawk men. Dad couldn't care less about their disapproval, but Cody knew it hurt Ma, even though she'd never said as much.

"He's as well as can be expected." Which meant Leroy Hawk wasn't happy and was making sure no one else was, either. The wind shifted direction, whipping around them with a blustery gust. "You'd better get back inside, ma'am, before this wind knocks you off your feet."

"Tell your mother she's in my prayers. You are, too."

"Thanks." He'd willingly take any prayers he could get, for within hours of crossing the Canyon Springs city limits, anger and resentments he thought God had put to rest resurfaced. And now, finding Paris living here... He hadn't expected the ambitious Dalton Herrington to settle down as a small-town doctor.

For a moment he thought Sharon might try to hug him, but apparently his expression prevented that. Instead, she fixed a look on him that said she understood more than he gave her credit for, then she headed back to her store.

Mrs. Dixon had always gone out of her way for his mother, for which he was grateful. It still galled, though, to know people were aware of your lack. That people—like Paris—knew you and yours were struggling and in need of a handout.

But, God willing, not much longer.

"Oh, sweetheart, this dress is breathtaking on you." Saturday morning, the well-coiffed Elizabeth Herrington stepped back to better view Paris in the three-way mirror outside the dressing rooms of a Canyon Springs boutique. "If only Dalton were here to see you."

Paris stiffened, avoiding Elizabeth's misty-eyed gaze in the reflection before her.

"I don't know..." She swished the skirt from side to side, the exhilaration she'd felt when she'd slipped into the floor-length gown evaporating at the mention of Dalton's name.

She didn't fault Elizabeth, though. Widowed not long before the loss of Dalton, she'd loved her only son dearly and generously included Paris in that all-embracing affection. Right from the beginning, when her mother died when Paris was fourteen, Elizabeth had stepped into her best friend's shoes to comfort and guide, to treat Marna and Merle Perslow's daughter as if she were her own. What could possibly have been more natural, more gratifying for her efforts, than to have the girl she adored grow up to marry her only son?

But Elizabeth's fondness had been undeserved. She had no idea Dalton would still be alive...if it hadn't been for Paris.

"I'll think about it." She turned her back to the sales associate to be unzipped.

Elizabeth frowned her disappointment. "It's only a few weeks until the charity event. In this dress you'll be the belle of the ball. It fits as if made for you, and the black velvet sets off your dark hair and fair complexion to perfection."

That's what Paris had thought, too. At first, anyway. Now the dress had lost its luster.

"Please hold this until you hear from me," Elizabeth instructed the sales associate, not questioning that her instructions would be followed even if it might cost the boutique a sale. There were certain advantages to being a Herrington in this town.

Paris returned to the dressing room to change into her street clothes. As much as she loved Elizabeth, as good as Dalton's mom had always been to her, would the dear woman ever let her live her life outside the confines of a relationship with her son?

Maybe this shadow world was Paris's penalty for having attempted to go against family wishes three and a half years ago. Which made what she planned to do now—leave Canyon Springs—seem all the more disloyal to those who loved her.

Once outside the shop, Elizabeth motioned her toward Dix's Woodland Warehouse. "Let's take a look at Dix's seasonal items. I love how it's decorated this year. I think Sharon's daughter has played a huge part in that."

Newly married Kara Kenton was an interior designer, a local girl who'd escaped for a time to Chicago and made her mark on the world. Paris didn't even know where she herself would start if given such an opportunity. She had many interests. Events planning. Gourmet cooking. Photography. Her unfinished degree was in elementary education. How could she choose?

Unlike yesterday, this morning the sun shone in a brilliant blue sky. Although still chilly, the wind had abated and Paris had donned a fitted wool blazer rather than a heavier jacket. Such crazy, patchwork weather in mountain country.

"Isn't this wreath beautiful?" Elizabeth stopped to admire the door decoration as they stepped up onto the porch at Dix's. "It would be perfect in my foyer, don't you think?"

"If it's not for sale, I imagine you can commission one from Lucy Hawk."

"That poor woman, being married to that lowlife Leroy." Elizabeth discreetly lowered her voice as she held open the door to the store. "He got what he had coming, but it will make life more difficult for her. Those sons of his haven't lifted a finger to help, either. They should be ashamed of themselves."

Paris bit back the impulse to defend Leroy's youngest. But she couldn't speak to what Cody's intentions were. Taking sides with a Hawk—any Hawk—wouldn't be advisable.

Once inside the store, they greeted proprietor Sharon Dixon who was dressed in a Christmas-themed sweatshirt, her head topped with a jaunty Santa Claus hat. Then they moved eagerly through the store to take in the abundance of Christmas wares mixed with the usual outdoor gear and general-store staples.

While Elizabeth wandered off, Paris moved to the Christmas tree in the center of the raftered room where tiny fairy lights and dozens of handmade ornaments were arranged in a heartwarming display. She had a collection of mountain-themed decorations and, as always, was eager to add one more. This year's selection would be particularly special for her as, if all went as hoped, it would be her last as a resident of Canyon Springs.

"Parker will be in town for the holidays," Elizabeth pointed out when she eventually rejoined Paris, her arms laden with Christmas merchandise.

"That's nice." Paris avoided her gaze. Dad had also mentioned Dalton's cousin Parker a time or two in recent weeks, expressing pleasure that the up-and-coming attorney might return to Canyon Springs to partner in the same law firm with city councilman Jake Talford.

As if this town needed another lawyer.

But Paris wasn't interested in being railroaded into a relationship with Parker Herrington.

"You *are* going to need an escort for the Christmas gala, you know."

"Actually," Paris said, "as the head of the committee this year, I'll be behind the scenes more often than not, seeing to details of the event. I don't want to be tied to someone with the expectation that I keep them entertained."

Her best friend would be home soon and, as far as she knew, didn't have a date for the gala, either. Maybe they could hang out together. As always, the high-spirited Delaney Marks would pitch in on anything that needed doing—like keeping Paris sane.

Elizabeth pursed her lips. "Parker is capable of entertaining himself and would be a strong complement to your talent for hosting social events such as this."

"Elizabeth, I—"

"Ho ho ho!" a low, masculine voice called from the front door. "Look what I found, Sharon. Ma had a stash of finished ones out in the shed. There's more in my truck."

Startled, Paris turned to see Cody making his way to the checkout counter, his arms laden with beribboned wreaths. Hope sparked. If she could ditch Dalton's mother, maybe now would be an ideal opportunity to talk to him regarding a unsettling phone call she'd received earlier that morning about his mother's role in the Christmas gala. Considering the nature of that untimely call from a committee member, she should never have given in last night to what she thought was

God nudging her to contact Pastor Kenton and agree to take on the weddings.

Elizabeth raised a brow disdainfully as she lowered her voice to a whisper. "Isn't that one of those Hawk boys?"

"Maybe he's here to help his parents."

Elizabeth sniffed. "That'll be the day."

Sharon clapped her hands in delight. "Lucy had these made up? Why didn't she bring them in? Customers are begging for more."

"I imagine she intended to, but with everything that's happened in the past week…" He shrugged, then motioned to the wreaths he'd placed on the counter. "Being kept in the cold shed, they still look and smell as fresh as you could hope for."

"They do look nice. I'll get busy calling people on the waiting list." Still smiling, Sharon placed her hands on her hips and looked up at him. "Aren't you the finest of Santa's helpers, doll."

With a laugh, she impulsively whipped off her holiday hat and stood on tiptoe to secure it on Cody's handsome head. Startled, he glanced uneasily around the store, no doubt to ensure no one had observed the indignity of his impromptu elf act.

Paris couldn't help but smile, but she didn't anticipate the knee-buckling impact when his dark-eyed gaze collided with hers.

Chapter Three

Cody groaned inwardly. Not because Paris caught him with the silly hat on his head, but because she was more beautiful today than she'd been yesterday. How was that even possible?

He swallowed the lump forming in his throat as the seconds ticked, taking in her trim, shapely figure, the brightness of her expressive gray eyes, the delicate curve of her sweet mouth...

Then, coming to his senses, he broke eye contact when he realized she wasn't alone. A frowning Elizabeth Herrington stood beside her. Her mother-in-law.

He sheepishly removed the ridiculous hat from his head, then handed it to Sharon. "I'll get the rest of the wreaths out of the truck."

"Do that, doll. I'll move these to a back room. It's warm in here with that woodstove blazing away."

He nodded, his eyes averted from Paris, then headed outside. He let down the tailgate and lifted the light-weight tarp to reveal half a dozen more wreaths. Well, it could have been worse. It could have been Paris's husband who caught him staring awestruck at his beautiful wife. Her mother-in-law catching him in the act was bad enough.

Mrs. Herrington was no doubt aware that Merle Perslow had warned him off more than once as a teenager and that a stipulation of that job offer twelve years ago included keeping his distance from his daughter. That's what had set off Cody's temper that day. That and the man's patronizing air that he was doing the community a favor by hiring the son of Leroy Hawk to keep him off the streets and out of trouble.

He didn't have long to wait until, from the corner of his eye, he caught a package-laden Mrs. Herrington and Paris exiting the store. Deep in conversation, the older woman didn't glance in his direction, but Paris clearly spied him, then quickly looked away.

Counting slowly to one hundred to ensure they'd walked down the shop-lined street, he'd no sooner lifted the remaining wreaths into his arms when he saw Paris heading briskly back in his direction.

"Good morning, Cody." Her voice came somewhat breathlessly when she halted before him.

"Paris." He nodded an acknowledgment as he placed the wreaths back in the truck bed, his heart beating faster at this unexpected chance to speak with her.

"I'm sorry to bother you, but I got a call earlier this morning about your mother."

He frowned. "My ma? Is something wrong?"

"I'm hoping not." She clasped her gloved hands in front of her, her expression troubled. "It has to do with the annual Christmas gala. I'm the committee head this year."

He was more than familiar with the event, but managed not to grimace. It was a charity dinner and dance that had been a community tradition since long before Cody's family had moved to Canyon Springs. It was for a good cause, of course. But he'd been mortified more than once when his father insisted he line up with other underprivileged children to receive a token toy or item of winter clothing as society's elite looked on benevolently, proud as peacocks of their generosity toward the community's needy.

Needy. It was all he could do to keep his lip from curling at a word reminiscent of a poor Dickensian urchin timidly holding out a bowl for cold porridge. How he despised the image.

He cleared his throat. "You'd mentioned yesterday that my mother is helping. She's making a few decorations, right?"

"More than a few, I'm afraid." A tiny crease formed between Paris's brows. "Some on the committee are concerned that, with your father's illness demanding so much of her time, she won't be able to fulfill her obligations."

"Exactly how many decorations has she agreed to make?" Dad might not always make good on promises, but no one would ever accuse his mother of that. Maybe, though, he should have asked permission before carting off to Dix's the stash of wreaths he'd found in the shed? He'd thought he was doing her a favor.

Paris slipped her hands into her jacket pockets. "Unfortunately, it's more than that. She's overseeing the decorating this year. The props. Christmas trees. Centerpieces. The works."

He gave a low whistle. "I'm surprised she took that on, but I doubt she'll be able to do it now. She's at the hospital almost around the clock and there's no telling how long Dad will be there. I suggest you look elsewhere for a volunteer."

"That's just it. She *isn't* a volunteer." Paris hesitated, as if reluctant to continue. "She's been contracted for a design she submitted several months ago, and she received payment in advance for her time and materials."

Cody flinched. He hadn't expected that. His mother must have needed the money badly. Why hadn't she told him?

"I can reimburse the committee, Paris. That's no problem."

Or it wouldn't be if things worked out as he and his business partner hoped.

Paris offered a feeble smile. "That's thoughtful of you, but the gala is three weeks from tonight, and I've been told nothing at the staging site has been touched in over a week. There's always a last-minute scramble, but usually by this time things are coming together. A few committee members are concerned that she intended to have your father build the sets. And now…"

Leroy Hawk volunteered to do something of that nature? No way. Ma must have had another plan.

"If I reimburse the committee, can't you get someone else to take over?"

A flicker of irritation lit her eyes. "I'll certainly do my best if it comes to that. I know I should talk to your mother directly, but when I saw you here…"

With Dad's situation demanding her every waking moment, Ma probably lost track of time. But he could tell this turn of events had unsettled Paris. The charity event was a huge responsibility on those young, slender shoulders.

"Let me talk to her. And don't worry about it, okay?" He met Paris's gaze with a firm one intended to reassure. "I imagine she has everything under control, but hasn't had time to update the committee."

"Thank you." She tilted her head, the expression in her eyes conveying her gratitude—and reminiscent of the look she'd given him the day long ago when he'd flown to her aid on the playground. "Your mother has my cell phone number, but I can give it to you, too, so you can get in touch with me."

He pulled out his phone and punched in the numbers she recited, then gave her his. But as he watched her head off down the street, he knew this exchange would be far sweeter if she wasn't married to Dalton Herrington.

Back inside Dix's, Sharon motioned for him to follow her to the rear of the store with his armload of wreaths. "I thought you'd fallen down a hole or something."

"No, no holes." Except for the gaping one in his heart.

Inside the storeroom, Sharon took one of the wreaths and placed it on an empty shelf. "How long will you be in town?"

"I'm not sure." He handed her another wreath. "Dad's situation is uncertain and I can't talk to his boss until Monday. But there's plenty to keep me busy at my folks' place in the meantime. Ma hadn't said a word about it, but Dad's let things go since I left."

"You know that I still check on her, don't you? I make sure she's doing all right."

"It's good to know there are people I can count on to make sure Dad doesn't get out of line." Cody grimaced. "Pastor Kenton does the same. Ma and I communicate through occasional phone calls he arranges at the church office. It's better for Ma that Dad not be aware of that."

"I figured you'd keep in touch with her. While life isn't easy being married to your father, I feel certain Lucy hasn't come to any physical harm. God's kept watch."

"He has. But He's had help from the sidelines, as well." Cody placed the last wreath on a shelf. Confession time. "This isn't something I'm proud of, but the night before I left town I told him if he ever laid a hand on Ma, I'd find out about it…and come back to kill him."

Startled eyes rose to his.

He met her gaze without blinking. "I meant it, too, and he knew it."

Sharon offered a dry smile. "It sounds as if I have more to thank the good Lord for in regard to Lucy's safekeeping—and your father's—than I originally thought I did."

"Amen." Cody cracked a smile of his own. "And I don't use that word lightly."

She tilted her head in question.

"It's a long story, but suffice it to say that my name is now recorded in God's Book of Life."

"Well, I'll be." Before he could stop her, she reached up to loop her arms around his neck and pulled him down for a quick hug. "Happiest day of your mother's life."

"And my old man's luckiest."

Sharon chuckled. "You've always been a good boy, Cody. Deep down, I mean. You had some rocky years and I know things were rough what with your father and those two brothers of yours setting the stage. This may never be a place you want to call home, but I know your mother's thrilled you're here now to help out however you can."

He ducked his head. He wasn't worthy of Sharon's praise. He wasn't in town because he wanted to be but because that scripture he'd come across last weekend had punched him in the gut. *Anyone who does not provide for their relatives, and especially for their own household, has denied the faith.*

Yeah, he'd seen to Ma's needs as much as he could, as much as she'd let him. But God had impressed on him to be here as His representative in the flesh this time.

"Well, I'd better get going. There's lots of work to be done at their place." He needed to find out what was up with Ma and the charity event, too.

"You *are* a regular Christmas elf, aren't you?"

"That's me." But they both knew this had never been his favorite season. It always brought too many reminders that he wasn't as well-off as the other kids in town. Too many humiliating opportunities for his dad to send him around for handouts.

Sharon gave him an apologetic glance. "I'm sorry if I embarrassed you in front of Paris and Elizabeth with this silly hat." She waggled her head to send the puffy white ball swinging.

He laughed and snatched it off her head, then popped it on top of his. "No problem. I'm sure I'm the most handsome elf this town has ever seen."

"I imagine you're the most handsome one *Paris* has ever seen."

"I don't know about that." He handed the hat back to her. "I imagine her husband can hold his own—if supplied appropriate headgear, of course."

Sharon's forehead creased. "Her husband?"

"Dalton." Why was she looking at him as if he'd lost his mind? "Dr. Dalton Herrington?"

"You *have* been gone a long time, doll." She placed a gentle hand on his arm. "Paris never married Dalton. He died. Didn't you know?"

"A tuck here and there and it will be a perfect fit," Paris reassured Macy Colston late Saturday afternoon as they exited the Sew-In-Love shop where the final fitting of the young woman's bridal dress had taken place. Low, slate-gray clouds once again hinted at a possibility of snow, the Northland's weather change-able from one minute to the next.

"Thanks again, Paris, for stepping in to take over for Reyna. With all the traveling for my *Hometowns With Heart* blog and my family scattered across the coun-try, I've probably depended on her more than I should. Hopefully I won't infringe on your time too much."

Paris patted the leather portfolio tucked under her arm. "Thankfully, Reyna is extremely organized. Your wedding will be utterly charming with the 1940s theme. I love that Jake's agreeing to wear a fedora and has a friend with a vintage car. So dashing—and romantic."

"He's being a real sport. You have no idea the lengths a man in love will—" Macy brought herself up short, an apologetic look darkening her eyes. "I'm sorry, Paris. Of course you know. Hearing women babble on about their fiancés and weddings can't be easy. Please forgive me if I've been insensitive."

Paris shook her head, determined not to allow a stab of guilt to affect her response. "I love your excitement at God's gift of marriage. That is in no way being insensitive to what happened to me."

When she and Macy parted, Paris headed to her SUV where she paused to leave a phone message for Abby Diaz, suggesting a time for a face-to-face meeting. She'd already spoken with Sharon and hopefully assisting the two of them would be no more time-consuming than Macy and Jake's wedding appeared to be.

With the strong possibility that she might be compelled to dive into decorating for the Christmas gala, she'd need every spare minute she could get. She should have foreseen that this could happen when she'd first heard of Leroy's setback, and not agreed to take on the weddings.

She glanced at her watch. Cody hadn't called yet. Had he forgotten he'd promised to talk to his mother? Should she call to remind him? No. That sounded teenager-ish, as if she wanted an excuse to talk to him.

But what she could do in the meantime was drive out to Pine Shadow Ridge, a gated community which Perslow Property Management oversaw. Its impressive

clubhouse would once again be the site of the Christmas charity event. She could confirm that there was
no sign of Lucy Hawk's recent decorating activity. In
fact, she *should* have confirmed it before speaking with
Cody. What if that committee member was wrong?
Sharlene Odel often thrived on conflict. What if things
were right on schedule and Lucy took offense at Paris
not trusting her?

Not far outside the city limits, Paris slowed to take a
sharp turn before heading up a blacktopped, tree-lined
lane. Ahead she spotted the stone gatehouse and the
security gate where an older-model pickup nosed up to
the wrought-iron barrier. The gatekeeper had stepped
out of his shelter, shaking his head and motioning for
the driver to back up. Harry Campbell knew all the
residents and vendors authorized to come and go. Apparently this one didn't pass muster.

Allowing adequate space for the truck to back up,
Paris put the SUV in Park, adjusted the heater and settled in to wait. Hopefully Harry would get this straightened out quickly and she could be on her way.

But…wait. Wasn't that truck similar to the one
Cody had been driving? Turning off the ignition, Paris
stepped out into the nippy late-afternoon air. A few
snowflakes kissed her cheeks as she approached the
gatehouse, and Harry's polite but firm voice reached
her ears.

"I'm sorry, sir, but like I said, you have to move.
You're blocking those who are authorized for entrance."
Harry glanced in her direction, then motioned apolo-
getically toward the truck. "Sorry, Miss Perslow."

At the mention of her name, Cody poked his handsome head out the driver-side window to look back in her direction.

"Paris, please tell this guy I'm legit. Like I told him, I'm here on behalf of the Christmas gala."

Did he intend to personally check out the status of his mother's work, to see how bad it was—or wasn't?

"He's legit," she confirmed as she came to stand by the irritated gatekeeper. Then she cast a cool glance toward Cody, who flashed an I-told-you-so look in Harry's direction. "It's customary, Mr. Hawk, to have authorization in advance. Harry wouldn't be doing his job had he let you in."

No doubt Harry had taken one look at Cody's weathered vehicle and decided this man had no business there. He'd know Leroy, of course, and could easily have gone to school with one of Cody's troublemaking brothers. A Hawk was a Hawk in this town, with a one-size-fits-all reputation.

She nodded to the gatekeeper. "Thanks, Harry. I'll vouch for him."

But was that wise? She had to keep reminding herself that Cody might have been a much-maligned boy who'd always been kind to her, but she had no idea who he was as a man.

Harry nodded and returned to the gatehouse, then the massive gates slowly opened. She glanced at Cody.

"Do you know where you're going?"

He shook his head and grinned, a heart-stopping flash of white teeth in his tanned face. "Why don't you lead the way, Miss Perslow?"

Back in her SUV, endeavoring to quiet the now-skittering beat of her heart, she watched Cody ease his truck through the gate. Then she followed until he pulled over to let her pass. The tree-lined lane curved among pines and boulders, a gradual incline that wouldn't give anyone too much wintertime grief. The majority of residents vacated after Labor Day, of course, not returning until early summer. But diehards remained throughout the year or returned on winter weekends to ski nearby slopes and cozy up to a roaring fireplace.

When they reached the top of the rise, the log-and-stone clubhouse came into distant view through the pines, but she took a sharp right turn down a narrow blacktopped road marked "Private." When she finally reached the large steel structure where heavy maintenance equipment and supplies were housed, she shut off the engine and got out as Cody pulled in beside her.

As he approached where she stood next to the substantial building, his dark eyes assessed his surroundings.

"This is new. And I'm guessing that was the clubhouse I glimpsed before we turned off. The foundation was being poured about the time I left town."

She'd forgotten he'd have still lived in Canyon Springs when the project was getting underway. Motioning to a door off to the side, she held a keycard to the security pad next to it. Cody reached for the latch and opened it for her.

"Thanks," she said as she stepped into the dimly lit interior, noting that the workers had left for the day. She felt along the wall for the light switch just as Cody reached for it, too, his warm fingers brushing hers as together they illuminated the high-ceilinged space. She pulled back as a shot of awareness bolted through her.

Catching her breath, she pointed across the spacious interior to the far corner. "We've set up an area for your mother to work. Since you've come to take a look, I assume you've talked to Lucy?"

"I phoned her."

Please, God, let Lucy be able to finish this project. This was supposed to be a special Christmas. My last one as a resident of Canyon Springs. But everything is snowballing out of control. Please?

She took a steadying breath. "And?"

"And..." Cody's brows formed a sympathetic, inverted *V.* "She can't follow through on it. Dad's too sick. She needs to be there for him."

"But she signed a contract. Accepted payment."

"Yes, she's well aware of all that."

"Well, then, what—?"

"What am I doing here? I wanted to see how much she's done." Cody glanced toward the work area, then once again leveled a steady gaze on Paris. "And see how much *I* have left to do."

Chapter Four

A soft, startled breath escaped Paris's lips. Cody wasn't sure if that was good or bad. All he knew was that it pierced his heart and made him more determined to make good on his mother's commitment to the holiday gala. For Ma. For Paris.

She shot him a confused look. "You're taking over for your mother?"

"She feels badly about letting you down. Being unable to fulfill a promise isn't something she takes lightly."

He still marveled that Ma said Dad had agreed to help out, to do the construction for her. That sure wasn't the Leroy Hawk he knew.

"She asked you to do this?"

"I offered to do it when I realized how upset she was."

When I sensed how upset you would be.

"But your mother is an artist."

Cody chuckled. "That she is. And I'm not a half-bad one myself, if you'll recall."

He'd once garnered the courage to waylay Paris as

she walked home alone from school one afternoon. He'd shown her a sketch he'd done while observing her from a far corner of study hall. The drawing was one of many where he'd done his best to capture her expressive eyes and her shimmering dark hair draping over her shoulders.

That day she'd stared for a long moment at the sketch he'd handed her, telling her she could keep it. She'd blushed furiously, thanked him, then hurried home without a backward glance.

Had she kept it? Or tossed it in the trash?

"You are," she said softly, her cheeks even now tinged a delicate pink, "a very good artist."

So she did remember.

"Ma has the staging designs worked out. All I have to do is build them. Everything will be true to the original plan the committee approved months ago."

She glanced uncertainly toward the work area, then at him. "Don't you have a job you have to get back to?"

He could tell it embarrassed her to ask. The older Hawk boys hadn't been known to stay with anything long. Where were they now? In Texas again? New Mexico? Barry had been in and out of who knows how many marriages and had done time in jail for violation of a restraining order. Carson had been in and out of trouble with the law as well and fathered more than a few illegitimate children.

"I do have a job, but it's flexible enough at the moment to let me remain in town a few weeks to help my mother. And *you*."

From the look in her eyes, he shouldn't have added that personal postscript. But it didn't much matter whether she liked it or not. He wasn't going to let Ma down and allow her reputation to be dragged down to the level of his dad and half brothers.

"Ma's subcontracting the project to me. If you'll make sure Harry the Gatekeeper knows I have approval so I can come and go here and at the clubhouse as time allows, I guarantee the staging will more than meet your expectations and your deadline."

He'd do it if he had to work twenty-four hours a day.

Could she tell that he had no expectations tacked onto his offer of assistance? Neither of them had alluded to that long-ago night when he'd poured out his heart to her, but it hung like an invisible barrier between them. As much as he'd like to spend every moment of his time in Canyon Springs with Paris, even with Dalton out of the picture he wouldn't attempt to insert himself into her world again as he'd done twelve years ago.

Doubt colored her eyes. "I'm not sure—"

"I'd say you could think it over and get back to me later." He nodded toward the work area as his eyes remained locked on hers. "But there's no time to accommodate much thinking, let alone much 'later.' I need to get crackin'. And you need to get on out of here and let me get to work."

Cody's authoritative words still echoed through Paris's mind on Monday morning as she poured herself another glass of orange juice. They'd been spoken as if he were the boss and she an unwelcome intrusion on his valuable time.

You need to get on out of here and let me get to work.

She should have protested, should have told him the contract was with his mother, not him, and that the committee would make alternate arrangements. But what choice did she truly have with the gala now fewer than three weeks away? Bristling under the surface, she'd nevertheless obediently departed, stopping off at the gatehouse to inform Harry of Cody's project work and to authorize the use of Lucy's keycard.

She *should* be relieved. A decorating disaster had been averted at the midnight hour. Everything would be finished on time if Cody was true to his word, and there would be little need to interact with him. He'd made it clear he could handle it on his own and would brook no interference that might delay him in meeting his mother's obligations.

So why was she feeling anything but relief?

"Something on your mind, sweetheart?" Her father rose from the breakfast table to gaze out at the thickly pined acreage from the French doors of his sprawling log home. It had been her home again, too, ever since she'd cut short her junior year at Northern Arizona University and returned when Dad had what he referred to as "my ticker episode." After Mom's death, he hadn't taken good care of himself and had worked too hard. Following a heart bypass and a change in lifestyle facilitated by the diligence of his daughter, Paris hadn't returned to school—a decision she was increasingly coming to regret.

Dad turned away from a light flurry of snow that lent the view a Christmas-card beauty. "You seem distracted this morning."

"I'm mentally planning out my day," she said lightly,

instinctively knowing her father wouldn't approve of Cody offering his services on behalf of the charity event. He'd hear of it soon enough, though, because she'd have to tell the committee tonight. Some—like Elizabeth—would doubt the wisdom of permitting him to take part. Trusting the job to the talented Lucy Hawk was one thing. A Hawk male was quite another.

She'd have to be prepared for pushback.

"Don't feel obligated to help with those weddings," her father stated, assuming that was the issue troubling her. "It's okay to change your mind. There's not a soul in town who would fault you for not lending a hand."

"No, but…" Paris smoothed the cloth napkin in her lap. What Dad said was true. Anyone who'd read the local paper's gushing front-page article in which her engagement had been announced—and later experienced the shock of Dalton's death reverberating through the community—could guess at the pall which descended on her at the prospect of weddings.

"I think, though," she continued as her father leaned in to kiss her on the top of her head as he'd done since she was a little girl, "it's time I got over my aversion to weddings."

That's the conclusion she'd prayerfully come to Friday night and now, with Cody seeing to the decorating, she could once again conclude it was the right decision. Things had gone well enough with Macy on Saturday, hadn't they? Except for those awkward moments when the soon-to-be bride apologized for her perceived insensitivity. Unfortunately, Paris's strategy of wedding avoidance had only served to draw sympathy she didn't deserve.

Dad studied her a long moment. Widowed fourteen years ago when her mother's multiple sclerosis had finally taken its toll, he was a still-handsome man in his early sixties, his dark hair silvering at the temples. He'd caught the eye of more than a few women since Mom's passing. But not only had he not remarried, he never dated, unless you counted occasionally asking a friend or business associate to accompany him to an event. Most often he went alone. Not that anyone could ever replace Marna Perslow, but Paris had always thought Elizabeth would be a perfect match. Why, after her husband's death, had Dad never acted on what she sensed might be a mutual attraction?

Dad had to be lonely at times and that's likely why he threw himself too fully into his work, a fact that worried her at the thought of leaving him on his own when she left Canyon Springs. This morning a crease had formed across his forehead when she'd mentioned Cody Hawk's scheduled appointment and it hadn't yet smoothed.

"Don't let our good pastor pressure you," he said. "Sharon is entirely capable of handling things on her own and the other two young ladies can call on family and friends if needed. Everyone in town understands the pain weddings bring to you."

Actually, there *wasn't* a soul in town who understood her pain. Not the true source of it, anyway. Would involvement with the weddings, as her pastor had suggested, help her heal?

Nevertheless, she nodded as her father headed to his study, then she checked the time. With the office assistant out again today, she needed to get there by eight to cover the phones and front desk. But she'd promised to give Dad a hand with paperwork for sales he'd be closing on this week, so she could conveniently be in the back room when Cody arrived at nine-thirty.

Why couldn't she stop thinking about him?

She'd been surprised to glimpse him in church with his mother yesterday. But to her irritation, throughout the service—and afterward—she couldn't keep her thoughts from wandering to that long-ago night when he'd told her he loved her. Had always loved her. Would love her forever.

She gave a soft, scoffing laugh as she headed up the stairs to her room. *Teenagers.*

But her heart beat more quickly as she recalled in excruciating detail how he'd stared down at her that night. How she'd leaned in ever-so-slightly toward him, certain he'd kiss her. Even though she'd dutifully turned him down, she'd been mesmerized by the powerful yearning in his black-brown eyes.

But he hadn't kissed her.

Instead, he'd quirked a smile and stepped back as if pleased with what he'd read in her eyes. He'd brazenly delivered his line about her one day begging him to marry her. And then he was gone, leaving her stunned.

Cody had been clear on his long-term intentions that night. But what was he thinking now? And why did the prospect of his continued interest—or lack of it—unsettle her so?

"Thank you for your generosity, Mr. Perslow. But the Hawk family no longer takes charity. I'm more than willing to pay Dad's share of the insurance premium."

Cody sat across the desk from the owner of Perslow Real Estate, trying to figure out where the generous response of his father's employer was coming from. He'd expected resistance, maybe even an argument, but neither had been forthcoming. Even though Paris's father wasn't obligated by law due to the fact that he had fewer than fifty employees, he seemed more than willing to make concessions to accommodate Leroy Hawk.

"That's a commendable sentiment, Cody, but it's a nonissue. This isn't charity. I'd extend this offer to any employee who'd worked for me as long as your father has."

Sixteen years. That's longer than Dad had worked anyplace in his whole life. Even in Canyon Springs, he'd drifted from job to job for several years until Merle Perslow hired him on full-time when Cody was in eighth grade. Dad could be a diligent, skilled worker whose productivity outshone just about anybody— when he wasn't on a drinking binge. Cody grudgingly handed it to Mr. Perslow for his willingness not to see Dad's stroke as an opportunity to immediately kick him off the payroll.

Cody leaned forward. "I appreciate that, but you are aware, aren't you, that my father's situation may not be..." He hadn't seen Dad yet—concerned that his sudden appearance might trigger another stroke—but he didn't like to think of the robust Leroy as permanently disabled, his mental adeptness impaired and motor skills incapacitated. "His recovery is uncertain."

His likelihood of survival was still unclear.

Mr. Perslow gave a brisk nod. "Then we'll cross that bridge when we come to it, won't we?"

This was odd. Genuinely odd. But Cody had prayed for days that Paris's father would, if nothing else, be willing to let Cody continue paying his father's portion—or all—of the insurance premiums. He'd prayed, too, that his dad's position would be held open should he eventually be able to return, and that a paycheck would be forthcoming until it was determined if he had to go on permanent disability. Merle's response was more than Cody could have hoped for.

He stood and extended his hand to the older man who also rose to his feet. "Thank you...sir."

A faint smile touched Mr. Perslow's lips as they gripped hands, no doubt remembering the last time Cody had been in this office and flung that term of respect less than respectfully.

"Will you be in town long?"

Why did that question sound more loaded than a casual inquiry? "For a few weeks at least."

"I see." The older man cut him a sharp look as he ran his hand through his hair. The flecks of silver weren't the only thing indicating that twelve years had passed since their last meeting. He appeared older in other ways now. He was still trim and tanned, but there was a general air of world-weariness that had been present throughout their brief conversation.

Then, unexpectedly, a flash of the old Mr. Perslow lit his features as he pinned Cody with an uncompromising look. "My daughter's heart is fragile. There's someone else coming into her life now. Don't mess it up."

Cody's eyes narrowed as the icy words hung between them. A warning. It was almost as if he knew

Cody had lain awake the past two nights since learning Paris hadn't married Dalton after all.

Even his days had been consumed with getting his head around this unexpected revelation. Sharon hadn't mentioned Paris's involvement with anyone, so Mr. Perslow could be lying about that. Then again, he wouldn't be surprised if she was seeing someone three and a half years after the death of her fiancé. Men must have lined up around the block, waiting for a suitable period of mourning to pass so they could make their move.

Hadn't he been contemplating that himself?

But now, as his resentful gaze met her father's, it became suddenly clear why he'd been so accommodating of Cody's requests on behalf of Leroy Hawk. His concessions had been a bribe to stay away from his daughter.

Before Cody could garner a response, the phone on the desk rang. Mr. Perslow frowned as he glanced down at the illuminated display, obviously irritated at the interruption. Then with a final cutting look at Cody he lifted the receiver, his tone at once warm and welcoming.

"Donald! Let me guess. Your wife has visions of a Canyon Springs Christmas dancing in her head and the two of you want to take another look at that condo."

Cody quietly walked out into the hallway and closed the office door behind him. He should have known Paris's father hadn't gone soft, that his generosity held an edge. A cunning purpose.

A muscle in his jaw tightened as anger flared and a too-familiar sense of shame pressed in. It was the same feeling he'd had when Paris's old man had caught him, at age sixteen, gazing longingly at the beauty of his fourteen-year-old daughter. In no uncertain terms, he'd let Cody know that a Hawk had no business "looking on the high shelf."

Cody had continued to look, if covertly. But even that last night when he'd longed to cup her beautiful face in his hands, to kiss her trembling lips, he'd held himself back.

Remembered he had no right.

Now to have her father suggest he'd barge into Paris's life and mess things up galled, and the fresh reminder that he was barred from pursuing her burned deep into his gut.

"Cody?"

The soft, questioning word echoed down the hall, jerking him from his thoughts. He turned away from the door, his spirits lifting at the vision before him. Hands on her slim hips, Paris's wide gray eyes studied him with open curiosity and, even in blue jeans and a bulky fisherman's sweater, she exuded a striking refinement, a delicate femininity. High-shelf material, indeed.

"Good morning, Paris." She hadn't been at the front desk when he'd arrived.

"Did everything go okay?"

"Your father's been...very helpful." He moved down the hallway to where she stood just inside the waiting room.

A dark brow rose. "I know you had concerns about your dad's situation."

"All addressed." With an unacceptable rider tacked on.

"I'm glad." She looked behind her where a middle-aged couple sat in the waiting area, admiring the Christmas tree. Then she again looked up at Cody. "Do you mind if we step outside for a few minutes?"

Although he hadn't knowingly made any promises to Mr. Perslow, they had shaken hands and it wouldn't bode well if her father saw him with Paris so soon after their conversation. Cody couldn't risk the insurance for Leroy Hawk being cancelled. Not until he had time to assess other options.

Nevertheless...

"Lead the way."

Chapter Five

Paris reached to the coatrack for her gray wool jacket.

"May I help with that?"

She glanced up uncertainly, but Cody's kindhearted expression reassured. She nodded and he held out the coat behind her, taking care not to touch her as she slipped her arms into the sleeves.

"Thank you."

She started toward the door, then stopped, returning to the front desk to pick up a lidded, holiday-designed box, about twice the width of a shoe box. What had gotten her so flustered that she'd almost forgotten what she intended to give Cody?

They stepped outside where snowflakes danced merrily in the air, almost in time to the holiday carols coming from the overhead Main Street loudspeakers.

"What can I do for you, Paris?"

He looked especially handsome this morning, but seemed somewhat on edge. Had things really gone as well with her father as he said they had?

She held out the box. "These are cookies for your

mother to share with the hospital staff—and something extra for her, too."

He took the box from her, his expression uncertain. "Thank you."

"I remember her bringing homemade cookies those times my mother had to be hospitalized and how much the staff enjoyed them. I don't imagine your mother has any time to bake right now, so…"

He still didn't look as if he knew what to make of her gift. Almost suspicious, if she had to interpret his expression. But then life had probably taught Cody not to trust anyone.

"No, she doesn't have much time for herself these days." He placed his hand on top of the box. "She says the nurses have been great. Dad's not the easiest patient to care for, so she'll enjoy having something to give them as a thank-you."

Good. He finally got it.

"I imagine your dad was surprised to see you, wasn't he?"

"He…" Cody hesitated, as if unsure how his response would be taken. "He doesn't know I'm here yet."

Surprised, her brows arched. "You haven't gone to see him?"

He gripped the box more tightly. "I drove Ma to the hospital in Show Low a few days last week and on Sunday. But we're trying not to hit him with anything that might bring on another stroke."

"Like you suddenly showing up after twelve years," she said softly, the tension flickering through his eyes making her wish she hadn't brought up the subject in the first place.

"Right." He stared down at the cookie box and she could sense his emotions swirling through him. Dread at the thought of again facing his abusive father and shame that she might not think him a good son for putting off that inevitable encounter.

"I personally think that's a wise decision on your and your mother's part." She placed her hand on his forearm and his head jerked up, his eyes searching for truthfulness in her words. "You have to put his well-being first. There will be plenty of time for the two of you to get reacquainted."

Cody's grip on the box relaxed a fraction.

"Ma's mentioned to him a few times that I might come to visit. He doesn't react one way or another, so we're thinking I should stop in soon and see how it goes."

"Hopefully well. I'll be praying so."

"Thanks."

He glanced around, as if realizing they were talking in a public setting, as though suspecting someone might be observing their chat. What would be wrong with that? But she withdrew her hand from his arm and he took a step back.

He cleared his throat as his gaze again caught hers. Softened. "I've been remiss in not expressing my sympathy for your loss, Paris."

Oh, no, not now. She didn't want this conversation to be about her, about concern for her grief.

"I knew you'd gotten engaged four years ago and assumed you and Dalton married. Until Sharon Dixon told me on Saturday about the car accident."

His mother hadn't told him years ago? He hadn't

known when he'd come to her father's office on Friday? Why ever not? Everyone in town knew about it.

"Dalton was a good guy," he added.

"Yes, he was." At least Cody wasn't a gusher like many who assured her they understood her loss, who wanted to reminisce about her fiancé as a young boy, a teen, a man.

Cody lifted the lid on the cookie box, the mouthwatering scent of homemade molasses cookies sure to tempt even the strictest of dieting medical staff. A small envelope lay on top, inscribed to Lucy.

His smile quirked. "So you think you can trust me to get these to the hospital uneaten?"

Relieved at the change in subject, she playfully placed her hands on her hips. "You'd better, mister."

The corners of his eyes crinkled. "Or what?"

"Or… I'll tell your mother, and then you'll be in big trouble."

"That's a threat intended to make me shake in my boots?" He grinned, then bumped the envelope with his finger. "What's in there?"

"Gift cards to Wyatt's Grocery and the gas station. I'm sure with the expenses your father is incurring and the many trips to—"

"Thank you, but Hawks don't take charity." Cody's smile dissolved as he snapped the box lid closed and thrust it toward her.

Charity? What was he talking about? She gently pushed the box back, her eyes firmly meeting his. "This isn't charity. It's a gift for your mother to use where she needs it most."

He opened the box again and extracted the envelope. "I'll take the cookies to her, but not the gift cards."

Confused at his reaction, she put her hands behind her back, refusing the envelope he held out. "I don't want them back. You're being silly."

"You think so?"

"Your mother does nice things for people in this town and this is a small way of showing appreciation in a practical way."

"I value your concern but, like I said, Hawks don't take handouts anymore." His jaw hardened. "If there's anything she needs, I'll see that she gets it."

She folded her arms. Why was he being so stubborn? "This isn't a handout."

"Let's not quibble over semantics, Paris," he said quietly as he tucked the envelope in the snug space between her folded arms, then gave the box lid a firm pat. "I'll see that Ma gets these. Maybe minus a cookie or two."

He winked. But his attempt to inject humor fell flat with her.

"Please don't be this way, Cody. You know I—"

"Your thoughtfulness is appreciated. Let it go at that." He lifted his hand for a lighthearted salute, then turned away, the cookie box tucked under his arm as he headed down the street.

Stubborn, pride-filled man. Why was he acting as if she'd likened his mother to a panhandler on the street?

"Cody!" It was all she could do not to stamp her foot like a two-year-old in a tantrum.

He lifted his hand again in a parting wave, but didn't stop or look back. Kept right on walking.

She drew an irritated breath. She hadn't even had a chance to ask him how things were going with the Christmas project, if he still thought it doable or if she needed to recruit additional volunteers.

But she wasn't about to chase after him.

Conscious of Paris's exasperated gaze and guilt-ridden for not having yet visited his father, Cody climbed into his truck. He brushed the snow from his hair, hoping the high country didn't get heavy snow while he was here. He had his eye on a new Ford F-150 but, with his vehicle in the shop, he'd been forced to commandeer one of his business partner's old junkers. It couldn't be counted on in significant snowfall.

He checked for traffic and backed out, but didn't allow himself to glance in Paris's direction. Then he pressed his foot to the accelerator and headed for his folks' place.

He didn't think of it as home.

Dad and Ma still lived in a double-wide trailer that they'd settled in when Cody had been in ninth grade and his half brothers—who only lived with their father when their mother periodically kicked them out of her place in New Mexico—were long gone.

Looking back, where had his folks gotten the money for a down payment? He wouldn't ask. Better not to know. Leroy Hawk had done time in Texas for forging his employer's signature when Cody was a second grader. Another time for attempted extortion.

How had Ma endured it?

He knew it was foolish, but he couldn't help but feel responsible. When he was a kid he'd overheard her telling someone he was a preemie, but it didn't take a mathematician to figure out his folks had to get married. Maybe if he hadn't come along, Ma would have married someone more deserving of her.

Cody shook his head as he rounded a treed curve, the windshield wipers beating a sporadic rhythm against the lightly falling snow. By the time he'd entered school here midautumn of fifth grade, he'd been pulled in and out of schools in three different states and five different towns. It was amazing he'd managed to graduate at all. He owed that to his mother—and to his own stubborn streak.

And speaking of stubbornness... He glanced at the box on the seat beside him. Had he been wrong to turn down the gift cards for his mother? Paris meant well and he hadn't intended to hurt her feelings as he suspected he had. God only knew how many people had slipped a little something extra to Ma in the years he'd been gone. After his departure from town, he hadn't had much to spare for her at first. He should be thankful, not resentful, that people cared.

Paris couldn't have known her thoughtfulness would push a hot button. Touch his pride. He'd overreacted.

Lord, I've got to stop taking things like this so personally, seeing it as a slap in the face every time someone is moved to an act of kindness on my or my family's behalf.

As he pulled onto the property that his mother had optimistically named Hawk's Hope in deference to a Canyon Springs property-naming tradition, his cell phone chimed.

"Yo, Trev. Any word yet?"

"Not yet," Cody's business partner, Trevor Cane, confirmed, "I hoped maybe you'd been contacted directly."

He could picture his stocky, well-groomed friend pacing the tiles of his Phoenix patio. It would be a balmy sixty-five degrees down there today, quite a contrast to the mountain country a few hours north and six thousand feet higher.

Cody chuckled. "If I get the call, you'll know when I know. That wouldn't be anything I'd keep to myself."

"I guess I'm getting antsy. Do you think we'll hear anything soon or is that wishful thinking?"

Cody was antsy, too, although he wouldn't admit it to Trevor. So much rode on this business deal, and hearing a "yes" would sure be the answer to a truckload of prayers.

"It might not be until after the first of the year. I advise you to sit back, relax and enjoy your family while you can. If this goes through as we hope, there's going to be more than enough work to keep us both occupied for some time to come."

"How much longer will you be up there?"

"At least until Christmas. Things are still touch-and-go with Dad."

He glanced toward the trailer. He'd started cleaning up the property, clearing out old tires, broken equipment and other assorted junk. But there were repairs still to be made to the trailer itself, fencing and outbuildings. Maybe one day, though, he'd get Ma that cabin in the pines Dad always promised her.

Cody reached for the cookie box, then stepped out into the lightly falling snow. "Ma's running interference between Dad and the hospital staff, trying to keep him calm and them from calling the cops."

Nicotine and alcohol withdrawal and a stroke on top of that. Not a nice combo.

"But the good thing is—" Cody gave a bitter chuckle as he unlocked the front door and stepped inside, his nostrils flaring with distaste at the lingering scent of stale cigarettes "—his right arm is incapacitated, so he won't be swinging it at me anytime soon."

"Man, it had to be tough growing up that way."

For almost a dozen years, he and Trev had been as close as God probably intended real brothers to be. He hadn't had any contact with his half brothers since he'd been in middle school and they'd gone out on their own. But his friendship with Trevor had more than made up for that lack.

"Yeah, well, I guess this is where I'm supposed to say growing up like that made me who I am today. Right?" Cody placed the cookie box on the dining table.

Trevor huffed a laugh. "That's one way of looking at it."

It was the only way to look at it, otherwise it made no sense. No sense at all. Just like coming back to town and discovering Paris hadn't married…

As if picking up on his line of thought, Trevor ventured deeper. "So, did that dream gal of yours and her hubby come home for Thanksgiving?"

Even though he'd long ago faced reality and dated a number of women since leaving Canyon Springs, when Paris had gotten engaged his friend and his friend's new wife had been there to pick up the pieces. They'd reeled Cody back in when he'd foolishly acted out in ways for which he was now ashamed. Trevor and Maribeth had played an instrumental role in directing his steps toward God, for which he'd be forever grateful.

"Actually...she's living here. But not married." He navigated his way across the room to slide open the door to the rear of the property and let the cold December air hit him full in the face.

"You're kidding. She's divorced already?"

"Nope. Never married." He stepped onto the snow-wet deck. "The guy was killed in a car accident before the wedding."

Trevor gave a low whistle. "Have you talked to her?"

"I have."

"And?"

He ran his hand along the deck railing, brushing off the thin layer of snow with his bare hand and noting a need for a good sanding and paint job. "Apparently she's involved with someone else now."

"Sorry, bud. The timing stinks. But I hope by seeing her again you got closure. You know, that you now recognize she's no longer the girl of your adolescent infatuation."

Cody drew a long breath. Trev was right. Paris was no longer the girl of his teenage fantasies.

She was the woman of his grown-man dreams.

Chapter Six

"Remember to stop and smell the roses, Paris," Dad playfully admonished on Thursday morning when he'd caught her staring at her lengthy "to do" list. "Or the pine trees, rather. Remember, this *is* the Christmas season. Ho ho ho."

She smiled indulgently. That was easily said by someone who didn't lift a finger to help with holiday preparations. When Mom had been alive he'd left that up to her. Now it fell to his daughter.

"By the way, honey, great breakfast as always. Thanks." He gave her a thumbs-up, then headed off to work for an early morning meeting.

Guilt gnawed at his words of appreciation. He'd be fending for himself soon enough…would he make the effort to eat healthy or resort to processed foods and dining out?

With a sigh, she again picked up her list from the kitchen counter. She had more than enough to keep herself occupied all day what with Dad's open house taking place tomorrow afternoon and evening. While he was okay with some items being catered, he preferred the homemade touch and enjoyed bragging about it.

Paris had completed the grocery shopping after work yesterday and decorated the house over a series of evenings this week. Yes, there were still more than enough activities to fill her day even though she'd deliberately not scheduled any property showings. And yet...

Before she knew it, she was driving through the gates of Pine Shadow Ridge in the predawn light. Despite Cody's reassurance, as the event's head she should monitor his progress and report back to her fellow committee members. As suspected, there had been more than a few unhappy campers at Monday night's meeting when she'd enlightened them on Cody's role.

If Dad had heard about it, though, he'd kept silent, which made her think he was still in the dark. That wouldn't last long, though, so she needed evidence to back up the wisdom of accepting Cody's assistance.

Inside the maintenance building, she stopped to speak to a few men who were adjusting a snow blade on a pickup truck. Then she made her way to the far corner where each year a makeshift workshop was set up for the Christmas event. Stacks of lumber, sawhorses, paint cans and brushes were now organized in an orderly fashion. Cody's touch, no doubt, as they hadn't appeared as well-arranged on Saturday. He'd already framed a number of the log cabin facades Lucy had illustrated in her design.

A High Country Christmas.

That theme had been Paris's idea. It seemed appropriate for what would likely be her last in the mountain town she'd grown up in. She ran her hand up the side of one of the sturdy frames as a knot tightened in her stomach. She didn't know what she planned to do when she left here. Return to school? Get a job—doing what? Continuing to sell real estate? She only knew that, as hard as it would be to leave, it was time to say goodbye to Canyon Springs.

"Well, Paris—" A low masculine voice close behind startled her from her reverie. "Do things meet with your approval?"

By the fact that she was here at this hour, it was evident she didn't trust him.

It was clear, too, from the guilty look in her eyes, that she'd come early thinking he wouldn't be here so she could snoop around. But he'd been up at his usual hour, touching base with Trevor who was also an early riser. Now he had a window of time to make progress on the project.

Despite their differences of opinion on Monday, however, you wouldn't catch him complaining about Paris keeping him from his work as he'd done the last time she'd been here. Dressed in a plaid skirt and tall suede boots, the rest of her was bundled in a fawn-colored, faux-fur jacket that made her look as huggable as a teddy bear.

She smelled good, too.

"Good morning, Cody. You're coming right along here, I see."

He smiled to himself, noting she'd ignored his somewhat accusatory question. Nor did she broach the subject of the rejected gift cards, where their last conversation had ended. "This part is going fairly quickly. It's the painting and detail work that will be most time consuming."

That would also be the part the committee would eye most critically.

"I was wondering if you'd like a quick tour of the clubhouse where the gala will be held. I didn't show you around on Saturday."

"Thanks, but I gave myself an unguided tour after you left. I needed to take measurements and get a feel for the space to make sure Ma's designs-come-to-life are proportionally appropriate."

"Then you're a step ahead of me." She turned again to the framing he'd completed. "So you'll fill in the openings with fabric or canvas you can paint?"

"Actually, I think I can do better than that." He stepped to a worktable where his mother's sketches fanned over the surface. "I've checked out options to attach lightweight tubing to the framework. Then a troweled-on substance that sticks securely to the surface will add a loglike texture. It should then be easy to spray paint a base color with only highlights and lowlights added by hand for further dimension."

Paris's eyes brightened, envisioning what he was talking about, and his heart lifted in gratification that she got it. He wouldn't have to defend his strategy or try to talk her into it.

"I like that idea, Cody."

Paris smiled up at him and his heart further lightened. That smile had been his sought-after reward for more years than he could count. You'd have thought its power to sway him would have diminished. But maybe his reaction to it was merely a residual teenage crush, a lingering flicker of hope that had dogged him for too many years?

Who was the man she was seeing now anyway? No doubt he'd be a prominent member of this community or a neighboring one. Did he know him? Who could he ask without appearing too interested?

"It's not that your mother's original plan isn't a good one," she added, "but the three-dimensional aspect will add so much."

He basked in her approval. "That's the plan."

A smile touched her lips and he got the impression she was relieved. She might not yet trust him—after all, she didn't know him now any more than he knew her—but he was determined to prove she could count on him. To prove a Hawk was as good as his word.

"I know your mother appreciates having you here. You know, to help with the Christmas gala and with your Dad's situation, too."

"I'm doing my best."

Did Paris recall the bad blood between father and son? The bruises he'd once revealed to her? He sure remembered how as a grade-schooler she'd cautiously reached out gentle fingers to caress the swollen, purpled skin along his rib cage. How tears had pooled in her eyes. He hadn't wanted her to feel sorry for him, though, and never showed her again. Never spoke of it.

Cody pulled his thoughts back to the present and, as if determined to lighten the mood, Paris cut him an almost playful look that caught him off guard. "I suppose—"

"Paris! I thought that looked like your SUV. What brings you out here so early this morning?"

They turned to see a man not many years older than Cody striding toward them, the superior quality of his wool jacket and the dismissive look he gave Cody spelling out his economic equality with Paris.

Cody's eyes narrowed. Was this the man she was seeing?

"Hello, Owen." Paris's smile widened as if genuinely happy at his arrival, but when the man reached her side, she didn't fling her arms around him or plant a kiss on his lips when he leaned in to hug her. But that didn't mean this Owen guy wasn't the one Mr. Perslow had mentioned as "coming into her life."

"Now, don't you look adorable in that furry jacket, my dear." Owen's eyes warmed as he gazed down at her. "Like a cuddly teddy bear."

Paris laughed, but Cody gritted his teeth at the assessment mirroring his own. No doubt this Owen character noticed her shapely booted legs as well, but knew better than to comment on them. At least in front of Cody.

"Owen, I want you to meet Cody Hawk," Paris said, laying a hand on the newcomer's arm. "Cody, this is Owen Fremont, one of the newest investors in Pine Shadow Ridge."

"Hawk, did you say?" An arrogant brow rose as the two men shook hands, both of them obviously sizing each other up and finding the other lacking.

"Yes," Paris continued, unaware of or choosing to ignore Owen's haughty tone. But at least she hadn't introduced the guy as her boyfriend or fiancé, so there was a good chance their relationship hadn't been signed, sealed and delivered. "Cody's mother is the decorative designer of this year's Christmas gala and he's helping us out while he's in town."

"I see."

Probably more than Cody wanted him to see. It wouldn't take a genius to recognize that another man had taken notice of this very attractive woman.

Paris motioned to the wooden structures next to her. "Cody's framing up the faux log cabins for our high country Christmas theme. He's brimming with ideas."

"I'm sure he is," Owen said dryly, casting a subtle warning glance in Cody's direction before turning again to Paris. "So you're not working this morning? We could do breakfast at the clubhouse, if you like."

Obviously Cody wasn't included in the invitation.

"I'm sorry, but I've had breakfast and I do have to go to the office for a while. Then I have a mile-long list of things I have to see to." She noted the time on her watch, then snuggled her jacket collar more closely around her neck. "I came out early hoping to catch Cody so he could update me on his progress."

Would that be a regular visit he could count on?

"Some other time, then." Owen offered his arm. "May I see you to your car?"

Paris hesitated, glancing uncertainly at Cody, then nodded and slipped her arm into Owen's. "You're doing a great job, Cody. Your mother—and the committee—will be pleased."

"Thank you."

But Owen didn't look pleased in the least, and a surge of satisfaction welled up in Cody. No, he wouldn't attempt to mess things up for Paris, but maybe the self-satisfied Owen would manage that on his own.

"Let's be on our way, then." Owen tugged at her arm. "I know you don't want to be late for work."

"Thanks again, Cody," Paris called back as the pair made their way across the open space toward the door.

Cody watched grimly as they exited the building. Owen Fremont. A city slicker with cash to burn and a greedy eye on Paris. At least the guy she was involved with wasn't someone Cody knew. That would have been even harder to stomach.

"Better put those eyes back in your head, Hawk." An amused voice echoed through the high-ceilinged space.

Cody swung around to see it was Jim Harper who'd called out to him from where he was tinkering with the snow blade on a pickup truck. Jim had been in school with him, an okay guy but not one Cody had been friends with—probably because he'd caught him ogling Paris on occasion. But they'd visited this week and seemed to get along fine now.

Cody cupped his ear. "What's that?"

Jim laughed. "You heard me, buddy. You don't stand a chance and you know it."

Shaking his head, Cody waved Jim off good-naturedly, then turned to start on the next few hours of work. He'd like to get the framing of the cabins done by tomorrow, then move on to securing the mock logs. He couldn't stay here all day, though, as he'd told Mom he'd stop in to see Dad.

Man, he didn't look forward to that first encounter.

He placed a board across the sawhorses, recalling the pretty picture Paris had made in her furry jacket, her dark hair loosely tumbling over the collar, her eyes bright and soft lips smiling her pleasure at his progress.

He took a labored breath and reached for another board.

Jim was right.

He could dream those teenage dreams all he wanted, but they wouldn't go any further. Even if that Owen dude hadn't been staking his claim, Cody didn't stand a chance. What could the prettiest woman in town, who'd once handed him a box at a community food bank, possibly see in him?

Lord, why'd You have to call me back to Canyon Springs right now? Why'd Dad have to go and have a stroke so Ma can't follow through on her commitment?

Cody let out a pent-up breath. He needed to buck up and face reality. God likely had a sweet gal tucked somewhere out of sight who'd been impatiently waiting for him to get his act together. He'd been slow coming to God and slow to allow God to heal the animosity he'd long felt toward his father and was only now coming to terms with.

Maybe facing his teenage feelings was a test, something that had to be done to set him free to love and be loved by the little lady God had in mind for him all along. He wouldn't want to miss out because he couldn't grow up and let go of an adolescent infatuation.

Was reality finally sinking in or was he subconsciously backing off because he feared Paris's father would rescind offers made on Dad's behalf? Cody wasn't yet in a position to take on the medical bills, long-term care or any debt his folks may have incurred through the years.

Either way, Paris clearly wasn't in his future.

He reached for a hammer and nail.

He could do this. Guard his heart. With God's help, anyway. It would be easier, though, if Paris didn't come around again.

But he couldn't bring himself to pray that she wouldn't.

Chapter Seven

"Oh, the weather outside is frightful…" Paris hummed the final bars of a favorite Christmas tune as the windshield wipers slashed away soggy snowflakes.

Although menacing clouds had descended, the highway wasn't too bad. With all she had to do for tomorrow, she hadn't planned to make an afternoon trek to Show Low. But she'd gotten a call from Reyna and promised she'd stop by the hospital before the weekend, drop off a few things she needed and discuss details of the upcoming weddings.

She was thrilled the Christmas gala preparations were coming along because of Cody, as suddenly all three brides needed her attention. The dress Sharon ordered online three months ago was abruptly unavailable. With so many motels and rental properties closed for the winter, Abby was having difficulty finding enough rooms for Brett's huge family. And Macy's mother suddenly refused to make the trip to Arizona, which wore on the bride's increasingly frazzled nerves.

"Why," Paris said aloud as she slowed to enter town,

"do people put themselves through this? Why not elope and save themselves the grief?"

In her case, however—had things not ended in tragedy—*not* eloping would have been a blessing. Seven months of attending to ceremony, reception and honeymoon details finally gave God the time needed to catch her attention. All the preparations had to be undone, of course. Reservations canceled, deposits forfeited. Her gown and the dresses she'd purchased for her bridesmaids donated to charity.

But *had* it been God, or her own fears that brought her up short? Paris adjusted the wiper speed as she stared through the streaked windshield at the gloomy day. Should she have gone through with the wedding, keeping her mouth shut and not asking Dalton to return for a heart-to-heart talk? Had she been too self-centered, thinking only about what *she* needed out of the relationship rather than focusing on what she should be putting into it? *Could* she have made Dalton happy?

There were no answers—and never would be.

Once inside the medical center, Paris asked directions to Reyna's room. Fighting back the sounds and scents that reminded her too vividly of her mother's frequent hospital stays that last year of her life, she silently whispered a prayer of thanksgiving that Mom had passed away quietly in Canyon Springs. Although he never said as much, Paris believed that's why Dad built a new home a few years later. While she found comfort in the memories shared during her mother's last days in hospice care, Dad likely wanted relief from them. To not walk into a room and remember…

As she stepped out of the elevator, a feminine voice with a soft Texan twang called to her.

"Miz Perslow? What brings you here? Your father is okay, I hope."

She turned to see Cody's mother, Lucy Hawk, who was maybe a decade younger than Dad. Not surprisingly, she looked tired today and it was tempting to cheer her with the gift cards Paris had tucked in her purse. But no, she wouldn't risk appearing disrespectful of Cody no matter how misguided his opinions might be.

"I'm here to see Reyna Kenton."

"Bless your heart." Lucy's gaze warmed as she brushed back her sandy-brown, chin-length bob. "She's in need of cheering up. She hopes to go home soon, but her doctor isn't making promises."

"She certainly doesn't want to be released prematurely and wind up back here again."

The older woman's gaze softened to a tenderness directed at Paris. "Which is why it's such a blessing you're stepping in to help with the weddings at Canyon Springs Christian. I know it's not easy for you. Many difficult memories."

Paris redirected the conversation before it veered toward memories of Dalton. "Cody said there hadn't been much change in your husband's condition."

"No, unfortunately. I do thank you for being understanding about my inability to follow through on the Christmas gala."

"You couldn't know this would happen to your husband. But you'll be pleased to know Cody is making rapid headway."

Lucy smiled at the confirmation. "I don't know what I'd do without him right now, but he has important things needing attention elsewhere."

Like what? And why was she wondering if those important things had to do with a woman?

"I doubt," Paris pointed out, "that Cody would do anything he didn't want to do."

Lucy laughed. "True."

"Did I hear my name taken in vain?"

Cody stepped out of the elevator, an insulated cup of coffee in his hand, and Paris's heart gave an unexpected leap. He was dressed as he had been that morning, in jeans, work boots, a red flannel shirt and a black insulated vest. His attire set off his rugged good looks to perfection.

She'd enjoyed their brief visit earlier in the day, although it ended awkwardly with Owen Fremont insisting he walk her to her car. They didn't know each other that well, but Owen could be pushy at times.

With a grateful smile, Cody's mother accepted the lidded cup he handed to her. "Paris tells me you're making strides on the project I dumped in your lap."

He shrugged. "I volunteered, remember?"

"You did." Lucy's eyes flickered briefly to Paris, their expression hinting that something disquieting had crossed her mind. Then she again looked up at her son, injecting a teasing lilt into her words. "I intend to inspect everything to see how closely you've followed my design."

"Great. Two women looking over my shoulder." But from that lazy smile, he didn't appear too bothered by it.

Lucy glanced at the wall clock. "I'd better check on your father again. Thank you for the coffee. They keep this place like an icebox."

Her son's brows lowered. "How late do you plan to stay today? The sun sets shortly after five and you know how the roads can get after dark. I'll follow you home."

She leveled a troubled look at him. "I'll only be here long enough for you to see your father…and to deal with what may come of that."

The corners of Cody's mouth dipped. "I'll be in there in a few minutes."

Lucy's apprehensive gaze flickered again to Paris, then back to her son. "Take your time."

Something was bothering Ma and it wasn't only Dad. Looking down at Paris in her teddy-bear jacket and stylish boots, her French-braided hair and makeup enhancing the natural beauty she'd been born with, he had a feeling he knew what it was.

But Ma didn't need to worry. He had things under control and his heart under wraps.

"I take it you're here to see someone—and not my old man."

A smile touched Paris's lips. "Our pastor's wife, Reyna. She's being treated for pneumonia."

"I heard about that at church on Sunday. Sounded bad."

Paris glanced down the hallway as if casting for a topic to continue the conversation. Or maybe a way to end it? He should help her out since Owen wasn't around to lend a hand this time.

"I guess I'd better join my mother so I can get her back on the road before dark."

"I'll be praying, Cody." Paris looked up at him with surprising understanding. "I know this can't be easy."

Sort of like the past she was confronting by helping with the weddings? When he'd stopped by Dix's on his way here, Sharon commented that Paris hadn't involved herself with weddings since Dalton's death, but she thought overseeing three upcoming events was a good sign that Paris was healing.

"Walking into Dad's hospital room isn't something I look forward to, but it's one of the reasons I returned to town—to make my peace with Leroy Hawk." From the second Ma called about Dad's stroke he knew, like it or not, God was giving him a warning. Dad could easily have died, an opportunity like today forever lost.

Paris impulsively caught his hand in both of hers. She gave it a quick squeeze, then released it. "Everything will be fine."

She smiled, her eyes beaming encouragement. Then she turned away and headed down the hall.

He moved in the opposite direction, the fingers of the hand she'd clasped now gripped tightly as he took his time walking to Dad's room. He'd never held her hand before, but he'd always wondered how it would feel in his.

Nice. Real nice.

At his father's open door he halted out of sight, inhaling the sharp, antiseptic odors around him. Dad had only gotten out of ICU this week, but was situated not far from the nurses' station. Would he turn his face away in silence at the arrival of his son or shake his fist in red-faced anger?

You called me here, Lord. Here I am.

He rapped his knuckles on the door frame as he stepped into the room. "Hey, Dad."

As his mother looked anxiously from father to son, Cody's gaze raked the sterile surroundings. Unlike rooms of other patients he'd passed on the way to this one, there were no balloon bouquets, no flowers. No get-well words of encouragement tacked above the bed. No family photos, posters or cards.

Just cold, bare walls.

A muscle tightened in Cody's throat as he drew his thoughts from the cheerless environment and forced himself to look his father in the eye. It was the first time since the night Dad, angered that Cody had turned down Mr. Perslow's job offer, had kicked him out of the house. Almost as big as his father by then, he'd caught Dad off-guard when he backed him against the garage wall and told him that with any luck they'd never see each other again—unless Ma wasn't treated right and he was forced to return and make good on his promise.

Please don't let my showing up cause another stroke.

The man now staring him down struggled unsuccessfully to sit up in bed. Leroy Hawk, while still broad-shouldered and brawny, was no longer the powerful, menacing man of Cody's memories. His face was severely drawn and pale, his eyes shadowed and sunken into their sockets. His right arm lay motionless, helpless, at his side.

Cody had known it was bad. His mother had warned that Dad retained impaired movement on his left side, but the right was entirely immobile. His speech patterns were hesitant, slurred, the words not always what he intended to say. Once-sharp mental faculties had dulled.

But Cody hadn't been prepared for the reality of it.

Ma placed a gentling hand on his father's arm, and Dad ceased his fruitless efforts to gain a seated position and settled back against the pillows. But his eyes never left Cody's, their expression ever-changing from the moment he'd stepped through the door.

Surprise. Anger. Humiliation. Resignation.

"Come…" The intended smile was a grotesque grimace as Dad struggled for garbled words. "…kill… me?"

Most might not make out what he'd said. But Cody knew. A sense of shame for the teenage threat he'd made stabbed his heart. Then again, he shouldn't have been forced to issue the ultimatum. That was Dad's doing.

"Naw." Cody swallowed, then managed a half smile as he motioned to the bed with its tubes and monitoring paraphernalia. "Looks like you came close to doing a good job of that on your own."

"Did…didn't I?" The laugh emanating from the drawn-down, misshapen lips wasn't much more than a puff of air.

Cody took a few steps closer, but halted when his father's expression darkened.

With a tight smile, his mother patted Dad's arm again. "Cody's taken a few days off work to come check on us."

The wheezing sound might have been a disbelieving snort.

Ma's gaze flickered apologetically to Cody.

"I talked to Merle Perslow," Cody ventured, hoping the assurance that things on the work front were secure might give Dad peace of mind. "The paychecks will keep coming. Your insurance is covered. He's being pretty accommodating."

Dad's lips curled downward and a glint of self-satisfied humor lit his eyes. "Just…bet…is."

Cody glanced at his mother, hoping to receive a cue from her. Maybe a topic of conversation he could pursue or a hint that he should move on, that more shouldn't be expected of today's visit.

"Well, Leroy, it's time Cody and I head out. It's been snowing off and on this afternoon and Cody doesn't want me driving alone after dark. He'll follow me back home."

Dad grunted, then felt along the bed with his left hand until his fingers reached those of his wife. He squeezed them in a weak grip as he struggled to smile. She smiled back.

A knot jerked in Cody's stomach at that unexpected gesture of tenderness. He'd forgotten that when Dad hadn't been drinking, he'd treated Ma like a queen.

"You're ready then, Ma?"

She slipped her hand from her husband's and stood, then leaned over to kiss him on the forehead. "You behave yourself tonight, Leroy. Don't give the night staff any trouble, you hear me?"

A sound that might have been a laugh escaped Dad's lips. "Back…tomorrow?"

"If the weather holds."

"I'll beg, borrow or steal a four-wheel drive," Cody assured, "if that's what it takes to get her here, Dad."

His father's now-drowsy gaze met Cody's, but he didn't reply. Then he closed his eyes and sank farther back into his pillows.

Cody's mother smiled sadly at her husband for a long moment, then picked up her coat and purse from a nearby chair and followed Cody into the hallway. He slipped his arm around her as they headed silently to the elevator.

Once inside the enclosed space, Cody pressed the down button. "He didn't seem overjoyed to see me, but at least he didn't keel over when I walked in."

"He was happy you'd come." His mother patted his arm. "I could tell."

Yeah, right. Ma was only trying to make him feel better, attempting to ease the shock of seeing Dad laid up like that, his face and limbs distorted, his mobility drastically impaired. It was worse than he'd imagined. An outdoorsman, Dad had always been robust, active. Fit. He'd been fast on his feet and threw a mean punch.

The elevator doors opened on ground level and Cody motioned to his mother to exit first. "He has to hate being here. Being like that."

Ma nodded as Cody helped her into her coat. "Thank you for coming today. I thought things went well. God is good."

"I don't want to make a nuisance of myself, but I'd like to come back. You know, if you think that would be okay."

Today had been a start, but he and Dad had things

to talk over. He wouldn't push it, though, and risk upsetting him.

"It would be more than okay, but don't feel you have to be here every day or provide transportation for me. I don't expect that. Seeing to the Christmas gala is what's allowing me to be here now. I can't thank you enough."

"I'll do anything I can to help. You know that."

Ma paused as they reached the exit to the parking lot. "Paris is a sweet girl. Beautiful inside and out."

"I agree on both counts."

Her eyes hesitantly met his. "You will be careful, won't you, Cody?"

Did she, like Merle Perslow, think he'd barge in and disrupt Paris's relationship with Owen? That he wouldn't be sensitive to what she'd been through with the death of her fiancé? "What do you mean?"

"We've never talked about it, but I know you've cared for her ever since you were a boy."

That obvious, was it? Cody forced a chuckle. "There's probably not a kid in existence who hasn't lived through a crush."

"No. But I don't want to see my big boy get hurt."

So, like everyone else on the planet, she didn't think he stood a chance. That he'd only wind up harming himself if he didn't steer clear of the pretty Paris Perslow.

"You don't need to worry. I'm a grown man now."

"I know that. I just—"

He leaned over to give her a quick hug. "You still see me as a fifth grader being sent home the first day of school for misbehavior on the behalf of a cute third-grade girl."

She smiled up at him. "You walked through the door with a bloody nose and stars in your eyes."

He imagined it impossible for a male of any age not to get stars in his eyes when he looked at Paris.

He gave his mother another reassuring squeeze. "Stop your worrying, Ma."

There was nothing to worry about. Not a thing.

Chapter Eight

The soothing piano notes of "O Little Town of Bethlehem" drifted back to the kitchen where Paris had dropped in to check behind the scenes of the open house.

"I don't know who he is, Paris," Carrie, one of her teenage helpers stated, "but if you don't want him, I get dibs."

"What are you talking about?" Paris laughed as she removed another tray of hot water chestnuts wrapped in bacon from the oven, their sizzling aroma scenting the air. She couldn't seem to keep the warming dishes filled with them. Next year she'd know to double the popular recipe.

No. Not next year. She wouldn't be here to play hostess for the open house.

Pushing aside a ripple of unease, she set the tray on top of the stove and turned to where Carrie peeped out a front window of the log home's kitchen. Dressed in black slacks and a white shirt with a satin bow tie, her hair pulled back with an ebony ribbon, Carrie and the other two girls hired for the open house looked efficient and neatly attractive. All tattoos that might offend her father's more conservative guests were concealed by the crisp, long sleeves.

"Please tell me he's not married, Paris."

"Who?" Paris squeezed in beside Carrie to peer between the wooden slats. Ponderosa pines rose in silhouetted majesty in the fading daylight and solar fixtures along the walkway to the cabin's broad porch glowed softly. Leafless aspens sparkled with tiny fairy lights winding up their white trunks. A few more guests who'd left their cars along the curving drive approached, laughing and bundled against the cold, but she recognized all of them.

"You don't mean Sharlene Odel's cousin, do you?" She couldn't imagine anything about the middle-aged Andy that would elicit oohs and aahs from a seventeen-year-old girl.

"No." Carrie rolled her eyes, her tone offended.

"I don't see anybody else."

"Where'd he go?" The teen maneuvered for a better view. "Oh, there he is. To the far right now, coming up the drive along the trees. It looks like he's heading around to the side door."

A guest coming in the back way, to the entrance between the house and garage?

Paris angled for a better look, then her breath caught.

Cody. And he was carrying something.

Suddenly self-conscious as she listened for a knock at the side entrance, Paris moved back to the stove and picked up a spatula to sweep the water chestnuts into a bowl.

"Who is he?" Carrie pressed. "Do you know him?"

Paris handed her the serving bowl. "His name is Cody Hawk."

"Cody," the teen whispered, her eyes going dreamy. "Is he—?"

Paris laughed. "No, he's not married."

Or at least she assumed he wasn't. She couldn't help but notice he didn't wear a ring, but that didn't mean he wasn't spoken for.

"In that case, I'll be back in a minute—with my wedding gown." Carrie batted her eyes in an exaggerated manner. "I've got to meet this guy and set the date before Madison or Brianna spot him."

Carrie spun toward the door, then abruptly halted, her forehead wrinkling. "Did you say Cody *Hawk?* Like as in *Leroy* Hawk?"

"I did."

Everyone in town knew Leroy or had at least heard of him and his boys by reputation—even this girl a decade younger than Paris. Poor Cody.

"He's one of Leroy's sons."

Carrie groaned, her once-eager expression now crumpling. "You're kidding me, right?"

Paris shook her head.

"Just my luck." The girl grimaced. "There's something majorly wrong with a world that gives a man who looks like that to a father like Leroy Hawk."

Paris couldn't agree more.

Dejected, Carrie again turned away, then paused. "What's he doing here at your party?"

A firm knock sounded at the side door.

"He must be making a delivery."

Carrie sighed. "Great. The hired help. I sure know how to pick 'em."

As the girl departed, Paris whipped off her holiday chef's apron, smoothed the skirt of her dress and hurried to answer the door off the utility room that linked the house to the three-car garage.

"Cody. This is a surprise." Illuminated by the soft lantern light of the log home's rustic outdoor fixture, his hair shone a glossy black and emphasized the strong planes of his face. Alert brown eyes met hers and her heart beat a faster clip as she opened the door wider. "Please come in. It's cold out tonight."

"I'm here only long enough to drop this off." He nodded to the cardboard box in his arms.

"What is it? I'm not expecting a delivery." And certainly not from Cody.

"I was down at Dix's a short while ago and Sharon mentioned you'd called earlier today saying you needed this for tonight. But no one had come by to pick it up."

She stared at him blankly, noticing how his five o'clock shadow skimmed a firm jaw and his lips curved upward ever so slightly as if something amused him.

He raised a dark brow. "Ginger ale? For the punch?"

"Oh!" Paris gave a halfhearted laugh. "I totally forgot. What's that tell you about how this day has gone?"

"I imagine you've been busy, if that line of parked cars leading all the way down to the road is any indication. Your annual Christmas open house?"

"That's right."

So he remembered Mom and Dad always hosted one. It had been a gathering of family and close friends, the community's movers and shakers and those out-oftowners who'd done significant business with Perslow Real Estate and Property Management. The family of Leroy Hawk, of course, had never been invited.

"At your old place, Dad and I used to wrap the trees and porch railings with lights. Remember? We'd line the perimeter of the yard and driveway with luminarias and set up the crèche scene out front."

Suddenly she envisioned the handsome, well-built teenager working alongside his dad the weekend after Thanksgiving. She'd spied on him more than once from her upstairs window.

"It always looked beautiful. Mom loved it."

"She was a real kid about Christmas, wasn't she?"

"She was. She'd start listening to Christmas music in October while she planned the open house, made homemade decorations and tested out new recipes."

"Some of that rubbed off on you, too, as I recall." Cody's smiling gaze met hers at the shared memory. "I remember she used to invite neighborhood kids to sit on the porch with her while she read the Christmas story and gave out sugar cookies. You did that after she passed away. Do you still do it?"

She shook her head, a pang of melancholy touching her heart as she motioned to the treed property surrounding the isolated log home. "No. There are no neighbor kids out here."

"That's a shame." He shifted the box in his arms. "That's where I heard my first Bible stories as a kid, listening in while I helped Dad with the yard work."

Before he'd been hired full-time, Leroy Hawk had done odd jobs for the Perslows and others around town, often taking his son along when Cody wasn't in school. Sometimes it seemed, even when a young boy, that Cody did much of the work while his father wandered off for a cigarette or shot the breeze with another neighbor.

"Mom did love everything about the season," Paris continued as more memories surfaced. "Decorating the tree and fixing the food. Playing every Christmas tune she knew on the piano. Sledding and cross-country skiing. That was when I was pretty young though, before the MS got bad."

Cody's expression softened. "You still miss her, don't you?"

"I do." In many ways it seemed like only yesterday that Mom was here, yet at other times it seemed like forever since they'd last spoken, since they'd held each other. How she wished she could have her mother here now, to have grown their relationship into that of adult friends.

Abruptly aware of the chill swirling in around her ankles, she stepped back from the doorway. "I'm sorry. I've left you standing out in the cold."

"No problem. I'll set this inside the door—unless you want me to take it on in to wherever you want it." His dark eyes met hers in question.

Dad hadn't been happy when Elizabeth told him last night that Cody was helping with the Christmas gala and he might not be any happier to find Cody on the premises this evening. Through the open door behind her, she could hear Carrie and her friends chattering as they entered the kitchen. Hopefully the teen wouldn't carelessly voice aloud her disappointment in the good-looking "hired help."

"Right by the door would be fine."

He leaned in to set the box on the terra-cotta tiles, gave it a shove to the side, then stepped back.

"I hope your open house is a success." He glanced toward the car-lined drive, now deep in shadow except where illuminated by solar fixtures. Another cluster of chatting guests made its way up the gradual incline. "Looks like more arrivals are heading this way."

"It's fun seeing old friends and hosting Dad's clients."

"Enjoy." He nodded a farewell, then headed back down the drive.

"Cody?"

He turned almost expectantly. "Yeah?"

"Thank you for making the delivery." She took a quick breath. "And for remembering Mom."

He smiled that slow, lazy smile of his, his eyes filled with understanding. "Anytime."

Cody strode along the side of the dimly lit driveway, nodding to another knot of guests heading up to the log home. He didn't know any of them, but they smiled a warm greeting. His own thoughts weren't on the house party, though, but on how stunning Paris looked tonight. Her hair had been swept atop her head, a few loose tendrils gently framing her face. A simple, charcoal-gray dress and pearls at her neck set off her breathtaking beauty.

She said it was a surprise to see him, but if she thought it weird that he'd made the delivery, she hadn't said so. He'd stopped at Dix's at the end of the day when Sharon had taken notice of the forgotten carton on the counter. She'd picked up the phone to call Paris, but with only a moment's hesitation Cody volunteered to drop off the box, saying he imagined everyone at the Perslow's was caught up in party preparations.

The time he'd taken for the detour had been well worth it.

With a grin, he kicked a pinecone, sending it scuttling down the drive ahead of him. When it came to Paris he was still looking for ways to help her, to please her. To draw her admiring gaze.

Mentioning her mother hadn't been an intentional ploy to gain her favor. But she seemed to appreciate that someone fondly remembered Marna Perslow at Christmastime. It had to have been hard these fourteen years, a young girl prematurely cut off from the loving influence of a mother like hers.

"Hawk!"

Cody's attention jerked from his reverie, his senses on alert at the sharp tone of a male voice. The light strings wrapping the pine trunks cast spotty shadows along the dark, forested drive and it took a moment to identify the source of the voice that had halted him. Up ahead a man leaned casually against the door of Cody's truck.

Owen Fremont.

Great. Cody strode on toward him, determined not to let the puffed-up man cow him because he possessed money and social status—and the assumption that he'd netted Paris.

When he approached, Owen pushed himself away from the truck, but didn't extend a hand in greeting. "Leaving the party? The night's still young."

The query didn't deserve a response. Owen knew, if for no other reason than how Cody was dressed, that he hadn't been in attendance. Unknown to Owen, though, he'd spent the past decade mixing with business and social acquaintances of his friend Trevor's exceedingly well-off parents. Had he been invited tonight, he'd have held his own just fine. Offering explanation to this joker didn't set well, but he nevertheless answered politely enough. "I was making a delivery."

The other man nodded as if satisfied that Cody hadn't overstepped his bounds. "Fine people, the Perslows."

"They are."

"With an impeccable reputation."

"That, too."

Owen slid his hands into the pockets of his neatly pressed trousers and shrugged a topcoat-clad shoulder as he gave Cody a calculating look. "I don't see any point in beating around the bush, *Mister* Hawk."

Cody folded his arms. "Then let's hear it."

Owen gave a soft laugh. "I've done some checking around since Paris introduced us yesterday morning."

"And?"

"I have no doubt you already know what the reputation of a Hawk is like in this town."

"Why don't you tell me?"

Owen grinned. "I don't think that's necessary, do you? I'm not here to disparage your family. I'm certain there's little I can share that you aren't aware of."

"Well, then?"

Owen pinned Cody with a challenging look. "I merely want to bring it to your attention that Perslows and Hawks don't—how should I put this?—mix. And Paris—"

"You can leave Paris out of this."

"Oh, but we both know we can't, don't we? So I'm asking—as one *gentleman* to another—" even in the dim light, Cody didn't miss Owen's mocking smile "—that you keep in mind a woman's reputation in a small town can too easily be tarnished by even the most innocent behaviors on the part of, let's say, a man who admires her?"

This jerk was so full of himself it wasn't funny.

Cody stepped around him and opened the driver-side door to his truck. He climbed inside, then looked back at the smirking man who'd had the effrontery to warn him away from Paris. Owen must not be that confident of his own standing with her or he wouldn't try to run off perceived competition. Was he beginning to realize money couldn't buy everything, including a woman's heart?

"I'm relieved you're aware of that hazard of small-town living, *Mister* Fremont," Cody said, his tone dry, "and that you intend to mind your manners around Miss Perslow."

Cody slammed the vehicle's door, started up the truck, then drove off without a backward glance.

Open her eyes, Lord. Soon.

Chapter Nine

"I can hardly believe that in less than two weeks I'll walk out of here as Mrs. Brett Marden." Abby Diaz sighed happily as she and Paris looked around the sanctuary of Canyon Springs Christian Church early Saturday morning. An overcast day, with little natural light illuminating the space, it was nevertheless cheerfully decorated for the season with greenery and red velvet bows. There wouldn't be much to do in that respect for the evening wedding except to light candles.

"Are you nervous, Abby? Even a little bit?"

Did other brides have nagging second thoughts? Or was she the only one who ever doubted she'd be the kind of wife her fiancé deserved?

"You mean am I getting cold feet? No way." Abby laughed and shook back her black hair. "I have absolute peace about marrying my cowboy."

Absolute peace. Paris hadn't had that as her own wedding day approached.

"So are we finished here?" Their meeting had taken longer than Paris anticipated and she was cutting it close for her next appointment. "We can stop by Kit's Lodge next week to review final details for catering the reception."

"Perfect," Abby pronounced, then cast Paris a sympathetic look. "But I know helping with my wedding has to be difficult for you. I'm sure that—"

"I'm thrilled to be helping you," Paris quickly cut in. She gave the bride a hug and, as soon as Abby departed, she returned to her own vehicle, disappointed that she wouldn't have time to swing by Pine Shadow Ridge and check on Cody's progress.

She glanced skyward at the slate-gray clouds, then headed in the direction of Main Street. It felt weird at times to be around a guy who'd declared his love a dozen years ago, when neither of them were much more than kids. Did he now find his youthful confession embarrassing or did he shrug it off? Was he relieved nothing had come of his adolescent declaration and that he hadn't been stuck with her for the past decade?

It had to have taken courage on his part to speak up those many years ago. Courage—or madness. They hadn't run with the same crowd in school. In fact, Cody didn't really run with any crowd. He'd been a loner. Did being around her now feel uncomfortable to him, too, remembering how she'd turned him away that night?

She wouldn't have dared do otherwise, of course, no matter how her heart clamored for his kisses. Dad would have locked her in her room and she'd never have seen the light of day before she turned eighty. Thankfully, Cody seemed to prefer leaving that episode in the past. But it still felt strange. Awkward. And she couldn't help wondering what *would* have happened had he kissed her that night…

Shaking off the memories, she found a parking space not far from Dix's Woodland Warehouse.

"Sorry I'm late, Sharon," Paris called as she entered the store. She rounded a display of outdoor gear on her way to the office at the rear of the building, then drew to a halt.

Cody looked up from where he perused the contents of one of the shelves. "Good morning, Paris. You're starting your day early."

She willed her suddenly hammering heart to slow at this unexpected encounter with the very man she'd been thinking about.

"I just met with Abby Diaz at the church and now I'm here to see Sharon. The dress she'd ordered for her wedding fell through, but I think I've found something online that she'll like. It's in stock and available for express shipping."

"I'm a big advocate for shopping locally, but the internet can sure come through in a pinch."

"It can." She took a quick breath and offered a smile. "Thank you again for delivering the extra ginger ale last night. We did end up using most of it."

"I was happy to help."

When he'd departed, she'd regretted not insisting he come inside in spite of how her father might have felt about it. Not being dressed for the occasion, he may not have wanted to join the other guests, but he might have enjoyed sampling the appetizers in the kitchen and visiting with Carrie and her young cohorts. Who knows, maybe after spending time in his company Carrie would have regretted so quickly dismissing a Hawk as undesirable. Most people didn't realize how fortunate they were to be born into a well-respected family, not being forever judged due to negative familial associations.

As Paris was well aware, the past and people's preconceptions could be a heavy burden.

"I know why Paris is here," Sharon called as she came from the back of the store, "but is there something I can help you with, Cody?"

"I'm picking up refills for my staple gun." He reached for a box.

Sharon tilted her head in interest. "I heard you were taking over the Christmas gala decorating for your mother. An answered prayer—right, Paris?"

Paris's attention flickered to Cody. "I don't know what we'd do without him."

"He was a skilled craftsman, even as a teenager. I'd give about anything to have a work shed like the one he built for his mother."

"It's nothing fancy, Sharon." Cody dismissed her comment with a shrug, but Paris could tell he was pleased by the compliment.

"You don't think so? The workspace and built-ins make it a hobbyist's dream." She nodded in Paris's direction. "You'll have to get him to show you."

Would he? He didn't look to be so inclined.

"With Cody in charge of the staging," Sharon added as she gave him an approving nod, "Bill and I are especially looking forward to this year's gala."

Cody caught Paris's eye, questioning what he thought he'd heard. Sharon and her fiancé would be attending the charity dinner and dance?

While both were established business owners in Canyon Springs, the holiday event had long been a gathering of the socially prominent moneyed elite of local townspeople and neighboring communities. It had been a private affair, not city-sponsored, an exclusive celebration as they bestowed their year-end tax deductible donations on behalf of the less fortunate. A tight-knit clique from what he remembered.

"You won't be disappointed," Paris assured Sharon. "Lucy's design is fabulous and it's apparent from what I've seen that Cody's rendering of it will be one to remember."

Sharon gave him a considering look. "Keep in mind, Cody, that Paris is gifted herself when it comes to bringing this type of thing to life. You might wield a mean hammer and saw, but don't hesitate to recruit her if you need help with the decorative details."

He again caught Paris's now-discomfited gaze, suspecting the last thing she needed was one more thing to do, and that doing anything with *him* would fall at the bottom of her wish list. He gave her an understanding smile. "I think she already has plenty on her plate this season."

"Not the least of which," Sharon admitted, her eyes now fixed on Paris, "is the added burden of helping those of us less adept with wedding preparations. Give me a few minutes to make a phone call, doll, then come on back and let's get that dress ordered and free up the rest of your day."

When Sharon disappeared into the office and shut the door, Paris turned to Cody with a penetrating look.

"If I'm not mistaken, you seemed taken aback when Sharon said she'd be attending the gala."

"Sharon and Bill may be long-established residents but not, shall we say, the crème de la crème of Canyon Springs society."

"They're well-thought-of."

"I'm not questioning that."

"But you are," she said evenly, "questioning how they'd fit in?"

He shrugged. "I'm wondering if they wouldn't find the event an uncomfortable one."

He could tell by the flash in her eyes that he'd stumbled on *her* hot button. He should have kept his mouth shut.

She tilted her head, as if weighing her words.

"You know, Cody," she said softly, aware as he was, that they weren't alone in the store, "you're not going to like hearing this, but you're very judgmental. Did you know that? You're prejudiced against people you don't even know because they're better-off than you."

"Whoa, there." He drew back with a forced smile, keeping his own voice low. "Prejudiced? Judgmental? I think that's a little harsh, don't you?"

Paris leveled a troubled look at him. "No more harsh than you thinking that because someone has money and social standing that they are innately snobbish. That's as far from the truth as you can get."

"You think so?" A too-familiar bitterness welled up inside. "Try standing on a stage in your patched jeans and worn flannel shirt with a roomful of elegantly dressed strangers staring at you. Looking down on you while someone passes out token gifts to the town's 'needy' kids."

Paris opened her mouth to respond, but he cut her off. "Those gifts didn't make a dent in their wallets, didn't inconvenience them in the least. But they got a warm, fuzzy holiday feeling before heading back to their big fancy homes, thanking God they and theirs were more *deserving* of His blessings."

A flicker of pity flashed through Paris's eyes, only to be quickly replaced with resolve. "I'm sorry you experienced that, Cody—or interpreted it that way. The committee no longer distributes gifts to kids at the gala itself. They haven't done that since you were a kid. But even when they did, you're mistaken about the spirit in which those gifts were given."

"Come on, Paris. You can't have been blind to it." She was too compassionate, too sensitive to have over-looked it.

"Are you saying my *mother* was like that? For years before her health prohibited it, she played an instrumental role in ensuring the gala was a successful fund-raising event." Paris's eyes darkened with emotion. "Do you think she looked down on those in need, on those who'd suffered from financial setbacks or from doing nothing more wicked than being born into the 'wrong' family? That she gave only so she might feel, as you put it, all warm and fuzzy?"

Cody glanced around the store to make sure no one was paying attention to them. Man, he'd opened a can of worms trying to get Paris to understand where he was coming from. She was taking everything he'd said the wrong way, twisting it around.

"Of course I don't think that of your mother." He

kept his voice low. "You're taking this too personally. Out of context."

At the sound of bells jingling above the doorway as another bevy of customers entered, she gave him a sharp look. "Am I?"

Before he could respond, she lifted that stubborn chin of hers and brushed past him, heading to the back office as the heels of her boots clicked sharply on the hardwood floor.

Hours later, anger and disappointment still welled up as Paris made her way down the festively decorated Main Street. Laden with packages and shopping bags, she wove her way among the smiling holiday shoppers, attempting to be thankful for the eye-opening conversation she'd had with Cody. How foolish she'd been for toying with the idea that he might still be interested in her. For having any interest in *him*.

She glanced at her watch. Noon. She'd better hurry or she'd be late to set things up for the two-o'clock tea at the church. Being so busy, she hadn't been her usual organized self. Cody's presence during this holiday season hadn't helped either, leaving her anxious and unfocused.

Whoever would have thought he'd harbor such thoughts of good people who had done so much for others? His youthful experiences were unfortunate, but to imply that her mother and others like her were pretentious and patronizing, condescendingly looking down their noses at those who were less well-off, was so unfair.

Mom believed she and Dad had been financially

blessed so that they might bless others. How often had she told Paris and the gala committee that God had expectations of those to whom He'd given much—that they weren't to be containers of God's gifts but channels to others of His blessings.

And to resent that? To think ill of well-meaning people?

"Paris!"

She turned to a cheerful female voice, spying her best friend dodging cars in her dash across Main Street, her tumble of long blond hair flying behind her.

"Whew!" Delaney Marks laughed as she leaped to the safety of the sidewalk. "Where is this traffic coming from? This *is* Canyon Springs, isn't it? I didn't take a wrong turn?"

Paris laughed. "No, you didn't get lost. You're really home for the holidays."

"I was worried there for a moment."

"When did you get back?" Her friend hadn't been in town for months.

"Yesterday."

"And you didn't call me? Didn't come to our open house?"

"I had other obligations last night. But I'm here now. Should we stop in for hot cocoa and a chatfest at Camilla's?"

"I wish I could." Paris nodded to the packages in her arms and the shopping bag handles looped in the crooks of her elbows. "But I have to get this stuff to the church. The ladies' Christmas tea is this afternoon and I want to make sure everything's ready. Are you going to it?"

"No. But…" Delaney leaned in close, her voice a soft hiss in Paris's ear. "Don't think you can slip away without telling me about *him*."

Paris drew back. Even as teens, she'd never divulged her feelings for Cody to her friend. "Him who?"

Delaney's voice remained low, her eyes dancing with mischief. "You know… Cody Hawk."

"Believe me," Paris said, her face warming as she pulled away from her friend and started off down the street once again, "there's nothing to tell."

Except that she'd been stupid for thinking that he might still have a thing for her, and that with the passage of time they could bridge the differences in their upbringings, which had separated them as teens.

Delaney quickly caught up with her. "Nothing to tell? That's not what I'm hearing."

Dismayed, Paris halted. "What are you hearing?"

"Not just hearing. But seeing." Delaney fanned her hand in front of her face as if she might swoon right then and there. "Oh. My. Goodness. He is one hunky guy."

"You've seen him?"

"Yeah, coming out of Dix's earlier this morning. Jacquie pointed him out. No wonder you're willing to risk stepping over to the other side of the tracks."

"Who says I'm doing that?" Maybe she *had* been contemplating the idea, but not after that run-in with Cody a few hours ago.

"Kirsten mentioned it. Jacquie, too. Of course, they're claiming to be concerned that you're dishonoring Dalton's memory, risking tarnishing your reputation. But personally, I think they're just jealous."

"There's nothing to be jealous of."

Delaney cast her a disbelieving look. "Kirsten says he was seen slinking away from a side door at your place last night and that you've been rendezvousing with him at Pine Shadow Ridge."

Small towns. Paris gritted her teeth as she juggled the packages in her arms. Dropped one. Delaney picked it up and handed it to her.

"Cody made a delivery for the open house and he's helping his mother with the Christmas gala decorations. Since you've obviously caught up on the local gossip, surely you've also heard she can't do it herself because his father had a stroke?"

"Yep." Delaney grimaced. "Brought on by alcohol abuse and a lottery ticket bust."

Amazing. Her friend had barely been in town twenty-four hours and she had the scoop on everything, even if the piece about Cody was distorted.

"So, Paris..." Delaney looked furtively around them, her eyes again twinkling. She could be so lovable— and exasperating. "Is he a good kisser?"

Her breath caught unexpectedly at the prospect of Cody's warm mouth on hers. Aware from the heat rising up her neck that her face was probably crimson, she swatted playfully at her friend.

And sent the armful of packages tumbling in all directions.

She groaned.

"Could you use some help?" a familiar male voice called from behind her.

Dread mingling with an inexplicable lifting of her spirits, she turned to see Cody striding across the street toward her.

Chapter Ten

Paris didn't look overjoyed to see him. But no matter. He had an apology to make and there was no time like the present.

Cody crouched at her booted feet and gathered the scattered packages into his arms. Then he stood, looking down into her apprehensive gray eyes. After their misunderstanding this morning, he wasn't surprised at not receiving a warm welcome. But their earlier conversation had been an overdue wake-up call for him. As much as he'd like to believe that the past twelve years lessened the impact their different backgrounds made on their lives, that theory had proven to be untrue.

"Thank you, Cody."

She reached for his armload, but he gripped it more tightly. "Where are you heading with this? To your car?"

"Yes, but—"

"Where's it at?"

He glanced around for the SUV, suddenly becoming aware of a cute blonde woman off to the side looking up at him with open amusement. Was she going to stand there and stare at him or go on about her business? He had something he needed to say to Paris and didn't want bystanders eavesdropping.

"There it is, Cody," the blonde said, standing on her tiptoes to point to a spot over his right shoulder and down the street.

He frowned. She knew him? Did he know her?

"Uh, thanks." He glanced at a rosy-cheeked Paris who motioned to the other woman.

"Cody, this is my friend Delaney Marks. She moved here shortly after you left town. Delaney, this is Cody Hawk."

Good. He didn't know her so there would be no expectation of catching up on old times with someone who'd stuffed him in a box of preconceptions labeled "loser."

But he still needed to be alone with Paris.

"Nice to meet you, Delaney." He'd offer his hand to her but couldn't risk scattering the packages once again.

She beamed up at him. "And it's *wonderful* to meet you."

Wonderful?

Paris cut her friend a sharp look, then turned to him. "If you're sure you wouldn't mind…" She motioned in the direction of her vehicle.

"Lead the way."

He followed, looking back only once to see the Delaney gal still rooted in place, thankfully not inclined to join them. Catching his eye, she wiggled her fingers in a merry wave. Blew him a kiss.

Flirty little minx. He squared his shoulders and fo-

cused again on Paris as, shopping bags looped over
her arms, she made her way to her SUV. When they
reached it, she lifted the tailgate, placed her bags inside
and then stepped back to give him room to do likewise.
He took his time divesting himself of his burden, taking care to arrange the packages where they wouldn't
tip or slide.

"Looks like that does it." He stepped back and lowered the tailgate, checking to make certain it latched
securely.

Her gaze met his uncertainly. "Thank you, Cody."

"You're more than welcome." He cut a glance back
to the spot from which they'd come, confirming there
was no sign of the blonde. Then he leaned a hand
against the edge of the SUV's roof. "I guess we got
off to a bad start this morning."

Paris smiled faintly, shaking her head. "Let's not
revisit it, okay?"

"I'm not intending to revisit it. I want to apologize."
He ran his thumb along the door window's chrome,
gathering his thoughts. "I didn't mean to imply your
mother—or any of the others—operated out of selfish
motives with their charity work. The annual Christmas
gala funds many critical projects throughout the year."

"Yes, it does."

He cleared his throat. "I had no right to say the things
I said. I'm sorry, Paris. I hope you can forgive me."

"You only said what you thought."

"What a *kid* thought." His eyes narrowed. "A kid
whose worthless dad was always pushing him forward
to get whatever he could from those who were willing
to share from their own abundance. A kid who'd been

humiliated time and time again in front of adults and his peers as he lined up for freebies."

Her gaze softened. "I know that couldn't have been easy."

He glanced down the street, then caught her eye again. "Do you remember the year I was a junior—you were a freshman—when you and your Dad distributed food boxes? You gave one to me."

She nodded slightly, her expression solemn at the recollection. He remembered it like yesterday.

"I had a big fight with Dad before I went that afternoon," he continued, forcing away the memory of a blush that had tinged Paris's cheeks when her startled gaze met his that day. "He told me if I didn't go, I could forget about coming home. Ever."

A soft whimper escaped her lips. "Oh, Cody—"

He held up his hand to stay her words. He wasn't looking for sympathy. He wanted her to understand why he'd said—stupidly said—the words he'd uttered that morning.

"When I saw you there with your dad, with a few of our classmates, I wanted to die on the spot. I was so ashamed. Dad had a job. I was working when I could. We had food and clothes—or we would have if he didn't periodically drink it all away."

He took a deep breath and let it out slowly. "After we talked this morning, I went back to the project and hammered out my anger on that poor defenseless wood." He gave a halfhearted chuckle. "In the process I came to realize what you heard this morning was a mortified kid's way of coping. And… I'm sorry, Paris."

Their gazes held for a long moment, the hustle and bustle of shoppers fading away as he focused on her.

"It's okay," she said quietly. "I should apologize, as well. I shouldn't have—"

"No. You had every right to say what you'd said. I never intended to slander good people who help others in need. I was wrong."

She didn't respond, a sadness in her eyes. *Pity?* Once again he felt as he had that day when she'd handed him the food box. He fisted his fingers and lightly rapped the top of her vehicle.

"So, that's it. All I have to say."

And without bringing himself to look at her again, he turned away and strode back across the street.

When she left the church late that afternoon following cleanup of the ladies' tea, Paris ignored the chiming of her cell phone except to confirm the caller ID. It was Delaney, no doubt wondering what conversation had ensued with Cody.

She wasn't ready to talk about it with anyone. Not even her best friend.

Throughout the long afternoon of pouring tea and serving holiday cookies, her mind had drifted to him repeatedly. Not only to the Cody who'd stood apologetically before her earlier that afternoon, but to the Cody she'd known through the years.

The Cody who'd been among a handful of boys roughhousing on the playground, but who had been the only one singled out to be sent to the principal's office.

The Cody who'd been made fun of when he'd come to school in a too-small coat and who subsequently chose for the remainder of the winter to brave the cold with only a knit cap, scarf and gloves.

The Cody who'd missed out on participating in school sports he probably would have excelled at, maybe would have received a college scholarship for, had he not been working alongside his dad when he wasn't in class.

In many ways, through no fault of his own, his life had been an uphill battle.

Now upstairs in her room, she stepped into her walk-in closet and lifted a fabric-covered box from a shelf. It was in the roomy container that she kept the treasures nearest and dearest to her heart. A photo of Mom and Dad on their wedding day lay on top. Below that snuggled a small cedar box containing, among other things, her first wristwatch, class ring and the sparkling chandelier earrings Mom loved to wear at the holidays. Below lay a leather-bound journal. She'd never kept a diary, but she'd written poetry. Opening the book, she removed a piece of paper tucked between the pages and carefully unfolded it to reveal a pen-and-ink portrait.

Gazing down at the girl she once was, she vividly remembered the beautiful autumn day Cody had run to catch up with her as she walked home from the high school. He'd startled her when, eyes dark and attentive, he'd carefully torn the sketch from his newsprint pad and handed it to her.

"For you," he'd said, his voice low. Almost gruff. "You can keep it if you want to."

Looking down at it, then back up at him, their gazes had locked for a heart-stopping moment. She'd been embarrassed. Thrilled. Unable to breathe. Incapable of saying anything more than thank you, she'd broken their too-intimate visual connection and hurried the rest of the way home. She didn't dare look back.

Although they'd later seen each other at school, they didn't speak more than a few words until that night a year and a half later when he'd shown up on her doorstep. But she'd thought of him often. Dreamed of him. Prayed for him.

She ran her finger across the still-dark ink of the sketch, gently refolded it and slipped it back into the journal. Then she turned to the pages where, in her own distinctive cursive she'd penned one of many free-verse poems she'd composed during her adolescent years. More than one written with Cody in mind.

I look at you sometimes...
And wish I could read your voice.
Or better still, your smile.
So gentle, tender and quick to please,
Most Sweet, I feel awed when you bestow it on me.
I belong to you and am thus honored—
Or could it be only my imagination?
I look at you sometimes
And I wish...

Paris quickly closed the journal and returned it to the box. Then, with a weary sigh, she leaned back on the pillows propped against the headboard of her bed and closed her eyes as the day faded into twilight.

Delaney said people were talking about them. Making wrong assumptions. Cody was helping with the

Christmas gala, that was all. How could they construe that as dishonoring Dalton's memory?

Anger sparked. Did this town expect her to never find someone else to love? Was she to be permanently bound to her dead fiancé? Or even worse, did they expect her to settle for someone who she had little in common with beyond their single status and the level of their family finances and social standing?

But what those who criticized an innocent relationship with Cody didn't understand was that, even if she threw caution to the wind and took up with the former "bad boy"—*if* he would have her—she didn't deserve his love, a home, a family. Hadn't her selfishness ensured Dalton would never see his own dreams fulfilled?

"Lord," she whispered, the ache in her heart weighing heavily, "I'm coming to care for Cody, but what am I supposed to do?"

Chapter Eleven

He hadn't seen Paris since Saturday, when he'd helped her load her vehicle and apologized for his regrettable outburst. But that was just as well. He needed to focus on the job at hand, and an uninterrupted dawn-to-dark day on Monday and most of today had given him a huge leap in progress. If all went well, he'd be working on the cabin roofs by noon.

Sunday, naturally, had been spent with Ma, and another brief visit with his father. The ministrokes Dad had suffered in the weeks since the major one continued. He'd rally one day, then seem to lose ground the next. It wasn't looking good and, in spite of Cody's conflicted feelings about his father, his heart ached for his mother.

Unexpectedly, though, as the days passed since his return to Canyon Springs, less and less Cody felt the need to press his father to right the wrongs done to his son. Felt less the need to demand an apology, to hear him admit his mistakes and ask forgiveness. Cody recognized that wasn't likely to happen, and the issue God pressed upon him wasn't one of his father's responsibility, but of his own.

Extending forgiveness when it wasn't asked for wasn't only to absolve the one who'd done the wrong but to free the one who'd been wronged.

Cody pulled the filtering mask over his mouth and nose, adjusted his goggles and angled the free-standing light for better illumination. Then he finished spray painting the base color for the tubing "logs." He noted with satisfaction that the spackle underneath the grayish-brown gave off an even better woodlike effect than he'd originally hoped.

"You've sure been putting in long hours," Jim Harper said as he stopped by to inspect Cody's work. He often paused to chat a few minutes when he came in the maintenance building for the workday ahead. "Looks like this year's gala is going to be impressive."

Cody paused and pulled the filter down to dangle around his neck. "Are you going?"

Jim snorted. "Are you kidding me? What would I be doing hobnobbing with the town's elite? Are *you?*"

"No plans to." In fact, it hadn't even crossed his mind. Even if the gala was no longer strictly a high society event, tickets wouldn't be cheap and would have sold out months ago.

"Come on, Hawk. You mean Paris doesn't have you measured for a penguin suit and your shoes polished to a glossy shine?"

Cody shrugged off the good-natured teasing with a grin. "I'm glad you're deriving some amusement from this, Jim."

His friend slapped him on the back. "Much appreciated, pal. Much appreciated."

With another laugh his former classmate headed off and Cody pulled on the filter once again. No, he wouldn't be going to the charity event and he hadn't heard Ma mention attending, either. But surely she'd been invited, hadn't she? Regardless, he'd slip her over here once the clubhouse was decked out in its finery. Although she'd teased him about overseeing his work, she hadn't yet come by to take a peek at his progress.

The remainder of the day flew by and he had a good running start on the cabin roofs before finally calling it quits at close to eight o'clock. It had snowed this evening—maybe three or four inches—and was still coming down. He needed to get back to Ma's, get some supper and give his business partner a call.

He stepped into the parking lot and firmly pulled the auto-locking door closed behind him when a blinding glare halted him in his tracks. He turned his head slightly to the side and lifted his forearm to shade his eyes, attempting to make out the vehicle that had pinned him with its piercing lights.

Irritated, he waved them away with his free arm. "Hey, knock it off!"

The lights abruptly shut off, but his eyes were still adjusting when he heard the sound of the vehicle's door open and saw a shadowy figure step out. The door closed again.

"Sorry about that, Hawk."

Merle Perslow, if he wasn't mistaken. But the scornful tone of his voice belied the apology and Cody didn't make any attempt to respond to the mocking words.

"So, you think you'll make the deadline?" The man approached, now visible in the faint pool of light provided by the door's overhead fixture. He halted a few yards away from Cody.

"I see no reason why not."

Paris's father gave a cursory glance around the parking lot. "I can think of a few myself."

"Sir?"

Merle tilted his head, eyeing Cody. "You'd be further along if you focused on the work at hand and limited your distractions."

Cody took a slow breath. "With my father in the hospital and my mother in need of assistance, I'm giving as much time to the project as I can. I'm confident things will meet the committee's expectations."

"Your efforts to help your family are commendable. But we both know that isn't the distraction I'm referring to."

Paris.

Merle's brows lowered. "I thought on the day you came to see me about the status of your father's employment that we'd come to a mutual agreement."

Cody met the belligerent gaze with a blandly innocent one. "There were strings attached to those concessions?"

"Cody, Cody, Cody." Merle gave a bitter chuckle. "You haven't changed since you were a teenager, have you? You still have your eye on a grand prize you're not even in the running for."

Is that how he saw his daughter? A prize to be awarded to a man who fit his idea of who and what Paris needed in her life? Nevertheless, Merle's casual dismissal of him stung, as if being brushed away like an annoying gnat.

"I agreed to fulfill my mother's contract and that's what I intend to do," Cody said quietly, having no intention of getting tangled up in a confrontation with this man. He was Paris's father and for that reason alone he'd show him respect.

Merle smirked. "That was a convenient windfall for you, wasn't it? You know, with your mother reneging on her contractual obligations."

Cody tensed at the inferred slur on his mother's integrity.

"Surely you can't believe Dad's stroke was deliberately timed to release her from her responsibilities."

"Of course not. But..." Merle raked his hand through his neatly groomed hair, then he fixed a challenging glare on Cody. "Look, let's stop dodging the issue here. You're seeing more of my daughter than is required to get this job done. I want that to stop."

"I've rarely seen your daughter."

Merle's mouth twisted into a grimace. "That's not what I'm hearing."

So Owen Fremont had gotten in his two cents' worth? What better tactic than to manipulate Paris's father into running off the competition.

"I'm speaking the truth, Mr. Perslow."

"Truth?" Merle snorted. "That's a foreign language for a Hawk, wouldn't you say?"

Cody managed a shrug, keeping his temper in check. Unlike in his younger days, he wouldn't give Mr. Perslow the satisfaction of getting him riled. "So you've come here to tell me you've rethought your position on Dad's situation?"

Merle waved him away, his expression darkening. "We both know your father's 'situation' is immaterial. I'm here to make it clear there's only so much I'll take of the games Hawks play. You got that?"

Without waiting for a response, Merle leveled a final glare, then swung around to march back to his SUV, snow crunching under his boots.

Fists clenched, Cody watched in seething silence as the arrogant man climbed into the Lexus. This time Cody didn't flinch when the headlights again hit him. But when the engine gunned to roaring life and the vehicle lurched forward, his muscles tensed as he prepared to make a running leap into the nearby stand of ponderosas.

But the SUV only made a tight circle, then headed out of the parking lot, the glow of its taillights illuminating the still-falling snow.

"Look out, Paris!" The warning was accompanied by a feminine squeal of laughter as a snowball smacked into the windshield she was endeavoring to clean off.

Paris bent to scoop up a handful of snow from the church parking lot and packed it tight in her gloved hands. Then, attempting to keep her balance on the frosty surface, she sent the frozen missile sailing over the SUV's roof to the vehicle next to her. Missed.

"You throw like a girl!" Delaney taunted as she ducked into her car and pulled the door shut. Then she started the engine, flipped on the lights and made a face at Paris out the driver-side window as she negotiated her car from its parking spot.

"Isn't it great to have Delaney back?" Kara Kenton called from where she was scraping ice and snow from her rear window. Snow was falling faster than they could clean it off their vehicles.

"Oh, yeah, great." Laughing, Paris brushed the frozen crystals from the front of her jacket. Her friend had a more accurate aim than Paris could ever hope to have.

"We'll gang up on her soon," promised Olivia McGuire as she climbed into her own vehicle. "Drive carefully, ladies. I just got a call from Rob and he says it's slick out there."

"Where are the men in our lives when we need them?" Kara pouted aloud and a half dozen women scattered throughout the parking lot responded with their own laughing protests. Everyone was in high spirits after Abby Diaz's bridal shower. Her fiancé had gallantly picked her up afterward and most of the guests had also departed, but a number of the women had stayed to clean the church's kitchen and fellowship hall. Unfortunately, another snow squall moved through as they worked, depositing a fresh, frosty layer.

Paris used her snowbrush to again swipe at her windows, noticing that a pickup truck was slowing to a crawl on the street parallel to where she stood. Recognition dawned and before she could stop herself, she waved.

Cody.

To her surprise, he pulled into the parking lot—or rather slid in—and came to a halt not far from her. The next thing she knew, he'd bounded out of the truck with a long-handled, heavy-duty snowbrush and ice scraper combo. Booted feet wide apart and slowly raising the metal-handled, retractable device over his head as if it were a massive barbell, he gazed around the parking lot.

All eyes were riveted on him and Paris couldn't help but smile. Tall, handsome and broad-shouldered with snowflakes lighting in his glossy black hair, he looked as if he could take on the world.

"So, ladies!" he called out in that low, yummy voice of his, a grin broadening, "whose car is first?"

A chorus of feminine cheers ensued as he was enthusiastically waved forward. In no time at all, he'd removed the snow from a handful of vehicles, cleaning off even the hard-to-reach tops of the SUVs. One by one the smiling ladies departed, waving happily.

And then, at long last, he turned to her.

She hadn't seen him since Saturday, hadn't dared let herself stop by Pine Shadow Ridge to check on his progress. Touched by his willingness to apologize, she was nevertheless still confused about how she felt about him, and decided avoidance was the most sensible route to go. He'd only be in town a short while longer. There was no reason to get tied in knots attempting to find answers to questions that were better left unasked.

He approached her slowly, almost warily, probably feeling as self-conscious as she did. Their last encounter had ended awkwardly. In fact, their last two meetings had ended on a less-than-comfortable note.

"I think you made a few fans tonight," she said, injecting a lightness into her tone. He laughed and the sound sent a delicious warmth flowing through her veins.

"Never hurts to have fans." He fiddled with the snowbrush, pulling the handle to its maximum length. Then he methodically pushed the snow from the top of her vehicle off the far side as he'd done for the other ladies.

"How are things coming on the project?" she ventured.

"The cabins are painted down to the details and frosted plexiglass windows inserted so light coming in from behind will give the illusion of an interior aglow." He gave the heavy snow on top another push, making it look easier than she knew it to be. "I'm working on the shingled roofs now."

"The trees are scheduled to be delivered next Monday."

"Live trees, with burlap-wrapped bases, right?"

"Just like in your mom's design." She tucked her snowbrush under her arm and thrust her chilled hands into her pockets. "We have door prizes—attach a tag under plates on each table and, depending on where people sit, they win anything from the centerpiece to a wreath to a tree to take home to plant in their yard. There's no point in the decorations going to waste."

He cut her an amused look. "Do you think anyone wants to win one of a dozen faux cabins?"

Paris smiled. "You might be surprised. As sturdy as you're building them, they may make clever holiday yard ornaments. Or the committee may choose to put them in storage for use again another year."

"I could see your mother setting them up as an entire woodland village in her front yard."

Surprised, she gazed up at him. "That sounds exactly like what she'd do."

He gave the snow another shove. "I liked your mom, Paris. I felt really bad when she died. I don't think I ever got the chance to tell you that."

Tears unexpectedly pricked her eyes and she again pulled out her snowbrush and swiped halfheartedly at one of the windows before placing the brush on the hood of her SUV. She missed Mom more than ever at this time of year. "You know, it's funny, but the night before she died…"

She'd never told anyone this. Why was she bringing it up now? Cody turned to give her a nod, encouraging her to continue.

"I dreamed…" She couldn't help but smile at the memory. "I dreamed Mom and I were walking in the forest with Dad. It was a beautiful snowy day with big fat fluffy flakes coming down around us. Mom was laughing and *dancing* around in the snow. Can you believe it? Twirling with her arms outstretched like a little kid."

Paris laughed and stretched out her own arms, marveling at the still-vivid dream.

"That sounds like a good dream to me," Cody said softly. "One worth remembering."

"It was, it really was. But then, all of sudden…" She swallowed, determined not to cry. "All of a sudden in the dream I realized that Mom wasn't in a wheelchair anymore. She wasn't using a walker or a cane. I grabbed Dad by the arm. Pulled him close and whispered, '*Look,* Dad.'"

Her voice broke as a single tear slid down her cheek and Cody set the snowbrush aside to reach for her hand.

She drew strength from the gentle grip with which he held her. "I... I said, 'Look, Dad. She's okay now. She's okay.' And it was like the happiest day of my life."

Her eyes sought Cody's compassion-filled ones.

"And then I woke up." She shook her head slowly. "I prayed it was a sign God would heal her, that we'd have a miracle."

"But it wasn't to be," he said, his voice gentle.

"No. That afternoon... Mom died."

"I'm sorry, Paris." Cody's voice came in a ragged breath as he opened his arms to her.

Chapter Twelve

What was he thinking? Her father all but threatened him with bodily harm if he didn't stay away from his daughter. Yet here he was, standing under the church's parking lot lights for God and the whole world to see, holding her as if he'd never let her go.

He shifted his arms more securely around her, savoring the scent of her as he placed his cheek against her soft hair. He didn't get a sense that she was crying, that there was a need to dry tears, but only that she sought a reassuring comfort of strong arms around her.

His arms. Not Owen Fremont's.

How many years had he dreamed of holding her this way?

"That dream?" she said softly, her voice muffled against his jacket, for she'd slipped her arms around him in response to his own embrace.

"What about it?" he whispered.

"It was God's gift to me, don't you think? To remind me there will come a day when Dad and I *will* laugh together with Mom in the presence of God."

"You will."

"Jesus promises He'll dry every tear and there will be no pain or mourning or death."

"No debilitating MS."

"No. No more." She pulled back slightly to look into his eyes. "How do people live without that promise, Cody? Without the reassurance God gives to get us through the loss, the pain?"

His chest tightened as he looked down at her, into her dewy eyes. At her sweet, kissable mouth. But now wasn't the time or place to be thinking thoughts like that. With effort, he lifted his gaze to the cascade of snowflakes coming down from above.

"It's not a way I'd choose to live now, apart from Him. I did for way too long, certain I had all the answers. That I had life figured out and it didn't include God."

"I'm glad you let Him find you, Cody. I know it must have been hard to recognize the love of a Heavenly Father when your only example of fatherhood was—"

"Leroy Hawk?"

Contrite eyes met his. "I'm sorry, I didn't mean—"

He placed a gloved finger to still her lips. "No, it's true. For the longest time the last thing I wanted was anyone in my life who called himself father, heavenly or not."

Should he tell her what the turning point had been? What had pushed him into God's welcoming embrace? The crust of his hard, rebellious heart had finally broken open when he'd learned of her engagement to Dalton Herrington III.

But he didn't want to remind her of Dalton. Not now. Not when he was holding her close.

As if only now becoming aware of how she pressed against him, she stepped back, a self-conscious, apologetic smile playing on her lips. Reluctantly he released her and the cold night air rushed in to replace the warm place she'd filled, both in his arms and in his heart.

"Thank you, Cody," she said, ducking her head almost shyly. "For listening. When you said you liked my mother, I—"

She motioned helplessly.

"I did like your mother." And he cared for her daughter even more.

"I guess I'd better get going before Dad places a call to search and rescue."

Her heading home might not be a half-bad idea. He sure didn't want Mr. Perslow looking for her and finding them here together. Despite the dismissive comment about his father's situation being "immaterial," he didn't trust her father not to renege on his agreement as he seemed to think Cody had.

"Maybe I should follow you, make sure you get there safely."

"Thank you, but…"

She took another step back, obviously now embarrassed for breaking down in front of him, clinging to him. Time had passed since they were teens, but not much else had changed. In the eyes of many, including Paris and her father, he remained the bad boy to her good girl. What is it he'd brazenly announced to her the night she'd turned him away? That one day she'd beg him to marry her?

No, he didn't see that happening. Ever.

"Why don't you pop inside and get your car warmed

up?" he suggested. They'd stood there so long, another layer of white had settled on the windows from stem to stern. "Get the defroster going while I give your windows a final cleaning."

All too soon, he had her windows cleared, ever conscious that she was watching him from inside the warmth of her vehicle and thinking about…what?

Him?

She rolled down her window, snowflakes lightly catching in her dark hair. Her luminous eyes met his. "Thank you again, Cody. For everything."

And then, as always, she was gone.

What had gotten into her last night? And what must Cody think of how she'd behaved, wrapping her arms around him and holding on for dear life? She was glad he didn't have any idea what was going through her mind as she looked up into his compassion-filled eyes, at his firm, inviting lips.

Or at least she hoped he didn't have any idea.

Could he feel her heart pounding as she'd pressed against him? Did he sense her confusion in those vulnerable few seconds when she'd drawn back from him after having poured out her heart about the dream?

But how good it had felt to be held in the security of his arms. What would it be like to be embraced like that for a lifetime? Knowing that someone was there for you no matter what, that they had your best in mind?

Someone like Cody.

She made her way through the snow outside the maintenance building at Pine Shadow Ridge shortly after noon, clutching a holiday-trimmed insulated box in her gloved hands. Turkey sandwiches with brie and cranberries, fresh and hot from Camilla's Café. Home-made sweet-potato chips.

She'd taken the afternoon off, but after last night should she be here, dropping in on Cody like this? At Abby's bridal shower, Sharon Dixon mentioned he'd confided the need for assistance in the making of pine-cone wreaths and, well, she could assist as easily as the next person, right?

But as Delaney had pointed out, people were be-ginning to talk about her and Cody, even though there was nothing to talk about. Neither of them had done anything that could remotely be considered out of line. And even though as a teenager he'd professed his un-dying love, he hadn't given any hint that he still cared for her, hadn't taken advantage of her vulnerable state last night as many men would have done.

But it was probably getting around that he'd come to everyone's aid at the church—and that the two of them had been the last ones in the parking lot when the others departed.

She glanced back at her SUV. Should she leave the sandwiches by the door, drive away and then call to let him know she'd dropped them off?

But she'd no more thought of that alternative when the steel door opened and Jim Harper stepped out. His eyes brightened as he gave her a friendly nod and held the door open for her. "Good afternoon, Miss Perslow."

He eyed her and the insulated box with interest.

"Hello, Jim. Would you mind—?"

She started to hand off the box to him, but he leaned back in the open door.

"Hey, Hawk!" he hollered loud enough to wake the dead. "Special delivery. *Real* special."

Paris's cheeks warmed as Jim swept her a low bow and motioned her inside. The door closed behind her and, as her eyes adjusted to the interior's relative dimness, she saw Cody approaching, a puzzled look on his handsome face.

"Hello, Paris. What brings you out here?"

He sounded surprised, but not particularly pleased. Had he thought that by her forward behavior last night she was playing games with him?

"Sharon said you could use help with the pinecone wreaths. That's something I can do." She held out the insulated box, suddenly questioning why she'd thought to make such a personal overture as bringing him a meal. "And I thought…you might be hungry and would enjoy something hot for lunch."

He ran a hand through his hair, uncertainty flickering through his eyes. Obviously he didn't know what to make of her offer to help or the noontime delivery.

"Or," she said quickly, "you could save it for your dinner tonight."

He accepted the box. "No, no, lunch sounds great. Thanks."

She peered around him to the well-lit area in the far corner of the building. A small army of faux cabins lined the walls. "Maybe while you eat, you could get me started working on the wreaths? I have the afternoon off."

He grimaced. "I wish I'd known you were coming. Unfortunately, the frames, glue guns and supply of dried pinecones are at my folks' place."

"I guess I should have said something last night." But cradled in his arms, she hadn't been thinking of pine-cone wreaths. "Do you have anything else I could do?"

Nice going, Paris. You're practically begging him to find you a reason to stay while he consumes the meal you forced on him. He probably hates brie. And cranberries.

He glanced back at the work area. "Maybe I can find something…"

"Don't worry about it, okay? I didn't mean to in-terrupt your work. I thought, from what Sharon said, that there would be something I could do. It's been awhile, but Mom and I used to make pinecone wreaths together."

He tilted his head. "I remember that."

"You do?"

"Yeah. Dad and I'd come the weekend after Thanks-giving to set up the lights and lawn ornaments. Your mother invited us inside for cocoa and cookies. You both had your hair in ponytails tied with metallic gold ribbons, and pinecones spread across the kitchen table."

Paris laughed. "That's right. I'd forgotten."

She didn't think there was a single encounter with Cody she didn't remember. Yet here was one he re-called right down to the details.

He looked at the box still clutched in his hand. "You know, I could sure use someone who is wreath-savvy right about now. I hate losing the opportunity to make use of your time and talents when you're available."

"Could we go get the pinecones and the rest of the stuff? Then we could come back here and I could get to work."

He rubbed his free hand along the back of his neck and she abruptly realized she'd basically invited herself to his folks' place. Sharon mentioned last night that it was in a state of disrepair, so he probably wouldn't care to have visitors even if only long enough to pick up pinecones.

He shook his head. "This isn't the most comfortable place for doing that kind of work. Even with that space heater back there, it's cold. Drafty. I don't want you catching a chill at Christmas."

"I may not be Laura Ingalls Wilder," she teased, suddenly wanting to convince him she was up to the challenge, "but I do come from sturdy pioneer stock."

A smile quirked as he gave her an appreciative head-to-toe evaluation that sent the blood in her veins thrumming.

"What about…" Cody studied her thoughtfully. "Ma will be home early this afternoon. She has business in town to take care of so she's cutting her hospital visit short. We could head over to her place and recruit her for pointers. It's been awhile since I've made wreaths, so I could use a refresher."

"I could, too." She'd never been to Cody's parents' place and, in fact, was surprised he'd taken her suggestion to retrieve the supplies a step further. "I can drive while you eat."

His forehead wrinkled. "It might be better if we both took our own vehicles. That way neither of us has to come back here if we don't need to."

Plus, it might not be wise to be seen riding around town together. That would definitely feed the gossip mill.

"Are you sure you have time?" She felt as if her arrival had disrupted his plans for the day.

He shrugged. "It will be a good break and I really could use the help."

Thirty minutes later, Cody having consumed his lunch as he put away his tools, they headed out. She followed his truck to the outskirts of their community.

The neighborhood the Hawks lived in was one she'd rarely passed through. Its winding, graveled road wove through the towering trees among a hodgepodge of modest—and sometimes run-down—frame homes and trailers. Here and there beribboned wreaths or a plastic holiday yard ornament reminded that Christmas came to this part of town, too. When Cody pulled into the driveway of a double-wide trailer, she followed close behind.

He approached to hold open her door. "Let's grab pinecones from Ma's stash and find us a place at the kitchen table."

"Sounds good."

Together they walked through the snow to the back of the property where Paris was surprised to see the shed Cody had built wasn't a stark shelter for lawn mowers and garden hoses, but a cute wood-framed structure. Painted a creamy yellow, it boasted glass windows with white shutters and window boxes to showcase flowers in the summer months.

"This is adorable, Cody. No wonder Sharon wishes she had one, too."

"You like it?"

"I love it."

He looked pleased. "Ma needed a place to call her

own, a place to work on her craft projects and gardening. Dad later put in electricity and heat for her."

"You're a talented man, do you know that?"

"Thanks." He reached for the doorknob and opened it wide to reveal a shadowed interior.

She eagerly stepped forward. "Oh, Cody, this is—"

An unexpected sound of movement from inside cut her words short and Cody protectively reached out to halt her.

She looked up at him uncertainly, her voice a whisper. "Do your parents have a dog?"

Frowning, he shook his head. "Maybe it's a mouse or squirrel."

They listened intently. Then the sound of movement came again, the scraping of something on the concrete floor. Not at all animal-like.

"Who's in there?" Cody called in a tone intended to intimidate.

No response.

"Ma should keep the door padlocked," he muttered under his breath, then stepped closer to the open doorway. "Whoever you are, come on out of there and show yourself!"

A rustling, crunching sound came from a far corner, outside their line of vision.

Cody nodded to Paris to step away from the door, then he again raised his voice. "I *said*—"

"Don't shoot, mister!" came a childish cry. "I ain't armed."

Paris and Cody exchanged a startled glance. Then together they leaned in to look through the doorway.

Chapter Thirteen

With a sense of relief, Cody flipped the light switch. Then he stepped farther into the shed, cautiously looking in the direction where Ma kept pinecones sealed in thirty-nine-gallon garbage bags. There, atop overstuffed plastic bags where he must have fallen, a boy defensively clutched a weathered backpack to his chest.

Cody's breath caught as he looked down into a mirror image of who he'd been as a five-year-old. The same shape of face, raven-dark hair and black-brown eyes filled with suspicion.

"Hey, there, young fella," Cody said softly, not wanting to further frighten the boy. "Who are you? And what are you doing here?"

For a long moment, their eyes locked and Cody got the distinct impression this kid had seen more than his share of the less-than-pleasant side of life, that he had every reason to be leery of Cody's sudden appearance in the doorway.

Oblivious of the pinecones being crushed under his weight, the boy clambered to his feet and slung his backpack over his shoulder. Then his chin jutted defiantly, his words tinged with a Texas accent. "I'm Deron Hawk. *D-E-R-O-N*. Who are *you* and what are *you* doing here?"

A Hawk.

Cody glanced to where Paris had joined him, reading immediately from her shocked expression that she'd seen the resemblance, too. The kid could be Cody's...

The boy stared unflinchingly from Cody to Paris and back again, but with a sinking feeling Cody recognized a too-familiar bravado that sent him hurtling back in time to his own childhood. He dismissed the boy's challenge for what it was. The kid was scared.

But from the looks of him, he was without a doubt a Hawk. Likely one of his brother's kids.

"I'm Cody. Cody *Hawk*. And this is Paris Perslow." He squatted to the same level as the boy and held out his hand for an introductory shake—which the glaring child didn't take him up on.

Cody glanced up at Paris, then back at the boy. "Well, Deron, can you tell us your dad's name?"

For a moment he thought the youngster wouldn't respond and he could almost sense Paris holding her breath. Did she really think the kid might be his? But apparently Deron was digesting Cody's words for, after a long pause, he thrust out an ice-cold hand for a man-to-man shake.

Where were the kid's gloves? His hat? The too-large jacket didn't look to be more than a layer of denim with a flannel lining and his sockless feet were thrust into well-worn tennis shoes.

"My dad is Carson Hawk and I'm here to see my

granddad." The boy's eyes narrowed. "You don't look like a granddad."

Cody sensed Paris's smile.

"No, I'm not your granddad. I'm your dad's brother. Your uncle."

A flicker of uncertainty broke through the facade of the boy's bluster. "I'm supposed to stay with my granddad."

Stay? Did Ma know about this? In the midst of Dad's illness, had she forgotten to tell him of the anticipated arrival of her step-grandson, Cody's nephew?

Doubtful.

"Your grandfather…isn't here right now." No need to tell about the hospitalization. "Where's your dad?"

Deron shrugged, avoiding his gaze. "Dunno."

Cody didn't like the sound of that. "So he dumped you off here and—"

"Cody." Paris touched his shoulder and he looked up at her. "He's tired. He needs to get warm and something to eat."

He looked back at the boy. He did look tired. Cold. Hungry. "What did you have for breakfast?"

"Potato chips." He announced the fact as if proud of it.

"What about lunch?"

The boy lifted a shoulder as if the question was of no consequence. "Dad said granddad would feed me."

So he'd been dumped at the trailer since at least noon. Probably considerably longer.

Cody drew in a resigned breath. "What do you think about coming inside? Warming up? I imagine we can rustle up soup or a sandwich. You can eat while we let your grandfather—and your step-grandma—know you're here."

Alarm flashed through the boy's eyes as his glance darted toward the open door. For a moment, Cody feared the kid might take off. But the look disappeared as quickly as it had come and Cody rose slowly to his feet to place a reassuring hand on Deron's shoulder.

His brother's kid. Exactly what Ma didn't need right now.

"Paris?" His gaze met her troubled one. "Why don't you lead the way?"

Once inside the trailer, Paris settled Deron on the sofa, one of Ma's handmade afghans tucked in around him. Cody peeled out of his jacket, kicked up the heat a few notches, then headed to the adjoining kitchen to dig out a can of chicken noodle soup.

As he heated the soup, he could hear Paris's soothing words of reassurance. Promises that Deron was safe here. Praise for his bravery. Confirmation of his welcome.

Not too much later she joined him, her voice low. "He looks so much like you, Cody, I have to admit that for a moment I thought—"

"No worries," he likewise whispered. "There are no Cody Hawk juniors running around out there. And I guarantee you if there were, they wouldn't be abandoned on someone's doorstep."

They both glanced toward the living room where, warmed by the crocheted blanket, the exhausted boy now appeared to be dozing.

"So you think his parents abandoned him? That they didn't drop him off for a day or two?"

"You heard the kid. He said he's supposed to stay with his granddad. He doesn't know where his father is."

"But surely—"

Cody cut her off with a shake of his head. "I've never been interested in the lives of my half brothers, but I've picked up enough from Ma to know that Carson's left behind a string of women and offspring."

"But his mother...?"

"I'm sure we'll learn more soon enough."

Compassion filled her eyes. "It's so sad."

That was a nice way of putting it. If she'd ever doubted that Hawk men truly deserved their tarnished reputations, that they'd merely been victims of bad PR, Deron's unexpected arrival should still those doubts.

"Here," she said, gently pushing him aside and taking the spoon from his fingers. "Let me finish with this so you can call your mother."

"She should be on her way home by now. I won't call her while she's driving."

"Do you think she was expecting...company?"

He shook his head as he searched the cabinets for saltine crackers. "No, and she sure doesn't need this on top of everything else."

Paris's expression softened even further. "He was trying hard to be a tough little guy, wasn't he?"

Cody nodded. "You saw through it, too? He's scared to death."

"I can't imagine how parents could—"

"Hey!" a boyish voice demanded from the living room. "What's with the baby?"

Cody glanced to where Deron was now standing by the sofa, the afghan clutched around his slim shoulders.

"What baby is that, Deron?"

Poor kid. Regardless of whether or not Carson and the kid's mother had any intention of retrieving him, he'd see to it the boy had more appropriate winter wear. That was easy enough. But none of them were prepared to take on raising a kid. Certainly not Ma, what with Dad's situation. What were they going to do with the little guy?

"What baby?" he asked again when Deron didn't respond.

The boy pointed to the ceramic nativity scene displayed on the coffee table. "*That* baby."

Cody caught Paris's look of alarm. The kid must be even more exhausted than they'd originally thought.

"That's baby Jesus," she reminded gently.

Deron's brow puckered. "Who is Jesus?"

Who is Jesus? Even the next day, Paris couldn't shake off Deron's question. To think that a boy his age, a kindergartner, hadn't any inkling of the birth of God's only son into the world seemed unimaginable. For a brief moment, she'd thought he might be teasing them, but one look in his dark, perplexed eyes quickly put an end to that assumption.

For Deron, Christmas was no more than Santa Claus and a red-nosed reindeer.

"You look pretty serious there." Cody glanced at her from where he'd laid down four ladder-back chairs in the bed of his truck. Paris had found them at the secondhand shop on Main Street that afternoon, intending them for a cozy holiday vignette at the clubhouse. Cody had been gracious enough to stop his work at Pine Shadow Ridge and meet her at the store to pick them up. "What are you thinking about?"

"Deron." She slipped her hands into her jacket pockets. "About how he didn't have a clue who Jesus is."

"I probably wasn't much more knowledgeable at that age than he is." Cody tossed a tarp across the chairs. "Ma didn't meet God herself until I was in high school. Even then, Dad wouldn't let me go to church with her—except, of course, the times when he thought we could get 'our fair share' from the congregation."

He shook his head.

"That's why you never went with your mother?"

"Right. The first time I probably heard the whole Christmas story—shepherds and angels and wise men and the works—was when I was a youngster and your mother read it to the neighborhood kids. I got included because Dad could hardly tell his employer's wife to take a hike."

"Really? That's the first time?"

"It was the first time it had ever been clear to me, not a jumbled kaleidoscope of disjointed stuff."

"Do you think I explained the true meaning of Christmas well enough to Deron?" She couldn't tell if any of it made sense to the boy. He listened, but didn't ask any questions, although he seemed fascinated by the nativity scene. Had she made the story sound as real as it truly was, not another fairy tale?

"You did an exceptional job," Cody said as he finished securing the tarp. "You kept it simple for a boy that age. Now we'll have to make sure we help him build on that foundation."

We.

Why did she like the sound of that? Cody probably meant it in a general sense, of course, not a personal one. Or maybe "we" meant him and his mother?

"My brother phoned the house late last night and talked to Ma." Cody adjusted the ball cap on his head. "Typical, though, that even when he heard about Dad's situation, he didn't offer a word of sympathy. He didn't care about the imposition on Dad's second wife at a time when she has her hands full. He's taking advantage, knowing Ma can't bear to turn Deron away."

"Did you talk to him, too?"

"No. But this morning he faxed documents to the school confirming that Ma and Dad will soon be Deron's legal guardians. It doesn't seem my soft-hearted mother has much of a choice."

"So he's going to stay? Poor little guy. Does he have siblings?"

"It sounds as if there are one or two older ones and a new baby. I guess a kid his age is too much to deal with for Carson's latest lady." He grimaced. "Ma's going to see the school guidance counselor to find out what's best—enrolling before Christmas break or after."

"Where is he today? Did your mother stay home with him?"

"No, he's with a next-door neighbor who has twin boys a year younger than him. Ma needed to talk to Dad without little ears listening in, and I can't drag him out to the maintenance building around heavy equipment and power tools."

"Maybe… I could help?" She couldn't bear to think of the child spending his day among strangers. Of course, she—like Lucy and Cody—was a stranger, too. But still…

He frowned. "What do you mean?"

"I'm pretty good with kids and I have several years of college toward an elementary education degree."

"Really? I didn't know that."

"Long story. I didn't finish. But children don't run in the other direction when they see me coming."

Cody folded his arms, the corners of his eyes crinkling. "Paris, there isn't a soul on the planet who would run when they saw you coming."

Warmth crept into her cheeks at Cody's candid compliment. "I could watch Deron once in a while. That way you wouldn't have to take off from the project and your mom could still spend time with your dad."

"Like you don't have enough to do?" He gazed thoughtfully at her for a moment, as if contemplating her suggestion, then shook his head. "Thanks for the offer, but we'll manage."

Disappointed, she watched as he started toward the driver-side door, ready to head out to the clubhouse with the chairs.

"Cody?"

He paused, his hand on the door latch. "Yeah?"

She took a few steps toward him. "May I come along?"

Uncertainty flickered in his eyes as he quickly took in their Main Street surroundings. How many times had she seen him do that, as if suspecting they were being spied upon? Was he aware people were talking about them, so he was trying to be respectful of how his presence might incite gossip?

Heat crept into her cheeks as the moment drew out. She shouldn't have asked to tag along. But after yesterday, sharing in the discovery of Deron and spending the evening making pinecone wreaths with his mother, it seemed the wall between them had crumbled slightly.

But apparently not enough.

Then his dark eyes swung back to her, and he nodded.

"Sure. Come on."

Chapter Fourteen

J̲ust a few nights ago, Paris's father had tracked him down and made veiled threats that should have sunk into Cody's brain. Yet today he found himself, bold as brass, driving down Main Street in his old loaner truck with the most beautiful woman in the world right beside him.

There is only so much I'll take of the games Hawks play. You got that?

Games Hawks play? What had he meant by that?

Cody cranked up the heat with an unsteady hand, but the shaky sensation didn't come from Merle Perslow's vague words of intimidation, but from the reality of Paris seated next to him.

He should have said no. It might have hurt her feelings, but she seemed oblivious to the fact that others had taken notice of the handful of moments they'd shared in recent weeks. People like his old classmate Jim Harper. Harry Campbell at the gatehouse. Paris's father.

Owen Fremont.

As they headed down the highway, he furtively

glanced to where Paris gazed out the passenger-side window.

How many others had seen them together just now? He hated to think his presence, no matter how blameless, might blemish her standing in the community. She was young, innocent, and apparently didn't fully grasp the fact that a good reputation, once tarnished, couldn't easily be replaced, or she wouldn't have invited herself to ride along.

That's what Owen had tried, in his clumsy, selfish way, to get through to him and the point her father was undoubtedly trying to make. If he had to do it again, he wouldn't volunteer to fulfill Ma's contractual obligations. He'd pay the committee double—even triple— what his mother owed and wash his hands of it. But no, he'd let pride get in his way. Pride and the niggling hope that he might see Paris on occasion.

"Look, Cody!" She pointed up ahead, to the side of the tree-lined road. "Deer!"

He checked the rearview mirror for traffic, then slowed to pull off the road and cut the engine. A buck and two does lifted their heads, looking curiously in the direction of his truck.

"They're beautiful, aren't they?" she whispered.

"They aren't something I see on the streets of Phoenix, that's for sure."

In rapt silence they watched the wildlife move slowly out of sight, then he started the truck and pulled onto the highway.

"You know, Cody, you've never told me what you've been doing the past twelve years. You mentioned Phoenix and your mother alluded to the fact that you have important things to attend to elsewhere. But that's all I know. It makes you somewhat a man of mystery."

Cody laughed. "I'd hardly call myself mysterious."

"What *have* you been doing with yourself?"

He'd already made clear he hadn't left a trail of women and kids behind him like Carson. But did she wonder if he'd gone from job to job, wandering aimlessly in this old relic of a pickup, one step ahead of the law?

He settled his ball cap more firmly on his head, keeping his eyes on the road. "A dozen years. That's a lot of territory to cover in a short jaunt to Pine Shadow Ridge."

"Try the CliffsNotes version."

So she really wanted to know? It wasn't every day that a woman like Paris asked to know more about him.

"Well, let's see…" His memory flew to the last time he'd seen her before leaving town, the night he'd shown up on her doorstep. No, he wouldn't start there. "Long story made short… I hitchhiked down to the Valley of the Sun. Then—"

"You *hitchhiked* to Phoenix? Cody, that was a dangerous thing to do."

He lifted a shoulder, dismissing her concern. "Not so dangerous when you're picked up by a talkative old rancher who is glad for the company and grateful for help unloading a cantankerous bull at an outlying ranch down there."

Paris shook her head disapprovingly, but he continued. "Turns out that ride was a godsend. The ranch was owned by a prosperous building contractor who happened to be desperate for workers who could handle a hammer."

"Then what?"

"That contractor's son, Trevor, and I hit it off and, before I knew it, the family basically took me in as a second son." He never would have foreseen that there were people in the world who would believe the best of him.

"I'm sure they saw what a hard worker you were."

His heart swelled. She recognized that? Had she seen that when he was growing up?

"Mostly I think they saw what a messed-up kid I was and how easy it would be for me to fall into the same destructive patterns as my half brothers. Trevor's folks were authentic Christians, not just a Sunday-morning variety, and recognized I needed tough love and a strong foundation to stand on."

"You were almost eighteen when you left here, weren't you? So, shortly after that you gave your life to God?"

Cody cut her a regretful look. "Nope. It would be another eight years before it finally sank in that the relationship the Cane family had with God was one He was offering me, too."

"That's a long time."

"I had a lot to be grateful for to Arden and Mona. And Trev, of course. But I had a rebellious heart, Paris. A heart that, despite Arden's loving example, had me convinced God fit the mold of Leroy Hawk. Unforgiving. Unpredictable. Untrustworthy. As we've touched on before, I couldn't make peace with the two extremes of fatherhood—what I'd lived versus what the Bible claimed."

He let his foot off the gas and slowed for the turn to the gated property. "Suffice it to say, our Heavenly Father eventually won me over. That was about three years ago."

A glance in Paris's direction caught her pensive expression as she stared out the window.

"So you do construction work?"

"I'd just finished my business degree when the building boom bottomed out, and Trev and I searched for other opportunities. Loans weren't easy to come by, but we did our research, picked out neighborhoods that had a good chance of revival and started flipping houses."

Paris turned to him. "So you're buying homes and fixing them up to sell for a profit?"

"And our risk is paying off. The housing market is stabilizing and prices are on the rise. We have a growing, competent team—made up of returning veterans and craftsmen who'd been hit hard by the economic downturn—so we're doing less of the labor ourselves and spending more time on the management end. In fact…" He and Trev hadn't shared this with many outside Trevor's immediate family, but with Paris's interested gaze now focused on him, he couldn't resist. "We have a major investor we're waiting to hear back from any day now. Trev and I'd like to branch out from the Valley and see where we could go with this statewide."

"Wow!"

She sounded as excited about it as he felt. Did she recognize that, while he might not yet be running in the same financial circles as her Owen Fremont, this poor kid from Canyon Springs had made good? "Yeah, we're pumped about it."

"I can see why. Do you think—" Her cell phone chimed, cutting her short. She pulled the phone from her pocket and glanced down at the caller ID, then back at him. "I'm sorry, Cody. I should take this."

A muscle tightened in his jaw.

Owen, no doubt.

Chapter Fifteen

"I took the liberty of picking up that velvet gown for you," Dalton's mother said, getting right to the purpose of her call. "I'll drop it off in the next day or two."

Paris self-consciously turned slightly away from Cody, but before she could respond, Elizabeth continued.

"By the way, I spoke with Parker's mother…and confirmed he'll be in town the weekend of the gala."

"Elizabeth, I thought I—"

"Now, now… I merely inquired about his plans while he's here and she's certain he wouldn't be opposed to acting as your escort."

"I already told you I don't need an escort," Paris stated, acutely aware of the man beside her. "I'm going to be far too busy for that."

"Nevertheless, consider the dress an early Christmas present. But don't wait too long to make up your mind about Parker. He's a nice young man with excellent prospects."

As soon as Elizabeth uttered a stiff goodbye, Paris shut off her phone. "You wouldn't happen to own a tux, would you, Cody? And be free the night of the Christmas gala?"

How did *that* pop out of her mouth?

He gave a halfhearted laugh as they headed toward the clubhouse nestled in the trees. "It sounds as if Mrs. Herrington has someone lined up for the occasion already."

Paris slipped the phone back into her pocket. "She won't let it go. She and Dad keep pushing Parker at me."

Cody's forehead creased. "Parker?"

"Parker Herrington. Dalton's cousin."

"But why would they… I thought… Aren't you seeing Owen Fremont?"

She almost choked. "Are you kidding me? No way."

"I have to admit I'm relieved to hear that."

He was? "Unfortunately, Elizabeth has already bought the dress."

He cast her a startled look. "A wedding dress?"

"No, silly." Paris made a face. "A gown for the Christmas gala. Are you sure you don't have a tux squirreled away someplace?"

How had she garnered the courage to even think such a thing, let alone boldly ask him? But it made sense. She was the head of this year's committee. Cody was the decorative designer in his mother's stead. Who could possibly object?

"From the side of the conversation I heard," he said, injecting a teasing tone into his words, "it doesn't appear as if an escort will get any personal attention from the prettiest gal at the event. So, what, if you don't mind my asking, would be in it for me?"

Paris perked up. If Cody would come with her, that would relieve her from being saddled with Parker and would keep Owen at a distance, as well. "Great food. Live band. Hearing the oohs and aahs as everyone admires your artistic endeavors—how great you look in a tux."

Cody pulled the truck up beside the clubhouse and cut the engine. "You've never seen me in a tux."

She raised a brow. "I have a vivid imagination, Mr. Hawk."

A smile tugged at his lips and her heart rate sped up in an almost giddy rush of expectation.

"So," she challenged, looking him in the eye, "how about it?"

He'd give anything to waltz Paris around the dance floor in front of the astonished faces of the town's elite, but there was no way he'd indulge in a dream like that. Even if she was too naive, too idealistic, to recognize it, a move like that would be social suicide. He couldn't allow her to do that to herself.

Reluctantly he broke eye contact to open the driver-side door, buying himself a few moments to gather his thoughts as he made his way to let down the truck's tailgate. Paris joined him as he untied the tarp.

"It would be fun, Cody, wouldn't it? To see everyone enjoying your hard work? Your mother turned me down when I invited her but, if you were going, maybe she'd be willing to come, too."

No fair dragging Ma into this. But he still couldn't put Paris at risk. Couldn't risk, either, having Merle Perslow cut short the compensation he'd agreed to for Dad. In another few weeks, maybe a month, Cody might be in a more secure position financially to field that possibility, but in the meantime...

"I appreciate your invitation, Paris." He raised the tarp off the chairs. "But once I wrap up this project, I've got to head down the mountain and relieve my business partner. He's been carrying much of the load since I've been up here."

He lifted down a chair and glanced in her direction, regret stabbing at the disappointment reflected in her eyes. Was he nuts for finding excuses not to escort her to the charity event? But he didn't really have a choice. He cared too much for her.

"You couldn't stay in town a few extra nights?"

The committee made arrangements for a breakdown crew. There would be no need for him to oversee that. Once he set everything up Thursday night, made sure everything was in working order, he could hand the reins to others.

He lifted down another chair, not meeting Paris's hopeful gaze. "Trevor's been a good sport about my absence, but he has little kids and with Christmas fast approaching…"

"Yeah, little kids and Christmas." She appeared to force a smile, as if at last giving up on her ill-thought-out campaign to get him to the gala. "I guess you'll have to contact Santa, won't you? Let him know where Deron is this year."

Cody almost dropped the third chair. "Santa?"

"You planned to buy him a gift anyway, didn't you?"

"I hadn't thought about anything beyond getting him warmer clothes." He should have taken care of that this morning before Ma sent the boy off for the day. The kid needed new socks, underwear and several changes of clothes in addition to winter outerwear. No way was he shipping his nephew off to his first day in Canyon Springs' kindergarten unless he was dressed as well as any kid in town.

"That jacket he had on didn't look suitable for a high-country winter," she agreed. "He didn't bring much in the way of personal items or toys with him, either. Did you notice? Only a pocketknife and a baseball."

"Yeah, and I took the knife away from him. He was none too happy with me, but I didn't figure Ma's neighbor would want him showing it off to her twins or getting into any mischief with it."

"No, I imagine not."

Cody turned back to the truck and lifted out the final chair. "Where do you want these?"

"Just outside the cloak room, next to the oak side table. I can show you." Paris picked up one of the chairs and Cody hefted the other three. "I'll place a battery-operated lantern on the table and it will make a cozy area where people can sit to remove their boots should it decide to snow."

Once inside, Paris showed him where the chairs went. Then, before he knew it, he'd ushered her back into the truck and dropped her off at her SUV. If anyone had taken notice of Paris when she'd climbed into his truck, their brief journey and swift return couldn't ignite too much talk.

Could it?

"I don't like this color."

"You don't like blue?" Cody looked down at his nephew, who shrugged impatiently out of the navy insulated jacket they'd found at Dix's Woodland Warehouse Friday morning. What kid didn't like blue?

"Well, then, what color do you want?" For a kid who'd shown up on their doorstep with next to nothing, he sure was picky. They'd gone through this with the shirts, jeans, underwear and socks at the discount store, too. Cody didn't look forward to tackling boots today, but more snow was in the forecast.

The boy pointed to another jacket.

"That's blue, Deron."

"Uh-uh. Not the same kind."

No, royal wasn't the same as navy. Apparently the kid knew his crayon colors.

Cody knelt to help Deron into the jacket, zipped it and then turned him from side to side to make sure it fit well.

"So, does this one work for you?"

Deron nodded, a grin widening as he lifted his hand for a high five, and Cody's heart did a three-sixty in his chest. This little guy's parents had dumped him on strangers and he could smile like that?

Deron had been slow to warm up to Cody. He'd kept his distance, which led Cody to believe Carson had more in common with Leroy Hawk than he'd hoped. Anger sired anger. Abuse, abuse. But he hoped that smile would be the first of many.

The bells above the door announced yet another shopper as Cody hustled to get Deron to pick out his final items. Their shopping excursion was taking way too much time, but the boy wasn't inclined to be rushed. Cody thrust a pair of brown gloves at him, but the boy immediately pushed away his offering.

Here we go again.

"I like that coat, Deron," a familiar female voice chimed in.

Cody glanced at Paris, noticing with pleasure that her cheeks were rosy from the cold, a red scarf snuggled at the neck of her teddy-bear coat. He'd tossed and turned last night, thinking about her invitation to the gala. But he kept coming back to the same conclusion. He couldn't escort her.

But would that force her to invite the Parker guy?

Paris reached for a red knit cap, then knelt down by Deron. "Ooh, I like this one."

"He doesn't like navy blue," Cody supplied, pleased he could share that insight.

She gave him a perplexed look. "This isn't navy blue, is it?"

"No, no, I meant..." His words faded as their gazes held. Suddenly he had no idea what he'd meant or what he was doing in Dix's looking at kid gear.

"Paris." Deron patted her arm to get her attention. "Uncle Cody says I can have gloves *and* mittens."

She focused again on the boy. "He does, does he? Maybe you can get red ones to match this hat."

"Okay." Deron turned back to the rack without argument.

What was the deal with that? Cody had battled him every step of the way that morning. Did his nephew think the pretty Miss Perslow was a more reliable source of fashion advice?

"These!" Deron triumphantly held up a pair of red fleece-lined mittens in one hand and insulated red gloves in the other.

Cody grabbed a red wool scarf from the rack and handed it to Deron, but the boy turned to Paris, his eyes questioning. She nodded and the kid looped it happily around his neck.

Go figure.

At least now he had some ideas of what to get his nephew for Christmas. Not that the kid asked for anything. He'd actually been unusually quiet, his eyes rounding at the floor-to-ceiling kid stuff at the discount store. It now seemed wise, however, to run his ideas by Paris if he didn't want to wind up with one disappointed kid on Christmas day.

"Well, let's get going, bud." He placed his hand on Deron's shoulder as Paris rose to her feet.

"Now we're going to get boots," the boy informed her, lifting hopeful eyes to hers. "You can come, too."

Chapter Sixteen

Paris glanced uncertainly at Cody, who looked slightly startled at his nephew's announcement, then back at Deron. "Thank you for inviting me, but—"

"Paris?" Cody raised his brows in appeal. "Believe me, the whole ordeal will go faster if you come."

She laughed. Poor guy. "Okay. Let me pick up a few things here and we can be on our way."

They paid for their purchases, then out on the street Deron reached for her hand. Her heart melted at the unexpected gesture of acceptance. Did he miss his mother? Did he wonder why he'd been thrust into a world of strangers?

But she was even less prepared when he grabbed hold of Cody's hand with his free one, and suddenly the three of them were linked as a unit. As a family.

Cody glanced at her and she could tell that he, too, was touched by the child's openness but discomfited by the happy domestic scenario. Nevertheless, they moved past the shops, hands still held.

"You two have such a cute boy," a teenage girl gushed as she and a friend paused outside a store.

Cody's eyes met Paris's as a wave of mortification mixed with pleasure washed through her. It was an easy enough mistake to think Cody's nephew was his son, of course, but fortunately, Deron appeared oblivious of the comment as he skipped along between them as if he hadn't a care in the world. Kids were amazing. So resilient.

Inside one of Canyon Springs' outdoor gear shops, she and Cody consulted comfortably, almost as if shopping together for a small boy were an everyday occurrence. Paris couldn't help but enjoy these fleeting shared moments. Cody was a good and generous man, ensuring that a nephew he'd never laid eyes on until a few days ago was well outfitted.

Watching uncle and nephew together, she couldn't help but remember how very little Cody had materially as a kid, yet how proudly he'd held up his head in spite of cruel jeers. Clearly, if he had anything to say about it, Deron's experiences in Canyon Springs wouldn't be anything like his uncle's.

They quickly found Deron a pair of quality snow boots. Waterproof and lined for warmth, they were perfect for tackling snowdrifts and slushy puddles the boy would no doubt find his way into.

"See? That wasn't so bad," she whispered to Cody at the checkout counter.

A corner of his mouth turned up. "You got off lucky, woman."

She yelped a soft laugh and the young male clerk looked up at her with a smile. She smiled back. In fact, she still felt like smiling at everyone she saw as they exited the store. It had been a long time since she'd felt like this.

Unburdened. Free. Happy.

She glanced at Cody who was exchanging teasing remarks with his nephew, the fact that it was in his presence that she was feeling this way not lost on her. There was something about him...so competent, responsible, caring. With him she felt a sense of security that she'd not felt with any other man.

As good of a person as Dalton had been, as much as she'd cared for him as a dear friend, she hadn't experienced that sense of peace and belonging that she increasingly felt when in the company of Cody Hawk.

Which was crazy. He would be in town only a short while longer. Obviously he didn't share her budding feelings or he'd have accepted her invitation to the gala. Or did he not recognize she was opening the door, even if only a crack, for him to step through if he wanted to?

"How about a cup of hot chocolate, Paris?" Cody studied her, as if wondering at her lengthy stretch of silence. "Deron says he's game."

"Me, too." But she didn't feel as over-the-top giddy as she had a few moments ago.

Even if Cody did share her feelings, what kind of future could they hope to have together? Dad would never welcome a son of Leroy Hawk. Nor would the broken-hearted Elizabeth receive him with open arms. How could Paris live with letting down those who loved her?

"You okay?" Cody cocked his head as he held open the door to Camilla's Café, the scent of fresh-baked bread and cookies wafting onto the street.

"I'm fine." Pushing back her coat cuff to look at her wristwatch she gasped, then stepped away from the door. "I can't believe it. It's almost eleven-thirty."

"So? Have soup and a sandwich instead. My treat."

"I have to meet Macy and Jake at Kit's Lodge. We're having lunch, then meeting with the caterer to go over details for their Saturday wedding. Tonight's the rehearsal dinner, too." She lifted the shopping bag. "I'd gone out to pick up a few things when I ran into you and Deron. I need to drop these off at the office before my appointment and make certain nothing pressing has come up in my absence."

Was that disappointment in Cody's eyes? It certainly was in Deron's. But her own feelings were mixed. As delightful as time spent with these two handsome males might be, she had to get her head back in the real world.

"You hafta come." Deron's forehead creased as he tugged on her sleeve, his eyes troubled.

"I wish I could, but you'll still have fun. Camilla's makes the best hot chocolate in the whole wide world." She sneaked a glance at Cody. "Make sure your uncle gets you whipped cream on top. With cinnamon."

"Doesn't that sound good, Deron?" Cody placed a consoling hand on the boy's shoulder when he didn't respond. "Thanks again, Paris, for playing shopping assistant."

"You're welcome."

"I may call on you again to talk *C-H-R-I*..." Nodding toward Deron who was still frowning up at Paris, he let his words drift off. Then he turned his nephew toward the open café door. "Come on, kid, let's see what this place has to offer."

Disappointed at missing out, even though it had been her own decision, Paris didn't linger outside but hurried back to the office.

Please, Lord, help me to stop thinking about Cody Hawk.

"Paris is your girlfriend, huh?" Deron licked the last of the whipped cream from the rim of the hot chocolate mug, his watchful eyes on Cody.

Where'd his nephew get an idea like that? He glanced around, hoping no one had overheard. Paris didn't need to be the focus of gossip and he sure didn't want Deron's vocal assumption getting back to her father via the Canyon Springs grapevine. He lowered his voice. "No, she's not my girlfriend."

"How come?" his nephew pushed aside the mug and reached for a remaining French fry that had accompanied his half sandwich. "You can have more than one girlfriend. My dad does."

Cody held back a look of disgust at Deron's matter-of-fact assessment. His half brother's lifestyle wasn't one to which a little boy should have had to be exposed. That was one point in Leroy Hawk's favor. To Cody's knowledge, Dad never stepped out on Ma, and he'd even managed to settle himself down once they'd come to Canyon Springs.

"Paris is a friend. All girls who are friends don't have to be girlfriends."

"Oh." Deron swirled the French fry through a

mound of ketchup, then looked up at Cody with one
eye squinted. "But she'd be a good girlfriend, huh?"

She'd not only make a good girlfriend, but a good
wife. A good mother. Cody shook his head as he folded
his napkin and placed it on the table, dismayed at how
easily those conclusions had slipped into his mind.

"Yeah, Deron, she would make a good girlfriend."

The boy smiled as though satisfied with his uncle's
response. But as Cody knew too well, hoping, wishing and praying didn't always make dreams come true.

It was all she could do not to collapse at the conclusion of Macy and Jake's wedding reception Saturday
afternoon. One wedding down. Two to go.

Thankfully, she wasn't responsible for cleanup and
didn't intend to pitch in, as she often did at weddings
in the past. She was tired.

And a little melancholy.

It had been a lovely ceremony and celebration afterward, the Christmas colors a beautiful contrast to the
bride's vintage dress and the snow-white tiered cake
with its holly accents. The bride's mother had even
shown up after all. But, throughout, Paris's thoughts
drifted to Cody. To Dalton. Back to Cody.

So what should she do now? Crashing at home held
vast appeal but, with a few hours of daylight remaining,
she returned there only briefly to change clothes before making her way to Pine Shadow Ridge. Last week
Cody had set up worktables for her in the clubhouse
ballroom, but had he settled her there on a pretense
of it being more comfy than the maintenance building when he really wanted to keep her at a distance?

It was dark by the time she secured a final pinecone with a generous dab of hot glue, then stepped back with a sense of satisfaction to view another completed wreath. Cody might not want her hanging around, but she knew he appreciated her assistance with the smaller decorative items while he focused on the larger ones.

Somewhere in the building she heard the echoing sound of a door closing and heavy footsteps on the tiled hallway floor. She turned, her heart beating faster in foolish anticipation as Cody stepped through the door.

His dark eyes lighted on her. "How'd the wedding go?"

"Beautiful. I imagine Macy's blog will feature a few photos this week. You should check it out."

"I may do that." He moved to the worktables to study the growing stock of wreaths, the fresh scent of the outdoors clinging to him. "How long have you been here?"

She turned back to the table and picked up the glue gun, determined to start another wreath tonight. "About three hours."

Cody leaned down to unplug the glue gun. "Then it's time to call it quits."

"If I want to get these done," she said, plugging the device back in, "I have to squeeze in the time when I can."

"*Have* to? Volunteers come in this week for the final push. It will get done. Do you mind my asking why you're packing your days with nonstop activity? Sharon says you got roped into the weddings at the last minute. Why didn't you say no?"

She shrugged. "I guess I want everything to be perfect for the brides and grooms on their special day."

And to somehow drive away the dark cloud of guilt that had hung over her for three and a half years.

"Perfect?" The corners of Cody's mouth turned downward. "That's a high bar you've set for yourself, don't you think? You're going to burn out before Christmas even gets here. You should take a day off to rest."

"Maybe *after* Christmas." She looked around at the spacious, raftered room, picturing all that remained to be done. "The trees arrive on Monday. Do you think they'll decorate themselves? That the faux gift packages to go under them will pop into their paper and bows on their own?"

"No. But where's the time for peace on earth?"

"I don't have—"

"No excuses." He took the glue gun from her hand, uplugged it once again, then placed it in its stand. Striding to where she'd tossed her coat and scarf over the back of a chair, he looped the scarf around his neck. Then picking up her coat, he turned to hold it open so she'd only have to step up and slip her arms into the sleeves. "Come on, Paris. It's a beautiful night out there. I have something I want to show you."

Chapter Seventeen

Despite his assurances that they were on-target to meet the deadline, Cody couldn't afford to lose an evening of work. He'd driven over to see Dad that afternoon—another awkward visit—and had just returned to town. But Paris was wearing herself out and something was clearly troubling her. As tragically as her wedding plans had ended, how could the trio of beaming brides and grooms *not* get to her?

He lifted the open coat invitingly, an idea having surfaced that would get her mind off whatever was weighing her down. "So what are we waiting for, hmm?"

She hesitated, indecision flickering in her eyes, then at last a weary smile curved. "Okay. You win."

He helped her into her coat, then they took a few minutes to straighten things up before stepping outside into the crisp night air. He cupped her elbow, guiding her toward his truck.

"Where are we going?"

"Wait and see."

Once they settled into the still-toasty-warm vehicle, he started the engine and flipped on the headlights. With the dashboard faintly illuminating the interior, he drove out of the parking lot and down one of the residential property's streets.

"I got good news today." It was hard to keep the elation out of his voice.

"What would that be?"

"My business partner received a call from that potential investor I told you about." He glanced in her direction. "It's a go."

"Cody!" Her eyes lit up as she squeezed his arm. "That's not good news, that's *wonderful* news. I'm so happy for you."

"We're pretty pleased to have reached this milestone." Trevor had been flying so high when he'd called that Cody could hardly pry the details out of him. "It's not without risk, but it's a promising start."

"Very promising, I'd say. From what you've told me, you and your partner have put a tremendous amount of time, muscle and brainpower into your business. Maybe now you can reap the rewards."

"That's what we're hoping." It would certainly put him and Trevor on more solid ground financially, which would no doubt delight Trev's wife. It would bolster Cody's ability to care for his folks, as well. Maybe to buy a home, settle down...

He slowed for a turn down a winding side street, headlights piercing the darkness. Not a single house showed signs of life. "It's really quiet around here in the winter, isn't it?"

"It is. But it's nice, too. While I enjoy the tourist

activity during the summer, there's something special about Canyon Springs when we're basically back to the locals."

"I'd forgotten what a contrast the seasons could be here, not only weatherwise, but the vibe, as well."

Ah, there it was—the cul-de-sac he was looking for. With the thick stand of trees now blocking streetlights, he drove through the undeveloped area, then pulled the truck to a stop in the middle of a circular pavement that marked the end of the street. Cut the engine.

Paris poked him playfully in the arm. "This is what you wanted me to see, Cody? A dead end?"

"Oh, ye of little faith." He stepped out. "Stay right where you are."

He snagged three heavy Mexican blankets he kept stashed behind the seat and draped them over his arm. Then, having shut the door, he loped around to the passenger side to help Paris from the truck.

"What are you up to?" He could hear the curiosity in her teasing tone.

"Hang on." Leading her to the front side of the truck, he then wrapped one of the big blankets around her shoulders.

She gave a startled gasp as he lifted her up to sit on the truck's hood and motioned for her to scoot back and lean against the windshield where he tucked another blanket behind her.

"Oooh. The truck hood is cozy warm."

"I figured it would be. I just got back from Show Low." He moved to the opposite side and pulled himself up on the hood to settle in beside her, then spread the last blanket across their legs.

"Tell me again what we're doing here?" She sounded nervous now.

"I find the dark is usually the best place for star-gazing." He leaned back against the windshield and pointed skyward. "Agree?"

Together they lifted their eyes to the heavens.

"Oh, my," Paris whispered.

At the more-than-mile-high elevation, devoid of artificial lights, starlight popped out against the inky blackness overhead in breathtaking clarity. Hundreds of them. Thousands. Millions. Sweeping across the universe in a display that put man-made holiday lights to humble shame.

"'Lift up your eyes and look to the heavens,'" Cody softly quoted the verse from the Book of Isaiah. "'Who created all these? He who brings out the starry host one by one and calls forth each of them by name.'"

"Can you imagine?" Paris kept her voice low, clearly as awed as he was by the magnificence above. "Not only having the imagination and power to create the stars, but to name every single one?"

"Amazing, isn't it?" He made a sweeping motion to the starry host above. "The Good Book says God has clearly made Himself known to mankind, His eternal power and divine nature, through His creation."

A ripple of awareness of that truth coursed through Cody as he stared into the night. But he was also acutely aware of Paris, the brush of her coat sleeve against his, the ever-so-faint scent of her perfume. For quite some time they gazed in rapt silence at the display above.

"Cody?" Paris finally broke the stillness.

"Yeah?"

"Did you miss Canyon Springs?"

"I can't say I did. I missed Ma, of course, and…" He glanced at her, softly illuminated in the dim light. "And another special person."

She looked away, sensing the significance of what he'd said. *Good going, Hawk. Back off.* She might not be seeing Owen and was being pressured to get involved with Parker, but that didn't mean she'd want *him* in her life. Besides, as her father had often reminded him…*you have no business looking on the high shelf.*

He cleared his throat. "I kept in touch with Ma, but basically cut myself off from the past."

Or he'd tried to, anyway.

"I rarely looked at the online paper for local news," he continued. "And I forbade Ma to fill in the blanks. I didn't want to be kept apprised of the comings and goings of folks in Canyon Springs. That's why…why I didn't know about Dalton's passing."

He heard her soft intake of breath at the mention of her fiancé's name.

"I know it's been rough," he continued gently. "It's taken courage to go on without someone you love, to commit to helping those brides after your own loss."

"Please, Cody, not you, too." She abruptly drew the blanket more closely around her shoulders and shifted away from him to again stare into the night.

He should have kept his mouth shut about the weddings. About Dalton. "I didn't mean to upset you. I'm sorry, Paris."

She shook her head. "No, don't apologize. It's just that…"

"Just what?"

She sighed, but didn't look at him. "Everyone treats me with kid gloves, as Dalton's grieving widow. Elizabeth. Dad. The entire town. Everyone pitying me. Now *you*."

He studied her a long moment, weighing his words. "I feel badly about your losing Dalton. But I can't say that I *pity* you. Not if you mean that I think of you in a negative sense, think lesser of you because of your situation."

Like someone might pity a kid growing up on the wrong side of the tracks?

She turned to him. "My situation? You have no idea what my situation is. Nobody does."

As he'd suspected, unresolved grief. The weddings had resurrected it in a way she hadn't been prepared for. "Why don't you tell me, then? I'm a good listener."

For several long moments he didn't think she would respond. Then came a soft sigh.

"Nobody understands, Cody, because..." He felt her gaze piercing into his, sensed the struggle she was having to get the words out. "Nobody knows I'm responsible for Dalton's death."

His heart jolted. "Say again?"

"You heard me." Her voice quavered. "If it weren't for me, Dalton would be alive today."

Her words made no sense. He'd gone back and read the coverage of that tragedy. Every detail. Nothing indicated she was at fault. "He died in a car accident, Paris. Hit by a drunk driver. You weren't even with him."

"No...but he came home days earlier than planned because *I* asked him to. Don't you see, Cody? He came home early and was hit head-on by that drunk."

Cody groaned as he slid his arm around her, pulling her close. She didn't resist, but slipped her hands free of her blanket to cling to the front of his jacket.

"It wasn't your fault, Paris. It's not."

"It is. I asked him to come home early because…" She drew a ragged breath. "I wanted to break up with him."

She intended to break up with Dalton? Why?

"I woke up one morning a few weeks before my wedding day, looked around at happily married couples and realized something was missing in our relationship. Suddenly I recognized we weren't well-matched despite our similar backgrounds and the fact that our parents were so excited about joining our two families."

"Had you been pressured, like you're now feeling with Parker?"

She shook her head. "I wouldn't call it pressured. It was more like encouraged. Expected. I'd gone along willingly, eager to please. It wasn't as if Dalton and I didn't like each other. Everyone in town thought we'd make a perfect couple."

"But not you?"

"I did at first." She gave a little sigh. "It's hard to explain, but our getting together was assumed. Like a son and daughter who unquestioningly join the family firm. I threw myself into wedding preparations, attempting, I know now, to shut out that still, small voice trying to get my attention."

"I can relate to that." How many years had he allowed his relationship with Dad to figuratively press hands against his own ears to block out God's persistent call?

"Suddenly my eyes were opened that when we talked on the phone, we never talked about anything that mattered to either of us. Only about the wedding plans. That's when I realized I wasn't what he needed in a wife."

"Nor was he what you needed in a husband," Cody said quietly. "Don't forget, Paris, your needs are equally important."

"I'm coming to recognize that now, to ask myself what kind of marriage is it if you can't share from the heart. From the soul? You know, if you don't know each other well enough to trust each other with that part of yourself? But after our engagement announcement, I'd focused on planning that one stupid day out of my entire life. I tried to please everyone around me, rather than listening to what God was trying to tell me."

"What did Dalton have to say about it?"

He felt her shrug. "I got a sense that he might have misgivings as well, but I didn't have the opportunity to tell him what I've told you. I wanted to do that in person, face-to-face. So I'll never know for sure."

"Men aren't dimwits. I imagine he sensed you didn't feel the way a bride should feel and welcomed your request to come home early. He may have wanted out, too, but—like you—he knew there would be repercussions in the family and he didn't want to hurt you."

She burrowed closer to Cody as if to absorb his reassurance. He gently stroked the length of her silky hair as she pressed against him. So warm. Fragile.

"You're not responsible for Dalton's death, Paris. He chose to come home when he did, just like someone wrongly chose to drive drunk that night. You need to forgive yourself."

Was she listening to what he was saying? Really listening and allowing God to heal her broken, fearful heart?

Paris slowly lifted her gaze to the starry expanse that clearly spoke God's presence and His love to those who chose to hear. He sensed her relax against him, to accept a peace long absent, held at arm's length by her refusal to receive it.

Thank You, Lord. Thank You.

Cody's drew her closer, his head now resting gently against her hair.

"It's not that I didn't care for Dalton," she whispered into the night. "I did. But not...not the way I'm coming to care for you."

There. She'd said it.

Cody's arms tightened around her, but he didn't respond.

What must he think of her? She'd admitted to being responsible for her fiancé's death, then almost in the next breath confessed to having feelings for Cody. A depth of feelings that Dalton had never inspired. But her statement was true. There was a peace here in Cody's arms that she'd never found in Dalton's, a sense of God smiling down on her. On them.

She drew back to look at him. His eyes were closed, almost as if in prayer. Was he asking God how to respond to her shocking confession?

"Cody?" she said softly, her fingers tightening on

the front of his jacket, brushing the soft wool of the scarf he'd earlier flung around his neck. Her scarf.

He opened his eyes and her breath caught. Compassion filled his gaze…and something else. He'd always looked at her in a way other boys—and later men— never had. But his eyes now met hers with a vulnerable, questioning intent, as if he wasn't sure he'd correctly understood what she'd told him.

She nodded slightly, a tiny smile encouraging.

"Paris?" he said softly, his gaze flickering from her eyes to her mouth and back to her eyes. And yet he still hesitated.

She grasped the edges of the scarf looped around his neck and tugged him gently toward her, a teasing lilt in her tone. "What are you waiting for, Mr. Hawk?"

His dark eyes sparked at her challenge, a corner of his mouth turning up. Then he once again closed his eyes and leaned in to touch his lips to hers.

Chapter Eighteen

No business. No business. No business.

His heart almost exploding from his chest and Merle's derisive words hammering through his brain, Cody nevertheless enveloped Paris in his arms, his mouth joining hers in a tender dance of love.

How long he'd dreamed of this moment. Dreamed of her soft lips pressed against his as her hands wound around his neck to draw him even closer. Or maybe he *was* dreaming. Right now. This very minute. But if he took it slow, savored every precious second, could he keep himself from waking? Could he stay right here with her in his arms forever?

Too soon she pulled back slightly and he cupped her face in his hands, loath to let her go, as his thumb caressed the scar he knew to be on her lower lip. At the quick intake of her breath, he leaned in again to touch his lips to that corner of her mouth, then drew back.

"Do you remember the day we first met, Paris? On the playground?"

Still breathless, she nodded.

"You were the sweetest, most beautiful girl I'd ever known."

"And you were my hero come to life."

He swallowed, not daring to believe that startling revelation. "I was?"

She nodded again. "From the very beginning."

"I… I never knew that."

"You were. You *are*."

He *had* to be dreaming. This was Paris Perslow snuggled in his arms, confessing secrets of the heart he'd never imagined hearing. He closed his eyes and touched his lips to her forehead, willing himself not to wake.

Please, not yet. Not yet.

"Do you remember," she said softly, "the night you came to see me before you left town?"

"Yeah. That's the night you sent me packing."

"I didn't want to. You said you loved me, remember? And I so badly wanted you to kiss me."

"Then why…?" He'd laid his heart at her feet that night. Ripped it right out and dared offer it, only to have her push him away. She'd loved him twelve years ago?

"Because…" She ducked her head, almost as if in shame. "I knew my Dad would never…"

Cody's spirits deflated. "Because I was the son of Leroy Hawk."

She nodded and, heart heavy, Cody pulled away to slide off the driver's side of the hood. Then he walked to the other side to help her down, as well. It was colder now. He needed to let her get home and then he needed to get back to work.

Tucking the blanket more securely around her, he gently tilted her chin to look up at him. "I'm still the son of Leroy Hawk, Paris."

"I know."

"Nothing's changed."

"But it has," she said, reaching for his hand as if sensing his heart pulling away. "*We* have."

"Have we? You're still the beautiful belle of Canyon Springs. I'm still a no-good Hawk."

Her grip tightened. "You're a Hawk who now walks with God. A man who's proven himself to be a trust-worthy man of integrity, a savvy business professional, a kindhearted man who looks after his mother and now a nephew."

His heart swelled at her words of praise. She saw that in him? "But what about you, Paris? You say I've changed. But have you?"

She'd turned him away once. Cracked open his heart. While she'd returned his kisses tonight, did she have it in her to stand up to her father? And even if she could, did he have it in him to ask her to?

"I'm no longer a sixteen-year-old, Cody." She pulled her hands free to cross her arms, her chin lifting as if daring him to contradict her. "I'm a woman who is coming to realize I've spent too much of my life at-tempting to please people because I was afraid if I said no, they wouldn't love me. I've allowed others to dictate how *they* think God wants me to live my life rather than allowing Him to get close enough to me so that I know and trust His voice. Is that enough change for you?"

"Paris—"

"Once, a long time ago," she cut in, looking him in the eye, "you told me you loved me. Do you...still?"

The love he'd confessed twelve years ago was only a shadow of what he understood love to be now. While an important part of it, love was more than ramped-up hormones and wild crazy feelings. So much more.

"I do, Paris. I've always loved you."

She blinked rapidly, then drew a shaky breath. "I love you, too."

He opened his arms and without hesitation, Paris stepped into them, slipped her arms around his waist and laid her head against his chest.

"What do we do now, Cody?"

"What would you like to do?"

"I think... I'd like to spend the rest of my life with you."

He gazed skyward, searching for answers. For wisdom. Here in this moment, alone together, all things seemed possible. All mountains could be climbed, all challenges overcome.

But he knew that wasn't real life. He was still a Hawk. Her father had harbored animosity toward him for as long as Cody could remember. Townspeople would be shocked that Paris would replace their beloved Dalton with a kid from the wrong side of town. A kid whose despised father drank too much, and whose half brothers left disreputable reputations in their wake.

"We should take it slow," he said at last, hating the thought of it. He'd marry her tonight if he had the power to snap his fingers and make everything right in their world.

"Because you don't believe I've changed, do you?" she said softly.

He looked down at her. "Of course I do."

"No. Right now you're thinking that at the first sign of disapproval I'll turn my back on you."

"I wouldn't blame you if you did. It's not going to be easy, Paris."

She tightened her arms around him. "The best things in life aren't always easy."

"No."

"But you don't trust me, do you? You don't believe when I say I love you, that I love you the way you say you love me." A determined gleam flashed in her eyes. "Come to the Christmas gala with me next week. Be my escort."

He stiffened. That was too public a venue for their first appearance as a couple. "Paris, I don't think—"

"Who's the scaredy-cat now?" She raised a delicate brow.

He frowned.

She laughed softly. "Ruffled your fur, did I? Come on. I think you'll discover your perceptions of this town are highly distorted."

Dare he tell her of the suspicious looks he'd encountered in recent weeks? How many times her father had warned him away?

"Paris—"

"You say you love me. Come. Please, Cody? For me?"

"*Something* is going on." Delaney's dancing eyes narrowed as she caught up with Paris in the parking lot after church Sunday morning. "I demand to know what it is."

"What are you talking about?"

"All during the service you had this secret smile thing going on." Delaney did her best to imitate it.

Paris laughed, her face warming under her friend's intense scrutiny. "It's Christmas. I'm happy."

"I'm not buying it. It's that Hawk guy, isn't it? Come on, fess up."

Paris glanced around to make sure no others exiting the church were within earshot, then took a deep breath. "He's going to be my escort for the Christmas gala."

Delaney gave a little yelp. "Get out of here. Are you kidding me?"

Paris shook her head, joy bubbling. It was fun to share happy news for a change. To remember how it had felt to be held by Cody. Kissed by him. She'd never felt like this before. Ever.

"Wow, Paris. I'm jealous." Delaney leaned in close, lowering her voice even further. "I absolutely cannot wait to see him in a tux."

"I'm looking forward to that, too." To her surprise, he said he owned one—that he'd attended a number of business and social functions in recent years with his business partner and his partner's parents that called for one. How many more things there must be that she didn't know about the grown-up Cody—or that he didn't know about her. He was right. They needed time to get to know each other.

But, hopefully, not *too* much time.

Delaney's smile widened. "I saw his mother in

church this morning, but not him. Has he gone to the Valley to pick out a ring? Hmm?"

The prospect of an engagement, while enticing to think about, was premature. "Actually, his dad isn't doing well so he's in Show Low this morning. I guess Leroy's kidneys are in worse shape than originally thought."

Delaney's smile faded. "From a lifetime of over-drinking."

"Probably."

"That's rough." Her friend gave Paris's arm a quick squeeze. "Look, I have to run, but we've got to get together. Soon. I want to hear all about Cody Hawk."

When Delaney departed, Paris drove home and fixed herself a light lunch—Dad was at his folks' house but Cody had promised to call her when he got back to Canyon Springs. She'd finished straightening the kitchen when the call came shortly before noon.

"How's your father?"

"Not doing so great. One of his kidneys is pretty well shot. The other isn't far behind. His doctors are considering removing the worst one, but they're hesitant with him still having ministrokes."

"I'm sorry, Cody."

"Yeah. Bad situation."

"How's your mother?"

"Hanging in there. She stayed home and took Deron to church this morning, but she just left to go see Dad. I don't like getting such a late start, but I'm taking the little guy with me to the Valley to get my tux. It will be a down-and-up trip and dark before we get back, but I thought you might like to go."

A long excursion with Cody? A chance to see his place? "I'd love to."

"Would you mind if we took your SUV? Deron's small for his age so I bought a car seat for him and it doesn't fit that well in my old truck."

"That's fine."

"You're home right now? By yourself?"

She knew he wanted to know if Dad was there before he showed up on her doorstep. "Just me. But why don't I come get you guys?"

That way Cody's vehicle wouldn't be sitting in the driveway at her place all afternoon. She scribbled a note to let Dad know she'd be out and taped it to the door leading from the garage to the utility room. He'd be certain to see it there if he returned before she did. Then she was off to pick up Cody and Deron and within thirty minutes they were heading down the mountain, Cody in the driver's seat.

"This is a sweet set of wheels," he commented a considerable distance from town, finally getting a word in edgewise. Deron, unlike his somewhat reticent uncle, revealed a gift of gab once he felt comfortable with those around him. From the moment Deron was fastened into the car seat behind them, the questions had been nonstop. Where had Paris been? Where were they going? What was a tux? Why were the trees so tall here? Was it going to snow again?

She'd fielded them all, enjoying the boy's chatter. How could his parents give him up like that? Did they intend to come back for him? Ever?

Farther on, once they'd dropped off the Mogollon Rim, the ponderosas were a thing of the past. The rugged terrain's vegetation changed rapidly from the scrub oak and fragrant pinyon pine to ocotillo, prickly pear and majestic saguaro cactus. Deron's questions multiplied. Was Cody enjoying seeing their world through the eyes of a child as much as she was?

They reached Cody's home by three-thirty, an apartment in a shady, well-cared-for complex where she stepped out of the SUV to the delightful sound of birdsong, then assisted Cody in releasing Deron from his car seat.

"This is beautiful." She opened her arms wide, drinking in the sunshine and almost-seventy-degree temperature.

"Do you have a dog, Uncle Cody?" Deron asked, pushing eagerly past them as they entered the second-floor apartment.

"No, no dogs. Maybe someday when I get a place with a big yard or acreage."

Deron went off to explore and Paris found herself examining Cody's quarters with as much interest as the little boy. Flavored with a bold but tasteful color palette and Southwestern accents, the furniture was simple, the space uncluttered. Masculine. Like Cody.

"This is nice," she said, stepping through the French doors and onto the balcony as Cody returned with his bagged tux, shirt, tie and shoes. He placed them on the back of the sofa, then joined her, motioning for them to sit at the patio table.

"I'm not here a whole lot, but it's home." His warm gaze lingered on her. "For now."

Suddenly shy, she glanced through the open door behind them. "Where'd Deron get off to?"

"He found my video games. He can't hurt them and they can't hurt him. All G-rated."

Cody having correctly read the concern in her question, she relaxed in the padded chair. "I can't believe the contrast in the weather between here and a few hours north. While the summertime heat isn't anything I'd care to deal with, *this* I could handle."

"You'd consider leaving Canyon Springs?"

That would be an issue, wouldn't it? Where to live, assuming Cody's suggestion to "take it slow" ended where she hoped and prayed it would.

"I already decided to leave." At his raised brow, she quickly amended, "Even before you came back, before...us... I knew I needed to start somewhere fresh."

"Where do you plan to go?"

Did he think her future might be in opposition to his? That she'd be dashing off to adventures in New York City? Europe?

She smiled. "I hadn't gotten that far. But I've known deep down that this will be my last Christmas in Canyon Springs. It's too hard living in Dalton's shadow."

Cody tenderly took her hand in his. "I'm hoping together we can drive that shadow away, Paris."

A tingle of happiness raced through her. He hadn't rethought things in the hours since they'd parted last night. He hadn't changed his mind about them. "Me, too."

"Hey, Aunt Paris!" Deron called. "You gotta see this."

"Sounds as if you're being paged, *Aunt* Paris." An amused Cody squeezed her hand. As they stood, he glanced at his watch. "After you take a look at what he has to show you, we'll need to hit the road."

She sighed. "I'd hoped to see the houses you're flipping."

"I wish we had time to drive out to Trevor's folks' place, too, so you could meet them."

"Maybe another time?"

"That's a promise."

Before heading back to the mountains, they stopped for burgers and fries, enjoying the remaining warmth of the day from the restaurant's patio. Deron didn't sleep on the way home as she—and probably Cody— had hoped, so there was little opportunity for conversation of a more personal variety.

Was that a taste of parenthood?

As they topped the Rim, snowflakes danced hypnotically in their headlights and, once they ushered Deron into the trailer and his car seat was removed, Paris got behind the wheel. Cody slipped into the passenger seat beside her for a sweet good-night kiss, then she headed home with his admonition to call him when she got there safely.

Still flying high from their afternoon together, Paris pulled into the garage, made a brief call to Cody and then let herself in through the side door. Seeing him with Deron today, she had no doubt he'd make a great dad. He had infinite patience and encouraged the boy to talk and share his ideas, to explore things that interested him.

Still smiling, she'd barely stepped into the darkened kitchen when a stern voice reprimanded her.

"Just where have you been?"

Chapter Nineteen

"Dad!" Paris's fingers found the light switch, illuminating the space.

Her father stood in the doorway across the room, arms crossed and a look of disapproval on his face. "I've been worried about you."

"You didn't see my note?"

"I saw it. And I also got a call from someone saying they saw Cody Hawk driving your SUV and you sitting in the passenger seat."

Who'd ratted her out? Sometimes living in a small town was akin to having a camera trained on you every time you stepped out the door. She placed her purse on the kitchen table and peeled out of her coat, resigned that the time had come—earlier than she'd hoped—to have a heart-to-heart with her father.

"We went to the Valley to pick up his tux."

"What does he need a tuxedo for?" His expression was wary, as if suspecting the answer to his question.

"He's…" *Spit it out, Paris.* "My escort for the Christmas gala."

Her father shook his head. "Honey, we both know that isn't a good idea."

"Cody is *not* Leroy. He's nothing like his father or his brothers. He never was."

Dad stretched out his hand toward her. "You may have lived here your whole life, sweetheart, but there are things you don't know about those people. Things that are not nice."

"I'm aware of his half brothers' reputations. The auto theft. Drugs. Drinking. Illegitimate kids. But that's not Cody, Dad. He's nothing like them."

"You think not, but—"

"The apple," she quoted, "doesn't fall far from the tree?"

"There's considerable truth in that statement. More than you know."

"Cody's a God-believing man who's overcome his unfortunate background. A man with a kind and generous heart. A man who—"

Who loves me. A man I love.

Why couldn't she bring herself to say those words? To tell Dad the truth? But she didn't want to make him angry, to hurt him.

"I fully comprehend that Cody is the type of man who's undoubtedly caught the eye of many a lady through the years. But he has no business talking you into taking him to the gala and risking your reputation."

Paris endeavored to keep her voice even, respectful. "He didn't talk me into anything. I asked him to be my escort and it took considerable persuasion on my part for the same reason you're pointing out. He was concerned for me."

"Clever tactic."

"No, Dad, it wasn't a tactic. Cody cares for me."

Dad shot her an exasperated look. "Of course he does. You're a beautiful young woman. No doubt he 'cares' for your financial and social standing, as well. But if he thinks worming his way into the gala will fling open the doors of opportunity here in Canyon Springs, he's highly mistaken."

"He's not looking for opportunities in Canyon Springs. He's a businessman in Phoenix. A successful one."

"That's what he's telling you?"

"I believe him."

Dad held up his hand. "Regardless, I don't want you going to the gala with a Hawk. I love you, Paris. You know that. But you have no idea of the repercussions that will ensue if you persist in this."

A sharp retort on the tip of her tongue, her response nevertheless came softly. "For me—or for you?"

Her father drew in a sharp breath. "Parker Herrington will be in town this week and that's who will be escorting you."

She took a step toward her father. "Dad, please try to—"

"This discussion is over. Good night." He abruptly turned away and left her standing alone in the kitchen.

"Can I come, too, Uncle Cody?" Deron looked up from the breakfast table early Monday morning as he spooned up another bite of cereal, his dark eyes eager. "I can eat fast."

Cody zipped his jacket, then placed a hand on Deron's shoulder. "Not this morning, bud. I have a lot of work to do and there's no place there for little boys to play."

"I can play outside in the snow. I have boots."

"Now don't nag your uncle," Ma chided gently as she sat down across the table from her step-grandson.

She smiled at Cody, obviously pleased that Deron continued to warm up to him. He seemed to be adjusting better than expected, soaking up the attention they gave to him. It would be good to get him in school, but local education officials still awaited the records Carson had promised. So it would again be a half day with Ma and a half day with the neighbor.

It was still dark when Cody headed to his truck, his thoughts drifting, as always, to Paris. He never would have dreamed when he'd wakened on Saturday morning that by evening he'd have her in his arms.

"She loves me, Lord." With a chuckle, he shook his head as he slipped behind the steering wheel. Although they hadn't much time for conversation with Deron aboard Sunday afternoon, their shared smiles that had sent his heart soaring proved she hadn't changed her mind. And yet...

They were meeting for lunch today, but why did he feel as if the other shoe was yet to drop? God orchestrated this unexpected turn of events, yet he found himself afraid to revel in it for fear of it being snatched away.

What kind of ungrateful slob was he, anyway? How would he feel if Deron wouldn't wear his new coat and boots for fear his uncle would grab them back? Cody let out a gust of pent-up breath and started the engine.

"I trust You, Lord. Forgive my unbelief."

Backing to the end of the driveway, he abruptly slammed on the brakes as his back-up lights illuminated a dark SUV pulling across the base of the drive, blocking his way. What in the—?

His heart jerked with recognition. A Lexus. Cody cut the engine and stepped out of the truck, doubting Mr. Perslow was here to welcome him into the family.

Merle left his vehicle running, its headlights cutting a swath down the graveled road, but he stepped out to join Cody in front of his SUV.

Cody rammed his hands into his jacket pockets. "I take it this isn't a social call."

"How much, Hawk?" Merle pulled out his wallet and opened it, his hand poised above a thick wad of bills.

"I don't understand."

"How much will it take to get you out of my daughter's life?" He motioned to his wallet. "There's more where this came from. Let's settle this once and for all. No more nickel-and-diming."

What was he rattling on about? "I don't want your money, Mr. Perslow."

"No? But the bottom line is Paris isn't yours for the taking. I thought I made that clear. I'll protect her no matter what, so name your price." Merle's eyes narrowed in an uncompromising glare. "Make no mistake, you and yours will not be allowed to prey on my innocent daughter. I won't have her involved in the games Hawks play. You got that?"

A ripple of uneasiness clawed its way up the back of Cody's neck. There was that reference again to Hawks playing games. And what was that "nickel-and-dim-ing" allusion?

Leroy.

"I don't know what you're talking about. I care deeply for your daughter. I think you know I always have."

"You're telling me you *love* her?" Merle made a scoffing sound. "I'll concede the fact that you've always *wanted* her, but love? The only Hawk who knows anything about love may be your mother and even that might be a stretch."

Cody held his tongue. How much had Paris told her father about them? That he was her escort for the gala—or everything?

Merle waved his wallet. "Let's get this over with. How much?"

"I told you," Cody said, stepping away from the vehicle, "I won't take your money."

The older man's lips tightened as he rammed the billfold into his back pocket. "Just remember, Hawk, you'll be sorry if you show up at the gala with my daughter. Real sorry."

Paris's father got back into his Lexus and Cody stared after the SUV as it headed down the road. There was nothing Mr. Perslow could do that would make him disappoint Paris by backing out of the gala. She'd take it that he didn't trust her, didn't believe in her love. But he had no doubt Paris's father, although misguided, cared for his daughter. How could he win the man's trust? How could he make him understand that he loved her, too?

But Merle had made several points that were more

than disturbing. As much as Cody needed to push ahead, his work on the Christmas gala would have to wait.

It was time to pay another visit to Leroy Hawk.

"I'm sorry, Elizabeth, but I'm not going to the gala with Parker." Hoping for a sign of support, Paris glanced across her bedroom to where Delaney stood holding the gown Elizabeth had delivered that morning. A slight nod bolstered her determination to stand her ground.

"But *Cody Hawk?*" Dalton's mother stared at her, aghast. "Sweetie, you can't show up with him. Your reputation will be in shreds before you're even seated." Elizabeth appealed to Delaney, her eyes beseeching. "You're her best friend. Tell her I'm speaking the truth."

"I think," Delaney said gently, "that you're speaking the truth as you know it and that you have Paris's best at heart. But when two people are in love—"

Elizabeth gasped and spun toward Paris. "*Love?* What is she talking about? Don't tell me this Hawk has convinced you he's in love with you."

"He not only loves me, but I love him, too."

"Oh, my—" Shaken, Elizabeth lowered herself to Paris's bed. "Surely you're not intending to marry a son of Leroy Hawk?"

He hadn't proposed in so many words, but the expectation was there, wasn't it? "We haven't made any decisions yet."

"Marriage or not, I can't imagine your father approves of any of this. A Hawk escorting you. Dating you."

"He will. Eventually." But doubt crept in. She'd read

that morning in *Dear Abby* about a family that cut off contact with a grown son due to his choice in a marriage partner. But Dad wouldn't do that to her, his only child, would he?

Elizabeth motioned helplessly. "Sweetie, I know you were badly hurt when Dalton died, that you've been lonely. I've only recently come to realize that, which is why I've encouraged you to see Parker. But there are any number of young men who would be vastly more suitable than Cody Hawk. Don't do this to yourself. Nothing good can come of it."

The two women stared at each other, Elizabeth in obvious anguish and Paris's heart torn asunder. She knew, had always known, that caring for Cody Hawk would carry a price. But Dad…and now Elizabeth, who'd always been like a second mother to her? Would neither support her and Cody together?

"We've cared for each other ever since we were kids." Paris pressed her hand to her heart. "I know in here that it's right. That God's in it."

Elizabeth rose, tears pricking her eyes. "You're saying you were in love with this man when you promised to marry my son?"

"No, no, I mean—"

Elizabeth waved her off and moved to the hallway door, then turned with sorrowful eyes. "Please don't tarnish Dalton's memory, Paris. Don't drag my son's name into the mire to be forever associated with a woman who gave herself to a Hawk."

She disappeared out the door and Paris drew a shaky breath as her gaze met Delaney's. "That went well, didn't it? I didn't mean to upset her like that."

Her friend slipped the gown's hanger over a hook on the closet door, then smoothed the velvet skirt. "You'd have to tell her sometime."

"I know, but—"

"She loves you, Paris. She'll always love Dalton. Losing you now to someone who isn't her son, regardless of whether it's to Cody or another man, is like losing Dalton all over again. That's how closely the two of you are entwined in her heart."

"Maybe Cody is right, then? Going to the gala together is too much too soon?"

Her friend approached with a determined look. "You love him, right?"

"I do. I think a part of me always has."

"And he loves you. There's no shame in letting the world know of the happiness God's brought into your life."

Paris sat on the bed, the heaviness in her heart weighing her down. "But all it's bringing into the lives of others I love is hurt and anger and disappointment with me. Surely that can't be of God."

"God's ways are not always our ways, Paris. Maybe there are lessons He wants them to learn here, too."

"But it's bad enough that Dad's angry Cody will be escorting me. He's going to be furious if Elizabeth tells him how I truly feel about him."

Delaney folded her arms. "And what if he is? You have to be prepared for that. That is, unless Elizabeth and your father are making you rethink things…?"

"No. Never."

"Well then? Once they see how happy Cody makes you, once they come to know him and the kind of man that he is, how could they object? It may take a little time—or maybe a lot. But mostly you need to be certain that God's in this, that you're not—as Elizabeth implied—merely longing for a replacement for Dalton and any man will do."

"Cody isn't *any* man, Delaney," she said more sharply than intended.

"I didn't think so." Her friend smiled, not taking offense.

"You've met him, but I want you to spend time with him, to get to know him. I want you to recognize for yourself what an amazing man he is. How God has worked in his life."

Delaney rolled her eyes. "Spending time with Cody will be such a hardship."

"So, you don't think I'm making a mistake?"

Delaney gently grasped Paris's upper arms and, drawing her to her feet, looked her square in the eye. "I told my mother I've never seen you so happy in all the years I've known you. Does that sound like I think you're making a mistake?"

Joy bubbled as Paris hugged her friend, remembering she was to have lunch with the love of her life today.

And yet…a nagging voice still questioned.

Would Cody think it was a mistake if her friends and family cut them off—or when he thought about spending a lifetime of holidays in their disapproving midst?

Chapter Twenty

"Look, Dad, Mr. Perslow made strong insinuations about 'games Hawks play.' He brought up being 'nickeled-and-dimed' and told me flat out that 'you and yours' won't be allowed to prey on his innocent daughter."

"Still trying...get hands on her?" What sounded like a chuckle emanated from his father's misshapen lips. "Pretty gal, ain't she?"

Irritated for inadvertently bringing Paris into the conversation, Cody didn't respond.

"Ain't she?" Dad said more forcefully. "And you... want...bad."

Cody had no intention of discussing his relationship with Paris with his father. Like Ma, Dad had recognized Cody's interest in Paris many years ago, but his commentary had always been mocking of Cody, disrespectful and suggestive. He didn't like that then and he'd have none of it now.

Dad snorted, amusement lighting his eyes as he motioned for Cody to come closer. "Can get her...for you, son."

Cody stood rooted to the floor. "What do you mean?"

"Her daddy…" His father smirked. "Ain't what… pretends…be."

He tensed as his worst fear took deeper root. The "nickel-and-diming" reference Paris's father had made was too reminiscent of what he'd remembered as a boy from one of his dad's incarcerations.

Extortion.

He took a steadying breath. "What do you think he's pretending to be?"

"Faithful family man." Dad gave a lame attempt at a leering wink. "But extra… Extracurricular…activity on side."

A knot tightened in Cody's chest. Paris's adored father, a church deacon, was having an intimate relationship with someone outside of marriage?

"You've been blackmailing Merle Perslow."

Dad shrugged, a sly smile tugging at his lips. "Job… security."

No wonder Paris's father met him with hostility upon his return to Canyon Springs. Looking back at each of their encounters, it was clear he had it in his head that Cody was a part of this, too.

Dad bought a new truck a few years ago. That was likely the start of it and he'd been "nickel-and-diming" Merle ever since. He'd have derived immense enjoyment from it. "For how long?"

The older man squinted, thinking back. "Fifteen… years?"

Fifteen years? Paris's mother would still have been alive. Merle had cheated on Marna Perslow? The saintly woman who'd given so much of herself to her husband and daughter and the community?

"I don't believe you." But as much as he didn't want to, there had to be truth to it. A man like Merle Perslow wouldn't succumb to blackmail easily. There had to be evidence. Something concrete. Cody had to get his hands on it.

Dad's eyes narrowed. "Photos…can prove."

"I want to see them."

Dad's chuckle turned into a deep, rasping cough and his face reddened.

Cody reached for the water glass on the bedside table, but his dad waved him off with his good hand. He coughed a few more times, then slid himself down from where Cody had earlier propped him on a pillow.

"You go…now."

He was being dismissed? Just like that? "Where are the photos, Dad?"

The older man turned away, his mumbling voice barely audible. "For me…know."

And for you to find out?

"I've got to get going, Paris. I had to run an errand and got behind on things at the clubhouse."

Paris sensed Cody's restlessness as he glanced out the front window of Camilla's Café for what had to be the hundredth time. He'd been late meeting her and seemed on edge throughout their meal. Was being seen with her in a public place making him nervous? If lunch could do that, what would happen at the gala a few nights from now?

"Are you having second thoughts about escorting

me?" She hadn't breathed a word about her encounters with Dad and Elizabeth, hoping the turmoil would resolve itself soon. There was no point in giving Cody any excuses to back out.

He didn't meet her gaze as he paused to take a sip from his water glass. "No, of course not."

"Because if you are…"

"Nope. Not me. What about you?"

"I'm looking forward to it." She'd leaped the highest hurdles by telling Dad and Elizabeth she'd be going to the gala with him. "Is everything okay? You seem distracted."

He placed his glass back on the table. "I have a lot on my mind."

"Is it anything it would help to share with me?"

He cut her a sharp look that immediately softened. "I'm concerned about Deron. And Dad and Ma. I need to get this project behind me so I can focus on their issues and my company."

And on the two of them? Had it only been a few days ago that they'd first opened their hearts and tentatively talked about a shared future?

"Were the volunteers there to decorate the trees this morning?" She folded her hands on the table. "I haven't had time to stop by."

"What? Oh. I assume so. I haven't been out there yet. Like I told you, I had an errand to run. In Show Low."

"To see your Dad?"

"Right."

Calling his father an "errand" seemed odd, proving that something was troubling him.

"Are you going straight to Pine Shadow Ridge from here? I was thinking maybe we—"

"I have another thing or two to attend to first." Apparently recognizing the vagueness of his excuse, he offered a reassuring smile and reached across the table to take her hand in his. "Maybe we can get together tonight? A late dinner?"

"I can't. I'm meeting with Abby and Brett at Kit's to finalize the catering for their Friday-evening wedding."

"Tomorrow night, then?"

"Choir practice."

"Wednesday?"

"A gift exchange at the office." She sighed, then perked up. "Would you like to come?"

"I doubt your father would care to have me there." He ran his thumb across the back of her hand. "I'm assuming, of course, he now knows we're seeing each other? You haven't mentioned how that went."

"He knows we'll be at the gala together." Should she confess to Cody that she hadn't yet told Dad their relationship was much deeper than attendance at a charity event?

A crease furrowed Cody's forehead. "How'd he take that?"

"He wasn't happy. But Delaney assures me that once he gets to know you, he'll come around."

"Your friend's an optimistic soul."

Paris smiled. "Always."

Cody gave her hand a gentle squeeze, then stood. "I'll give you a call later."

But he didn't say when.

It was with a sense of foreboding that Paris watched

him pause at the cashier, then push open the glass-paned door. Snowflakes filled the air, swirling around him. Yes, it was beginning to look a lot like Christmas.

But it sure didn't feel like it.

Cody stood in deep shadow outside the clubhouse Saturday night, oblivious of the cold for which his tux provided little defense. He and Paris had taken separate vehicles since she needed to come early to meet with the committee, caterers and staff. But in a matter of minutes he'd join the continuous stream of arriving guests and step through the doors to meet her at the agreed-upon time.

Right now, though, he needed to find his bearings. It had been a rough week, starting with Dad's sickening revelation about Mr. Perslow and fearing each time he spoke with Paris that she could read his every anxious thought—every spark of anger directed at her father and his own.

Fifteen years ago, Dad wouldn't have had a digital camera. He still didn't own one. But where would he have stashed the incriminating photos *and their negatives?* Repeated searches of the garage and trailer had left Cody empty-handed. That the photos were incriminating, he had no doubt. Merle Perslow was smart enough to know Leroy Hawk could shout his accusations from the rooftops and no one would listen to a word he said.

Unless he had rock-solid evidence.

Knowing what he did about her father had made Cody uncomfortable around Paris the past several days. She sensed it and he could tell it confused her. But until he found those photographs and destroyed them, he'd feel part of Leroy Hawk's vindictive scheme and her father's infidelity.

Cody glanced skyward into the star-filled night—a night like the one when he'd first kissed Paris. Would he ever be able to bring himself to tell her the truth? Or would this ugliness stand between them for a lifetime?

Please, Lord, don't let my coming to this event cause negative repercussions for Paris.

He waited a few minutes more, allowing the stragglers to enter, then squared his shoulders and went inside. Now, standing in the foyer and looking down at a beautifully gowned Paris, his spirits rose. God was in this. Everything would be okay.

"I'm sorry I was tied up with the wedding last night, but I'm glad you brought your mother to see her design come to life." Her hair piled atop her head and earrings sparkling, Paris smiled up at him. "What are she and Deron doing tonight?"

"Ma's at a gathering with her Bible study group and her next-door neighbor is keeping Deron. The kids were out in the front yard building a snowman when I left."

Paris's brow wrinkled. "What's going to happen to him, Cody?"

"I don't know. But I'll tell you one thing—if Dad ever comes home, I can't leave the little guy there. Dad might not be able to swing his fist like he used to, but he could still do emotional damage."

"I can't understand why I promised never to tell anyone about the way he treated you. What kind of friend was I?"

He looked into her troubled eyes. "We were only kids, Paris. That's in the past now. But, whatever it takes, I won't let Dad's temper ruin the future of another child."

She glanced around to make sure no one was watching, then stepped up on her tiptoes to kiss him on the cheek.

He grinned. "What was that for?"

"For being the most loving, kindhearted man I've ever known."

He straightened his bow tie. "And the most handsome?"

"Definitely. I'll be keeping an eye on you tonight so none of the other ladies attempt to steal you away from me."

"There will only be one woman in there who I'm interested in." He offered his arm to her. "So are you ready to set the tongues wagging?"

"I am if you are." She linked her arm with his and together, with bated breath, they entered the ballroom.

It was probably his imagination that the room fell silent when they stepped into the raftered space that had been transformed into a rustic winter wonderland. It was probably all in his head, too, that the hush was swiftly followed by a soft buzz as guests turned to whisper to their tablemates.

Nevertheless, he nodded a warm greeting to those they passed on the way to their reserved table near the front of the elevated stage, reminding himself that the beautiful woman on his arm had chosen him, out of all the men on the planet, to join her tonight.

Black-and-red buffalo plaid tablecloths topped with

glass-encased candles set a mellow mood with the overhead lights dimmed. An open space in the middle of the room would serve as an after-dinner dance floor.

"Cody." Bill Diaz rose from his seat to shake hands as they passed by. "Good to see you. You, too, Paris."

"The decorations are out of this world," Sharon Dixon chimed in. "Absolutely breathtaking."

"They are, aren't they?" Paris smiled up at him, her eyes shining.

"So this is the young man responsible for this magnificent craftsmanship?" Former city councilman Reuben Falkner stepped forward. For a moment Cody hesitated. Mr. Falkner had more than once chased him off when he'd taken a shortcut home from school through his property.

Cody shook his hand, only to be tapped on the shoulder and drawn into another conversation praising his and his mother's work. Astoundingly, the warm welcomes continued as they wound their way among the tables. Only a few times did he catch a fleeting frown or see someone deliberately turn away from them.

Owen looked disgruntled, but managed not to sneer.

All too soon, however, they arrived at tables reserved for those who'd played a major role in making the Christmas gala the charity event of the year. Among them, one table away from where he and Paris were to be seated, was an exquisitely dressed Elizabeth Herrington and her escort for the evening, Paris's father.

Elizabeth and Merle. A cold, invisible finger pressed against Cody's spine. Would hers be the face he'd see in the photographs Dad stashed away? The woman Paris loved like a second mother? No, it couldn't be. On top of her father's betrayal of her mother, that would be too cruel.

Mrs. Herrington nodded regally, too well-bred to publicly shun him, but Mr. Perslow didn't rise to shake his hand like the other men at the table did.

To his relief, he and Paris were seated with their backs to Elizabeth and Merle. But he could still feel the man's steely gray eyes boring into his back, a reminder of his promise that Cody would be sorry if he appeared at the event with Paris.

However, the evening was off to a promising start, with Paris and her committee extending a formal welcome to the guests and thanking them for their generous donations that would sustain community charities throughout the year.

Throughout dinner, he joined the conversation around the table, answering questions about the creation of his mother's decorative designs. It was gratifying as well to share details regarding his and Trevor's business expansion and several at the table expressed interest in learning more about a possible investment of their own.

"Didn't I tell you everything would be fine?" Paris whispered in his ear.

"You did. And—" he whispered back, unable to keep from teasing her "—I haven't felt the least bit neglected by the gala's committee head. Not long ago I thought I overheard her insisting she wouldn't have time to deal with an escort."

"I already told you what my responsibilities for the

evening are." She gave him a playful smile. "Keeping at bay the women who have their eye on you."

He grinned, nodding to the band members gearing up for after-dinner dancing. "Maybe I can bribe them to play only slow numbers."

She nodded at him with approval and his heart rate ramped up a notch. Being seated here by Paris, announcing to the world they were a couple...it still didn't seem real. He turned toward the front of the ballroom where dozens of the high-school-aged waiters and waitresses converged on the stage piling festively wrapped boxes and pushing beribboned scooters, go-carts and bicycles.

"What's this?" he whispered to Paris as an unwelcome memory pricked his mind.

"They're displaying the gifts that will be distributed to children in the community."

He nodded, relieved—until he heard high-pitched, childish chatter at the back of the ballroom. His muscles tensed as he turned in that direction. In the dim light he could see two dozen giggling grade-school-aged children moving restlessly just inside the main double doors, some hopping from one foot to another in excitement.

Cody reached for Paris's hand, his gaze piercing into hers. "You said they didn't do this anymore."

"I—"

"Children!" Sharlene Odel called from the stage microphone, drawing Cody's attention as a knot formed in his throat. "Please join me up here."

With giggles and whispers, the kids quickly wove their way among the tables. But Cody wasn't seeing them, was barely aware of Paris's hand gripping his as a familiar, humiliating warmth crept up his neck.

His mouth going dry, Cody pulled his hand free of Paris's and reached for his water glass. Was it his imagination, or were people staring at him, remembering he'd been paraded to the front with the other needy children in the past, being reminded that he had no business here among them and certainly not at Paris's side?

He didn't dare meet their gazes but kept his eyes trained on Sharlene, who was rambling on about the generosity of those assembled tonight.

In an effort to still his hammering heart, he prayed for every child crowded on the stage, focusing on each youthful face. Some were bursting with excitement, eyes dancing. Others appeared shy, withdrawn. Or embarrassed. He prayed they'd hold their heads up proudly. Prayed they had a family who loved them and who shared God's love with them. Prayed they'd one day break out of the cycle of poverty.

There was no shame in being poor—Jesus had been far from rich—but there *was* shame in looking down on the impoverished, using them for entertainment. How could Paris have allowed this spectacle when she knew how he hated it?

Pausing on each face as his gaze slowly made its prayerful way through the throng on the stage, he was barely aware of Sharlene's words.

And then, as his eyes touched on a familiar boyish face, an invisible fist punched him in the gut. A blow that would have brought him to his knees had he been standing.

Deron.

There. At the far left side. At the back. Smiling uncertainly. Looking a little scared.

No. No. Please, Lord, no!

Instinctively, Cody rose to his feet. Paris grasped his arm in an effort to restrain him, but he shook her off. Looking neither left nor right, he strode to the stage and, to Sharlene's surprise, stepped up onto the platform. In a blink of an eye, he had Deron in his arms and headed toward a side door.

He only paused once to look back—into Paris's guilt-stricken eyes. And at Merle's smirking mouth.

"Where are we going, Uncle Cody?" Deron looped his arm around Cody's neck as they strode into the starry night. "The man said I could have a bicycle."

The man. Merle?

How could You have let Paris be a part of this, Lord?

"I'll get you a bicycle, Deron." His heart aching, he gave the boy a hug. "The biggest and best bicycle in the whole wide world."

Chapter Twenty-One

"Sit down and don't make a scene," her father's low voice warned as Paris tried to slip past him in pursuit of Cody, his grip on her wrist tightening. "There's been enough of that tonight. I hope you're happy."

Waves of icy cold flushed through her from the moment she'd spied Deron. Had her father played a role in staging this humiliation of Cody and his family?

She should have known something like this would happen. But Dad was right. She couldn't abandon the gala to chase after Cody, no matter how much she wanted to. From the look he'd leveled on her from across the dimly lit room, he wouldn't be in any mood to listen to anything she had to say anyway. He blamed her. And rightly so, if Dad had anything to do with this.

When Cody had stepped off the stage, Sharlene immediately drew the guests' attention to the excited children as she gave the go-ahead to open presents. Grateful for the continued distraction, Paris numbly returned to her seat to the sound of happy squeals and tearing wrapping paper.

Please, God, be with Cody. Please let him forgive me.

The remainder of the evening was a blur. As soon as the packages were opened, the band struck up a popular Christmas tune and couples milled onto the dance floor. Parker appeared out of nowhere to sweep her into dance after dance and others cut in throughout the night, including Bill Diaz, who was one of several who told her not to worry about what happened with Cody, assuring her everything would be all right.

If only she could believe that.

Dad didn't approach her to dance their traditional dance together. That was evidence enough of his guilt, wasn't it? Or was he merely angry with her because Cody had disrupted the evening? Perslows did *not* make scenes.

When late in the evening the band's final song came to a close, she and the other committee members stepped to the microphone to thank everyone for coming and wished them a merry Christmas. Others were in charge of overseeing breakdown and cleanup, so as soon as she could, she made her escape.

But she'd no more than stepped into the softly lit hallway that surrounded three sides of the ballroom when she saw Elizabeth standing off to the side. Shoulders slumped, she leaned against a window frame, staring out the floor-to-ceiling glass expanse and into the night.

As if sensing Paris's presence, she turned a tearstained face toward her. With only a slight hesitation, she stretched out her hand to beckon Paris closer and, when she approached, clasped Paris's hand tightly.

"I'm so very sorry. This is my fault and I can no

longer carry the burden of what I've done to you—and Dalton."

Dalton? "I…don't understand."

She tilted her head to gaze lovingly at Paris, blinking back tears. "No, no, you wouldn't. And when I tell you, you may never speak to me again."

"Elizabeth—"

"Hear me out. Please? From where I sat tonight I could catch glimpses of you throughout dinner, see the glow in your eyes when you looked at Cody. Hear the sparkle in your laugh. And suddenly I realized you really *do* love him."

"I do."

"He looked at you the same way, with respect and a gentle protectiveness." Elizabeth took a breath. "I know you've been lonely. I know I—and everyone else in town—remind you all too often of Dalton and haven't allowed you to move beyond your grief."

Why would she think Paris would never want to speak to her if that was her only confession? "Elizabeth—"

The weary-looking woman held up her hand to again halt Paris. "What I'm trying to say is…it's *my* fault that you lost Dalton."

Paris shook her head, not understanding any of this.

"Oh, sweetheart." Another tear trickled down the carefully made-up cheeks. "You see, I pressured Dalton to return home earlier than planned for the wedding."

A chill coursed through Paris.

"I'd filled the week with gatherings that would showcase *me* as the mother of the groom," Elizabeth rushed on. "I insisted he be here for them so I could show off the both of you. Make me look and feel important. He finally gave in to my persistence, to my sometimes angry haranguing. And…and it brought my dear boy home. Right into the path of a drunken driver."

Cody let the neighbor next door know he'd picked up Deron and got confirmation that, as when he'd been a kid, a rented bus had made its way through the neighborhood with gala volunteers knocking on doors and gathering children. Then he changed clothes, plugged in the lights on the tabletop tree they'd gotten for Deron and played a few board games with him.

But his mind wasn't on games.

"I like this popcorn, don't you, Uncle Cody?"

He ruffled the boy's hair and helped himself to the tin of caramel-covered popcorn. "Yeah. It's good."

He shouldn't have gone charging onto the stage. Maybe no one would have noticed a grandson of Leroy Hawk—who bore a striking resemblance to his uncle Cody. But he had been hurtled back in time, seeing himself standing there in front of the crowd with everyone staring, knowing he was Leroy's son, knowing he'd come for a handout.

Had Paris known they were going to resurrect the old custom? She hadn't denied it. But then again, he hadn't given her much of a chance before he'd shaken off her hand. In his first—and now-to-be-only—foray into Canyon Springs society, he'd hauled Deron off the stage, no doubt embarrassing Paris. To top it off, he'd not only humiliated her in front of her family and friends, he'd left her dateless for the remainder of the evening.

At the mercy of Parker and Owen.

"It's your turn, Uncle Cody."

"Oh, sorry, bud." He drew a printed card from the stack, then moved his playing piece forward on the game board.

Why'd he think he could fit in with that crowd anyway? He'd only been fooling himself. He'd be forever tainted in this town by his former poverty, his father's and brothers' reputations, and the shadow of the blackmailing of Mr. Perslow. By his own disastrous public performance tonight, as well. That should give the community's elite something to whisper about…and to negatively judge Paris for inviting him.

With the gala over, though, he was free to leave town and release Paris from any sense of obligation. If only he could find those photos, destroy them and somehow destroy the guilt by association that haunted him. It wouldn't make any difference in his doomed-from-the-start relationship with Paris, but he couldn't allow Dad to feather his own nest at the expense of another man's dishonorable deed.

The rattle of the front door announced his mother's return. Cody used the opportunity to communicate a silent "later" shake of his head, then he wrapped up his game with Deron and slipped out to the garage to resume his search for the evidence. He combed the rafters once more, pulled out drawers looking for anything taped to them and dug through bins of nails, screws and whatever else he could lay his hands on.

He *had* to find and destroy the photos and negatives—for Paris. That's the least he could do after what he'd done to her tonight.

But an hour's worth of effort was to no avail.

Defeated, he paused in the doorway, his hand on the light switch as he gave the workbench a final sweeping glance. The pegboard filled with tools. The jars and bins lined up. The hodgepodge of key chains and their shiny metal keys looped over hooks…

In a flash he was at the workbench, spreading out the handful of keys and studying their varied key chains. Most were likely freebies. Advertising for a local insurance company. The grain and feed store. A self-storage facility…

He picked up that one and studied it—a business in neighboring Hunter Ridge, about thirty minutes from Canyon Springs. The key chain was likely another promo item and the heavy-duty key dangling from it unrelated. But then again…where did Dad keep his boat? It wasn't on the property at the trailer, and he distinctly remembered Ma mentioning Dad had gone out on Casey Lake one last time for the season early in November.

Cody clenched the key in his hand.

Please, Lord, let this be it.

It was after midnight when Paris, still reeling from Cody's abrupt departure and Elizabeth's confession, let herself into the house. She'd attempted to call Cody several times throughout the evening, but he didn't pick up nor did he respond to her text messages. And now, standing in Dad's study as he defended his actions, she could only stare in numb disbelief.

"Blackmail? Cody is *blackmailing* you?"

Her father paced the floor in front of the fireplace.

"I didn't want to tell you, honey, but it's clear you'd never believe what I've been telling you all along about Hawks. They're bad news. Tonight was my way of publicly letting Cody know I'm standing my ground. I refuse to live any longer in fear of his and his father's intimidation."

"But Dad—"

Her father drew to a halt, his irate gaze fixed on her. "No matter the cost to myself, to my own reputation, I'm not going to give in to demands that place my daughter in the middle of their schemes."

Paris rounded the brightly lit Christmas tree and crossed the room to lay a comforting hand on his arm. "I know you're upset, but I'm not understanding any of this. What am I in the middle of? And what could you possibly be blackmailed for?"

Sometimes Dad drove a hard bargain, skated as close to the edge as the law allowed, but he always kept things aboveboard.

"The less you know, the better." He pulled away and moved to stand behind his desk. "Suffice it to say I made bad choices and, unfortunately, Leroy Hawk was witness to them. He's been toying with me—like a cat pulling the legs off a bug, one by one, getting his kicks out of making periodic demands and watching me squirm. Well, I'm squirming no more."

He slammed his fist on the desk, rattling the pen-filled cup holder she'd made for him in grade school.

"But what's this have to do with Cody and me?" None of this made any sense and certainly not the part about Cody playing a part in it.

"Don't you see? Leroy's out of commission and suddenly Cody's in town to pick up where his father left off. Only he's not demanding money, but demanding *you*." He raised his brows at Paris's sound of protest. "He's always wanted you, but he'll have you over my dead body."

"I told you, Cody cares for me. And I care for him, too."

With anguish-filled eyes, her father came from around the desk to take her hands in his. "He's using you to get back at me. He thinks my reputation, the respect of my family and community, means more to me than you do. But he's wrong."

"No, Dad. He loves me and—" she took a deep breath, garnering strength to meet her father's gaze "—I love him."

His grip tightened. "I know you *think* you do. I know he's convinced you he does. But honey, you have to listen to me. You have to know that if I could do things over again, if I could go back in time and make better choices, I would. No matter what happens, no matter what you might hear, you have to believe that."

She pulled away from him. "Cody wouldn't blackmail you. He wouldn't blackmail anyone."

A pitying gaze met hers. "I know you don't want to believe he's involved in this sordid business. I wish he wasn't. But he's trying to coerce me to hand over my reputation—or my daughter. He's gambling that my standing in the community, my good name, will win out and I'll give my blessing to his pursuit of you. But that will *not* happen. I love you too much."

If only she could get in touch with Cody. If only he could explain to her what was going on. Did his refusal to respond to her phone calls mean Dad was right? That he—and Leroy—recognized by what happened at the gala that her father was no longer willing to go along with extortion? So Cody had made himself scarce?

No. While she didn't doubt Leroy could be involved in blackmail, she refused to believe Cody was using it to force Dad to sanction a relationship with her.

Her father took a hesitant step closer. "I'm sorry to tell you like this, but I tried every way I could think of to avoid it. I've given Cody plenty of opportunities to back off."

A sliver of cold crept up the back of her neck. Why had Cody not said anything to her? Could that mean…? "You talked to Cody about this?"

"Several times. But I'm not taking it anymore. I'm not proud of what I did, but this has gone on long enough."

Paris moved behind a wingback chair, gripping the back of it as if to draw courage. *What's going on, Lord?*

"If this involves Cody and me, don't you think I have a right to know *why* you're being blackmailed?"

Her father's pain-filled eyes met hers, indecision flickering. Her hopes sank that he might be overdramatizing, blowing a minor indiscretion out of proportion.

"Please, Dad?"

He lowered himself into the chair in front of her, bracing his elbows on his knees and placing his head in his hands. The clock on the fireplace mantel ticked away the seconds echoing in the silence.

And then came a sob.

Struggling to breathe, she stared down at her father's bowed head and shaking shoulders. What had he done that would bring him to this brokenness? She moved to the side of the chair and knelt down to place a hand on his arm. "Dad?"

He drew a resigned breath, then turned tear-filled eyes to her. "I… I had an affair with a married woman."

Paris swallowed. *Elizabeth?* Her husband had died only five years ago. Had Dad, in his loneliness—? But Paris couldn't bring herself to ask. She didn't want to know.

"I'm sorry, sweetheart." His words came in a breathless rasp. "Can you ever forgive me?"

Aching deep inside as the father she loved fell from the pedestal she'd placed him on long ago, her heart nevertheless filled with compassion. She reached out to pull him into her arms, cradled and soothed him as she would a child.

Clearly, though, her father's shocking revelation was worthy of extortion and its exposure would impact his standing in the community, the church, his business.

That Leroy would take advantage of a situation like that, she had no doubt.

But please, God, not Cody, too.

Chapter Twenty-Two

On Monday afternoon, a brown envelope gripped in Cody's hands, the housekeeper admitted him into the Perslow's spacious home.

Paris hadn't tried to call him since the pleading messages of apology she'd left Saturday night, nor had he returned them. He intended to make his own apology face-to-face to make clear why a shared future was no longer possible. But the issues remaining to be resolved took precedence. Today he'd waited and watched until she returned to the office after lunch, then took his chances that her father might still be at home.

Yesterday afternoon he'd traveled to Hunter Ridge and at long last found the items he'd almost given up hope of finding. Initially he thought he'd once again come up empty-handed. But a prolonged search produced a zip-type plastic bag taped under a seat of Dad's fishing boat—a packet of photos and negatives identified with a discount store photo department in the Valley. Not surprisingly, Dad hadn't taken any chances having them developed anywhere nearby or delivered through the mail.

Yes, the photos were compromising, although not explicit. They caught Merle and his lady love entwined in each other's arms just inside the entrance to what appeared to be a remote cabin location. Innocent enough until you realized they weren't of him and his wife, and considered the date they were developed—a year before Marna Perslow's passing.

Even now, preparing to face Paris's father, he was filled with disgust. That anyone would cheat on Paris's mother and break vows taken before God was beyond his understanding.

"This way, Mr. Hawk," the housekeeper said when she returned to the foyer and motioned for him to follow.

When he stepped into the rustically appointed study, the housekeeper announced she was leaving for the day, then discreetly departed. Merle Perslow sat in a wingback chair next to the stone fireplace, its cheerful, welcoming crackle and the Christmas tree's bright points of light contrasting with the grim nature of Cody's visit.

Elbows propped on the arms of the chair and fingers tented, Paris's father acknowledged his presence with a nod. "Do come in and have a seat, Mr. Hawk. I've been expecting you."

Cody approached, but didn't sit down. "I won't be here long. Only long enough to drop off something I think you might like to have."

He tossed the brown envelope to the coffee table and caught Merle's flinch, the tightening of his jaw.

Yesterday he'd come close to destroying the contents of the packet. What purpose would keeping it serve?

But this morning, while Ma was enrolling Deron in school, he'd traveled to the hospital to show his father the evidence that his blackmailing days were over.

Dad hadn't been happy. He'd cussed out his son as best he could manage given his difficulties with speech, but he'd made his feelings clear. So another wall for God to tear down, a bridge to rebuild. If there was time.

On the drive back to Canyon Springs, though, Cody realized there might be legal ramifications for blackmailing Merle. Deciding what to do with the evidence used against Paris's father wasn't up to Cody.

It was Mr. Perslow's call.

Merle motioned to the packet. "I'm familiar with what I imagine you've brought to share with me. But no matter. I'm done with your and your father's manipulation. So don't expect to march in here and demand a blessing on a relationship with my daughter. There won't be one."

"I didn't imagine there would be." Cody held little hope that once Paris knew of his father's extortion that she'd want anything to do with Leroy's son. It was a nice dream while it had lasted, but clearly Hawks and Perslows weren't destined to make a match.

Merle snorted. "Then what are you doing here?"

"I'm returning personal photographs—and negatives—that someone of our mutual acquaintance has held in…safekeeping."

The older man's eyes narrowed. "Why would you do that?"

Cody stepped to the fireplace to look down into the dancing flames, then glanced at Paris's father. "There seems to be a serious misunderstanding between us. A misconception on your part. I've had nothing to do with the extortion my father has been involved in."

Merle motioned to the envelope. "Don't you think *this* in your possession contradicts such a statement?"

Not surprisingly, Mr. Perlsow wouldn't be easy to convince.

"Things you recently said led me to confront my father with my suspicions. It took some doing, but I tracked down the proof of what he shared with me, what he's been holding over your head. It's up to you what you do with it. I want no part of this ugliness."

"You expect me to believe these are the only copies?"

"It's my sincere belief that they are. But regardless, if you decide to press charges against my father, I'll testify on your behalf."

Merle stood, his expression uncertain. "Is this for real, Hawk?"

"It is." Cody folded his arms. "Make no mistake, Mr. Perslow, while I don't condone what you did, I have a feeling you've paid a heavy price for your wrongdoing. But I wasn't aware of what my dad was up to until a few days ago. I've had nothing to do with my father's scheming and I believe I've now ensured you will no longer be troubled by him."

Merle was silent a long moment as he stared down at the braided rug, digesting Cody's words. Then with a resigned sigh, he lifted his gaze to Cody's. "You're a better man than I am."

Cody shook his head. "Maybe, maybe not. I've done things I'm not proud of, too, sir. None of us are without fault."

But he'd never cheat on a woman he claimed to love. He'd never cheat on Paris.

"I take full responsibility for my role in this." Shoulders slumped, Merle wearily raked his fingers through his hair. "There wouldn't have been an opportunity for your father to exploit had I been a man of honor. If I'd been the man my wife and daughter believed me to be—the kind of man you apparently are."

How long had Cody yearned for Paris's father to recognize that about him? That, although a child of poverty and the son of Leroy Hawk, he was a man worthy of respect. *God's man*. But he didn't feel an expected I-told-you-so triumph at the acknowledgment. He could only feel pity for Merle Perslow, a man who'd been given so much and thrown it all away.

Merle let out a pent-up breath. "You were right, weren't you, Cody, those many years ago?"

"Sir?"

"You told me one day I'd be groveling at your feet. And here I am." He hesitantly extended his hand. "Can you forgive me for judging you by the behaviors of your father and brothers? For making a cruel spectacle of you and your nephew at the Christmas gala?"

Could he?

Forgive us our trespasses as we forgive those who trespass against us. His business partner's father always said it was a waste of time and energy not to forgive—a disobedience toward God.

"I can, sir." He clasped the other man's hand. "I'm serious about testifying should that be the path you decide to take. My dad's in no shape to be hauled through the court system and there's no telling what finding out about this would do to Ma. But I realize there are consequences for wrong choices such as my dad's made."

"His wrong choices are no worse than mine." Merle picked up the envelope from the coffee table, opened the flap and gazed down at the contents. "More harm than good would come from holding your father publicly accountable. I deserve the scandal, the disapproval and rejection by family and friends that would ensue. But Paris doesn't."

"No, sir, she doesn't."

Merle stepped to the fireplace and tossed the packet into the flames. It quickly caught fire, the corners curling and the contents soon consumed.

Their eyes met in mutual understanding, then Merle shook his head as if trying to clear it of cobwebs. "I don't deserve this. Being absolved. Forgiven for the way I've treated you since you were a boy."

"None of us *deserves* forgiveness, Mr. Perslow. Isn't that what Christmas is all about? The coming of the One who paid the price to make forgiveness, the restoration of our relationship with Him and others, possible?"

"Indeed it is. But it will take me some time to come to terms with the gift you've given me. My actions have haunted me for fifteen long years."

"Fifteen years?" A small, stricken voice whispered from the open doorway. "You didn't tell me *you* were married when you confessed to having had an affair."

Her father blanched as he swung around to where Paris stood. He took a halting step toward her, his hand outstretched.

"Sweetheart, I—"

An icy cold flooded her body as she instinctively stepped back, staring at her father as if at a stranger. "You cheated on Mom? That's why Leroy Hawk blackmailed you?"

"I—"

"Who was this woman?" She fought for breath, fought back the sensation that she was falling, tumbling into a deep, dark abyss. "Please don't tell me it was Mom's best friend."

Dad's eyes widened as he held up his hands in denial. "No, no, not Elizabeth. A woman who lived here only a short time. Neither you nor your mother knew her."

She turned to Cody, her eyes appealing for confirmation. He'd no doubt looked at the pictures Dad had thrown into the fire and knew the truth.

He shook his head. "It wasn't Elizabeth. No one I recognized."

She momentarily squeezed her eyes shut, fighting back tears of relief.

"Honey, I'm sorry." Her father motioned feebly. "Not a day goes by that I don't wish I could go back in time and change things."

"But how could you do that to Mom, Dad? How?" She fisted her fingers, her voice barely above a whisper. "And how dare you lie to me and imply that it was only the *woman* in your little affair who was married?"

"I have no excuses. None. Except that I'd do anything within my power to keep from hurting you."

A tiny whimper escaped Paris's lips. "Maybe you should have thought of that fifteen years ago. After what you confessed to me, I thought… I consoled my-self that in your grief over Mom's death, in your loneli-ness, you made a mistake. But that's not what happened is it?"

"I did make a mistake. The worst mistake of my en-tire life." He looked to Cody, as if appealing for sup-port. "Her mother's prolonged illness, watching her suffer, had worn me down and I selfishly reached out to another for comfort. But things went too far."

Paris pressed her hand momentarily to her mouth as a horrifying possibility leaped into her mind. "Mom… never knew, did she?"

"No, honey. No. I cut off the relationship after only a few weeks, so ashamed of what I'd done. But Leroy stumbled on us, used it against me. I went along with his demands to protect your mother. To protect you."

"And yourself."

"Yes." He bowed his head. "And myself."

"I don't know how I can ever—" Fearful of saying something she might forever regret, she spun away from him and ran from the room. But she'd just reached the foyer staircase when a firm grip on her arm drew her to a halt.

But it wasn't Dad. It was Cody, his distressed gaze capturing hers as he turned her toward him.

She struggled to free herself. "Let go of me."

"Paris. Calm down. Listen to me."

"I don't want to listen to you. I don't want to listen to any of you *lying* men."

His brow creased. "I've never lied to you."

"Oh, really?" She stared at him in disbelief. "A sin of omission is just as black as one of commission."

Confusion flickered in his eyes. "What do you mean?"

"How long have you known about my father's infidelity? How long were you going to keep silent?" She glared at the hands that held her captive. "And I said let go of me."

"Now, Paris—"

But he released her and she stepped back. "You found out last week, didn't you? I knew something was wrong. Why didn't you tell me? I've been worried sick that you were having second thoughts about us. Then you didn't return my calls. Accept my apology. So I was left to believe the worst, that Dad was right about you."

"I'm sorry, Paris. I didn't know what to do. I'd just pried everything out of my dad and was still trying to confirm the truth of it. Then when I did, when I found the evidence being used against your dad, I didn't think it was mine to tell."

He reached for her hand, but she pulled it away. "And just who else could I trust to tell me? Dad?"

"I knew it would hurt you, cause a rift in your relationship with your father."

"So were you *never* going to tell me?" At the guilty flicker in his eyes she turned away, but his hand on her arm stayed her and she reluctantly faced him again.

"Look, I'm sorry. I was wrong." His anguish-filled eyes met hers, imploring for understanding. "And I'm sorry for the way I left you at the Christmas gala. I wasn't thinking straight. I saw Deron up there on the stage and I overreacted."

"That was Dad's doing. Not mine."

"I know that now."

"I don't think I can ever forgive him for doing that to you and Deron, for how he implicated you in blackmail." She blinked back tears. "Or for what he did to Mom."

"I know it doesn't seem possible right now." Cody stared down at her, his eyes filled with understanding. "But you can. And you will. But it will take time."

She pressed her lips together, trying to still their trembling, hold back the tears. "I can't bear to speak to him. To see him. I don't want to spend another night under the same roof with him."

"I understand…but I think he needs you right now."

She stared. "You're siding with him?"

"I don't condone what he did, Paris. I thought the world of your mother. I'm angry with your dad and my dad. I'm just saying that fifteen years ago he made a mistake. A bad, bad mistake he's had to live with for a decade and a half. He's suffering."

"And I'm not?"

"That's not what I'm saying."

She impulsively reached for his hand, her eyes beseeching. "Then let's leave town tonight, Cody. Together."

Cody's breath caught. She still wanted him in her life even after learning of the role Leroy Hawk played in blackmailing her father? But there were other issues less easily resolved.

"I don't think that's such a good idea, Paris."

She squeezed his hand. "Why not? I'm not suggesting we do anything immoral, something we'd come to regret. I told you I planned to leave after the first of the year for a fresh start, remember?"

"Yes, but—"

"I can go back to school or get a job. Maybe get an apartment in the same complex as yours. Unless…" She tilted her head to look up at him with hope-filled eyes. "Unless you're ready to make things permanent."

He swallowed. "Permanent?"

"You know…?" She gazed shyly up at him, a blush tingeing her cheeks.

"Oh."

But, judging from the dismay in her eyes, that was an inadequate response to a woman who had marriage on her mind. To a woman who'd been led to believe that was his intent, as well. A weight settled into Cody's chest. How could he make her understand, yet not hurt her?

He took her other hand in his as well, his words measured. "I'm not sure making it…us…permanent is a good idea."

Apprehension flickered through her eyes, but she quickly rallied. "Why not? Dad can hardly object to you now, can he? I overheard enough of the conversation between the two of you to know he owes you. Even he recognized it and admitted he was wrong about you."

"The fact of the matter, though, is…" He was still the son of Leroy Hawk. Son of an alcoholic, an extortionist and a liar extraordinaire. A half brother to two men who had a rap sheet a mile long. People around here wouldn't be likely to forget that. And why should they when he couldn't?

"The fact of the matter," she prodded, tension evident in her tone, "is what?"

He ran his thumbs gently across the back of her hands. "As much as we'd like to ignore it, pretend it doesn't exist and won't have a lasting effect on us, we still come from vastly different worlds, Paris."

He'd given it a lot of thought and prayer these past few days. Yeah, he was a different man today than the angry, callow youth who'd left town a dozen years ago. But he still had a lot of growing up to do. Spiritually. Professionally. Paris deserved so much more than he could ever offer her.

"What are you saying?"

"I'm saying…we need to step back. Allow ourselves some breathing room."

She swallowed. "Breathing room."

"We both have a lot on our plates right now. You—your Dad's situation and working through that. Figuring out what you want to do with your future. And me—Ma, Dad, Deron and getting my business off the ground. Well, it's a lot, you know?"

"I see."

But she didn't. He could tell by the injured look in her eyes that she didn't recognize that even though it was killing him to say these things, he had to. For her own good. He couldn't bear to tear her away from a privileged life in Canyon Springs, tear her from her family and friends and all that was familiar. To ask her to journey by his side to a destination he couldn't yet see on the horizon and had no idea how it would all work out.

What if the business deal backfired and he lost everything he'd worked for? What if no one in this town could see beyond his past and, as Paris's father had long insinuated, his involvement with her tainted her reputation, her happiness, for a lifetime?

No, that might not be faith-filled thinking, but he had to weigh the possibilities, face reality.

"I'm sorry, Paris, I'd really hoped—"

She pulled her hands from his. Tears pooled in her eyes as she looked up at him, a disbelieving laugh escaping her lips. "You had me convinced you didn't trust me. That you were afraid I'd head for the hills at the first sign of opposition and break your heart. But it turns out *you're* the one who can't be trusted, Cody Hawk."

Before he could react, she dashed up the stairs, leaving him to stand staring after her.

Chapter Twenty-Three

Paris made her way slowly down the aisle with the throng of Christmas Eve churchgoers exiting the service. From her seat near the front of the church—Dad insisted she sit with him—she hadn't seen Cody tonight. Had he gone back to Phoenix, back to the world he'd lived in apart from her these past twelve years?

She said a silent prayer for him. For them. But there was no *them*. He'd made that clear.

Light snow had continued to fall all day, lending Bill and Sharon's afternoon wedding a season-suitable glow. But Paris had found it difficult to keep her mind on the touching ceremony.

"Sweetheart," Dad whispered as they moved down the aisle. "I'm going to Elizabeth's after this. Will you be coming?"

The Herrington and Perslow clans had shared a longtime Christmas Eve tradition of cocoa and cookies after the service. She only wanted to go home, but because Elizabeth had confessed her role in Dalton's return to town, she knew she should put in an appearance. Despite her own confession of guilt and their tears shed together, she wouldn't want Elizabeth to misconstrue that she held her to blame.

Paris gave a little sigh. She hadn't had a chance to tell Cody about that twist in events…how, because of her own long-held perception of responsibility for Dalton's death, she'd been able to comfort his equally guilt-ridden mother.

"Paris?" Dad touched her arm.

"Oh, sorry. I'll stop by for a little while. I'm pretty tired."

"No word from Cody, I take it?"

She shook her head.

"He cares for you, Paris. He has for a long time. He'll be back." Her father clearly wanted to say more, but they were still on shaky ground in their own relationship. He'd apologized repeatedly, not only for his unfaithfulness but for his misconceptions of Cody. For playing a role in keeping them apart.

She loved her father and had forgiven him as a matter of the will alone, a decision in obedience to God's expectation. But her feelings on the matter of his betrayal of her mother still clamored.

She now better understood, though, why Dad remained unmarried after Mom died. Just as she played a lonely, blame-filled role following Dalton's death, Dad had done likewise even after the passing of Elizabeth's husband. He'd no doubt feared that she, a woman Paris suspected he much admired, might somehow also become implicated in Leroy's schemes. And what man wanted to confess a past infidelity to a woman he wished to woo?

Her dad kissed her on the forehead. "I'm going to slip out the back way. I'll see you in a bit."

He departed and, heart heavy, Paris slowly made her way to the front foyer. She smiled and murmured responses to greetings of the season, noting with longing the many parents with sleeping infants in their arms and youngsters eager to get home "with visions of sugarplums" dancing in their heads.

At the door, Pastor Kenton took her hand. "Reyna and I can't thank you enough for handling the three weddings."

"I'm glad I was able to help."

He wiggled his brows. "I don't suppose you'd be interested in taking on the lead wedding coordinator role again?"

Was she? No. She'd proven to herself and her family and friends that she could do it. With God's and Cody's help, she'd begun to move beyond the tragedy.

"I'm afraid not, Jason. Besides, I think Reyna missed not being in the thick of things these past few weeks. She's a born romantic, if you hadn't noticed."

"Indeed I have. But thank you. And Merry Christmas, Paris."

She headed to her SUV in the far corner of the parking lot, the snow falling around her and crunching under her booted feet. The cries of holiday wishes from those departing the church rang hollowly in her ears.

Merry Christmas. Happy holidays.

She flipped the lock switch on the key in her hand and her vehicle momentarily lit up under a light layer of snow.

"Excuse me, miss," a male voice came from behind her, "but could you use help cleaning off your car?"

Heart racing, she turned slowly to Cody. Tall, handsome, with fluffy snowflakes lighting in his hair, he held up his trusty heavy-duty snowbrush.

She watched in silence as he effortlessly swept the inch-deep layer from her windows, the hood and the roof. Then he turned to her once again, his gaze as uncertain as she felt.

"So you didn't leave town after all," Paris ventured. "I thought maybe you had."

"Actually, I just got back from Phoenix. I didn't want to miss out on Christmas with Ma and Deron."

Of course he'd return for that. For them.

"So Santa has things covered?" He'd told her that day outside Camilla's that he'd be calling on her for assistance. He hadn't.

He squared his shoulders. "I think the jolly old elf has done all right for himself."

She offered a smile. "Good."

How delightful it would be to watch the little boy tear into his packages tomorrow morning, to see Cody and his mother joining in on the fun. But she and Dad would go to her paternal grandparents' house—her mother's parents were still on a month-long cruise—then on a round of afternoon holiday open houses.

Cody shifted his weight, his gaze again catching hers. "How are…things going with your dad?"

"It's awkward. We're handling each other with kid gloves. He's brokenhearted, ashamed. Yet I sense there's a relief there now that he's not bearing the burden alone, that he's accepting forgiveness." She took a quick breath. "But I still can't believe he did what he did. I love my dad and I've chosen to forgive him just as I know Mom would have. But I'm still struggling to come to terms with it."

"Give yourself time. This was a severe blow."

"I know, but it feels as if the foundation of my whole world has collapsed."

"But you know it didn't," Cody said softly, his eyes filled with compassion. "Jesus is your foundation, Paris, not your dad. You can stand firm on His promises."

She nodded. "I keep reminding myself of that."

He placed the snowbrush on top of her SUV and thrust his hands into his jacket pockets. "I'm reminding myself of those promises, too."

She tilted her head. "In what way?"

He scuffed a booted toe in the snow, a faint smile surfacing. "In case you never noticed, even after all those years living outside of Canyon Springs and giving myself to God, I still managed to return to town with a mountain-size chip on my shoulder."

"What? You?" She gave a little laugh. "Oh, surely not."

His smile broadened. "Go ahead. Make fun."

"Me? Never."

He shook his head, the momentary brightness in his eyes dimming. "I guess what I'm trying to say is that I have a lot of pride issues."

Memory flashed to the day he'd refused the gift cards intended for his mother. How he'd snatched Deron from the stage.

"Pride issues can get out of hand," he continued, his gaze riveted on her. "Issues I've used to justify holding people at arm's length and refusing to believe the best in them. Issues to defend keeping old wounds alive and rationalizing not trusting God…in matters of the heart."

A flicker of hope sparked.

"You've had a lot to overcome, Cody."

"That's no excuse." He took a step closer. "Not when pride and a bad attitude keep me from accepting the love of a woman I've long believed God made for me. And me for her."

Paris's throat went suddenly dry.

"I've made plenty of mistakes in my life", he continued. "Quite a few since returning to Canyon Springs. I know I've hurt you. Disappointed you. But no matter how you might feel about me now, I love you, Paris. I've always loved you and I'll forever love you."

A dizzying sensation raced through her. She'd thought when she'd turned her back on him and ran up the stairs, that she'd never see him again. And, yet, here he was, saying all the things she'd so desperately prayed she'd one day hear.

"I love you, too, Cody."

He reached out to cup her face in his surprisingly warm, bare hands. "Can you forgive me for being slow to become the man you need me to be? To be the man God wants me to be for you?"

She nodded. "I can and I do. But will you forgive me for not recognizing you were the man of my dreams twelve years ago? For not standing up to my father even when deep in my heart I knew the truth?"

"Done deal." His eyes smiled into hers. "But new rule, Paris. No regrets. That's all in our past, a past God used to bring us to who and where we are today."

She placed her hand over Cody's, her eyes never leaving his. "Is this where I'm supposed to beg you to marry me?"

"Mmm." He hemmed and hawed, pretending to consider, then grinned. "I might enjoy hearing that. But you know, I think I can take it from here."

To her astonishment, he dropped to one knee in the snow, reaching into his jacket pocket to produce a small, ornament-shaped box. Paris gasped as he opened it to reveal a diamond ring sparkling in the dim, snowy light.

He extracted it and took her hand, his gaze holding hers captive. "I don't know whether this is premature or twelve years late...but will you marry me, Paris Perslow?"

Breathless, she stared into his love-filled eyes.

"To have and to hold from this day forward," he prompted. "And all that other good stuff?"

She couldn't contain her smile. "I like the sound of that.'"

"That's a yes?"

"It is."

He slipped the ring on her finger, then she drew him back to his feet where they stood entwined in each other's arms as snowflakes danced in the dark around them.

He gently leaned his forehead against hers. "If God would have told me four weeks ago that by Christmas I'd be engaged to marry you, I never would have believed Him."

She pulled back slightly and brushed the snow from his dark hair, a coquettish smile forming on her lips.

"Would you have believed Him if He told you you'd not only have a fiancée by Christmas, but you'd be kissing her, too?"

He cocked a brow. "Is that a hint?"

"I think…it is."

"Then Merry Christmas, Paris." Eyes dancing, he gathered her more closely in his arms and touched his lips to hers.

Epilogue

Noisemakers sounded and confetti flew in the great room of the Perslows' home as Cody grabbed Paris's hand and pulled her aside for a kiss.

Paris. His love. His soon-to-be bride.

Thank you, God.

"Happy New Year, Paris," he said softly.

"Happy New Year, Cody." Her eyes smiled into his. "I still wake up each morning, wondering if this is a dream."

"Believe me, it's real." Cody leaned in again, certain another kiss would convince her, but her father laughingly tugged at his arm. "Come on, you two, there's plenty of time later for such as that. Let's have a toast."

With a regretful look at Paris, Cody handed her a punch glass, then lifted his as the other guests did the same.

"Thank you for joining me tonight." Merle beamed a smile around the room that made him look years younger than when Cody had first met with him only a few days after Thanksgiving. Was that what forgiveness did? Or the added fact that Elizabeth Herrington smiled at him with a special sparkle in her eyes?

"I want to take this opportunity to thank God for His many blessings," Merle continued, "and most of all for the gift of His son, Jesus Christ."

Several guests clapped.

"We all—I'm including myself here—daily fall short of the expectations God has for us. We miss the mark, sometimes by a long shot. But He loves us anyway." Merle shook his head as if in wonder. "I, for one, am humbly grateful for that gift."

"Amen," someone murmured.

"And now… I wish to all of you the happiest of new years." Merle lifted his punch glass, then turned to Paris and Cody. "And especially to my daughter and soon-to-be new son."

Cody's gaze met Merle's and he nodded an acknowledgment as Paris hurried over to give her dad a hug. Yes, a lot of healing remained to be done in all their lives and it would take time. Patience. Trust. But undoubtedly, God had been at work and would continue to work in them.

Following a round of renewed congratulations at their engagement, Cody led Paris to the front foyer where he snagged her teddy-bear coat off a wall peg and helped her into it. Together they slipped out onto the porch, into the chill, snow-filled night.

At the railing he stepped in behind her, wrapped his arms around her and pulled her close. For several silent minutes, they watched snow gently descend, settling on the ponderosa pine branches as fairy lights strung through the trees lent a surreal glow to their surroundings.

Cody could feel God smiling on them.

He gave his fiancée a hug. "I've loved you, Paris Perslow, since the day I first laid eyes on you."

"And you've always been my hero." She snuggled closer. "Yet it's only been in the past month that God turned over the tangled thread side of the tapestry of our lives so we can see the beauty of the pattern He's been working on."

He leaned his head against her silky hair. "Waxing poetic tonight, are you?"

"I always wax poetic when I'm around you. Someday I'll show you the poems I wrote when I was a teenager. You drew pictures of me and I wrote poetry about you."

Cody drew back. "You're kidding."

"No."

"I showed you one of my sketches, why didn't you show me your poetry?"

"Get real." She turned in his arms to face him, a teasing smile on her lips. "I was determined to squelch those stirrings of what I'd begun to feel for you. I was terrified Dad would find out, too."

"He seems good with it now. With me. Us." He frowned. "Or do you think it's an act because he doesn't want to lose you?"

She lifted her chin. "No, Dad's for real. God's opened his eyes to many things in recent weeks. When he called you son, he meant it."

"If only my own dad's eyes would be opened before it's too late." It didn't appear as if Leroy Hawk would be long for this world.

"Never forget that with God there's *always* hope."

"There is." His heart lightened at the assurance in

her voice, and his thoughts turned to the future. Their future. "I'm happy you feel the same way I do about renting a weekend cabin up here until we can, hopefully, relocate somewhere in mountain country."

He and Trevor saw real possibilities up here in the number of second homes thrown on the market during the recession. He'd be better able to cover the territory without such a long commute.

"And I'm all for taking Deron in if your brother and Deron's mother don't refuse us. But I have a strong feeling right here—" she pressed her hand to her heart "—that they'll be more than willing to let him go."

"Then he'll be our first kid."

"He will."

"You're going to fit right into his life, Paris. You're already fitting into Ma's. She loved the scarf and gloves and—" he cast her an apologetic look "—the gift cards."

Paris gave a soft laugh, then pulled back to look up at him. "Now, wasn't there something my dad said right before his toast? You know, about something we'd have plenty of time for later?"

Cody cocked a brow, his gaze locking with hers. "That may have been in reference to…kissing."

"Ah, yes, I remember now." Paris tilted her head playfully. "It's later now, isn't it?"

"I do believe it is." He tightened his arms around her waist, his heartbeat stepping up a notch.

"Well, then, what are we waiting for?" Applying gentle pressure to the back of his neck, she drew his mouth down to hers.

* * * * *

Receive one
FREE

Love Inspired®

eBook
with in-store purchase.

Enjoy a FREE eBook by following these simple instructions:

1. **Visit www.Walmart.com/loveinspired.**

2. **Select one title from the 8 free eBook options and add it to your cart.**

3. **Enter your promo code LOVEINSPIRED.**

4. **Read your free eBook instantly on the Walmart eBooks App!**

Offer valid from October 29, 2019, to March 1, 2020.

SPECIAL EXCERPT FROM

Love Inspired.

*Carolyn Wiebe will do anything to protect her late
sister's children from their abusive father—even give
up her Amish roots and pretend to be Mennonite.
But when she starts falling for Amish bachelor
Michael Miller, can they conquer their pasts—and her
secrets—by Christmas to build a forever family?*

Read on for a sneak preview of
An Amish Christmas Promise *by Jo Ann Brown,
available December 2019 from Love Inspired!*

"Are the *kinder* okay?"

"Yes, they'll be fine." Uncomfortable with his small
intrusion into her family, she said, "Kevin had a bad
dream and woke us up."

"Because of the rain?"

She wanted to say that was silly but, glad she could be
honest with Michael, she said, "It's possible."

"Rebuilding a structure is easy. Rebuilding one's sense
of security isn't."

"That sounds like the voice of experience."

"My parents died when I was young, and both my
twin brother and I had to learn not to expect something
horrible was going to happen without warning."

"I'm sorry. I should have asked more about you and
the other volunteers. I've been wrapped up in my own
tragedy."

"At times like this, nobody expects you to be thinking of anything but getting a roof over your *kinder*'s heads."

He didn't reach out to touch her, but she was aware of every inch of him so close to her. His quiet strength had awed her from the beginning. As she'd come to know him better, his fundamental decency had impressed her more. He was a man she believed she could trust.

She shoved that thought aside. Trusting any man would be the worst thing she could do after seeing what Mamm had endured during her marriage and then struggling to help her sister escape her abusive husband.

"I'm glad you understand why I must focus on rebuilding a life for the children." The simple statement left no room for misinterpretation. "The flood will always be a part of us, but I want to help them learn how to live with their memories."

"I can't imagine what it was like."

"I can't forget what it was like."

Normally she would have been bothered by someone having sympathy for her, but if pitying her kept Michael from looking at her with his brown puppy-dog eyes that urged her to trust him, she'd accept it. She couldn't trust any man, because she wouldn't let the children spend their lives witnessing what she had.

Don't miss
An Amish Christmas Promise *by Jo Ann Brown,*
available December 2019 wherever
Love Inspired® books and ebooks are sold.

LoveInspired.com

BASED ON A **HARLEQUIN** NOVEL

Love ALASKA

PREMIERE **UP**LIFTING MOVIE

Love will keep you warm.

COMING THIS FALL

 #uplifting